D1422862

534 634 19 X

THE END OF THE GAME

HOLLY WATT

RAVEN BOOKS

LONDON · OXFORD · NEW YORK · NEW DELHI · SYDNEY

RAVEN BOOKS
Bloomsbury Publishing Plc
50 Bedford Square, London, WC1B 3DP, UK
29 Earlsfort Terrace, Dublin 2, Ireland

BLOOMSBURY, RAVEN BOOKS and the Raven Books logo are
trademarks of Bloomsbury Publishing Plc

First published in Great Britain, 2023

A catalogue record for this book is available from the British Library

ISBN: HB: 978-1-5266-2560-1; TPB: 978-1-5266-2559-5; EBOOK: 978-1-5266-2562-5;
EPDF: 978-1-5266-6742-7

2 4 6 8 10 9 7 5 3 1

Typeset by Integra Software Services Pvt. Ltd.
Printed and bound in Great Britain by CPI Group (UK) Ltd, Croydon CR0 4YY

To find out more about our authors and books visit www.bloomsbury.com and
sign up for our newsletters

To Jago

1

Red lights flickered. A list of runners.

Torn Silk. Kittiwake.

Stunning Miller. Active Risk.

King Lawrence. Gentleman's Darling.

Dotted Daisies. Milaara.

A jumble of worlds, a babel.

And their odds, of course: all that glistening elegance boiled down to numbers twinkling chummily.

Twenty to one, and four to one, and five to four the favourite.

The crowd bustled around the bookmakers' boards. Cash handed over. A wink, a nod, a betting slip printed.

She could hear snatches of conversation.

Well beaten at Newmarket.

Sweating up a bit.

Stunning Miller wouldn't win if it started yesterday.

'Stunning' slightly slurred.

Casey looked across the racecourse. It was a beautiful day, the swathe of emerald grass unfurling under a bright blue sky.

'Enjoying it?' a man's light voice enquired.

'Of course.'

The hats were extraordinary. Coral petals and lavender feathers and a rainbow whirl of ribbons. The men wore morning suits. Waistcoats, duck-egg blue. Jackets, sloping to tails. Top hats the punchline.

Casey had read her instructions for the day – obediently – the giggles rising in her throat.

'You've been before, though.'

'Once.'

A microphone hidden in scarlet silk roses; a tiny camera in apricot pleats.

He read her smile. 'You were working then.'

'I'm working now.'

'I forgot.' He rolled his eyes. 'Now come and meet an old friend …'

Casey had known Nash Bexley since her first days working at the *Post*. Back when she was starting out as a very junior news reporter, he was the newspaper's political editor. Within a couple of years, he had ditched journalism to become a partner at Greville Polignac, one of the most successful public affairs companies in London.

'Nash knows what he's bloody doing.' The *Post*'s home affairs editor had stared crossly into his pint at the leaving do. 'Rats and sinking ships and all that. He'll be making a sodding fortune at Greville Polignac.'

'We're not sinking yet,' Miranda said firmly.

By then, Miranda was the head of the *Post*'s investigations team and Casey Benedict was working alongside her, chasing stories all over the world.

'It's only a matter of time,' the home affairs editor insisted.

For the past few weeks, however, Casey had been seconded to the politics team. The *Post* had a small office in Parliament, Nash Bexley's former hunting ground.

Away from the main office.

Away from investigations.

'Just for a bit,' Dash, the head of news, had insisted. 'We've got a new deputy politics editor coming over from the *Argus*, but the gits are making him work his notice. Plus it's going to be interesting, the run-in to the next election. You might enjoy it. And you could do with a bit of time off from investigations anyway. After … after last time.'

Within a few hours of starting with the politics team, Casey had received an email from Nash.

Congrats on the new role. We must have lunch.

Two days later, she met him at 6 Arundel Street, a private members' club in Belgravia. The waiter led her through a ruffled silence.

'How lovely to see you again, Casey.' Nash stood up as she approached, the suit impeccable, the sunny expression perfectly calibrated. Don't worry; not *that*. 'It's well worth escaping Westminster for this place. My favourite lunch spot.'

He was in his late forties, Casey guessed, and Nash had left the racket of Fleet Street well behind him now. The suit was Savile Row and his dark hair – salt and pepper these days – perfectly cut. Regular tennis at the Hurlingham kept him fit. He was very clean-shaven, his skin pink and polished. Despite his newfound grandeur, she still enjoyed his company. He was civilised and entertaining, telling the occasional very sharp joke.

That lunch was a smooth gambol through the fields of Westminster gossip. By the time the waiter brought their coffees, Nash had passed on three decent stories about his clients and two excellent ones about their rivals.

'We must do this again,' said Casey as she stood.

'Greville Polignac have a box at the Royal Opera House.' He helped her with her coat. 'Why don't you join us there next week?'

'I must get Dash to second me to the bloody politics team,' Miranda moaned when Casey called her as she trotted back towards the House of Commons. 'I'm spending the weekend in a soggy ditch in Caerphilly, trying to bust some godforsaken county lines deal.'

'Yes.' Casey grinned into her coffee. 'That doesn't sound anywhere near as much fun.'

The day at Royal Ascot had started with lunch. Quails' eggs and smoked salmon and deliciously delicate sandwiches. Cheese melting lazily under a hot June sun. Pudding was meringue with strawberries and cream.

'We're in Number One carpark.' Nash expected Casey to be impressed.

In the carpark, she found dozens of lunch parties under way. Nash's wife – Rosamund, blonde and glacial – had organised everything. The picnic unfolded like a conjuring trick. Dainty china and linen napkins, a crisp tablecloth covering the trestle table. A bunch of roses – pink and gold – gradually shed petals over the silver cutlery and crystal. People stopped by constantly. The chief executive of this, the chairman of that, the Earl of the other. All getting too hot in a carpark.

Casey remembered dodging into a petrol station a few months ago, halfway down the M3 to the next story. Tapping her foot as the tank filled, grabbing a Ginsters pasty. A couple of minutes later, her empty can of Red Bull had landed in the footwell. She suppressed a smile.

'You think this is all a bit ridiculous,' said Nash.

'It's theatre,' said Casey. 'Isn't it?'

'Of course.' He filled her glass with champagne. 'Now, I'd like you to meet the founder of ...'

This founder was in his sixties, tall and steely, the aura of power almost visible. He beamed down benignly, filled her glass with more champagne, and a few minutes later, Casey had another story, this time about an MP who was being rather too creative with his expenses.

As they chatted, she spotted Tillie Carlisle, a junior reporter at the *Post*, and waved. Tillie, she knew, had been invited by a very grand aunt.

'You're only allowed the day off,' Ross, the *Post*'s news editor, had snarled, 'if Auntie coughs on whether her son's having a run in the next leadership battle, okay?'

'Yes, Ross. Okay, Ross. On it, Ross.'

Nash was making his way around the different lunch parties. As he stopped to talk to a beautiful redhead, Casey watched his wife's eyes narrow very slightly.

'Coffee?' sang Rosamund Bexley when the chief executive had finished talking.

Nash's wife was immaculate in primrose yellow, her hat a twist of tulle and marabou. She was an unimpeachable hostess, ensuring every glass was full, and never permitting a pause in conversation.

4

'Rosamund's daddy's worth proper billions, I was told once,' Archie said, when he heard about Casey's invitation to the races. Archie had been Nash's deputy, replacing him as political editor at the *Post* after he left. 'Which Nash definitely appreciated. She did something like design handbags before they were married. Or that sort of thing anyway. Didn't last for long.'

'What's she like?'

'Well, she sharpened up quite a lot after they were married.'

That was why Nash had moved to Greville Polignac, Casey guessed. His wife had perhaps been amused by the raffish political editor at first, but that must have palled soon enough.

'We'd better hurry,' said Rosamund now. 'Or we'll miss the first race.'

Despite her refined exterior, she had a gleam in her eye, the glint of the true fanatic.

'Let's go.' Nash was on his feet too. 'I've got a good tip for that one, and I won five hundred on the colour of the Princess of Wales's outfit a couple of years ago, so you never know. Aquamarine, I think, this year.'

Casey didn't know much about racing. She admired the horses strutting around the parade ring, all glossy shimmer and nerves. The jockeys scurried out as the loudspeaker echoed over the stands.

'Dotted Daisies is looking good.' A French accent to her left.

'Active Risk hammered her by eight lengths at Newbury.' Arabic intonation, dismissive.

'Placed your bets, Casey?' It was Nash, top hat at a rakish angle.

'A fiver on Active Risk,' Casey said randomly, admiring the jockey's silks, white stars on bright purple.

'Number six.' Nash studied his programme. 'Interesting choice.'

'Better make it each way, then.'

'The others are up in the stands already,' he went on. 'Shall we head that way?'

They strolled towards the stands, Casey smoothing down her unfamiliar dress. Cressida, the *Post*'s fashion editor, had selected this outfit after Casey appeared next to her desk a few days earlier and pleaded.

'I do *love* Ascot.' Cressida had rubbed her hands together. 'And we're doing a feature about it too, so I've already called in various looks. I *suppose* you could borrow one just for the day. The hats are *fabulous* this year.'

The fashion editor's eyes had narrowed as they took in Casey's jeans and her unironed shirt. Cressida was a grumpy fairy godmother, defending the fashion cupboard with vigour. But that day she was smiling, and now Casey found herself wearing oyster silk and a hat topped by arching feathers. They bobbed gently in the breeze.

The stand in the Royal Enclosure was huge. Rows of seats overlooked the track, allowing thousands of people to watch the race. Behind the tiers of seats were all the bars and restaurants required by several thousand people on a day out. These were contained in a vast atrium, which soared up to a glass and steel roof. Walkways criss-crossed the space, with pairs of escalators rising through the void.

As the start of the next race approached, people hurried to their seats. Tags dangled from lapels in a range of colours because, no matter where you go, there's always a more exclusive circle. Everywhere, television screens showed the latest odds.

As they ambled through the atrium, Casey glanced idly at one of the bars where the staff were rushing to fill orders before the race kicked off. The horses were parading out to the racetrack now and the sound levels rose again.

'Hurry up!' a brunette bawled at her husband. 'You'll bloody *miss* it, you fool.'

And the husband ran, clutching his glass of Pimm's.

Nash caught Casey's eye, and they laughed together.

'I've got to place a couple of bets,' he said as they paused at the bottom of an escalator. 'Rosamund's most particular. You head up, I'll follow.'

It was the man's stillness that caught Casey's eye as she glided upwards. He was standing close to the top of the escalator, neat in his barman's uniform. Dark trousers, white shirt, shiny blue tie: anonymous. He had white-blond hair and wide shoulders.

In the bar below, Casey could see a waitress filling wine glasses, her face pink with exertion. Other bar staff were racing to pour pints, hand over crisps, hold out card readers. Their busiest time. But this barman just stood there, looking towards Casey as the escalator flowed relentlessly upwards.

He wasn't looking at her, she realised. He was staring fixedly at the man just in front of her.

From behind, the man was unremarkable. His tails tapered neatly and his black shoes were highly polished. He was thin, with slightly stooped shoulders and messy brown hair.

Still, the barman stared down. As part of the atrium's design, the architect had turned the necessity for escalators into a feature. Carving their way up through the hall, they drew the eye skywards. To Casey's left, a matching escalator purred smoothly back down to the ground floor. On her right side, there was nothing but open space, a swallow dive through thin air. There was no way out, she realised abruptly, a sharp fear flooding her veins. This was a trap.

The barman took a step towards the top of the escalator. People were stepping off in ones and twos. They were laughing, flirting, consulting their racecards. But the scene was all wrong. The barman was standing too close to the top of the escalator. A rock in a river, forcing racegoers to swirl around him. To the crowd, he was an inconvenience, nothing more.

But.

But all the other staff were buzzing, helpful as bees.

The man's eyes narrowed and one hand went to his pocket. Still the escalator rose. Efficient, incessant, normal.

And impossible to escape.

A shiver ran down Casey's spine.

She tried to push away the panic, the sudden burn of claustrophobia.

You're being ridiculous … Too many years …

I'm not.

He can't be.

He is.

Oh, don't be stupid.

7

Only a few seconds before they reached the top, only a few seconds before they were spat robotically into the ambush.

A decision of sorts.

'Excuse me.' Her voice, sounding too loud.

The man ahead of her turned around. He had a long face and deep-set eyes, a shy look about him. Black-rimmed glasses, maybe mid-thirties.

He did not look like a target.

'Check your watch as if I'm asking for the time and don't look round.' Casey smiled as she spoke, so it would look like an ordinary conversation. 'I don't have time to explain now, but there is a man at the top of this escalator and I think he is a serious threat to you. I'm going to come past you and distract him. You're going to have to jump across to the down escalator and make a run for it, okay?'

It was the man's reaction that confirmed her suspicions. She had hoped he would laugh, mock her, even: *crazy cow, mad bird.* But instead, it was as if a fear he had carried with him for years was abruptly, horribly real. He shrank from her, face draining of colour.

Not physically athletic, she thought. Not able to fight. A sitting duck.

'What's your name?' she asked quietly, with a steadying smile.

Either the question or the smile snapped him out of his stupor. 'Aidan,' he mumbled.

'Aidan, you have to let me pass right now,' she whispered urgently. 'I'll go ahead and distract him, and while I do that, you're going to have to make the leap. There isn't another option, okay? It will be all right.'

He nodded, face white. Twenty yards to go. The escalator hummed on, an everyday death trap.

Moving fast, Casey barged past him, nose crinkled, teeth bared, cackling loudly. She waved wildly at a point somewhere just behind the barman's head, mouthed, *I'm coming.* Pushed past a few more people, forcing her way to the top of the moving staircase.

Ten yards.

As Casey reached the top, she threw her arms wide. *Hello, sweetheart!*

The barman barely saw her, his whole attention focused on Aidan. In the bustle of Ascot, one more drunken woman was barely worth a glance.

'Must just grab a quick drink,' Casey squealed, and tripped heavily on the polished floor. As she fell, she grabbed at the barman's arm. 'Oops, sorry, darling.'

And Aidan leaped across to the other escalator.

2

There was a ripple of jovial laughter as Aidan jumped awkwardly, struggling for a moment with the rubber handrails sliding fast in opposite directions.

'Tally-ho!' one man shouted. 'Forgotten to place your bets?'

'You've broken my shoe!' Casey shrieked, clutching onto the barman. 'My *shoe!*'

She clung on for as long as possible, gripping so hard that tendrils of a tattoo appeared above his neat shirt collar. Aidan sprinted down the adjacent escalator, shoving his way past people. With a snarl, the barman pushed Casey so hard that she slammed against the glass barrier overlooking the atrium.

'Hey!'

People around them were beginning to realise something was wrong. 'You can't do that. Hey …'

But the barman was gone, racing down the moving stairs after Aidan. Only a few people were heading down now so he could leap several steps at once.

Aidan reached the bottom and darted across the atrium floor towards the racetrack. A flood of people were still making their way out to the lawns in front of the stands and he bobbed ineffectually among the crowd.

Casey peered over the edge of the barrier. He would be all right now, surely. He would have the sense to find a policeman, to seek help from one of the dozens of Ascot staff scurrying around the vast space. Surely …

Aidan didn't. Instead, he sprinted out through the big doors that led to the track. Swearing, Casey dashed out to the tiers of seating. Far below, thousands of people were milling around next to the track. They were drinking, laughing, craning to see the horses canter down to the start. Hundreds were making their way to the bookmakers' stands with their twinkling red numbers, to lay a final bet.

From here, Casey could just make out Aidan scuttling through the throng on the Royal Enclosure lawn. A pulse of fear. There were several figures following him, and they were moving fast, ruthlessly.

They might be security guards, she told herself, drawn by the shouts and the shoving. It wasn't very Royal Ascot, after all.

But they might not be guards.

Casey thought about the intensity in the barman's eyes. The raw ferocity of his movements. What had he held in his hand? A syringe? Or if he had access to the kitchen areas of the racecourse, a knife?

Far below, Aidan was moving to the left, towards a crossing where racegoers could stream across the course between races. But the runners were out on the grass now, powering gracefully down to the start. The marshals were closing the gates, halting the flow of people across the course for the duration of the race.

'Come on, Aidan,' she murmured. 'Just push through.'

But he was stalling, reluctant even in his terror to override the strict Ascot protocol. Instead, he ducked to the right, making his way back along the side of the track. The crowd was thick there, clustering as close to the winning post as possible.

From her vantage point, Casey could spot his pursuers. They were fanning out over the lawn, pushing their way through the throng. From the way they were dividing up the crowd, they were coordinating. Taking their time, getting eyes on every person on the lawn. Not easy. But not hard for professionals, either.

Aidan was veering towards the cheaper stands. By sheer luck, he hadn't been spotted yet. But he was panicking, Casey could see, fighting through crowds thick as porridge. People would be jovial,

11

immovable. And in the middle of all that, Aidan's panic would attract the attention of the most incompetent searcher.

Just then one of the pursuers spun around with a foxhound's urgency. The man began shoving his way across the lawn towards their quarry. There was no politeness here, none of Aidan's hesitancy.

Aidan wasn't going to make it.

Casey sprinted for the down escalator.

The atrium was almost empty now, the crowd compressed into the tiers of seating. Casey raced down the escalator, cursing the oyster-grey heels. Vaguely, she could hear the loudspeaker.

Kittiwake kicking up a bit of a fuss at the starting gate ... They're all in now though.

Casey bolted towards the cheaper end of the stands. The gate-keeper let her through, eyes flickering over the badge attached to her dress. She ran on. She couldn't see Aidan anywhere.

And they're off!

There was a roar from the crowd, an almost animal howl that brought her to a standstill. Where would Aidan go? she wondered. He hadn't headed for the carparks when it would have been easier to go that way. *Where?*

She leaped up the steps to the first tier of seating in this enclosure, using the height to get her bearings. The vast stands were angled so that they faced down the finishing straight.

She yanked her programme out of her bag, hunting for the course map. There was a pedestrian tunnel leading to the other side of the racecourse, she saw. But it would be too easy to cut him off there. He wouldn't try that, surely?

The loudspeaker was rattling through names now.

Milaara straight into the lead, then King Lawrence, Dotted Daisies, Kittiwake taking a strong hold ...

To Casey's right lay the Windsor Enclosure full of noise and revelry. That way? She could see a couple of Aidan's pursuers in there already, their eyes raking the crowd. It felt oddly as if two separate events were overlaid. One a cheery, jolly race scene, the other a world of hunters and prey.

Kittiwake can't find any space, being squeezed by Torn Silk as they ...

The stands were strangely quiet now, all eyes on the course as the horses thundered down the back stretch. Casey stared around frantically. Maybe the men had grabbed Aidan, hauled him away …

Active Risk's having a great run now as they come out of that turn.

A rumble from the crowd.

Casey checked the map again.

To the east of the racecourse was a sprawling golf course, and beyond that a helipad, which racegoers used as a taxi service back to London.

The helipad.

Could Aidan be scrambling through the enclosures trying to find his way to the helipad?

Dotted Daisies forced to take the long way round there …

If that was his plan, it wouldn't work. The golf course would be fenced off, protected from the crowds.

Casey gazed east all the same.

There he was.

In the far distance, she could just make out a small figure rushing through the Windsor Enclosure. She leaped forward.

His pursuers had seen him too. They were bolting after him, and they were so much closer.

Only one hope …

Casey pivoted away and darted through the grandstand, straight out to the open space beyond.

Gentleman's Darling's making a move now, but Active Risk is hanging on.

The roar of the crowd was swelling, thousands of people beginning to cheer. Past the grandstand were the turnstiles, and beyond them lay Ascot High Street and its prosaic red brick. Casey raced to the road. A taxi was waiting, engine humming quietly.

'That way.' She hurled herself in. 'Fast. Five times your usual fare.'

The driver – buzz cut, football shirt, chewing gum – looked back at her with a gappy grin. 'A pleasure, madam.'

As the taxi shot down the high street, Casey peered towards the bulk of the stands. She could hear the echoes of the loudspeaker, the dragon roar of the crowd.

Active Risk and Dotted Daisies are duelling it out. But Dotted Daisies looks to be tiring ...

And then she saw it: the briefest glimpse of Aidan.

'Pull over on the left, please.'

He was sprinting for the exit, dodging past a couple of vast marquees. Casey leaped from the taxi, waving wildly.

'Aidan! Here!'

A look of blind panic, a split-second of recognition. He changed course, racing towards the turnstile closest to her. But there was a man just behind him and he was far faster, closing the gap with every stride.

'Come on, Aidan!'

Gripping the bars of the turnstile, frantic with impatience, Casey glanced around and gasped with horror. The barman was sprinting down the high street towards them, white-blond hair flying. Two hundred yards: a few seconds away.

'Hurry!' she screamed to Aidan, and then to the gatekeeper manning the turnstile: 'That man there tried to snatch my handbag earlier! Call the police!'

She was bouncing on her toes, fighting the urge to flee and leave Aidan to take his chances. The barman was only a hundred yards away now, running flat out. Aidan was closer but slower, trying his best, precious seconds slipping away.

'Aidan!' Her voice broke. 'Hurry!'

It's going to the line ... Active Risk's holding on ...

Aidan was scrambling frantically, his shoes slipping on the tarmac.

Active Risk takes it! Then Dotted Daisies, Milaara, Gentleman's Darling ...

The roar of the mob crashed over them, all refinement stripped away.

'Come on!' she screamed.

The gatekeeper was looking around uncertainly – prepped to stop people getting in rather than breaking out. Aidan reached the heavy gate, throwing himself at the weight of the turnstile. Casey yanked it frantically from her side, trying to move the solid iron faster than its usual lugubrious pace.

The barman was nearly on them, reaching out, ruthlessly determined. There was something gleaming in his hand.

'A knife,' Casey screamed. 'He's got a knife!'

The turnstile creaked round, painfully slow.

Only a few strides away now.

Nearly there.

Through.

On the other side of the barrier, Aidan's pursuer shouldered the gatekeeper to one side, the uniformed man crashing ineffectually against the railings.

'Come on!' Casey leaped into the taxi, dragging Aidan in behind her. 'Go!' she screamed.

The car accelerated smoothly, speeding off down the high street. The barman slammed against its side as it powered away.

'Quickly,' Aidan begged the driver. 'They might follow us … I'll pay for any damage. They might have a car … They might … Please hurry!'

'I am, sir.'

Casey glanced back. A small group of men had gathered to one side of the street, staring angrily after them, but there was no immediate move to follow. She slumped back against the headrest.

'Bloody hell,' the driver said quietly to himself. But he kept driving, indicator clicking prosaically.

'Towards the golf course, please,' said Casey. 'Thank you.'

'Who on earth are you?' Aidan gasped.

He sounded slightly asthmatic, struggling to breathe through his panic.

'I'll explain later.'

He seemed to accept this, twisting his fingers together anxiously. An odd silence fell. They gazed out at the mundanity of Ascot town centre. Starbucks, Esso, Tesco Express. Gradually, Aidan got his breathing under control.

Casey turned on him forcefully. 'Who were those men? And why were they chasing you?'

Aidan sat back in the scruffy grey seat and chewed briefly on his thumbnail before answering.

'It's probably …' The words were cautious, tentative. 'It might be because of what I do.'

'What is that?'

'I gamble,' he said slowly. 'I gamble quite a lot.'

3

The helicopter began its descent to Battersea's heliport.

Aidan and Casey had sat in silence as the twin-engined Agusta roared away from the racecourse and tilted swiftly towards London. The flight lasted only fifteen minutes, the Thames a glittering ribbon beneath, the outskirts of London unfolding in a blur.

'Do you think,' the idea seemed to occur to Aidan for the first time as the helicopter touched down, 'that they'll try to do it again?'

Casey looked across at him. His brown hair was thinning and there was a sharp crease between his eyebrows. His forehead was slightly bulbous, face tapering to a narrow jaw. Bright, she thought, but the opposite of streetwise. In his morning suit, he was mildly pathetic, a schoolboy dressing up.

'They might,' she said shortly. 'You ought to go to the police. Those men were very … determined.'

He shook his head instinctively. 'No. No, I'd better not.'

She contemplated her bruised leg, remembering the speed, the careless violence, that gleam from something in the barman's hand. 'They meant business, whoever they were. Do you owe them a fortune?'

'No, that's not …' The rotor blades were slowing. Aidan looked at her again. 'What did you say your name was?'

'My name is Casey Benedict.' She had told him once already in the brief wait for the helicopter – he had a return flight booked, she'd guessed correctly – but he had been too deep in shock to take it in.

'And what do you do, Casey?'

'I'm a journalist.' No point in secrecy. 'I work for the *London Post*.'

'But not the sports pages?'

There was an edge of Essex to Aidan's voice. The Royal Enclosure was new, she thought. Perhaps his first visit.

'Investigations, usually. Politics at the moment, though.'

A flicker of eagerness in his eyes. 'Maybe you could … you know, investigate this?'

Casey's phone bleeped. Nash. *Casey, you've disappeared off the face of the planet! Got your Active Risk winnings. See you soon.*

'You're involved in gambling.' Casey knew she sounded dismissive. 'I don't really investigate that sort of thing.'

'Perhaps,' he said calmly, 'I should explain.'

From outside, the building was an anonymous industrial unit on a drab back street in Kennington. Just over the Thames from Westminster, it was only a short drive from the heliport. Aidan summoned an Uber as if the chase through Ascot had already slipped his mind.

Next to the industrial unit's front door, a few pigeons pecked hurriedly at a discarded carton of fried chicken. There was no nameplate and the grey walls rose to windows set high above Casey's head.

Security was an iris scan triggering a revolving door. Once inside, Aidan buzzed Casey through. They were straight into a functional lobby lined with coat hooks and lockers. No receptionist, no frills.

'This way,' said Aidan.

A short flight of stairs took them to a large room, high-ceilinged and busy. It was around forty yards long and thirty wide, Casey calculated, and there must be over a hundred desks, each with at least four screens. A wall of flickering technology divided each workspace from the next. The desks were cheap plywood: practicality trumping aesthetics. Above them, on a mezzanine level, there were more desks. The workspaces were maybe half full, almost all occupied by men in their twenties and thirties. They stared at their screens with a focused intensity.

'Is this a hedge fund?' Casey guessed. She had visited a couple before, finding them less glamorous than expected. Dozens of men riveted to twinkling computer screens, half the numbers red, half green. There had been the same hushed obsession, though, the same sense of transmuted ferocity.

'Sort of.'

'Do you work here, then?'

'Sort of. Come this way, Casey.'

Nodding at one or two people, he led her towards a glass-box meeting room. Again the emphasis was on convenience, not charm. There was a table, a few Blu-Tacked health and safety posters, and a view of a Kennington carpark. Two Bourbon biscuits on a chipped white plate; they had been there for an indeterminate period.

Aidan took a seat on one side of the table, its wooden veneer peeling slightly. He gestured Casey to the chair opposite. He was more confident now that he was in his own space, she saw, his movements less jerky than they had been at Ascot. Or maybe that had been from the flood of adrenaline and now it had eased off.

She waited.

'You journalists talk off the record, don't you?' Aidan tried out the phrase carefully. 'I can talk to you and you won't write about what I say?'

'We do that sometimes,' said Casey cautiously. 'Depending on what—'

'Can this be off the record then?' he persisted. 'All of it?'

He met her stare, wrinkling his nose to push his glasses back into place. His gaze was steady, his hands still, for once.

'Okay,' Casey agreed. 'For now, it can be.'

'Right,' he said. Then again, with more emphasis, '*Right.*'

There was a short pause. 'So,' Casey waved at the rows of desks, 'what are all these people doing?'

Aidan looked out at the flickering screens. 'Well,' he said, 'I suppose you could say that they're gambling.'

'It started with football.' As Aidan spoke, he was fiddling with the peeling veneer. 'I love the game, you see. My dad used to take me to matches. From right back when I was little, I loved the whole thing.'

Enthusiasm shone out of him, his eyes glowing.

'Football.' Casey struggled to match his fervour. She had absorbed a vague sense of which Premiership teams were doing well from the newsroom, but lacked any real interest. Dash – the *Post*'s head of news – regularly attended Chelsea games. Ross, on the other hand, venerated Spurs.

'A twat like him would support Tottenham,' the home affairs editor grumbled regularly. He was an Arsenal man, season ticket.

Casey would only know that a big match was underway when a sudden roar erupted across the newsroom at a crucial moment, and it emerged that half the office were surreptitiously watching on their phones.

'Do some fucking work,' Ross would bawl. 'You useless pillocks.'

'I was into Fantasy League,' Aidan went on. 'All that.'

'A lot of people are.'

'Yes.' A smile. 'Then one day, when I was about eleven, I was wandering down the high street with a mate and he suggested we put a bet on. He was a few years older than me, could get away with it.'

Casey thought of the betting shops lining every high street. The sweet-shop colours, the pavement covered in patches of chewing gum.

'And you won?'

'I did.' The memory still gleamed. 'Two quid on Everton, got five back. It was free money, seemed like.'

'A lot of people feel like that at first.'

'So straight away I put that fiver on Aston Villa to beat Blackburn Rovers.' Aidan's recollection was computer-precise. For him, it was just a matter of reaching for the right data. 'Three to one.'

'And Aston Villa won?' Casey hazarded.

'No.' Aidan laughed. 'I lost the lot.'

'Tends to happen.'

'That was my sweets for the week,' he said. 'So I took a step back.'

He was still wearing the morning suit, lolling back in his seat. He was swinging the office chair a quarter-turn one way, then a quarter-turn the other.

'Don't tell me,' said Casey. 'You worked out a system.'

'But,' Aidan's eyes met hers squarely, 'that's exactly what I did.'

*

'It was companies like Betfair – and its Asian equivalents – that changed things.' Aidan was leading her back out to the main room. 'Before that, you basically had to set up as a bookmaker to offer your own odds on a serious scale. Now, though,' he was standing at the shoulder of a twenty-something who was chewing gum frantically as his fingers pattered over the keyboard, 'anyone can act as a bookmaker.'

'Yes.' Casey was transfixed by the endlessly flickering numbers. 'I know that much.'

'Here,' Aidan pointed, 'you've got Tshakhuma playing Cape Town Spurs.'

'Who are they?'

'They're two South African football teams. Playing,' he focused for a second, 'in Jo'burg.'

'And people will bet on that?'

'People,' Aidan said, with supreme confidence, 'will bet on anything.'

'I'll take your word on it.'

'Critically for our purposes,' he went on, 'the odds of a win for Tshakhuma will shift during the game. So Tshakhuma could start at – let's say – ten to one, but then their striker starts having a blinder of a game and it looks like he might pull it out of the bag, so Tshakhuma's odds narrow down to five to one. Next minute, the star striker falls over and breaks his leg, and the odds shoot back out to twenty to one.'

'And you make money,' Casey worked out, 'because you've bet a tenner at ten to one, and then you lay off another tenner at five to one. So if Tshakhuma wins, you get a hundred pounds from the first bet, and you only have to pay out fifty to cover the second one. And the difference is your profit margin.'

'More or less.' He nodded.

'And when the odds go out again, you whack on another tenner.'

''Course.'

'But' – Casey glanced around the room – 'this looks slightly more sophisticated than that.'

'Well, that's because it is.'

A spiral staircase in the corner led to a mezzanine level. Casey followed Aidan up the stairs and they stood looking out over the office floor.

'I started by building software that snipes the prices,' he said. 'So as the market moves during the match, if there's a difference between two exchanges, my software snaps up the bet. It's all automated and even a small price shift can bring in a chunk of money.'

'And Betfair and the rest of them don't like that?'

'Not especially.' He shrugged. 'If you think about it, if my boys are winning ten grand over the course of the game, punters somewhere else are losing it. We reduce their likelihood of winning and that reduces their enthusiasm for playing, especially on that exchange.'

'It does if the punter's got any sense.'

'Well, yes.'

'So how do you get round that?'

A sideways smile. 'That's what that lot are up to.' He pointed to a group of workers in a corner of the room.

Probably generating thousands of different IP addresses, guessed Casey, so it wasn't clear that all these bets were being made from a single industrial unit in Kennington. And this unlovely office would have some of the fastest internet access in Europe, because when Tshakhuma's star striker broke his leg, the market would move fast, but it wouldn't move instantaneously. There would be the time it took for the television image to flash from Johannesburg to London. And the time it took for that information to be processed. And the time it took for Aidan's computers to place their bets. Seconds, maybe, for Tshakhuma's odds to jolt from sure-thing to also-ran? And in those brief moments, the fastest computer could pull in thousands. Millions, probably, on a big game, when vast sums were sloshing round the exchanges.

Aidan was waiting for the next question.

'That's not all you do, is it?' She met his eye. 'What else?'

'Off the record?'

'Not if it's illegal, Aidan.'

'The thing is,' he said, 'that what we're doing isn't illegal. Just … low-key.'

'How come?'

He blew out his cheeks as he considered how to explain. He wasn't patronising her, Casey decided. He was just used to people not being able to keep up with his thought processes.

'Okay,' he began. 'Sport isn't market-sensitive, is it?'

In finance, Casey knew, there were strict rules around market-sensitive information. If the chief executive of a utilities company discovers that his brilliant CFO has scarpered to Rio with a couple of million and a foxy PA, the market must be told as soon as possible, with everyone receiving the information at the same time. A careless leak can allow a select few to dump their shares before the rest of the market catches up, and that is regarded as unfair.

Around the world, these rules are enforced by financial authorities with varying degrees of success. Shares are bought and sold on stock exchanges, which are also carefully monitored. Abuse of insider trading rules can – very occasionally – lead to a lengthy jail sentence.

'I guess not,' said Casey. 'You don't have to make an announcement to the stock exchange about Tshakhuma's forward's tibia.'

'Exactly,' he agreed. 'It's all a bit grey.'

'So what do you do?'

'Well,' he said, 'imagine there's a big test match in Chittagong. Bangladesh's opening batsman strides out to the crease, the crowd goes wild. The first ball whizzes down and … he's out for a golden duck. The betting market is going to go absolutely doolally, right? The odds on a Bangladesh win will shoot up.'

'Yes.'

'So if we are able to know about it first, then we can make a lot of money.'

'And you know first because …' Casey stopped.

Pitchsiding, it was called, she remembered vaguely. If Aidan dispatched someone to the test match in Chittagong with an open line to the office, a signal could be sent at the precise moment the ball snicked the bat and hurtled to a triumphant wicketkeeper. By the time the television pictures showed the umpire raising his finger, the batsman trudging disconsolately back to the pavilion, Aidan's computers would long have finished their work.

It wasn't quite illegal. Observers were occasionally removed from cricket matches, grumbling and complaining. Pitchsiding breaches the terms and conditions of the ticket purchase, cricket authorities will say primly, as a watcher is escorted to the door.

But there might be 80,000 people in the stadium, all holding phones and all shouting randomly. It was almost impossible to police. Few sports authorities wanted to draw attention to the problem anyway. Punters like the illusion of fairness, at the very least, and sport's finances depend on punters.

'So I started using scouts at games more and more.' Aidan cracked his knuckles loudly. 'Television follows the action, right? 'Course it does because that's where the interesting stuff is happening. But my boy in the stadium is watching the whole field. So he can see that the Spurs striker's limping a bit, and that it's making him a tiny bit slow to the ball. The cameras don't catch the striker signalling to the coach that he's finished, but my boy does. And we know that if Spurs' star striker is subbed off, his team's chances will slide a bit. And with a scout in the stands, we can know that minutes before the rest of the market.'

'I see.'

'For us,' Aidan explained, 'it's not really about who wins or loses overall, it's about how the likelihood of winning and losing changes during the game.'

The small shifts in the market. Easy calculations for someone who thought in fractions, someone who found numbers infinitely more intelligible than emotions. Throughout the match, the odds would fluctuate, and Aidan's computers would hoover up the difference.

'So these guys ...'

'Almost every person in this room has a PhD in maths,' Aidan told her carelessly. 'Cambridge, MIT, Harvard. They're bright kids, this lot.'

'And this is what you're up against,' said Casey, 'when you plonk a fiver down on Chelsea to win?'

'Yep,' he agreed cheerfully. 'Exactly.'

4

'So who wants to kill you?' Casey asked conversationally. 'One of the betting exchanges?'

Her phone buzzed. Nash, texting.

Casey, are you OK?

I had to go home, I'm afraid. Terrible migraine. Sorry, Nash – it was such a lovely day. Thank you.

No probs. Get well soon.

'I don't think so.' Aidan frowned thoughtfully. 'I mean, we irritate them, but not that much.'

They were making their way back to the little office. Casey remembered again the ferocity of the barman, his fury. Hungry now, she decided to take her chances with one of the abandoned Bourbons. Aidan didn't notice.

'But your operation is soaking up,' Casey glanced around the dingy office, 'millions a year. It must be affecting the exchanges' business.'

Aidan didn't react to the figure. Right ballpark, then.

'I still don't think it's them,' he said calmly. 'I think it's the match fixers.'

A vague memory surfaced. The *News of the World*, years back. A man – oleaginous, sweaty – promising he could ensure three no-balls in a row as Pakistan faced down England at Lord's. Because, of course, there is a market over the next no-ball. There's a market for everything.

And on that occasion, the *Screws*' camera was there too: silent, relentless, capturing every word. Because there's a market for news, too, and it is just as aggressive.

A few years earlier, Casey and Miranda had done a quick story about match fixing. A small-time crook in the Midlands, jailed for a few months. That fixer had had links to Macau, the casino paradise across the bay from Hong Kong, where hundreds of millions shifted every week.

'Match fixers,' Aidan repeated. 'They're everywhere.'

'Tell me.'

'Right.' He took off his glasses, polished them with the front of his shirt. 'In football, for example, it can be hard to promise a win, because, well, that's what most teams are trying to do anyway, right? Realistically, it's quite hard to sign up all eleven players and guarantee a loss. It'd be expensive too. Not saying it doesn't happen, but it's tricky. But there will always be a decent market in the number of goals scored in a match. Two goals or less, three or more. Simple, right? And the odds for that shift a lot during the game. Your dodgy footballer might not be able to guarantee a win, but he and a couple of mates can probably make sure a lot of goals are scored, either by them or the other side.'

'It must take a lot of coordination,' Casey said drily.

'Yeah, sure. But at least it's not like tennis, where you've just got a couple of people facing each other over a net. Fixing tennis is an absolute doddle. The set-and-break mob, where the favourite goes a set down, and lets himself be broken in the second set too, and then – a miracle! – bounces back. That's the way you get the biggest price swings in both directions.'

'Devious.'

'I won't go near bloody horses, either. Never know what those things are going to do next.' He looked down ruefully at his morning suit.

'I'm sure racing has its own skulduggery,' said Casey.

''Course it does.'

'But you're not fixing matches?'

'No!' Aidan's eyes opened wide. He seemed genuinely startled. 'Never.'

'So why are they after you?'

Aidan stood. He walked into the main room and grabbed a laptop.

'Here.' He sounded earnest. 'This is where we really make our money.'

To Casey, the screen was gibberish. Rows of numbers and symbols.

'I built a model,' he explained, 'that predicts the chances of a win or a loss in a football game.'

Casey peered closer. 'How?'

'My model processes all the data. It looks at how this team has played against that team before. It looks at which players are on the pitch and how they've been performing. It analyses how those players have been doing in training because we've got scouts at those sessions too. It looks at the weather because that impacts on how they play. It looks at how far a team's travelled because their chances of winning drop by, say, three per cent for every fifty miles they are from their home ground. We can even find out if some of the players have been on a bender the night before and are absolutely hanging. And then the model grinds up all that data and spits out the odds of the win.'

'I see.' Casey wasn't sure that she did.

'So, here, you've got Pordenone playing Ravenna. They're both Italian football teams,' he added, seeing her raised eyebrow. 'Our model shows that Ravenna have got a seventy-eight point six per cent chance of winning, but look at the odds right now.' He pointed with a chewed fingernail. 'The rest of the market thinks Pordenone's going to clobber them. So we back Ravenna and, statistically, we've got a very good chance of cashing in, especially if we do it a thousand times a day.'

There wasn't a time zone that hadn't fallen for the delights of football, thought Casey. Aidan's was a twenty-four-hour operation.

'Only if you're sure about the model.'

'I am.' He spoke with absolute conviction.

'How accurate is it?'

A sparkle of mischief glinted in his eyes. 'Very. And it doesn't need to be right all the time to make money anyway. If it's accurate seventy-five per cent of the time, we still end up miles ahead.'

'So why's it getting you chased by men with knives?'

The sparkle disappeared. 'Because there's a sort of side effect to all this … It means we can tell when someone is fixing.'

'How?'

'Well, if the model shows a ninety-eight per cent chance of a team winning,' he said simply, 'and they get hammered, that means something's up.'

'You can't know that. Not beyond doubt.'

'I can.'

'You can't,' she pushed him. 'What if the whole team is fed a bowl of dodgy shellfish the night before? What if the star striker's girlfriend's ditched him that morning and he's heartbroken? Life isn't that predictable.'

'It is.' Aidan's mouth had gone tight. 'You just don't want to believe it. And even if it weren't, I don't assume someone is cheating on the basis of just one duff game. We track individuals and teams over months – years, even. And that means we can see the patterns. And that means we can tell who's doing what.'

Casey peered at the rows of numbers again.

'So what do you want from all this?'

'I want them to *stop*.' Anger spurted suddenly.

Casey regarded him thoughtfully. 'Why, especially?'

'When they fix matches,' he was still twitchy, the anger bubbling just below the surface, 'it produces junk data. That data feeds into my model and it's like – I don't know – it's like throwing grit into an engine. It *damages* it.'

The money, Casey saw, was almost a by-product. For Aidan, perfection meant the data functioning seamlessly: his model seeing into the future.

'I see.'

'It took *years* to build that model,' he said. 'I want it to be *perfect*.'

'Okay.'

Looking up, Casey realised it was evening. Outside, the drab street glowed in the summer twilight.

'So you'll look into it?' He sounded hopeful.

'You produced a list of dodgy footballers?' she guessed. 'Who's throwing games?'

'I was trying to do the right thing.' It sounded plaintive but true, she thought.

'Who did you give the list to?'

Guilt flickered over his face. 'Well ...'

'Who did you give it to, Aidan?'

'I ended up giving it to lots of people.' He was tracing shapes on the floor with the sole of his shoe. The black leather was still highly polished, even if the shoes hadn't been designed with sprinting in mind.

'Who exactly?'

'I started with CleanBet,' he said. CleanBet was a division of football's governing body, set up to monitor betting. As far as Casey was aware, its members spent a lot of time liaising over long lunches in Rome or Shanghai or Buenos Aires. Match fixing flourished regardless.

'What did CleanBet do?'

'Nothing,' said Aidan sulkily. 'I mean, they may have talked to a few footballers or something. Given them a bit of a going over. But nothing proper. Nothing *real*.'

'So what did you do next?' Casey could guess the answer.

'Well, after that, I told anyone who would listen,' he said. 'Guys I know at the betting exchanges. A few of the football correspondents. People like Griff Aitken at your own newspaper. And I told the boys on my team to keep their ears to the ground, of course. Everyone.'

'What team?' Casey asked.

'Fleethurst Wanderers.' Aidan blinked at her. 'Bought them a few years back.'

'You own a football team?' Casey glanced around the dingy room, recalculating. Not millions: tens of millions a year. Maybe even hundreds of millions.

'Sure.' He was unconcerned. 'Fleethurst Wanderers in League One. Hopefully, we'll go up this year.'

'Basically,' Casey doubled back, 'you told everyone you could think of?'

'Yes.' An apologetic grin.

'And one of those people,' said Casey, 'is very pissed off.'

5

'Casey!' Cressida's shriek echoed around the newsroom. 'What in God's name have you done to that Emilia Wickstead?'

'Emilia who?' Casey glanced down at the oyster silk. Sprinting across Ascot had done the dress no favours, she realised. A couple of the buttons had popped off and there was a tear in her left sleeve. Fixable, surely?

'And where the hell' – Cressida's voice went up an octave – 'is the *hat*?'

'The hat?' Casey's hands went guiltily to her head. A vague memory surfaced, of feathers spinning into the distance as she raced down an escalator.

'Your exquisite Jane Taylor hat!' Cressida vibrated with fury. 'It costs a *fortune*. Casey, I am *never* ...'

'But I had to. It was *important*.'

'You always say that. You absolute ...' Cressida searched around for an appropriate word, 'delinquent.'

Behind Cressida, Casey could see the newsdesk collapsing with laughter.

'Casey.' After letting Cressida land a few more choice insults, Dash threw out a lifeline. 'Can I have a word?'

Cressida was still raging as Dash closed the door to the investigations room behind them. Miranda grinned at Casey. Hessa, a junior reporter who had joined the team recently, was trying to hide her mirth. Tillie Carlisle usually sat at Casey's old desk but it was currently empty. The Ascot festivities would run late into the evening.

'Sorry about that,' Casey said to Dash.

'It's all right.' He was suppressing a smile too. 'Cressida'll calm down in a bit. Get anything good at Ascot?'

'I did, actually.' Casey brightened. 'Lucas Fairbairn – you know, the junior Treasury minister?'

'I do try to keep a vague sense of who's who in government,' said Dash. 'Even the lower echelons. I find it really helps me get the job done.'

'What's Fairbairn been up to?' Miranda cut through Dash's sarcasm.

'Some chief executive buddy of Nash Bexley told me that Fairbairn's renting a room in London,' said Casey. 'And claiming for it on his expenses.'

There was nothing unusual about that. As the MP for Easton in Warwickshire, Fairbairn was entitled to claim the costs of travelling to London to attend Parliament. He could rent a whole flat or a room in a house, and the taxpayer picked up the bill. There were strict rules, though.

'So?' Tough and bright, Miranda ran the investigations team with a ruthless efficiency. Her blonde curls and blue eyes made her appear charming and innocent, which was deeply misleading.

'I'll have to check this out,' said Casey. 'But apparently he is also in a relationship with the woman he is renting the room from. Esther Amaral, I think her name is.'

That would almost certainly lead to his resignation if it leaked out. Even years after the original scandal, any ambiguity over an MP's expenses remained toxic. Parliamentarians were banned from renting accommodation off plus-ones.

'So he's renting a room from his girlfriend?' Dash clarified.

'That's what this guy said.'

'How can this chief executive be sure they're together?' Hessa asked.

'Wouldn't say. You know it could be any number of ways.'

They all knew. One of the chief executive's employees might live next door, with a clear view into the neighbouring garden. Or there might have been a goodbye kiss in a thoughtless moment on the Tube one morning. Or Esther Amaral might simply have giggled the secret to a girlfriend, who told her friend, who told.

Eyes everywhere, always.

'Check it out,' said Dash. 'Sounds good.'

'Sure.'

'Anything else?'

Casey looked down at the torn oyster silk. 'Something a bit odd happened while I was at Ascot,' she began.

By the time she had finished, Miranda was laughing. 'Honestly, Casey. It was only meant to be a nice day at the races.'

'I know,' she agreed. 'Things got a tiny bit out of hand.'

'Aidan Gardiner.' The corners of Dash's mouth turned down. 'I haven't heard of him, have I?'

'I looked him up on the way over here,' said Casey. 'He definitely owns the operation in Kennington. And he also owns Fleethurst Wanderers. He's just very, very low-key.'

Dash picked up Miranda's landline handset. 'Griff?' he said. 'Dash. Pop over to investigations?'

The desks in the *Post*'s open-plan offices were roughly grouped into sections. News, Business and Sport were a chaos of notepads and old newspapers and abandoned lunches. Massive televisions dominated the main newsdesk, an endless swirl of information bannering across the screens.

A wide staircase led up a floor to the fluffier sections: Mags, Features, Books. Up there, the atmosphere was chattier, more congenial. There were bouquets of flowers and occasional birthday balloons tied to office chairs. It was on this floor that Cressida – still raging – ruled over the fashion cupboard.

Griff Aitken, one of the football correspondents, sat fifty yards from the investigations office. Within a few seconds of Dash's call, he was leaning against the doorframe, arms crossed, raising his eyebrows rather than asking the question.

'Have you come across someone called Aidan Gardiner?' Casey asked.

There was a brief pause as Griff tried to remember, while simultaneously trying to work out why they wanted to know.

'Should I have?' he said eventually.

'He emailed you a few weeks ago,' Casey expanded. 'With a list of footballers he reckoned were fixing matches.'

A hint of recognition crossed Griff's face. 'I think I remember,' he said slowly. 'I was going to have a proper look at it, but he sent it over in the run-up to the FA Cup final so it all got a bit submerged.'

'Can I see it now?' Dash asked briskly.

'Sure.' Griff pulled his phone out of his pocket. 'Aidan Gardiner, you said? I meant to …' His voice trailed away. 'Here.'

'Forward the email to Miranda.'

As the message came through, they all gathered round Miranda's screen. Even Casey recognised some of the names on the list of footballers.

'That's quite a line-up.' Dash's tone was neutral.

'I did check it out,' Griff said, only slightly defensively. 'I had a quick chat with this Aidan guy and I tried to make sense of it all. But it was only a computer program that generated a list of possibly dubious players. We would never have run something that libellous off some random program none of us could understand anyway.'

Griff was lolling against the wall again, as if standing was too much of an effort. He was tall, with untidy black hair and dark brown eyes. There were Welsh cadences in his voice, and an air of not being able to take anything too seriously. He'd been a reasonably successful football player himself in his teens, Casey remembered, and the athleticism was still there. In his twenties he had moved into journalism, where he combined sharp insight with a dry wit. His weekly column was very well regarded, she knew. In the summer, he wrote about horse racing too. As she looked in his direction, Griff's eyes flickered over the oyster silk, his eyebrows twitching slightly.

'Of course, we might not have run anything,' said Dash evenly. 'But it would have been helpful to have it flagged up all the same.'

Griff shrugged, unabashed, confident enough in his own abilities to let Dash's displeasure roll over him this once.

'Everyone has their pet conspiracy theories about football, you know?' Griff was scrolling through his emails. 'Like this one. Or this. We get dozens of emails like that in any given week. Hundreds. No one could read them all.'

'Sure.' Dash wasn't quite letting him off the hook. They all got hundreds of emails every day. The reporters filtered stories before they passed them on to the newsdesk, and sometimes they filtered the wrong thing.

'Who is Aidan Gardiner anyway?' asked Griff.

'Fleethurst Wanderers' owner.' Casey watched the pieces fall into place.

'Okay.' Griff held his hands up in what might have been an apology. 'I should have—'

'Aidan Gardiner also runs a betting operation,' said Casey, 'which appears to be fairly sophisticated.'

'I see.' Griff glanced at the list again. 'Well, that … okay. He didn't tell me that when I spoke to him. Might have been useful to mention it, you'd think.'

'Right,' cut in Miranda smoothly. 'What exactly can we do with this?'

There was a moment of silence.

'It is tricky,' said Casey thoughtfully. 'Griff's right. This list isn't enough. We'd need to catch the fixer in the process of actually fronting up a footballer, and I haven't even begun to think about how we'd do that. For all Aidan's data gathering, he's got nothing on who's behind it all. No target. He knows it's happening, nothing about how.'

Ross stuck his head in the door. 'Editor wants to see us, Dash.'

Nobody kept the editor waiting.

'Casey,' Dash spoke fast, 'focus on that Fairbairn story for now. Griff's right – this is all a bit theoretical. And for all we know, it could have been a case of mistaken identity. These heavies just took Aidan for someone who owed them a fortune or something.'

The glitter of terror in Aidan's eyes; the ferocity of the barman as he smashed Casey against the glass partition.

'Yes, Dash.' Sounding obedient.

The head of news departed, striding towards the editor's office.

The three investigative reporters contemplated Griff.

'All right.' He held up his hands again, laughing. 'I know what you lot are thinking. But the day-to-day stuff does keep me quite busy. We're not like this team, publishing a story every few months or so.'

'Sure.' Miranda's mouth was twisting into a smile. 'And I mean, it's sport, right? So crucial.'

'Oi!'

News reporters tend to regard themselves as the elite, which is not a view shared by the rest of the other sections. News thinks Business is boring. Business thinks News is illiterate. Politics chats to the Prime Minister every few weeks, and therefore thinks they are more important than everyone else. Everyone else thinks that Politics has dolly-drop stories dictated to them by some junior spad every afternoon and can barely be regarded as journalists. Business and News are united in thinking that Sport is full of obsessive simpletons. Sport thinks that sport is the centre of the universe and doesn't care what anyone else thinks.

'Seriously, though,' said Hessa. 'How could we prove it?'

6

Tillie and Casey watched with interest as the dark-haired woman made her way down the street towards them.

'Pretty,' said Tillie, and Casey nodded.

They were sitting in Tillie's car – a navy Polo – on a quiet back street in Islington. The woman walked straight past the car, heading towards Highbury Fields.

'I'll—'

'Yes.'

'Laters.'

Tillie slid out of the car and followed the woman down the road.

Casey stayed seated, fingers drumming on the dashboard.

'You've got to prove beyond all doubt that they're in a relationship before we front him up,' Dash had insisted, which Casey knew anyway.

But it was proving difficult.

Fairbairn was unquestionably living in the neat little cottage, halfway along a terrace not far from Arsenal stadium.

Casey had spent some time studying the estate agent's details from the last time it sold. When Esther Amaral had bought the house three years ago, it had been a dilapidated two-up, two-down. A month after she bought it, she had applied for planning permission to convert the attic into a third bedroom with an en suite bathroom. The rest of the house had been overhauled at the same time. Casey had found images on the website of a proud interior designer.

So it was perfectly possible that the MP was chastely renting one of the house's three bedrooms from Miss Amaral.

Casey scowled and ran through what they knew about Esther Amaral again. Not much.

Amaral had gone to a private girls' school in North London before heading for Bristol University. Now she worked in compliance in one of the big pension funds. Most mornings, she was picked up – 'so early,' Tillie had grumbled, 'so very, very early' – by an Uber and swept towards the City. In the evenings, late, she was dropped home. On Saturdays, a personal trainer waited in the dawn outside the house. Esther would bound out, glossy brown hair pulled back in a ponytail, slim figure in Lululemon leggings, and the two of them would jog off towards the park, spring-heeled.

Esther was always immaculately turned out. Hair blow-dried to a glossy swing with a thick fringe. A mask of make-up – mascara, eyeshadow, eyeliner. At the weekend, she pottered around Islington: popping to restaurants, ambling round galleries, seeing friends.

Esther never mentioned a boyfriend, Tillie reported, after plonking herself down at the next table in the local cafe. Not once in a whole long lunch with her girlfriends.

Fairbairn worked more erratic hours, but most Thursday evenings or Friday mornings, he headed for Euston and a weekend in the constituency.

In Parliament's bars, Casey put out feelers.

'I've never heard about a girlfriend,' said one lobbyist, shrugging.

'I always assumed he was gay,' cackled an MP's parliamentary assistant, mopping up a splash of white wine with a bar mat.

'Really? Why?'

'Well, if you don't hear anything ...' An expressive nod.

Because even now, there was secrecy.

'Why?' The lobbyist's raucous laugh. 'You interested?'

'God, no.'

*

'What about Fairbairn's own finances?' asked Ross. 'Why didn't he just buy his own place in London?'

'They seem to be a bit unusual,' said Casey. 'As a kid, he went to Drewsteignton, which some of his colleagues have given him crap about.'

'Typical champagne socialist,' muttered Ross. 'But then a bit of hypocrisy's always useful to us.'

'Except his parents lost all their money somewhere along the way. Fairbairn's spoken about it in the Commons – how devastating it was when his father went bankrupt. So I guess he's just never built up the deposit to buy his own place.'

'Boohoo,' snapped Ross. 'Now, are you any closer to proving they're actually in a relationship?'

'It's impossible,' Tillie wailed when Casey asked her again. 'I never see them out together. They've got those wretched wooden shutter things in the front window, and the moment they're home, the shutters slam shut.'

Peering in through windows was discouraged anyway.

After a couple more days of moaning, Casey offered to help Tillie one Saturday morning.

Now she waited in the navy Polo. Half an hour later, Esther Amaral reappeared, carrying a large, beribboned carton from the local bakery. Tillie trudged a hundred yards behind her.

The junior reporter climbed into the car and slammed the door.

'It's hopeless. Can't the source just tell you how he knows? That might give us something to go on.'

'It's probably best that we don't know how he knows.'

'It's never going to work, then. Just a waste of time.'

'Shall we give up?' Casey asked conversationally.

There was a flicker of hope in Tillie's eyes. 'Fairbairn's in Warwickshire now. Amaral's here. Esther's never shown any interest in trekking up to Warwickshire for the weekend, which is fair enough, if you ask me. And there's a party tonight that I'd—'

'Okay,' said Casey easily.

Tillie eyed her suspiciously.

'What?'

As she waited for Tillie to return to the car, Casey had been working her way through a pile of newspapers. 'Here.' She flicked through a copy of *The Times* and handed it to Tillie.

It was a list of notable birthdays. A Marshal of the RAF. A Formula One racing driver. The principal emeritus of the University of St Andrews.

'And Lucas Fairbairn,' Tillie read aloud. 'MP for Easton.'

'There is no way,' Casey was thinking about the Lululemon leggings, 'that Esther Amaral spends her Saturday evenings on her own, munching her way through a vast cardboard box of sugary carbs.'

'No,' said Tillie wistfully. The penny dropped slowly. 'It's a birthday cake in that box! She must be meeting up with him today.'

Casey let the silence lengthen.

'Tonight. Probably not in his constituency, because they've always been so careful. But where?' Tillie finished uncertainly.

Casey handed her a list. 'That's every nice hotel between here and Easton. Concentrate on the blissfully rustic ones first. Those lovely, remote country-house hotels. She may have booked a cottage, of course, but we might as well start with the hotels.'

'We can't just follow her from here?'

'We will if we have to,' said Casey. 'But it would be helpful if one of us could get to the hotel before her, in case we can spot Fairbairn checking in. Trailing someone isn't particularly easy, either. If we lose her today, we'll be back at square one.'

'Right.' Tillie squared her shoulders. 'I'll get started.'

They sat in the stuffiness of the blue Polo, working their way down the list.

Oh, hello, my name is Esther Amaral. I just wanted to check on my booking, because I got a weird email and I wasn't sure if it had been cancelled. Oh? I never was? Let me check and get back to you.

Hi there, my name is Esther Amaral. We're booked in for tonight, but I just wanted to check which spa services were available? Oh, we're not? I'll just …

Hi, Esther Amaral speaking …

'What if Fairbairn booked it?' Tillie fretted, after a dozen calls.

'On his own birthday? I doubt it. Possible, though.'

They kept going, widening the net.

Until finally, Tillie's eyes widened ecstatically. 'That's perfect.' She grinned. 'See you later.' She hung up. 'Lettaford Manor,' she recited. 'Not far from Chipping Norton.'

Casey pulled up the description on her phone. Imposing Cotswolds stately home, grounds landscaped by Capability Brown, Michelin-starred restaurant, award-winning spa.

'Brilliant,' bawled Ross when Casey rang him up. 'I do like a nice bit of colour in these stories. That sort of posh-twat hotel will really hold the page, too.'

'A snapper's on his way from Gloucester,' Casey told Tillie as she hung up on Ross. 'He'll try to get a shot of them arriving. Book your-self a room now.'

'With pleasure!'

Tillie would blend in effortlessly at Lettaford Manor.

'You scoot off to Oxfordshire straight away,' Casey added aloud. 'I'll try to follow Amaral from here. Then I can tell you when she's arriving. I'll call you if I lose her, too.'

'I'll take the train up,' Tillie said. 'You hang on to this car.'

'Thanks,' said Casey. 'See you in a bit.'

It was easy, in the end. Esther Amaral picked up her boyfriend from a nearby station, and the photographer snapped her car entering the long beech avenue that led up to Lettaford Manor. The two of them sat side by side in the little BMW convertible, Fairbairn half turned towards his secret girlfriend, both of them smiling delightedly.

They looked quite sweet, Casey thought, as she glanced through the photographs later.

When the couple walked into the hotel reception, Tillie was sitting in a plush armchair beside a big fireplace of honey-coloured stone. Her phone was recording before the car had even come to a halt.

Fairbairn carrying Amaral's bag.

Amaral carrying the beribboned cardboard box.

His arm round her waist, her hand on his back. Smiling at the receptionist. Grinning at each other.

The briefest of kisses.

Enough.

More than.

'They didn't come down to dinner,' Tillie reported later. 'I did, though. Guinea fowl with pancetta and prunes. *Delicious.*'

The photographer, less delightedly, reported that Amaral's car had stayed in the same place all night.

'They didn't come out of the hotel at all,' he reported grumpily. 'Tipping it down, that's probably why. Glad bloody Tillie had a nice time.'

The photographer caught them leaving together the next morning, Amaral still driving, the rainswept beeches looming as her indicator flashed.

It was Tillie who emailed the front-up letter to Fairbairn's special adviser.

The resignation announcement came through a couple of hours later, the Prime Minister sounding genuinely regretful that he was returning to the backbenches.

At the *Post*, the back bench whirled into operation, subbing the copy and tweaking the headlines as the paper's lawyer scribbled in red pen. He never typed his notes into his computer, preferring a printout and a shredder, just in case.

An hour before the website changed up, the phone on Casey's desk rang.

'Casey Benedict.'

'Um,' said a man's voice. 'It's Lucas Fairbairn.'

Casey pressed the record button automatically.

'Thank you for your statement, Mr Fairbairn. I can confirm that we have received it and I will make sure that its contents are fully reflected in the article.'

'I was wondering …' His voice trailed away. In her mind's eye, Casey saw the dark auburn hair, the scattering of freckles. Fairbairn had pale skin, with light brown eyes set wide apart. His walk was slightly shambling, and she'd never seen him with his tie done up properly. He must loosen his top button before he even left the Islington cottage.

'What?' she asked.

'Please don't mention Esther in your article.' The words came out in a rush. 'Please. She's a private individual. What I did … It was my fault, not hers. She's nothing to do with any of this.'

'I can't do that, I'm afraid, Lucas.'

'Please.' His voice sounded more urgent. 'It'll … It would be disastrous for her, being named. Her employers—'

'I'm sorry.' In the distance, Casey could see Ross prowling round the newsdesk, gesticulating angrily at one of the assistant news editors.

'But Esther's … She's no one!' Fairbairn said. 'No one knows who she is, and that's how she wants to keep it. Needs to keep it. Her privacy—'

'She is involved,' Casey said flatly.

She was pretty, too, crucially. The picture editor had pulled a photograph of Amaral off the pension fund's website: bright smile, pearl necklace, shiny hair with that thick fringe. A photograph inside the paper showed her in her leggings, bounding off towards the park.

'Lovely.' The picture editor had almost licked his lips. 'That'll look fantastic on the page.'

'Please. I'm … I'm begging you.'

'I can't.' Brusque but probably true. She could have before. It was too late now. The story didn't need the details about Amaral, not really. But if Casey tried to remove her name now, Ross would raise a mocking eyebrow and turn back to his newslist. Because the newslist was Ross's obsession. The newslist, the newslist, always the newslist.

'It'll be the only thing anyone remembers about Esther,' Fairbairn said desperately. 'For the rest of her life, when someone Googles her …'

'I am sorry.'

'Please. She's not involved.' His voice was rising.

'I can't—'

'I'm begging you.' It was a shout. 'Please don't do this.'

'I'm sorry.'

'You'll destroy her life.'

'Mr Fairbairn—'

'You people don't care, do you? We can all end up like that poor fucker in Holloway Road for all you care …' Fairbairn's voice stalled.

'What? Who are you talking about?'

But he had swept on. 'You just don't give a damn, do you? Not about anyone.'

'Again, I am sorry, Mr Fairbairn.'

'Please. Her family … It'll—'

'Mr Fairbairn, it's too late.'

'All right.' He sounded defeated, close to tears. 'All right.'

The phone line went dead. For a moment Casey just sat there, staring at the businesslike black handset.

And then the headlines blared.

Miranda, grinning, swept Casey, Hessa and Tillie out for champagne.

'My first scalp,' Tillie said, again and again. 'My first proper scoop.'

And Casey, perched in the glamorous bar, wondered why sadness swept over her.

7

Nash Bexley's email had arrived by the time she woke up the next morning. *Great work on Fairbairn, Casey! The git had it coming. Catch up soon.*

Casey squinted at the message and then dragged herself upright. She stared around the bedroom of the little flat in Tufnell Park. The laughter of the night before echoed briefly and faded away.

She thought about two people waking up just a few miles away. Waking in silence, heavy with dread. If they had slept at all, that was, with everything different now.

Casey had slept with the curtains open. As she looked out over the austere grey roofs, the rain sliced down.

She was still here: she hadn't moved out. Not after …

Because there was nowhere else for her to go.

There was before, and there was after. Same flat, same clothes, same job. Everything looked the same, and everything was different now.

I miss you.

Hopeless thought.

Ed's eyes, flecked with grey and green, blue and gold.

Ed's eyes, staring at nothing.

Thank you for your help, Nash, she typed slowly.

The movements to start Casey's day were automatic.

Coffee. Shower. Coffee. Dressed.

Then out into the grey of the morning and the clatter of the traffic. The rain splashed in the gutter and a thousand bobbing umbrellas flowed down the pavements. Past the greengrocer and the dry cleaner, past the estate agent and the Costa. And there was the squat Tube station, with its oxblood arches and Edwardian faïence. She marched along, swept towards the ticket gates by a stream of commuters. A man used to sell newspapers here, that loud shout: *Read-all-abaaaaht-it!* Not anymore, though. Long gone.

There was a shape close to the entrance. A man, slumped on the ground, a disillusioned lurcher huddled by his side. Could he possibly be sleeping through the chaos of the morning? Maybe. And Casey found herself reaching for her wallet. No change rattling around. A fiver? Sure.

That poor fucker in Holloway Road.

The memory jerked her to a halt.

In, Lucas Fairbairn had said in that chaotic conversation yesterday. Not *on.* And then a hesitation, as if he already regretted the words. What had he been talking about? Casey swam to the side of the flood of commuters, pulled out her recorder and played the call back to herself.

That poor fucker in Holloway Road. Brief pause.

He must have been talking about someone physically inside Holloway Road Tube station, not just somewhere on the busy road that sliced from Archway to Highbury. The Tube station was only half a mile from the little cottage in Islington; Esther and Lucas Fairbairn must use it all the time.

Who was Fairbairn talking about? Could it be someone who worked at the station?

Casey checked her watch. She needed to get in, update her story, see if there were any developments overnight.

It's probably nothing, she told herself. *In* or *on,* it's all the same.

That poor fucker in Holloway Road. Pause.

Get to work. Ross will be scribbling at his newslist, checking his watch.

There had been something in Fairbairn's voice, though. A tremor: I shouldn't have said that. Not to a *journalist.* Not to *her.*

She could pop by, maybe. Take a look. It couldn't be much more than a mile to Holloway Road. Wouldn't take long. But Tufnell Park was on the Northern Line and Holloway Road was on the Piccadilly Line and it would be quicker on foot. She contemplated the splashing rain. Unappealing.

She really should get into the office.

Curiosity won.

She started walking.

Casey slowed as she drew near to Holloway Road station. It was the same as any other busy London road. Sainsbury's, Sports Direct, squashed McDonald's coffee cups. A train rattled overhead, wheels shrieking, metal on metal. Commuters poured into the station.

Fairbairn must have been talking about someone who'd jumped here once. Because that happened often enough. A shriek of brakes drowning the screams. A Tube driver shuddering, nightmares forever. Commuters – cynical, weary, irritated – streaming off down another route. She could look up that death in the office.

There was a person slumped just inside the station, though. A tatty sleeping bag pulled high, a few coins in a battered hat.

Casey hesitated. She was intruding.

Sparse blond hair. Pale face. Fast asleep.

I don't know him.

She felt ashamed by the flood of relief.

Are you sure, quite sure?

Peering closer.

No, I—

She bent to drop another fiver into a battered hat, and as she leaned down, the man's eyes opened, just.

Casey came to a halt with a gasp.

They stared at each other. Only for a second, and then the flow of commuters built up behind her. She was nudged forward, down the lift, down the platform, down and down and down.

The train roared into the station and she was gone.

*

The Burma Road, the corridor in the House of Commons where most of the newspapers keep a dilapidated office, was busy that morning. The *Post*'s room overlooked Parliament Square, the chimes of Big Ben whiling away the days. Every other lightbulb in the narrow corridor had been parsimoniously removed, casting badger stripes of light and shade on the worn linoleum.

Casey made her way to her desk, clutching another coffee.

'Morning, Casey.' Archie, the political editor, glanced up as she walked in. 'Nice work on Fairbairn.'

'You could have bloody warned me,' Baz, the Whitehall editor, grumbled. 'Fairbairn was fifty to one to be booted.'

'What?' Casey stared at him. 'What do you mean?'

'I mean I'd have chucked a tenner on if I'd known you were about to off him,' Baz explained as if talking to an idiot. 'I'd have made a bomb.'

'You bet on ministerial resignations?'

'Sure.' Baz clicked his computer mouse and a betting website appeared on his screen with a jolly fanfare and a bright purple banner. 'Look at the odds on old Fossil at the moment, for example. Evens. I suppose with Fairbairn gone, the PM's going to have to do a mini-reshuffle anyway, so he might as well dump Fossil at the same time. Should have put a tenner on. Too late now.'

Miles Foscliffe was the Leader of the House of Commons, drifting further from the centre of power with every reshuffle.

'Miles Foscliffe. He—'

'Never really recovered from that story you did on him ages ago.' Baz nodded. 'His wife, having an affair with that bodyguard. You could have given me a heads-up about that one too, while we're on the subject.'

'But you know far more about who's likely to be in and who's likely to be out than the average punter,' Casey protested. 'It's basically insider trading.'

'You've got to be a bit careful.' Baz shrugged. 'Ladbrokes won't take bets from the *Banner*'s pol ed anymore, not after he bunged a grand on the leadership battle last year.'

Casey rolled her eyes.

Archie ignored Baz. 'The Attorney General's making a statement to the House later. Could you cover it, Casey? Bit dull, but the desk'll want five hundred words.'

She listened vaguely as Archie continued dividing up the day. One of the political correspondents was packed off in the direction of Dorset. 'Cate, can you take that? The Health Secretary's not speaking to Baz. Twat.' 'Who's the twat?' 'Both of them.' Another went to Shrewsbury. The sketchwriter was dispatched to Lincolnshire to cover a Cabinet Minister visiting a sausage factory: 'A *sausage* factory?' 'I know. Writes itself, really.'

The waters were already closing smoothly over Fairbairn's career. Back in the *Post*'s main office, Tillie was writing up the day-two story. By tomorrow, it would be a nib.

'You okay, Casey?' Archie finished up. 'You look a bit—'

'I'm fine.' She rubbed her eyes and focused on her computer screen.

'Sure?'

'Yes.'

She rang Miranda as she walked towards the Chamber.

'Hi,' Casey began, and then ran out of words.

'Casey?' Miranda said, after a short pause. 'You there?'

'Yes. Um …'

'I'm a bit up against it.' Miranda's voice was clipped. Casey could hear her footsteps, click-clacking down a pavement somewhere.

'Don't worry.' Casey hung up.

A moment later her mobile rang.

'Casey?' It was Miranda again. 'Don't be a dick.'

'It's Nick Llewellyn.'

'Nick Llewellyn?' Miranda took a whole second to place the name. 'Where on earth did you see him? Haven't heard a whisper in ages.'

'No.' Casey's throat closed up for a second. 'No, you wouldn't have.'

There was a pause. 'Well, where did you see him? Or did he get in touch with you about something?'

'He was in Holloway Road station this morning,' said Casey. 'In a sleeping bag.'

The footsteps hesitated for a moment. 'Poor bugger.'

47

'He's homeless, Miranda. He was completely alone.'

It had been one of the first stories they worked on together. Nick Llewellyn – then – was a fast-rising star in politics. Charismatic and witty, a young MP going straight to the top. Everyone said so. Casey had watched the Llewellyns working the room at party conference in Manchester. Mrs Llewellyn remembered everyone's name, smiling and smiling; he made jokes and sparkled. PM material, they murmured. Not this time but the next.

But he had also pushed through some special government funding for one of his donors. It had been the leaked emails between the civil servants and the MP that had been the coup de grâce.

'I heard that Selina Llewellyn started divorce proceedings the morning our article came out,' Miranda said carefully. 'Wasn't it her father who had all the money anyway? For all his poncing about, I don't think Nick Llewellyn started with much.'

'And Selina's daddy wasn't delighted by ...'

'No.' Miranda's footsteps were clicking down the pavement again. 'No, he was not.'

'They had two children, didn't they? Small ones.'

'Think so.'

'We ruined his life, Miranda.'

'He ruined his own life, Casey. He was an absolute idiot with all that Orbmond stuff.'

'Still.'

'I wonder what else went wrong?' Miranda pondered. 'I mean, MPs usually end up in PR or corporate affairs after that sort of thing. A scandal just proves they know how to play the game.'

'Was he a drinker?' asked Casey. Because many MPs were, and journalists more so.

'I never heard about a problem.' It could easily be hidden, though. Until it was far too late.

'Drugs?'

'Possible. Or some sort of mental breakdown?'

'I wonder ...' Casey said, almost to herself.

'So this was at Holloway Road?' Miranda asked, too casually. 'Not Tufnell Park?'

'Miranda. No.'

'Oh, come on, Casey. It's an interesting story. A cautionary tale, if you like.'

'It's dancing on a grave.'

'I'm just amazed no one else has spotted him yet.'

'He doesn't look like … You'd have to know him.'

'You don't have to do it,' said Miranda. 'I can send Hessa or Tillie.'

'Miranda—' Casey glanced at her watch. There were four hours until the Attorney General's speech. Miranda would dispatch a reporter as soon as this conversation ended. Keeping her talking, Casey hurried towards the entrance to Westminster station.

She hesitated as she came out of the Tube barriers. Nick Llewellyn was still lying in his sleeping bag, screened by the legs of passersby.

Casey stepped to one side and pretended to examine her phone.

A few years ago, Llewellyn had had rounded cheeks, manicured hands and a hint of a wink in his grin. His accent had shifted depending on the setting. Elongated vowels for Tory peers, dropped consonants for a visit to a factory. The consonants were firmly in place when he was working a room with Selina at his side.

Back then, his hair was dark blond, lightly gelled, luxuriant as it curved into a shape that was almost – but not quite – a quiff. Bright blue eyes that were disconcertingly sharp at times. He had spent a lot of Selina's money on suits, Casey guessed. Brioni, bespoke, or Anderson & Sheppard, and hoping the workers didn't recognise the cut.

Not her type, but she could see how the mix of charisma and energy and that undeniable intelligence would be catnip to the upper echelons of the party.

Today, the bright blue eyes were closed against the relentless tramp of a thousand feet that stamped and clomped until every step was a thump to the skull.

From across the narrow ticket hall, Casey watched.

The gold had gone from his hair now. It was longer. Thinner, too, patches of scalp peeking through, unwashed.

The apple roundness of his cheeks had disappeared, along with the jolly pink of his complexion. He had pulled the sleeping bag – purple, worn through to greying insulation here and there – up to his chin, and his head rested on a scruffy, dark green rucksack. Now in his mid-forties, he looked a decade older.

A deep breath, and she stepped forward.

'Hello.' She bent down next to him.

The blue eyes opened. 'Oh, do fuck off. I'm not in the mood for do-gooders today, thank you very much.'

'My name,' she said steadily, 'is Casey Benedict. I work for the *Post*.'

The eyes widened. He hadn't recognised her this morning, she realised abruptly. She had been just one of a hundred coolly curious faces, glancing carelessly, moving on.

Her name would have ricocheted around his head for months. Years, maybe. *Casey Benedict, that—*

But regardless, he hadn't known her face. Both Casey and Miranda avoided being photographed as far as possible. Casey was always nervous in the seconds before she went undercover: throat narrowing, palms wet. The last thing she needed was a photograph just a couple of mouse clicks away. *Aren't you that …*

No. Anonymity was everything, secrecy a habit.

'Well, you,' Llewellyn spoke with heavy emphasis, 'really can fuck off.'

He sat up as he spoke, straightening his legs out ahead of him and wrestling his arms and shoulders out of the sleeping bag. It restored his dignity very slightly.

'Can I get you a coffee, Mr Llewellyn?'

'No, you bloody can't.' It was the voice he had used in the Chamber, reverberating round the ticket hall.

'A sandwich, then?'

He eyed her suspiciously, and as a couple walked past, he spoke with ringing tones: 'You ruined my life, you bitch. Now you can leave me the fuck alone.'

The couple stared, faces riven by distaste. Casey turned so that her back was against the wall. She slid down until she was sitting on the cold paving next to him, stretching her legs out in front of her too.

'You can't stay here, I'm afraid, Mr Llewellyn.'

'Why?' He vibrated with anger. 'Why the fuck not?'

'A journalist from the *Post* is on her way.'

The blue eyes flicked towards her. 'You just said *you* were a journalist from the *Post*.'

'I am,' Casey said equably. 'But I thought you might rather not be found by the other one.'

He processed her words. 'Why are you telling me this?'

'I'm not really sure.' Casey found that she wasn't. 'But if we go to a coffee shop just round the corner or something, then the other journalist won't be able to find us.'

'I'll sodding leave, all right.' He was standing up now, folding the sleeping bag. 'But not with fucking *you*.'

'Fine,' she said. 'Well, see you around.'

He was picking up the rucksack now. There was a moment of hesitation before he leaned down to pick up the hat and the scattering of change. The morning's fiver had disappeared.

Under a shapeless khaki jumper and dark trousers, Llewellyn was sharply thin, and when he moved, she caught a waft of old sweat.

'What do you bloody want then?' he snapped. 'I don't need your pity.'

'Nothing,' Casey said. 'I don't want anything at all.'

'You're not making any sense.'

'No.'

'What, then?' He looked at her in exasperation.

'I suppose,' Casey tried to explain, 'that it feels as if the *Post* has done enough to you already.'

'That's one way of putting it. But I'm sure your charming colleagues won't mind another bite of the apple. Or another kick in the teeth, more like.'

'A cautionary tale.' Casey heard Miranda's words ringing in her head. 'But I don't think people really need this warning.'

'It's a bit niche, is it?' Llewellyn raised an eyebrow. 'Because how many MPs are really going to end up destroying their lives in precisely this way?'

They contemplated each other for a moment, the tension dissipating.

'A cup of tea, then?' For a moment, the old charm glimmered again. 'And everything off the record?'

The words that he must have used a hundred times almost made her smile. 'Of course.'

'And perhaps even a slice of cake.'

They wandered towards Highbury, stopping at random at one of the coffee shops that littered the Holloway Road. Casey caught the sideways glance of the barista – *will there be any trouble?* – before his gaze moved on to her and relaxed.

She left Llewellyn sitting in a leather armchair at the back of the shop, returning from the counter with tea and cake.

He contemplated her, head on one side.

'What do you want to know, then?'

'Nothing.' She put down the mugs.

'Rubbish,' he said. 'You people always want something.'

'And you people always want your story on the front page.'

'Fair enough.' His mouth stretched into a grin. One of his teeth was broken, ugly in the immaculate row. 'You want to know how I ended up here, don't you?'

'I suppose so.'

'Not for a story.'

'No. Just …'

A table away, a man was reading a copy of the *Post*. Casey could make out the photograph of Lucas Fairbairn and Esther Amaral turning out of Lettaford Manor's drive. She jerked her gaze away.

'Well,' he said, 'it's not as if I have anyone else to talk to.'

The loneliness in his voice clanged like a bell. Casey waited.

'Selina kicked me out after your story.' He spoke abruptly. 'Can't say I blame her.'

'Just because of the story?'

A pause. 'No.'

'Was there someone else?'

'Another woman?' He looked surprised. 'No, that was one thing that … Not a man either, before you ask.'

'What, then?'

Llewellyn stared at the slice of chocolate cake. 'The thing was,' he said slowly, 'I always liked a gamble.'

Casey's shoulders tightened. 'Of course you did.'

'What do you mean?' He glanced up sharply.

'Nothing. Sorry. Carry on.'

'Well, that's it, really. Gambling.'

'Tell me.'

He blew out his cheeks, glanced at the door, came to a decision.

'When did it start properly? Way back as a teenager, I liked the odd flutter. When we were dating, Selina and I would go to the races and we'd both enjoy the odd bet.'

'But that wasn't the end of it?'

He sipped his tea thoughtfully, broke off a piece of chocolate cake.

'No. No, it was not.'

Casey waited.

'It started off as an extra burst of excitement, you know? Adrenalin. But gradually it became a habit. It started to feel as if nothing was worth watching unless I had some skin in the game.'

He stopped. His eyes were unfocused, memories crowding in.

'So you started gambling more?'

'It began to feel as if something only really mattered if there was a bet on. And then I started betting on more than just the races. Tennis, cricket, anything. Bit by bit, I got deeper into it all.'

His eyes focused again. On the other side of the coffee shop, there was a framed film poster – *Rocky*, vintage – and Casey could see his eyes tracing the boxer's outline again and again.

'So you got addicted?'

He shrugged. 'At about the same time, gambling changed. You used to have to go to a shop or ring up your bookie. But suddenly it was on my phone, and that meant I could bet any time I wanted. Next thing, I got into poker online. Then I got into other games and suddenly it was—'

'And Selina didn't like it?'

'She didn't even realise at first. And I suppose I didn't either, not really. I was clever about it back then, or so I believed. But then one day you find yourself sneaking away from a family dinner for a quick game of blackjack in the bog. Or running late for a funeral because you've just got to finish that hand of poker. I remember hugging Arlo once, and using the moment that my hands were behind his back to refresh my phone screen. Checking a bloody cricket score, for God's sake.'

Arlo, his son. He must have been toddling when the story broke. The daughter, she remembered after a brief effort, was Saskia.

'People think gambling's all James Bond and poker in Monaco,' he said. 'But it's actually creeping out of your daughter's fourth birthday party to find out what Alianza Atlético's B team are up to against Cienciano.'

'Yes.'

'And then there was the money.' Llewellyn almost laughed. 'Oh, Christ, the money. You don't realise for a while because you win a bit here, a nice chunk there. And you only remember the wins, somehow. Even when you really force yourself to think about the losses, you tell yourself, "Just a few more bets, and I'll turn this around. Win it all back, and more. Just a couple more times." But then one day, I filled up my car with petrol and my card was rejected. I told the cashier she was being ridiculous, to run it through again' – as he spoke, Casey could hear the old arrogance in his voice – 'but back it came. No, no, no. I was stranded, like some … I had to ring Selina in the end. Told her there was some problem with my account so could I have her card details? And that was when I heard something in her voice. She *knew*.'

He paused and looked across at the man holding a copy of the *Post*. Cocked his head to one side as he read the headline, then raised an eyebrow at Casey.

'Yes.' Casey was frank. 'One of mine.'

He did the maths fast.

'So that's how you found out I was in Holloway Road.' When she didn't respond, he laughed. 'Now Fairbairn really *is* a fucking do-gooder. He stops by all the time. And there is a limit to how many Pret sandwiches one man can eat.'

'Tell me what happened after your cards were stopped.'

'I got home late that evening,' he went on. 'I drove straight there from that petrol station. It was a Thursday night, so it was all the way back to the constituency. Selina waited up. I remember parking the car on the drive and looking at the light behind the curtains in the drawing room, feeling this awful sadness descend.'

'What happened then?'

'To be fair, Selina tried to help. She sat me down that evening and worked out how much I'd lost in total. And it was only then that I realised it was hundreds and hundreds of thousands of pounds. I don't know how I hadn't realised before. It's extraordinary the way you can just ignore something. Pretend.'

'When did all this happen?'

'Oh, it must have been a year or so before you ... Before you wrote your article.'

'And what happened after that?'

'Well, I said I'd stop. And I meant it. Selina was beside herself. Reggie – that's her father – had given us a chunk of money for the kids' school fees, and I'd burned through that, as well as everything else. I didn't even realise I'd done it. Just kept telling myself that it would only take a couple of winning hands, and then I'd be back on top. I'd put all the money back and no one would be any the wiser.'

Reggie was Sir Reginald Armstrong. Back in the eighties, he had set up one of the world's largest interdealer brokerages, and was not noted for suffering fools with any degree of enthusiasm. Telling Sir Reginald that his grandchildren's school fees had gone up in smoke could not have been a fun conversation.

'But Reginald Armstrong sold off his brokerage for about fifty million just a few years ago,' Casey said aloud. 'There was plenty more where the school fees had come from, to be frank.'

For Selina, the adored only daughter.

'Sure.' Llewellyn nodded. 'But from then on, Selina had her eye on me. Reggie, too. We couldn't hide it from him, and Selina didn't want to anyway.'

'So you tried to stop?'

'I did but it was hopeless.' He shrugged. 'You don't understand. No one does. Everywhere you go there's something tempting you. Taunting you. Look, right there.'

He pointed across the street. Fifty yards away, through a blur of traffic, was a bright purple shopfront. The colour was familiar, thought Casey. Tip Top, that's what they were called. It had seeped into her unconscious, without her even realising. That bright purple on the shirts of a dozen football teams.

'Did you bet with them?'

The shortest of pauses. 'I bet with everyone.'

'Of course you did.'

'And the shops are the least of it,' Llewellyn went on. 'I'd tripped every algorithm on the internet by then, so I was constantly bombarded by adverts. Free bets here, special offers there. It was relentless, endless, all the fucking time.'

There was a chequered pattern on the tabletop. He was running his finger over the design again and again.

'So what happened?'

'Losses are a ghost,' Llewellyn said tonelessly. 'They're shadows that follow you everywhere you go. The only way you can stop gambling is by accepting that the losses are just that: a void. That all the money and energy and time you've spent gambling has gone, and you'll never ever get any of it back. My marriage, my career, my children's happiness, everything. It was all … just wasted. And there's still a tiny part of my brain that won't accept that. Can't accept it. That believes – really, truly believes – that my luck will turn a fraction, and I will get it all back again. I'm honestly convinced that I've cracked poker right now, and if I could just scrape together a few hundred quid to start off, I would win it all back.'

'Did you try therapy? Gamblers Anonymous?'

'Selina marched me off to all of it,' he said. 'Blocked me from the websites. Tracked my bank account every day. She's a good girl, Selina.'

Casey imagined her in those early days. The laughter at the race-track and the rainbow whirl of ribbons. And in the background, those red numbers flickering. Memories, shattered.

'But they didn't work? Selina's efforts?'

'No. Not for long.' His eyes gleamed for a second before he shut away the memory. 'As an MP, you can't really get away with anything … fun. But no one cared about me spending a few minutes on my phone every so often. It was my own private world.'

'So how long before you were back to gambling?'

'A few weeks? It distorts everything, you see. If I wasn't gambling, I was thinking about gambling, every single moment of the day. I'd had some big wins along the way, too. On some level, it seemed ridiculous to spend years working to earn it all back, when it would take three minutes to fix everything if Brocade Blue clobbered the opposition in the three-fifteen. I'd lost so much by then that it would have taken a lifetime to get back to where I started anyway.'

'What did you do?'

'I applied for credit cards that Selina didn't know about. Took out a loan. I opened an account with a new online casino. I remember, at one point, I was four thousand up, and I really did try to withdraw it. But those casinos are so quick to take your money and so very slow to make it available to you. By the time they gave me access, I'd already lost the lot.'

'And Selina found out again?'

'She was screaming at me when she did. Out-of-control furious. I think we were both starting to see that I couldn't stop, would never stop. That all her father's money ... It was just a drug to me. It should have given us a golden life, but as long as I had any access to it, I couldn't ... wouldn't ... It is an addiction.'

'And then what?'

'And then you ran your article,' he said. '"Orbmond, the MP and the lobbying scandal". And that really was the end.'

'What happened?'

A pause. 'She kicked me out. Reggie's lawyers negotiated the divorce on her behalf. They offered me a generous pay-out. A decent chunk with a cast-iron agreement that I had no further rights to any of the Armstrong cash. I signed it – because I had honestly convinced myself that this lump sum would be the basis of my new fortune – and, well, you can guess how that's turned out.'

Sir Reginald had been ruthless, Casey thought. Another man to whom money was no object might have rented a flat for his errant son-in-law, found some structure that provided him with the absolute basics. A supermarket delivery for groceries. Utility bills paid direct.

Anything to avoid Arlo and Saskia wandering down the street one day, and waking to the nightmare of their father passed out in a tattered sleeping bag.

But maybe Nick had called Sir Reginald's bluff one too many times. This was only the Llewellyn version of events, after all.

'Saskia and Arlo live down in Devon now.' It was as if he had read her mind. 'Their mother keeps them well away.'

'I see.'

'So is that what you wanted to hear?' He was running his tongue over his cracked tooth. 'That I would have ended up here anyway. Is this a form of absolution? Will you sleep better tonight?'

'I don't know,' Casey said, 'that you would have ended up here.'

They smiled at each other, their lives oddly entwined. Casey remembered the moment the *Post* went to press with that huge photograph of the Orbmond headquarters blazoned across the front. She remembered the very slight change in Ross's voice when he spoke to her. The way Dash started waiting for her to speak. That was the day that her career became real.

And the day that Nick Llewellyn's disintegrated.

A strange sort of symmetry, a zero-sum game.

His sharp eyes were fixed on hers; he had read her thoughts again. The intelligence of this man, that ruthless brilliance, it was all still there.

Still there, and utterly wasted.

'I can talk about it rationally,' he said. 'Articulately, even. I've done all the research. I know that it's the primitive reward centres in one's brain going haywire, rewarding the wrong thing with nice big hits of dopamine. It could just as easily have been drink, drugs, day trading, whatever. It just happens that my chimp brain rewards me hugely for gambling. I know everything there is to know about gambling addiction. But you put a fiver in my hat this morning, didn't you? And can you guess what's happened to that?'

8

Casey made it back to the House of Commons just in time for the Attorney General's speech. She had watched Llewellyn shamble off into the distance of Camden, rejecting her offer of a hotel room for the night.

'Where are you going?' she had called after him.

'Who knows?' He didn't look back. 'Regent's Park? I might go and look at all the pretty roses.'

Now she was sitting in the press gallery, staring out over the green benches of the Commons. They were sparsely populated today, just a doughnut of MPs around the Attorney General so that on television it would appear as if he were well supported by his colleagues, all industriously at work.

Casey's phone buzzed and she peeked at it discreetly. *Tillie says no sign of Llewellyn at Holloway Road. I imagine you got there first? Git.*

Miranda would not be delighted. And it was lucky she had sent Tillie, not Hessa. Hessa would have checked every coffee shop for miles around, a patient, relentless bloodhound.

As Casey wrote up the Attorney General's speech almost without thinking, her phone buzzed. Nash Bexley.

Fancy La Bohème *tonight? First night at Covent Garden?*

Casey thought about her plans for the evening. Skipping a yoga class, followed by a microwave meal in Tufnell Park and the cold remains of some television series. Hessa had accidentally spoiled the ending, too.

That would be great, she texted back.

Excellent.

She didn't feel brave enough to ask Cressida for an opening night outfit – not after the Emilia Wickstead debacle – so had to dash home to change. As a result, she only just reached the Opera House in time for a quick drink before curtain-up.

Nash's group was sitting around a table in the beautiful champagne bar. Far above their heads, the exquisite glass and ironwork fan-shape glittered in the fading light of the day.

'How lovely to see you again, Casey.' Rosamund Bexley stood up as she arrived. 'Let me introduce you to …'

She waved a hand towards the people at the table, a blur of faces.

'You must have a quick glass of champagne to celebrate the Fairbairn story.' Nash popped open another bottle. 'You absolutely nailed it.'

Casey found that she was sitting next to the businessman who had given her the original tip at Ascot.

'Nice work on Fairbairn,' he said.

'Thank you for your help.'

'I asked Tillie Carlisle if she could make it tonight,' said Rosamund Bexley. 'But she couldn't, which was a shame. She's such fun.'

'I think Ross has dispatched her to Scarborough for the evening,' Casey told her. 'A cliff collapse.'

'Where?' Rosamund looked confused.

They made their way to the box. Below them, the orchestra was tuning up. Casey had always loved that sound. A cacophony of squawks, a careless scale from an oboe, a brief ripple of magic as a flute ran through a phrasing. It held the beauty of a broken mirror, and a sense of alchemy as the notes began to spin to gold.

She leaned forward.

She wasn't looking for him.

But she was.

So it shouldn't have been a shock when she saw him.

But it was.

Opera, chess, racing, sailing.

His pastimes, known by heart.

Years ago, she had found him in an old *Who's Who*. An odd sort of pride when she discovered him in the big red book in the school library. It made him real in black and white.

The bare bones of his life. Clues.

His birthday, for one. So every year, she wondered about the cake and the party and the faces lit up by candles.

For he's a jolly good fellow …

Isn't he?

Opera, chess, racing, sailing.

She wasn't listed in the big red book, of course.

Of course not.

One son, two daughters, that was all. Two plus one equals three.

Odd one out. Odd. One. Out.

Later, she learned more.

He was predictable. Chambers at the same time every morning. Coffee from the same cafe as he walked to court. Venerated, these days. Venerable, even.

Maybe.

Every evening, there was a brisk walk back over the bridge. A quick step over the Thames, a ribbon of sky in the city.

The same train.

Back to the house with the mock-Tudor beams.

A mock-Tudor life, up to a point.

Two plus one equals three. Opera and chess, and you don't count.

Occasionally, she passed him on the bridge, quite invisibly. Will you know me? Could you ever say you're sorry?

She looked at him sideways and thought, *Is this why I destroy everything around me? Shattering lives. And the lives of those they love.*

Again and again and again.

Because they *will* remember me. They *will* know me. My name, anyway. Your name, maybe.

Chess: a game of sacrifice. And, yes, I can choose.

She went to the seaside, once, to watch him sail. A yacht, racing through the waves, and an ocean roaring behind her eyes.

Drowning in a sea of unshed tears.

She watched his life from the wings, noting every gesture. And scrambled into a costume that someone else had chosen. A mask, always.

On the edges.

On the edge.

That life, but half of it.

There was a girl with him tonight. Blonde, smiling, treasured. Her dress, a glint of red.

A half sister. Half a sister.

Like half a heart, quite useless.

King Solomon's leftovers, because he knew how to choose.

Half a sister, half a heart.

Half a brother, half a life.

Half a family, half a lie, half a truth and half a story.

So she wasn't looking for him.

Operachessracingsailing.

She wasn't looking for him.

But she was.

The roar of the crowd slapped her back into her seat. A deep breath, a sense of unreality, the sting of tears in her eyes. Two scenes overlaid, again.

Her thoughts darted to Nick Llewellyn. It felt impossible that she was here, in the plush seats of the Royal Opera House, with the crowd rising to their feet and the music surging, while somewhere out on the streets of London, he was settling down on the cold of the concrete.

It was impossible. Implausible.

True.

'Are you okay?' Nash asked, as they made their way back down towards the bar at the interval. 'You seem—'

'Did you ever find it difficult?' Her words emerged in a rush. 'That sense of … I don't know … breaking things. Again and again?'

He understood. 'The constant destruction? Hurling brickbats from the safety of the sidelines. Always criticising, but never having to find an actual solution. Yes,' a sideways grin, 'a bit.'

'How did you manage it?'

'By moving into corporate affairs,' Nash said drily. 'By the way, I've got a very good story to tell you about Swann Hopkins. You know, the pharmaceutical giant—'

'I saw someone today,' Casey interrupted him.

'You must bump into ghosts of stories past all the time. Who was it today?'

'Oh … someone I wrote a story about, years ago.'

'Okay.' Nash drew out the second syllable.

'He's homeless now,' Casey said bluntly. 'The man I wrote about. He's lost everything, just a few things in a rucksack. He was so alone, Nash.'

'The poor bugger.'

'I've ruined his life.'

'It's not your fault,' said Nash firmly. 'He just got caught out.'

'But Nick Llewellyn … It was my article that …'

And she was going to say more when Rosamund Bexley turned towards them cheerfully. 'More champagne?' she asked.

'Sure.' Nash's grin was back. 'While I tell Casey all about Swann Hopkins …'

9

Casey didn't want to go back to the box after the interval. It was Rosamund who noticed her hesitation, slowing her own pace to match.

'Nash mentioned you'd had a bad day at the office.'

The blue eyes were sympathetic.

'It's not just that.' Quite abruptly, a sense of exhaustion overwhelmed her. The words spilled from her mouth. 'There's this man in the audience, too … He's … Well, he's my father.'

She stopped talking sharply. But there were hundreds of middle-aged men in the audience, she told herself. No one would ever be able to guess. And it was a relief, almost, to hear the words aloud.

'A bit of family dysfunction?' asked Rosamund, a sympathetic twist to her mouth. 'Don't worry, I know all about that.'

'Do you?'

A nod, a smile. 'We don't have to go back to the box, Casey. We can just stay here and have another drink.'

'But we must. The music is so …'

'I know. But there are plenty of people enjoying it.'

For the first time, Casey could see why Nash had married Rosamund.

'My father and I …' Casey struggled to explain. 'We've never been …'

'Close.'

'No.'

'It must be hard. You lost someone too, didn't you? Recently. I read about it in the *Post*.'

A shape on the floor.

A silence that sank into her bones.

Eyes, flecked with grey and green, blue and gold. Staring at nothing.

Falling to her knees. Touching his face, his chest, his arm, so gently. Holding his fingers for a moment, as if she might lead him back.

'Yes.' Casey cleared her throat. 'A few months ago. Ed. His name was Ed Fitzgerald.'

'I'm really very sorry.'

'Thank you.'

They stood in the grandeur of the Opera House, a flurry of people heading past. It was an odd moment of intimacy.

'And your father …' Rosamund asked delicately.

'I never think about him,' said Casey. 'Well, mostly.'

'Really?' Rosamund raised an eyebrow.

'No, that's a lie. But … you know.'

'My father,' said Rosamund, 'was always travelling when I was growing up. He flew all over the world, making his fortune.' She spread out her fingers, palms down, inspecting her rings. 'If I got his attention somehow, I'd do or say anything to hold it. Have you ever grown hyacinths? I plant them every year because they're so beautiful in the depths of winter. That glorious smell fills the whole house … But I have to be careful; they'll grow towards the light if they're not staked. Leaning further and further, until they topple right over, and their stems snap, and they're ruined. That's how I always felt with my father: as if I were twisting towards the sun.'

'Parents.' Casey managed to smile.

'Quite.'

Casey couldn't sleep that night. She sat up and looked out over the rooftops. The orange of the streetlights was a hellish glow in the chasms below the dark roofs.

She was almost relieved to get a text message from Aidan Gardiner at 5 a.m. *I've thought of a way! Come to the Kennington office as soon as you can? I'm heading there now.*

There didn't seem any point in delaying.

Outside her flat, the streets were almost empty, the sky lightening slowly. The odd Uber was racing along, gaining precious seconds on the straight.

As she headed towards the station, she saw a glint of red. A fox, scurrying down the pavement towards her. It was mangy, thin, slinking close to the shopfronts. It froze when it saw her, the streets normally abandoned this early in the day. Then it spun away, disappearing between parked cars towards the emptiness of the main road.

A car came racing by. It didn't swerve. It probably never even saw the glint of red. There was a small thud, and a yelp that might have been a scream, and then the car raced on, disappearing round the corner as Casey ran towards the injured animal.

The fox was dying. Its back end had been flattened, crushed into the tarmac. Its front paws still scrabbled, clawing at the road. It was frantic to reach the cover of the parked cars. Frenzied, desperate, only half dead, the next car coming in a blur of speed.

A wheel smashed into the fox's head and the animal was obliterated. Shreds of fur, shards of bone. A spatter of blood, unidentifiable.

A mercy, of sorts.

A grey dawn broke over the roofs, and Casey stood still as one car after another slammed into the corpse. Over and over. Smashed until there was nothing left to see at all.

Later, she sat on the Tube, the memory going round and round her head. That fox had probably trotted down the same road every dawn. A familiar path, enjoyable. And then, one morning, she was there.

'Not your fault,' she murmured to herself. 'Not your fault.'

Not your fault.

Yes. Yours.

Aidan Gardiner was waiting in the lobby of the industrial unit as Casey arrived.

'Don't come in,' he said, as he came out through the revolving doors. 'We're going straight to Fleethurst.'

A black Mercedes was purring at the kerb, a chauffeur waiting patiently. Aidan hopped in, gesturing to Casey to follow.

'Where are we off to?'

'A training session. You'll see.'

'What's all this about?' She settled into the leather seat.

'I'll tell you when we get there.'

On a large billboard in the high street, Fleethurst described itself as a charming Surrey village, with a delightful sense of community. The communities were mostly gated, from what Casey could see from the black Mercedes.

'The boys love living round here.' Aidan saw her looking up the long gravel drives. 'Decent houses and nice and close to London. Helpful when you're trying to sign them up.'

It was still early when they arrived, driving against the traffic that was streaming into the capital. The Wanderers' training grounds were huge, the emerald green pitches rolling into the distance under a bright blue sky.

This wasn't the main stadium; that was a mile further down the road. Here, the focus was on the neat clubhouse – beautifully designed but small compared to the echoing amphitheatre where the Wanderers played in front of tens of thousands of roaring fans.

As she climbed out of the car, Casey glanced at a group of players sprinting between flags.

'Does the team train at this time of year?' she asked. She remembered – hazily – that footballers had the summer off.

'That's not the team.' Aidan laughed. 'Those are schoolchildren.'

Casey looked across again, her eyes adjusting to the scale.

'You certainly start them young round here.'

'It's a session for the local kids,' said Aidan. 'They go mad for it. Because that over there' – he paused for emphasis – 'is Jackson Harvey.'

Even Casey recognised the name. Griff Aitken had profiled Jackson Harvey at the end of last season. As far as Casey could tell, Harvey had been almost single-handedly responsible for propelling Fleethurst Wanderers to the top of their league.

A few months ago, he'd been called up for England – to the surprise of the Premiership – and performed with a confidence that belied his age. Only twenty-two, he was now tipped for the very top. Casey suspected that a substantial chunk of Aidan's Kennington winnings would be diverted to retain Harvey's services for next season.

The training session was drawing to an end now, the children jogging back towards the clubhouse. Parents waited in the carpark, gossiping in the early morning sun. As they drew closer, Casey could hear Harvey teasing the kids, his laughter ringing out over the ground.

The group reached a pile of rucksacks. Notepads mushroomed. Harvey's signature was a practised squiggle that spoke of a thousand requests.

As he scrawled, Harvey caught Aidan's eye and gestured towards the clubhouse.

'He won't be long.' Aidan was already turning towards the ultramodern building.

The interior was plush, with the hush of a first-class waiting room. Grey carpets and lots of chrome, the mud of the playing fields banished firmly to the changing rooms. The Wanderers logo was everywhere, with officious signs pointing in all directions. Sauna. Gym. Hydrotherapy Pool.

Aidan led Casey upstairs to a large lounge that looked out over the playing fields. A bar ran down one side of the room, tables and sleek chairs scattered about the high-ceilinged space. Aidan crossed the room to a table that was framed by full-length windows.

He didn't display any especial pride in the opulence of the surroundings, settling unremarked into his chair. A minute later, a waitress poked her nose round the corner, but there was no panicked rush to take Aidan's order, no nervousness. She greeted him in a friendly manner and took his enquiries after her son for granted.

A few minutes later, footsteps raced up the stairs and Jackson Harvey erupted into the room with all the energy of a sportsman in his prime. He sparkled with health, every movement a burst of power.

His maternal grandmother was from Nigeria, Casey remembered from Griff's article, but she'd moved to London years ago and married a builder from Lewisham. Jackson's father was Moroccan, and both parents were famously supportive, going berserk with delight on the sidelines of every game. Jackson's curly black hair had been twisted into neat locs on top of his head and clipped short at the sides. His face was broad across the cheekbones, with a strong jaw. Exuding exuberance, he grinned at Casey as he threw himself into a chair.

Very attractive, she acknowledged, and aware of the fact. He gave her a split-second appraisal: a man used to taking his pick. There was kindness in his eyes, but she sensed it might soon be subsumed by stardom.

'Those kids are exhausting, man.' He grinned at Aidan. 'They've bloody broken me this time.'

It seemed unlikely. Harvey kicked his feet over the chair's armrest and switched his focus to Casey.

'You must be Casey Benedict. Aidan's told me about you.'

'Yes—' She was interrupted by the waitress who came rushing across with some sort of smoothie.

'Thanks, love.' Harvey smiled up at her. 'My saviour.'

Blushing, the woman retreated to the kitchen again.

'Right.' The footballer turned unflinchingly towards Casey. 'I've got some thoughts about match fixing.'

10

'Jackson's brother,' Aidan began evenly, 'is Landon Harvey.'

The pieces fell into place. Landon Harvey's name had been almost at the top of the list Aidan had created from his database.

'I see,' Casey said carefully.

'Me and Lan don't always get on.' Jackson met her eye without flinching. 'He's nine years older than me, so we didn't hang out much as kids. And he's made some stupid decisions along the way, right?'

There was affection in his voice all the same.

'And now … Well, now he's got himself into trouble …' Jackson's voice trailed away.

'Why don't you start right back at the beginning?' prompted Aidan.

'This guy.' Jackson perked up as Aidan spoke, gesturing towards him. 'This crazy guy and his obsession with match fixing … Aidan gave me a proper going over when I was first signing with Fleethurst.' Jackson started laughing at the memory. 'I couldn't work out why he was so mad about the whole fixing thing. But he made me *swear* I wouldn't have anything to do with it. On my *mother*'s life.'

'And you personally have never been involved in match fixing?' Casey asked.

'Never.' Jackson spoke with emphasis. 'Not even close. None of the Fleethurst lot would get messed up with anything like that. Aidan would know before we even got on the pitch, apart from anything else.'

'So?' Casey waited.

Jackson hesitated again.

'My systems started flagging Landon late last year.' Aidan picked his words carefully. 'There was no suggestion of any problem with his playing before that.'

'I had no idea about any of it until Aidan came to me last week.' Jackson was nodding his head. 'Asking all about Lan.'

'What specifically did Aidan ask about?' Casey asked.

'Lan's been a moron,' Jackson said flatly. 'I went round to see him straight away and he admitted it all. He's been a fucking idiot.'

'What exactly has Landon done?'

Jackson stared out over the playing fields. 'Football's great,' he said slowly, 'but it can be tough, you know? When I was a kid, everyone thought it was Landon who was going to be the big star. He was always better than me. Just the *best*. So fast, so tough. Everyone thought he'd play for Chelsea, play for England, the whole bit.' The hero worship of his big brother echoed still. 'But he's been unlucky. Had a problem with his Achilles three years ago, and that's never been quite right since. And he probably spent a bit too much time in clubs when he was my age, if I'm honest. I think he sort of expected it all to come to him,' Jackson finished earnestly. 'And it never quite did.'

'Landon plays for Elmington now,' said Aidan. 'A couple of leagues down from us,' he informed Casey's raised eyebrow.

'Elmington.' Jackson shrugged. 'I mean … And, of course, Lan's burned through most of his cash. And he's on the other side of thirty now. For a footballer …'

A bleak future, quite abruptly.

'I'd help him out,' Jackson insisted. ''Course I would, always. My mother would go ballistic if I didn't. But it wasn't what Landon wanted …'

'So,' repeated Casey, 'what did he do?'

'This guy …' Jackson hesitated again, squirmed, glanced across at Aidan.

'Go on, Jac.'

There was an interesting dynamic between the two of them, Casey thought. It wasn't quite father and son: the age gap was too narrow for that. But Jackson clearly respected Aidan and appeared to be drawn to the older man's solemn intensity. She wondered whether Jackson had cast around as Landon drifted off the trajectory of the greats, and unconsciously sought out an alternative.

Jackson started speaking again. 'There was this guy who approached Landon.'

'Where?' asked Casey.

'At a club in Essex,' said Jackson. 'Close to the Elmington grounds.'

'What's the club called?'

'Mimi's. A lot of people hang out there. It's cool.'

'And what's the man's name?'

'Blake.' Jackson watched Casey's face as she waited. 'That's all I know, right? Landon never even knew his surname.'

'What did Blake ask him to do?'

'Well, the first time Landon just had to promise that he wouldn't score.'

'Landon's a striker,' Aidan expanded. 'And he's very capable. I checked it all out. Back in that first game, Elmington should have annihilated the opposition, and the chance of Landon being one of the goal scorers was pretty high. If you knew he definitely wasn't going to score, you could rake it in. And knowing he wasn't going to score would be enough to tilt the odds away from an Elmington win, too.'

'So Landon didn't score in that match.' Jackson bit his lip. 'He actually laughed about it, said he had to pass to one of his mates when he was right in front of the goal. Afterwards, the coach told him it was very generous.'

'And then what?'

'Next time, he had to guarantee a certain number of corners. He said that was a bit more hectic, but he managed it. And it just carried on from there.'

'I had a scout at one of the earlier games that Landon was fixing,' said Aidan. 'You can see when an unusual amount of money is moving in the market, so I told my guy to keep an eye on things, work out what was going on. He picked out Landon quite quickly. But you'd have to know what you were looking for, if you see what I mean?'

'Sure. And how much was Landon being paid for this?'

'A decent whack,' said Jackson. 'Very decent.'

'How were they paying him?'

'That was the clever bit. They told him to open an account with an online bookie, and then he'd play poker with a certain player at a specific time of the day. And that guy would lose a chunk of money to Landon in just a few hands, and a few days later Lan could cash out. It worked great, he said.'

And that guy might have been playing anywhere in the world, thought Casey, in complete anonymity. Online bookmakers were supposed to report suspicious transactions, but with millions flowing around the world every hour, a fortune could be laundered in a few minutes.

'Landon barely even knows how to play poker,' Jackson added.

'Is he still doing it? Fixing matches for this Blake character?'

'Not right now.' Jackson shook his head. 'He stopped doing it a few months ago.'

'I guess that CleanBet had a quiet word with Landon,' said Aidan. 'It fits with the timeline. Quite a few of the guys on my list seem to be playing straight at the moment. I don't think the football authorities did any proper investigating themselves, but that list was enough to give those boys a proper scare.'

'It would take nerves of steel to throw a match if you thought you were being watched.'

'It hasn't gone away, though,' said Aidan. 'We started to see dodgy patterns from some new guys within a few matches. It's endless.'

'So,' asked Casey, 'what's the plan?'

Jackson gave her a surprisingly wicked grin.

'Landon still has this Blake guy's number,' he said. 'So I thought I'd tell Landon to give him my number too.'

Casey blinked.

'It would be hugely tempting for Blake, whoever he is,' said Aidan. 'An England player at their beck and call. Imagine.'

Casey leaned back in her chair, eyes on the training pitches, giving herself time to think.

'It might be dangerous,' she said carefully.

Jackson's eyes gleamed. 'Yup.'

'Blake is likely to be the tip of a very nasty iceberg. And if they ever found out that it was Landon who stitched them up, it could rebound on him too, and badly.'

Jackson swung round, sitting forward, feet squarely on the ground. 'Maybe. But Landon's a big boy. He can look after himself.'

'How would it work, though?' Casey wondered out loud. 'Would we put a camera on you and send you in? Are you sure you'd know how to manage that situation?'

'You could come with me,' Jackson said calmly.

'As your PA?' said Casey. 'It might be a bit weird, me being there for something like that.'

'As my girlfriend.' Jackson's mouth twisted into a grin.

She was caught off-guard. 'I couldn't.'

'Why not?' Jackson was half flirting, half joking. Casey folded her arms.

'You're ...' She cast around. 'You're twenty-two.'

'So what?'

'I ...' Casey was irritated with herself for the hesitation in her voice. 'I'll think about what would work best. Discuss it with my colleagues,' she finished crisply.

Jackson gave her a slow smile. 'Sure.'

'I've got to take this call.' Aidan was looking vaguely at his phone. 'Won't be a second.'

Casey and Jackson watched as he wandered off.

'He's a good guy,' said Jackson.

'Do you understand his systems?' asked Casey. 'The way he bets?'

'Does anyone, really, apart from him? But I reckon it's how he identifies us.'

'Who?'

'The team,' said Jackson. 'His computers spot who's playing well and is undervalued by their current team. Then he snaps us up for pennies.'

'I suppose it makes sense.'

Jackson grinned. 'We all like to be told we're undiscovered geniuses.'

She laughed, enjoying him. 'And it's quite a few pennies, from what I gather.'

'Sure.' His eyes narrowed. 'You know, it could be fun, you and me going after Blake.'

Casey raised her eyebrows. 'Not like that, it won't be.'

'Why not?' His eyes were teasing, flirting.

'You're not my type.'

He leaned back in his chair, stretching. His jumper rose up a few inches and she forced herself not to glance down at his stomach. 'I'm' – a lazy smile, total self-confidence – 'everyone's type.'

'It's not how I operate, then.'

He was enjoying the rebuff. It was probably unprecedented, and this was a man who lived for a challenge.

'You never know.' His eyes gleamed at her. 'You just never know.'

'It might work.' The black Mercedes was purring back towards Kennington. Aidan was scrolling through his phone, pausing occasionally to send an email. 'Jackson's very bright, for all the footballer chat.'

'I'll think about it,' Casey repeated. 'We have no idea who we are dealing with. It could get very messy, very quickly.'

'You okay? You seem a bit off.'

'Do I?' asked Casey. 'There's this man I ... bumped into yesterday.'

'Who?'

'I wrote a story about him once. Years ago. He was an MP, in fact. And now he's ... well, he's lost everything. Through gambling.'

'Poor bastard,' said Aidan. 'It does happen a lot, though.'

Llewellyn, the losing party in one of the thousands of bets Aidan's operation made every day. For every win, a loss somewhere. That zero-sum game.

'Do you ever feel that compulsion?' she asked Aidan. 'When you're betting? That sense that you're not in control anymore?'

'No,' he said bluntly. 'I couldn't do it if I felt anything like that. For me, it's a mathematical thing, pure and simple. I accept there will be losses, that's baked in. It's just about minimising those.'

'But doesn't everyone who gambles think they have a system?'

'Sure. But, statistically speaking, mine actually works.'

'So there's no emotion?'

'Nope.'

'He's homeless now, this man,' said Casey. 'Living on the streets. It's so bleak.'

The black Mercedes had reached Wimbledon, purring past stretches of green common.

'Tell him to come and see me,' Aidan surprised her by saying. 'We've got a few jobs going. Nothing major, but it might get him back on his feet.'

'Really?'

'Yeah.' And Aidan went back to his phone.

'Did you mean it?' Casey asked again, as they climbed out of the car in Kennington. 'Honestly?'

Aidan was already ambling towards the industrial unit. 'Tell him to call me.'

'I don't think he has a phone.'

'Well, tell him to come round here, then.'

'I'll have to go and find him,' said Casey. 'Last time I saw him he was heading to Regent's Park, but he might be anywhere by now.'

Aidan peered up at the grey walls of the unit, blinking in the sunlight. 'Well, I'm here most of the time,' he said. 'Just send him down.'

Casey got out of the Tube at Great Portland Street and walked north to the grand gates of Regent's Park. It was the height of summer, people ambling along the paths and unfolding rugs on the lawns. The grass was wearing away here and there, patches of dust coned off. In the distance, stucco terraces gleamed with a wedding-cake charm.

Casey walked up the Broad Walk, past serried flowers.

Llewellyn might be anywhere, she thought. He might have abandoned Regent's Park altogether, meandering instead through the busy streets of the West End and the generosity of tourists. Or headed north, towards the great spread of Hampstead Heath. As she carried on up the Broad Walk, she could hear the grumble of a lion, trapped in London Zoo, and when she turned to walk along the zoo's perimeter, she caught the awkward sway of a giraffe, the acrid whiff of dung.

Where was he?

Now she had reached the canal, opaque and lined with brightly-painted barges. Through trees, she could see the hump of Primrose Hill.

Crimson tulips, silver dark clouds, and a city lit up by a storm.

Thunder and lightning, and you don't have to choose.

Those eyes.

That first kiss.

Not today.

No.

She turned away sharply.

I might go and look at all the pretty roses, Llewellyn's voice echoed in her head.

South again, then. Past the big pavilion and the huge playing fields. Past adolescent boys, kicking a football, Jackson Harvey bounding through their dreams.

Maybe Llewellyn had wandered towards the hustle of Camden?

No, he was still here, she was sure of it. Enjoying the warmth of a summer's day. Rejoicing in the beauty of the old park and the echo of a lost life. As she skirted the Boating Lake, a lawnmower roared and the smell of cut grass drifted in the air. A few minutes later she was at the gates of the graceful old rose gardens.

It was late in the summer for the roses. Still a few here and there: a second flush.

But Llewellyn was nowhere to be seen.

Frustrated, Casey slumped on a bench. She pulled her phone from her pocket. What was it that Nash had said about Swann Hopkins? Might as well knock out an email to the *Post*'s tough business editor while she had nothing better to do.

I'm swamped, but do you remember that heart drug Swann announced last month? Big fanfare etc. A contact of mine says he's heard of several people who've had minor heart attacks after taking it. They'll talk.

Casey gazed at the roses, interrupted by the ping of her phone a minute later.

Love it. Will get James on the case ASAP!

Back to the roses.

He might be back in Holloway Road ... He might have gone to a homeless shelter. She could try ...

A shadow fell over the bench.

'Hello,' said Nick Llewellyn.

They wandered back towards the Boating Lake. Carrying his rucksack, his sleeping bag neatly rolled up, Llewellyn might have been any tourist ambling round the park.

Walking slowly, Casey told him about Aidan's offer.

There was a brief spark of interest in Llewellyn's eyes, but as Casey watched, it faded.

'What?' she asked. 'It could be great.'

'I know.'

She understood, or thought she understood. It was the years thrown away. He'd gambled it all on black, and lost everything, and it was impossible to turn it around now. Unfixable, in his eyes.

'Think about it,' she persisted.

'I will.' She heard the lie.

One of the schoolboys scored a goal, racing down the grass, sliding along on his knees. The others crowded around him, roaring with simple delight.

'There isn't a way back.' Llewellyn was watching the schoolboys. 'Not for me. You don't understand. You can't live like this and then go back to a nice nine-to-five and tasty takeaway *pains au chocolat.*'

'You can, Nick. You can try at least.'

'No.' His voice was sharp. 'It's the fear. It gets ingrained in you. Embedded in your bones so deeply that it displaces everything else. It's a cancer you can't cut out because there'd be nothing left at all. All those hundreds of hours of being cold, of being scared. Of having nowhere to hide. Nowhere to close the door on the world and just *be*. It's not knowing whether the next footsteps will be those of someone looking for someone to kick ... or someone to punch. Or someone to fucking piss on. And, of course, it's all those hours thinking about everything I've lost.'

'But from here. From this moment right now, you could—'

'You're so naive,' he said roughly. 'You have no idea. Of the utter humiliation. Of the shame. I hate myself for what I've done. For what I've done to my wife, to my children.'

'You could still …'

'No. Stop it.'

He paused at a poster for the outdoor theatre. The Merchant of Venice, scowling fearfully over his shoulder.

'"In my school days, when I had lost one shaft …"' murmured Llewellyn. It took Casey a moment to recognise the play '"… I shot his fellow of the self-same flight, The self-same way with more advised watch, To find the other forth – and by adventuring both, I oft found both."'

Casey thought of the arrows streaking through the air, the second risked to find the first. And then the next, and the next.

Maybe it was all hopeless.

They wandered on. It was peaceful here. Trees lined the northern edge of the lake, casting a dappled shade on the freshly mown grass. A few boats bobbed brightly on the water, rowers laughing to each other across the water. They passed a man sleeping on his front, a Panama hat shading his head. He had been reading a novel, but had discarded it along with his shirt. There was a beautiful tattoo on his back, an olive tree twisted with age. A woman pushed a pram towards the boathouse cafe, a mewling sound coming from a pile of blankets. She looked tired, frayed.

'It's all so … normal.' There was longing in Llewellyn's voice. Casey thought he might say something more, but he let the silence drift.

They turned back towards the Broad Walk. The park felt near empty, Wednesday afternoon, everyone at work or school. The lake narrowed to a reed-choked ditch here and the grass had been left to grow, rambling into a tussocky tangle. A row of willows trailed their leaves in the water, creating a sense of privacy. There was a bench too, surrounded by green, safe from the bustle of London. Llewellyn sat down and looked across the narrow stretch of water.

'I'll go and get coffees,' said Casey. 'And some cake, maybe? From the boathouse cafe.'

He nodded, eyes half closed, face tilted up to the sun.

There was a queue in the cafe. Children, thrilling over the prospect of the colourful boats. Mothers, deciding between walnut or red velvet. Casey, when it was her turn, chose chocolate and Victoria sponge.

She meandered back towards the bench, where it was hidden behind its cool green curtain. As she walked along the side of the lake, she enjoyed the breeze, the neatly clipped grass, the laughter of the children.

A hundred yards away, the man in the Panama hat was walking away across the grass. White-blond hair, tall, a novel in his left hand. He was moving briskly, had nearly disappeared behind a clump of sycamores. Two mallards were bickering at the edge of the lake. One flew off, emitting squawks of disapproval as it lumbered into the air.

A jolt.

White-blond hair.

Don't be silly. Millions of people have blond hair. Coincidence, pure and simple.

White-blond hair.

Casey found that she had quickened her pace. It wasn't far to the bench now, where it waited peacefully behind its fringe of willows. Only another fifty yards and she would be able to see Llewellyn relaxing in the sun. Just a short distance and the shudder in her stomach would disappear.

White-blond hair. A tattoo on his back.

You're being paranoid. Enjoy this day. Enjoy the jingle of an ice-cream van in the distance, the willows weeping into the lake. Enjoy the swans drifting past with that picture-perfect elegance.

Enjoy all this.

White-blond hair. An olive tree twisted with age; silvery branches peeking above a neat collar.

Stop it. You're being ridiculous. Millions of people have tattoos.

Just a few more steps now anyway, no time at all.

Any moment.

Just coincidence.

Any second.

Llewellyn was gone.

Casey stood for a second, holding two coffee cups and looking at the empty bench. The cakes were heavy in a paper carrier hanging from her wrist.

A bit annoying of him to disappear like that, she tried to convince herself. Still, Miranda would appreciate the chocolate cake … Where was the nearest Tube? What time was—

There was a shape at the bottom of the grassy bank. In the shallows, at the water's edge.

Casey peered closer. That hadn't been there before, half submerged. The water was cloudy, almost mud, and the shape was blurred and distorted.

But.

A shock to her heart.

That was a slick of muddy hair.

It couldn't be.

A sodden khaki jumper; an awful stillness.

No, impossible.

A hand, just visible.

No.

A man, face down in the water. *Face down.*

'Nick,' she heard herself scream. 'Nick! Somebody, help us!'

11

The news that a former MP had drowned in Regent's Park dominated the front pages the next day. Hordes of police descended on the park within minutes, unfurling tape, setting up tents.

A detective, not unkindly, questioned Casey at length.

'You say you saw a man walking away from the scene?'

'Yes. He had white-blond hair, was wearing a Panama hat. I think I saw him at Royal Ascot too, back in June. That time, he ambushed a man I was … standing close to. He chased him and had a knife, I think.'

'You think?' The detective raised her eyebrows. 'Did you report all this in June?'

'No. We just … We got out of Ascot as fast as we could.'

'Could you give me a more detailed description?'

'Yes, I'll try. He was quite a long way away though. He has a tattoo on his back. An olive tree. Sort of gnarled, you know how they get when they're old?'

'How did you see the detail of this tattoo?' the detective asked. 'I thought you said he was quite a distance away when you saw him?'

'We passed him earlier, when we were wandering around the park. He was sleeping on the grass. Well, he probably wasn't asleep, in hindsight.'

'And you also saw this tattoo at Ascot?'

'I saw a part of it,' Casey struggled to explain. 'The edges of it poked up above his collar. At the back.'

'Okay, well, we'll return to that. So today you just came to the park to find Mr Llewellyn for a chat?'

'Yes, I wanted to … I wanted to know that he was okay.'

'But then you left him alone?'

'Just for a few minutes.' Bizarrely, someone had handed her the cakes she'd dropped, still in their paper carrier. The ice-cream van warbled in the distance, and again there was that sense of two scenes being overlaid.

'To go to the cafe?'

'If anyone was watching, it might have looked as if I wasn't coming back.'

'And when you returned, he had drowned?'

'That man must have—'

'Must have what, Miss Benedict?'

'Well, Nick didn't just fall in. And he wasn't suicidal.'

'Are you sure?' the detective said carefully. 'What makes you say that?'

Casey had scrambled down the bank, grabbing him by his shoulders, trying to drag him out of the water. But he was too heavy, too awkward. She scrabbled for her phone, dialling frantically.

Police, ambulance, now, right now … Regent's Park, just north of the Boating Lake. Come quickly. Help us, please.

'Nick,' she had screamed his name again and again, as if she might wake him. 'Nick!'

He was waterlogged, dead weight, impossible to drag out. Her feet slipped in the mud and she found herself sliding inexorably towards the water. Ended up holding his head, letting the water cradle his body, shouting at him to: *'Breathe, Nick. Breathe, please.'*

Close to, his face was a deathly white, rivulets of muddy water dripping from the sparse strands of hair. There was no pulse, no breath, the bright blue eyes half closed. She tried all the same, his lips cold against hers.

It was hopeless. Of course it was.

She screamed again, praying that someone would hear, and some-one would come. So that it wouldn't be her all alone, trying to hold on. So that he wouldn't slip away and sink into the silty depths and disappear forever.

Primitive, that urge.

It had been a team of runners who heard her, diverting at once to her aid. Good Samaritans – shocked, kind, clumsy. She didn't think fast enough to stop them from sliding down the bank to join her. Fifteen pairs of shoes and all those helpful hands hauling him out. Putting those years of first aid into practice, at last.

Useless, though, because he was very dead already.

'We can't tell exactly what happened yet.' The detective pulled a regretful expression. 'The footprints aren't clear.'

The paramedics had scrambled up and down the bank too. And it was a park – a public park – and anyone could explain away being there. A hundred children, a thousand dog-walkers. A man dozing under a tree with a novel. Anyone.

'I know,' Casey said again. 'But he didn't jump and he wouldn't have fallen.'

'Did you see anyone else in the area apart from this man in the Panama hat? We would like to speak to as many witnesses as possible.'

Her memories were a blur. A woman with a pram? Schoolboys playing football? It was hopeless.

'Why,' the detective tried again, 'would someone have wanted to kill Mr Llewellyn?'

'I don't know,' she muttered. 'I don't know.'

'Did he have any enemies?'

'He ... led a complicated life.'

'But for someone to kill him?' The detective allowed a note of surprise to creep into her voice, although any naivety must have been blasted away long ago.

Casey didn't mention Aidan Gardiner's offer to Nick Llewellyn. And she certainly didn't mention Jackson Harvey, knowing that even the most tangential reference to the footballer would cause the story to explode. *England ace linked to former MP's death.*

A glimmer of silver …
The detective waited.
A glint of red …
'I don't know,' she said in the end.

When the detective turned away, Casey checked her phone. Fifteen missed calls from Ross, a dozen from Miranda.

By the time she reached the office, Ross was in a frenzy. 'Not much point in having an eyewitness on our staff,' he spat, 'if she doesn't answer her bloody phone.'

Above his head, Selina Llewellyn was hurrying into her London house in Chelsea. Three different angles on the big television screens. Sky had the best viewpoint, Casey noted clinically: tightest in on the ex-wife's tears.

Selina Armstrong, she was once again, her maiden name blasted across the bottom of the screens.

Dash interrupted Ross's rant. 'Arthur can run through events with Casey quickly to update the site,' he told Ross firmly. 'And then, Casey, can we all have a chat in the investigations room?'

Arthur was the *Post*'s crime correspondent, an ebullient reporter who took great delight in the grisly detail of his job.

'Sure,' Casey managed. 'Of course.'

'Someone killed him,' she said as she sat down on the old sofa.

'How?' asked Ross.

'I think Nick Llewellyn was drowned by the same man who attacked Aidan Gardiner at Ascot,' she said. 'He did it while I was over by the cafe.'

Spoken aloud, the words sounded hysterical.

Casey caught glances being exchanged around the room.

'Why would the same person attack Aidan Gardiner and Nick Llewellyn?' asked Dash. 'There's nothing to link them.'

'I don't know,' said Casey. 'But I am sure it was the same person. He has a tattoo on his back. An olive tree. I saw it at Ascot, just the edges above his collar.'

Silence. Dash wrote something in his notebook.

'The police say there are no significant marks on Llewellyn's body.' Arthur's voice was even. 'There were a few bruises and so on, but nothing definitive. He drowned, according to preliminary assessments, but we're not allowed to use that yet.'

'Llewellyn was frail,' said Casey. 'Nothing like the man he used to be. It would be easy to—'

'What?' asked Miranda. 'Hold his head underwater?'

'Well, maybe. The bench was screened from the rest of the park by willows. And once he was below the path, he was out of sight. It might have been ages before someone spotted him. You know what London's like.'

'How long were you gone for?'

'Ten minutes, maybe? There was a queue.' Walnut or red velvet.

'But why then?' said Dash. 'Someone would have had to be watching, waiting for you to walk away.'

'I saw the man before we sat down. He was lying under a tree with a novel when we doubled back on ourselves. He could have been following us, waiting for his chance.'

Ross raised his eyebrows. 'Why do it in the middle of a park in broad daylight?'

'We were a long way from anyone else,' said Casey. 'No one could see that bench unless they were right next to it. If they were following him, they might have decided that, for central London, that was as isolated a place as any.'

'The police obviously think that Llewellyn just tripped and fell into the water,' Miranda said flatly. 'Or possibly drowned himself somehow. With his back story, it's possible.'

'But why there?'

'He could have spotted something in the water that he wanted to take a closer look at, and slipped. Some cute little ducklings could have bobbed past, for all we know.'

'We can put a line in Arthur's story,' said Ross. 'An appeal for witnesses. Man in a Panama hat … see if anyone gets in touch.'

'Fine,' said Dash. 'But we're appealing for that man's story, not suggesting he killed Llewellyn. I don't want the paper coming across as deranged.'

'I'm not some mad conspiracy theorist,' Casey protested.

'Sure,' said Dash. 'But you'll end up appearing like one if we don't phrase it carefully.'

'He didn't just die,' said Casey. 'I know it.'

The death of Nick Llewellyn was a big news story for two days. The coverage was larded with comment pieces about the tragedy of home-lessness, the Icarus plummet of a great political mind, the hat Selina wore to church on Sunday. Then it faded, as all stories do. A week later, the police had found nothing.

'They must have done.' Casey stared blankly at Arthur. 'There must be something.'

'They're going to put it down as accidental death,' he said. 'There isn't anything to suggest it was anything else, Casey, apart from a bunch of conspiracy theorists on the internet.'

'And that's it?' she asked. 'What about the yummy mummies at the cafe in Regent's Park? Have they talked to them about a man with white-blond hair?'

'A couple of the mums think they remember seeing a man in a Panama hat walk past, but nothing more specific. CCTV hasn't picked up anything. There are lots of exits from the park, and car access too.'

'I—'

'The police are floating the idea that it might have been something to do with Llewellyn's health,' said Arthur. 'Drugs or something. Felt dizzy, fell in, the end.'

Because that was the sort of thing that happened to other people, and *Post* readers would shrug – *well, what did he expect?* – and move on.

'The tox screen was clear,' said Casey. 'Nick didn't do drugs.'

'You spoke to him twice,' Arthur said reasonably. 'You don't know that.'

The crime corrrespondent was standing at the door of the inves-tigations room, notepad in one hand, attention halfway across the newsroom.

'So they're giving up?'

'Not exactly.' Exactly.

'Something happened to Nick Llewellyn,' said Casey.

'Apophenia,' piped up Hessa, unexpectedly.

'What?' Casey looked round, baffled.

'It's the tendency to perceive meaningful connections between unrelated things,' she explained. 'The human brain doesn't like randomness, so it's always searching for patterns. It's what drives a lot of gambling – people convince themselves that they can see patterns when they can't.'

'Thanks for that, Hess. So you think my brain can't accept that what happened to Nick was pure chance?'

'Maybe.' Hessa shrugged. 'Maybe not.'

'It's why we create gods.' Miranda leaned back in her chair. 'Because our brains simply cannot process the idea that it's all random. Sends you mad, just contemplating it.'

'So it's just that I *have* to believe these things are connected?' Casey wondered aloud.

'Possibly.'

'And it's why the house always wins. Because cold, hard logic will always outgun our optimistic little human minds?'

'No one,' said Arthur, 'could accuse you of being overly optimistic. Terribly deep, you lot are today.'

'Someone murdered Nick Llewellyn,' said Casey. 'I know it.'

12

Aidan sounded apologetic when he rang a few days later.

'I don't know if you've had a moment, Casey ...'

She was sitting in the *Post's* Commons office, staring vaguely at a protest down in Parliament Square. A few hundred people were demonstrating against the visit of some foreign despot, the police hovering warily around Winston Churchill.

I told you he was in Regent's Park, she thought. *You knew.*

'Work's pretty hectic right now, Aidan.'

'I was just wondering if you'd had any more time to think about Jackson's plan. Him contacting the match fixer.'

'No,' she said. 'I haven't. Not yet.'

'Ah. Okay.'

'I'll call you soon, Aidan.'

'Absolutely.' A pause. 'Thank you,' he said. 'For not mentioning you'd been with me and Jac. The morning of the Regent's Park thing.'

'Sure.'

Maybe I should have.

Casey hung up and looked back down at the demonstration. Someone had brought out a megaphone, his anger echoing around the old square.

She thought of the speed of the barman as he sprinted down the escalator.

She thought of the shape in the muddy water.

Lunch? she texted Miranda.

'I knew you'd go up to Holloway Road that day,' said Miranda.

'Miranda, I—'

They hadn't spoken for several days, which was unusual.

''S'fine.' Miranda prodded her sandwich suspiciously then her face softened. 'I'd like to say I'd have done the same, but we both know that's a lie. So what's up?'

Miranda reclined on the grass. They had met in St James's Park, lying in the shade of one of the huge London plane trees. Buckingham Palace slumbered in the distance, the Royal Standard drooping in the heat.

Speaking quickly, Casey outlined Jackson and Aidan's plan to hunt down the match fixer who had bribed Harvey's brother. By the time she had finished, Miranda was sitting up.

'Cressida would have so much fun turning you into a WAG.' Miranda was almost smiling. 'She still hasn't forgiven you for the tragic loss of that unbelievably expensive hat.'

'That's not my main concern.'

'No.' Miranda sobered up. 'But what if you're not actually mad and Nick Llewellyn really was murdered by this blond guy, whoever he is? You'd told Aidan that Nick was heading to Regent's Park, so Aidan knew where to find him. The blond guy could have been operating under Aidan's orders, for all we know, and now they're using Jackson as bait?'

'The blond guy was last seen attempting to attack Aidan at Ascot,' said Casey. 'I don't see why he would suddenly be carrying out Aidan's orders now. And I'm not mad, by the way.'

'Debatable.'

'Aidan's not the type anyway.' Casey tried to convince herself.

'You can't be sure of that,' said Miranda. 'You and Jackson going off somewhere random. The more I think about it, the less I like it.'

'I saw Aidan being chased at Ascot,' Casey said firmly. 'He was terrified, and he's not the sort of person who could act scared.'

'The gambling world can get pretty filthy, but wasn't that level of fear a bit suspicious?'

'Because ordinary Mr Smith doesn't worry about being assassinated on an escalator at Ascot?'

'Well, Lord Smith at Royal Ascot, but you get my point. You and I are never going to be able to understand Aidan's algorithm,' Miranda went on, 'even if he would show it to us, which he won't. So although he's telling us that he's after the baddies, and it's all Robin Hood and good angels, we have to take his word for it. He could be using us to take out his rivals. He could be—'

'*Cui bono,*' murmured Casey. The old question: who benefits?

'Quite.'

'The only thing that links Aidan and Nick is gambling.' Casey tried to soothe Miranda's fears. 'And millions of people all around the country gamble every week. Plus Nick's gambling must have been fairly limited for the last few years because he just hasn't had access to much cash, so even that connection's pretty tenuous.'

A fiver in a hat, gone in a moment.

The ghosts rose again and Casey's voice trailed away.

'Are you okay?' Miranda looked at her properly. 'You seem ...'

'I just keep thinking about all the stories we've done. Seeing Nick in that Tube station. All those lives ...'

A shallow grave, somewhere in Libya.

A plane, cartwheeling through the air.

And those eyes. Those eyes, flecked with grey and green, blue and gold.

'I know,' said Miranda. 'I know.'

'I miss Ed.' The words were so meaningless.

'You'll always miss him.'

Casey rolled over and stared up at the brightness of the sky.

It was as if the memories were glitter shards of mirror, cracked carelessly. As if they were fragments of sorrow, crystallised. At night, sometimes, she would pick them up carefully. Examine them one by one, turning them over and over, so that they caught the light, came alive.

She might even catch a glimpse of herself, maybe, in one splinter or two. The gleam of an eye, a fall of brown hair, a frozen sort of happiness. They were nothings, these remnants, quite weightless, sparkling on the floor.

But then she might turn clumsy and feel the glass bite deep. Stare almost in disbelief as the blood welled up. Scarlet beads, a line of pain.

In the daytime, she overlaid the memories, so carefully. Layers of lacquer, hard, bright and pretty.

Although sometimes the colours cracked, and she caught him in the corner of her eye, disappearing just as she turned.

In those places. Their places. Where he had waited for her, once, with a bunch of red roses.

She shook her head. Threw the pieces back to the floor and watched them shatter all over again.

Miranda was talking. Casey interrupted.

'Jackson thinks this'll all just be a bit of fun. Something to boast about in a bar after it's all over.'

'I'm sure he does.'

'He doesn't get it,' said Casey. 'That it could be really dangerous.'

'You said he was smart.'

'It's all wisecracks and flirting for him. He doesn't understand that you have to concentrate for every single second. And that if you let things slip, it can all blow up. Ed … Ed always understood.'

'Ed was a Marine, Casey. He was trained to plan for disaster.'

'Miranda, I keep thinking … I keep thinking about Libya. Ed and me, out there.'

The two of them, driving across the burning red of the desert. Side by side, smiling. Half an act, half in love already.

'I certainly can't imagine Jackson Harvey in Libya,' said Miranda. 'But this is different, Casey—'

'People *died* in Libya. That child … I still think about those parents, the absolute, unbearable tragedy of it all. And I watched. I stood there and watched. Oliver Selby himself—'

'*Selby. That* was his name. I was trying to remember the other day. Cormium chief exec. We never actually found out what happened to him, did we?'

'No,' said Casey. 'But we left him in the middle of the Sahara Desert with a bunch of angry mercenaries and no one's heard of him since, so ...'

'Shallow grave.' Miranda nodded.

'We abandoned him, Miranda. We left him out there to die.'

'We didn't have much of a choice. And he had been—'

'He didn't deserve to die.'

'Again, debatable.'

'It shouldn't have been our call. Whatever he'd done.'

'True.'

'And Ed ...'

'I know.'

'Ed was *killed*.' The word was still a shock. Still impossible. 'He's *dead*. And Jackson thinks this is all a bit of a laugh. A chat-up line, with a twist of adrenaline. Got all the Ferraris you need? Bored of sky-diving? Take yourself undercover.'

'It's up to you, Casey. No one is going to make you do anything. Dash is quite happy with you knocking out a couple of articles a day from the Politics office, forever.'

'I know.'

'But it isn't enough?'

'No. I suppose not.' Casey sighed and stared across the park. A small girl was feeding the ducks, scatters of bread and squeaks of excitement. 'How about you? Are you all right, Miranda?'

The briefest of hesitations. Miranda was tired, Casey saw. There was a tension around her eyes that hadn't been there before.

'I miss Tom,' she said bluntly. 'I told him to go, and he has. And now I'm alone, and I can't remember what I thought there would be instead.'

Miranda's husband had left their pretty house in Queen's Park one sunny morning. Moved out, moved on.

'I'm sorry.'

'I wake up and wonder, "Is this all there is? Is this all I wanted?"'

'You do something,' said Casey, 'and you don't consider ...'

'You can't possibly think through all the consequences.'

They sat silently for a moment.

'I don't even know,' Casey said moodily, 'if Dash will let me do any undercover again. He treats me as if I were—'

'I'll fix Dash,' said Miranda. 'If you really want to go. But I think it's dangerous. I think it's—'

'I want to go. How else are we going to work out what's going on with Aidan's match fixers?'

A half shrug from Miranda. 'Fine, Casey. Fine. But be careful. Because gambling isn't the only thing that links Nick Llewellyn and Aidan.' She cracked open her water bottle. 'The other thing that links them is you.'

13

Screams echoed across the water.

Two girls, giggling hysterically, collapsed into the swimming pool. As they fell, they tried frantically to keep their faces above the turquoise water.

'They're having fun, at least.' Jackson raised his glass to them, triggering more squeals of laughter. 'You got to love Spain, Casey.'

Walking into Neroli's with Jackson Harvey had been an education.

From the outside, the club looked underwhelming. It was in a slightly seedy two-storey building, which took up a whole block of a palm-tree-lined street in Marbella.

On the ground floor were shops, valuable retail, the club entrance flanked prosaically by an estate agent's and an optician's: *Oferta especial!* One storey up, white curtains were drawn across most of the full-length windows that ran all the way round the building. The club's name was picked out in pink neon letters, ten foot high, that glowed brighter against the sky as the evening darkened.

The entrance was a swirl of disco balls and leopard print. The greeter – a blonde in a cerise playsuit and a mass of diamanté jewellery – waved them up a flight of marble steps. There was certainly no waiting in a queue for Jackson Harvey. At the top of the stairs, the vast roof garden was open to the night sky, filled with a crowd of beautiful men and women. A large swimming pool stretched away, the glittering water surrounded by oversized four-poster beds veiled by billowing cream drapes. Groups of people lolled on these, swigging champagne and shouting to each other over the music, their eyes constantly sweeping the crowd.

At each corner of the pool there was a podium, a dancer in a black latex dress balanced on top. The dancers were spinning flaming torches, arcs of fire twirling to the beat of the pounding music.

As she walked in with Jackson, heads had turned and stayed turned. Casey could imagine the whispers.

Is it … ? Could be … Think so … It is!

Excitement shimmered around the pool. A second beautiful hostess in an electric blue catsuit led them to a cream-draped bed in the most prominent position in the club. Behind them, the dancefloor heaved.

'Champagne?' she offered.

'Why not?' Jackson grinned back at her. He threw himself onto a pile of pillows and patted one of them. 'Come on, Callie. Chill out.'

Casey perched on the side of the bed. Callie: that first syllable, enough to make her glance up. She felt twitchy, wary, on her guard. Looking for the snare within the trap, and half seeing Aidan out of the corner of her eye even though he was at home in Kennington.

Good luck, Casey, he had texted before she left, and she had peered at the few words, knowing there was no way to tell.

'What time did you tell Blake to meet us?' she asked briskly.

'Not for an hour or so,' said Jackson. 'So we can enjoy ourselves, babe. You look good in that outfit, you know?'

And Casey pulled a horror face at him, twisting her eyes and nose to make herself laugh.

'Shut up. I told you I hate it.'

Knowing Casey wouldn't listen, Cressida had given Miranda stern instructions for the evening's make-up.

'It's all about the contouring,' Cressida had insisted bossily during the trial run in the fashion cupboard at the *Post*. 'Start with liquid foundation, then the contour blender, then the powder highlight, right?'

'Right.' Miranda had squeezed her mouth shut to stifle laughter as she rubbed a range of creams into Casey's face. Once they had decided on the plan, Miranda had thrown herself into it, as she always did.

'The eyebrows have to be really strong, too.'

The day before they flew out, a beautician in Knightsbridge had applied fake eyelashes before a neighbouring hairdresser wove in a mass of hair extensions. 'Blonder,' Cressida insisted from the next chair along. 'More!'

'I'm turning bloody orange,' Casey had said, peering in the mirror.

'The spray tan's really deepening now,' Cressida said happily. 'Nails next. And a pedicure, of course.'

'Oh, of course,' Casey wailed.

'I thought you were meant to be good at all this.' Jackson was still laughing at her as he lounged back on the four-poster. 'Supposed to be an expert at blending in and that sort of thing.'

'Smile.' Casey grimaced at him. 'It might never happen.'

Jackson was so confident, so sure of himself. On a table beside the bed, there was a bunch of red roses. He reached out and grabbed one, handing it to her with a flourish.

Red roses.

For a second, Casey was pulled away. To a different smile that flickered only for a second. To that careless grace, and a fast boat racing over the blue of the Indian Ocean. Ed, laughing back over his shoulder as she squealed and clung on, her body armour tight against her sides.

She pushed the memory away.

Not now.

Not ever.

The hostess reappeared, with glasses and a bottle of champagne balanced on a tray.

'You all right, darling?'

The girl lit up at Jackson's words, her evening made.

'Gorge dress,' the hostess said to Casey. 'Gucci, right? Love the cut-outs, and those studs are amazing.'

Casey managed to take a sip of the drink and grin up at her. 'Thanks, hon, I got it in a fab little boutique just down on the beachfront.'

'Very nice.' The hostess whirled away.

Jackson smiled down at Casey. 'You see. I told you, it's easy.'

And she took another sip of champagne, and it was.

'Catch up with you later, right?' Jackson somehow managed to make the dismissal affable. Practice, Casey guessed. That had been the fourth group of girls to approach the four-poster bed in less than half an hour.

'Didn't it drive your ex mad?' Casey asked.

'She didn't love it.'

'But it is useful for us,' said Casey. 'Remember to ask Blake if we can go somewhere quiet because you're tired of being hassled.'

She had hammered it into Jackson before they arrived at the club. 'We have to be able to hear what he's saying,' she had insisted. 'None of it's any good unless the audio's decent.'

'I get it, Casey.' That slow smile. 'It's cool. We can go somewhere quiet any time you want.'

'Concentrate, Jackson.'

'Oh, I am.'

At last, a short man with a shaved head approached the bed.

'Jackson! My man! It's a fucking pleasure.'

'Blake, right? Great to meet you.'

Casey had stood next to Landon as he made the call a week earlier. She had caught the train out to Elmington and made her way to where Jackson's elder brother lived in a neo-Georgian mansion.

'It's rented,' murmured Aidan. 'And be careful with Landon. Jackson might trust him, but …'

Layers of trust and suspicion, bleeding into each other.

Landon, however, had dialled Blake's number with all the Harvey confidence.

Blake! Just thought I'd give you a call, dude, see how it's going … What you up to? Where are you, anyway? … Marbella? No way, man, that sounds amazing … You know what? My brother's out there next week. Yeah, Jackson. The baby of the family, right? I'll tell him to get in touch … And you know the other thing? He might be interested in …

Casey had watched Landon sitting there in his Balenciaga logo T-shirt, his Prada shorts, his customised Nike Airs. And wondered.

A few minutes later, he had hung up, smiling, and turned to her with a nod. 'Blake's well up for it. Said that Jac should give him a call when he's flying out, and he'll organise clubs, whatever.'

'He didn't have any suspicions?' Casey's eyes held Landon's. 'Even though you haven't called him for months?'

Because, above all, she didn't trust family. Didn't rely on the my-little-brother saccharine.

But Landon's eyes held hers. 'You're the one risking Jackson's life, okay? I'd never … But if it's what he wants to do …'

Later, Casey had listened back to the tape of the call again and again, probing the tone, the cadences. Blake sounded relaxed, confident; Landon, straightforward.

It was worth a try.

Now Blake clapped Jackson on the back.

'Good to see you,' Blake shouted over the blare of the music. 'Landon's told me so much about you. Those England games were outstanding.'

Blake was a gym enthusiast, Casey thought. The black T-shirt was tight over bulky biceps and a muscled chest. There was a dusting of stubble on the he-man jawline and he was heavily tanned. His eyes – slightly too close together – were green, his teeth a startling blue-white. As Jackson stood up, Blake bounced slightly on his toes: half repressed energy, half gaining a valuable couple of inches.

'Callie.' Casey held out her hand.

'Nice to meet you.' Blake's eyes barely met hers.

Girls were an accessory for Blake, she guessed. And here there were half a dozen parading past at any minute, teetering along the edge of the swimming pool in the highest of heels.

Unbothered, she lay back on the four-poster's pillows and listened as Blake and Jackson talked about music and clubs and football, always football. They were pals within minutes.

Finally, Jackson glanced down at her.

'I'm starving.' He rolled his shoulders, stretched out his neck. 'We're going to grab some food, Callie. Come on.'

'They'll bring it—' Blake objected.

'It's fine, Blake. We won't be hassled over there.'

Across the dancefloor was a dining area. The tables were raised a floor above the uproar of the club, perched on a structure designed to look like a treehouse.

'The restaurant will have emptied out by that time,' Miranda had reported back after a leisurely meal the night before. 'Even the Spaniards will be down in the club. It'll be much quieter up there.'

'Wonder what time it'll close?'

'It'll stay open,' Jackson had been listening in, 'for me.'

Now he put his hand out to Casey and pulled her towards him as she rose to her feet. His face was very close, and she had to smile, and peek up at him from under her eyelashes, and wonder – for a second – whether he was going to kiss her. Stomach twisting, half excited. He grinned, lifted her hand to his mouth and kissed it with perfect chivalry.

Blake led the way round the dancefloor towards the wide staircase that swept up to the restaurant.

As Jackson had predicted, the maître d' was already clicking his fingers, the waiters rushing to clear a table. Beyond the lights of the club, the Mediterranean was a black vastness, punctuated only by the glimmer of yachts.

'I want to sit over there.' Casey pouted. 'The music's giving me a headache.'

She was pointing to a table in the far corner of the open space, looking out over the darkened beach. Blake shrugged and led them across as the waiters whisked over with gleaming cutlery.

'I want to see the view,' demanded Casey, so Blake, shrugging again, sat with his back to the beach, Jackson and Casey opposite.

It mattered. If Casey sat facing the dancefloor, it would be impossible for the little cameras to make sense of a dark face silhouetted against the strobing lights of the club. But the cameras could adjust to the darkness of the beach, and as Blake turned to Jackson again, his face was lit up, bathed first in blue light, then in fuchsia.

'Very atmospheric.' Casey could almost hear Miranda's voice in her head. 'Livens things up nicely.'

'Where does the camera go?' Jackson had asked in fascinated curiosity when Casey appeared in the tight red dress.

When she showed him the pinhead camera replacing one of the tiny Gucci studs, he prodded it with a finger, delighted. 'That is *wicked*.'

'Here's yours.' She pulled a shirt from her suitcase and shook it out. It was slim fit, in a slightly metallic dark grey.

'No way.' He looked horrified. 'I'd never wear *that*.'

'Jackson.'

'I'll put that on if you'll take that off.'

'You have to wear dark colours.' She ignored the protests. 'The buttonhole camera is black. It would stand out too much against a pale shirt.'

Charmed by the miniaturised camera, he had agreed, grudgingly.

As the waiter reappeared with the menus, he also plonked a vase of white roses in front of Casey. She forced an appreciative smile.

'It's lovely to meet you, Blake.' As she spoke she fiddled with the roses, casually pulling the flowers out of her sightline. 'How long are you out in Spain for?'

'I'm here for the summer.' Blake turned his charm on her. 'I like hanging out in the clubs, catching up with people. Letting my hair down.' He rubbed his hand over his shaved head with a wry grin.

'What's your surname?' she asked. 'So I can follow you on Insta.'

Because his surname was crucial.

'Gibson,' he said. 'Blake Gibson.'

Casey was logged into the investigation team's Instagram account, which was ten thousand followers bought from a click farm in Shenzhen. Over several months, Tillie had added generic photographs of flowers and beaches and cheery crowd scenes, so that it could be adapted whenever required. For chatting with Blake, Casey had changed the account's handle to @heyheyitscallieee and uploaded a series of photographs from clubs across London. Even if he scrolled all the way back to the flowers and beaches, it would still be believable.

'Oh, there you are,' Casey said when she had found Blake online. 'Great pics! Ha – look at you, swimming with those dolphins! So what do you get up to back in the UK?'

She jumped as Jackson slid his arm around her waist, pulling her against him. His arms were rock hard. Without missing a beat, she ground her heel into his foot.

'Watch it,' he murmured into her neck. 'Aidan won't be delighted if you send me back injured.'

'He'll understand. Won't take long to update his algorithm.'

'Maybe.' He kissed her neck and she didn't move away.

'Bit of this, bit of that,' Blake was saying. 'I fix stuff for a few footballers I know, sort out their problems, that sort of thing.'

'Like what?' Casey squirmed away from Jackson, trying to concentrate.

But all Blake's attention was focused on Jackson, and the conversation swirled away again to Fleethurst's chances, and how Landon was doing, and what Jackson thought of the England back four. Until finally, Casey saw her chance.

'Fleethurst is *nice*,' Blake was saying. 'Classy. Have you bought a place down there yet?'

'I—'

'We *can't*,' Casey interrupted Jackson with a whine in her voice. Her foot nudged his, hard.

'Not yet, mate.' Jackson managed to look shamefaced. 'I will soon, though.'

'We can't because he's gambled it all away, can you believe it?' Casey said petulantly. 'Hundreds of thousands of pounds. Stupid mug.'

Blake was watching them closely.

'I've got years ahead of me,' insisted Jackson. 'It'll be fine, Cal. You'll see.'

'It really pisses me off. Him and his dickhead friends, gambling on crap, all the bloody time.'

Blake poured them more drinks, nodding sympathetically. 'It's easily done, mate. I know how it goes.'

'It's not good enough.' Casey put spite into her voice. 'He needs to sort it out. We're going to have to move to a crappy little house near Woking, rented and everything. It's *ridiculous*.'

Stillness fell over the table, Casey willing Jackson to silence.

'Have you ever …' Blake began slowly. 'Have you ever thought about—'

Once he started talking, Blake was efficient. He had done this before, Casey could tell, dozens of times.

Before she had flown out to Spain, Aidan had told her about the young footballers gambling on their phones in the back of the bus on the long drives to fixtures: in Manchester, Newcastle, Paris.

'It's the boredom,' Aidan had said. 'And once they arrive wherever they're going, they're stuck in hotel rooms for hour after hour. You'll find that one of the team gets hooked, and the next thing, they're all at it. Wayne Rooney was meant to have lost hundreds of thousands. And that's not a financial disaster for him, of course, but some of them lose more than they have, and next thing, someone like this Blake character appears, offering them a way back. And they're being told to think of match fixing as two fingers to the system that took their money in the first place.'

And soon, Jackson and Blake were laughing, and shaking hands. Jackson even managed a glow of relief. Blake ordered more champagne with a click of his fingers.

'No more for you,' Casey chided Jackson. 'What'll Aidan say?'

'Who's Aidan?' Blake laughed along. 'I thought Stjepan was the Fleethurst captain?'

'Aidan Gardiner,' said Casey. 'He owns Fleethurst?'

'Oh, sure,' said Blake. 'Him. Jackson, I've got to tell you about this one time …'

14

'It's not the whole story,' Casey fretted.

Miranda was sitting at her desk in the investigations room. 'You always say that.'

Casey kicked her heels against Tillie's desk. 'And I'm usually right.'

She had dragged a resistant Jackson to the airport. 'I promised Aidan that I would deliver you home safely. Like a badly behaved parcel, if you like.'

'Are we role-playing a sexy DHL delivery girl now?'

'We are not.'

'Look at that beach,' he protested. 'And my all-time favourite DJ's playing Neroli tonight. And you and I could have some real fun, Casey. You know you want to.'

'Come *on*, Jackson.'

'And we're flying *economy*?'

'You're worried because Blake didn't seem to recognise Aidan Gardiner's name.' Miranda took a sip of her coffee. 'He might just have been concentrating on someone else? Like – say – the England player sitting next to you.'

'It was a complete blank though,' said Casey. 'Unless Blake is the best actor in the world, he didn't know who Aidan was. If you try to have someone killed one week, you're probably going to remember their name the next.'

'Blake might just be the best actor in the world.'

'He's not.'

'Does it matter either way?'

'Yes,' insisted Casey. 'It means that Blake's just a random crook who didn't have anything to do with the attack on Aidan at Ascot. There's something else going on.'

'Does it really matter if Blake's not running a vast criminal empire? He's definitely match fixing. It's a great story already and the footage is brilliant. Blake's coughed to the whole thing.'

'But we've also got a dead ex-MP and an aggressive, organised ambush on a major gambler in a public place, with the blond barman – not that he *is* a barman, but you know what I mean – linked to both attacks. Blake's a dead end.'

Jackson was due to go wobbly on Blake, ringing him in a panic and pleading for reassurance.

'That way we can force Blake to prove what he's up to,' Miranda said with relish. 'Get the names of which players are going to be doing what in the pre-season friendlies, and there we go. Perfect.'

'We're going to miss it.' Casey rubbed her face. 'By rushing it.'

'Well, where does a story end anyway?' Miranda put her head on one side. 'You could go on forever, really.'

'Philosophy,' said Casey, 'doesn't suit you.'

'You think?'

Together, Miranda and Casey watched football matches, freezing the frame on the deliberate corners and sly penalties Blake had promised in advance.

And the next day Miranda rang him as he lounged by the pool in his Marbella apartment complex: *Mr Gibson, we would like to give you the opportunity to comment; we want to reflect your side of the story.* And listened coolly as his tone turned from charm to bluster to fear.

They called the footballers too. 'Oh, I don't think Viktor will want to comment on that,' said one PR airily. 'We're focused on his partnership with Juniper at the moment, that new line of trainers they're bringing out, yeah? I can send you Jpegs of those, no problem.'

'Mmm,' said Miranda. 'That isn't *exactly* how this is going to work.'

'I do love fashion PRs,' said Hessa as Miranda put the phone down.

A few hours later, the *Post* published the story, with its blaring headlines and its outraged comment pieces. As promised, there was no reference to Aidan. But there were several profiles of Jackson: the England ace, the hero, the star who fought tirelessly for justice.

I'll be advertising crisps soon, he texted Casey cheerfully.

Thank you, Jackson. We couldn't have done it without you.

I know you couldn't. Drink soon?

The footage of Blake – his face sharp against the black of the Mediterranean at night, the sapphire lights flickering across his cheekbones, the vase of white roses just tipping the edge of the frame – led every TV news bulletin.

And three days later, Blake Gibson disappeared.

15

Casey was sitting in the *Post*'s Parliament office when Miranda called.

'There's something about Blake Gibson breaking on the wires,' she said carefully.

'What?' Already Casey was pulling up the copy, hunting through the endless blur of news for the most recent reference to him.

Where … *Where?*

There.

The words were prosaic, devoid of emotion. The horror was all in her head.

Phrases jumped out.

Spanish police are searching for …

Blood found in his apartment …

Neighbours heard shouting …

Not seen since …

'What's happened, Miranda?' Casey managed. 'What's happened to Blake?'

A glint of red.

A glimmer of silver.

Shuddering, she read the news bulletin again, searching for a clue that wasn't there.

Not your fault.

Not your fault.

Yes. Yours.

'It's all very unclear so far.' Miranda's voice was deliberately crisp. 'And Christa's having to look after an ill child, so she can't get down to Marbella.'

Christa was the *Post*'s Madrid correspondent.

Casey's fingers curled into her palms. 'Is Blake dead?'

'I don't know. I don't … But, yes, the Spanish police obviously think it's a possibility, or they wouldn't be appealing for information like that. He's only missing, officially.'

'I'll go out there, if Christa's tied up.'

'Okay. Casey …'

'What?'

'Be careful.'

Blake's apartment was shabbier than Casey had expected. Like Neroli's, she thought: shoddy in daylight. Thousand-euro champagne sprayed in the air; nylon drapes gone grimy. She peered through peeling gates at the swimming pool, grey scum floating in one corner.

A bored Spanish policeman pointed out the flat to her, a corner of the fourth floor in an ugly six-storey block.

For a moment, Casey stood in a dusty patch of shade, the sun searingly bright against the walls, and then she looked away.

A small pack of journalists had taken themselves off to a cafe across the street to observe the comings and goings at the apartment block's entrance.

'No point in boiling alive out there,' said the *Daily Mail*'s Madrid correspondent, stirring a coffee briskly.

'You did the original Gibson match-fixing story, didn't you?' said the man from *El País*. 'Good hit, that was. And it looks like somebody wasn't exactly delighted with him.'

Not your fault.

'Any more colour to come from your investigation?' asked the *Daily Mail*. 'Got to say that I fancy the absolute pants off Jackson Harvey.'

'He very much feels the same way.'

Back in London, Jackson's PR team were working hard to offset the darkness of Blake's disappearance. *Just shows how risky it was, right? Heroic, really, when you think about it.*

'I'll bet. So there's more to come?'

'A bit,' said Casey. 'Yes.'

Tillie was going through the footage again, for new clips to shunt out to the broadcasters. New, that was all that mattered. Previously unseen. Sapphire lights, white roses and an emergent sense of pathos.

And the *Post*'s watermark plastered over every news bulletin, unbuyable advertising.

'Not sure this story needs that much more colour,' grimaced one of the BBC reporters, eyes on her phone. She was flicking through the leaked police photographs of the apartment: blood smeared across the floor, a scarlet spatter on the walls.

'But no corpse to be found,' said *El País*. 'The police *hate* it when that happens.'

'There's a lot of Mediterranean right over there.' The BBC fiddled thoughtfully with her recorder. 'Gibson could be absolutely anywhere.'

'Do you think there's anything more to come today?' asked an earnest reporter from the *Guardian*. 'Only if there isn't, I fancy a swim.'

At the press conference later on, the police were not forthcoming. Because they didn't know anything, Casey guessed, aloofness a veil over ignorance. Like the rest of the pack, she spent the evening and the next day trying to track down any possible witnesses. The neighbours hadn't seen anything. No, they hadn't poked their noses out to investigate the screams. No, they hadn't called the police, not then. It was the cleaner, knocking timidly, who had found the sprays of blood.

'It is his blood type,' a policeman confirmed. They were waiting for a DNA sample from his mother.

'Enough that he's definitely dead?' asked the *Mail* briskly.

'We are not sure,' the policeman said. 'He could still be alive.'

But only just, they all thought. Only just.

There was a lift from the flat to an underground carpark, and no CCTV. Casey used the repurposed @heyheyitscallieee account to trawl through Blake's Instagram, contacting the people who commented most frequently on his photographs.

'Hi, I'm getting in touch from the *London Post*,' again and again.

A couple of them were tearful. 'We always had the best nights out with him.' 'We had such a special connection.' 'I had no idea that …' 'Please get in touch, Blakie. Please' – but none of them had heard from him, none of them could even guess at what had happened.

Casey messaged Jackson, asking him to put an appeal on his social media for any information to be sent to a generic *Post* email address.

No problem, he messaged back. A short pause. *Please take care, Casey. I can't believe they think he's dead. Fuck. We only met him for a few hours, but …*

I know. I am sorry, Jackson.

Take care, he wrote again.

I'll be fine.

His bounce returned. *And tell me when you're back, too. We can go out. Have some real fun.*

Can't, Jackson. I don't fancy being photographed by a hundred paps. I do too much undercover work.

We'll go somewhere private, then. Very private.

I'm not the WAG type, Jackson.

Honestly. No one else has a problem with it. Another brief pause. *Anyway, WAG is sexist. You're better than that, Casey.*

She laughed out loud.

I have to work, Jackson.

Laters, darling.

Casey put down her phone, filed her story thoughtfully – 'Mystery surrounds …' – and then headed back to her hotel.

'Was it a punishment for being caught out on camera?' Casey said to Miranda when she called her from the desk in her hotel room. 'Or a warning to other match fixers?'

'Or did Blake know more than he should? More than we realised. And now he's been very effectively shut up.'

'But what did he know?' Casey drummed her fingers on the desk. 'Perhaps we've just killed off our only lead.'

'I think Aidan used you to track down Blake and then had him killed,' Miranda said bluntly. 'To stop crappy data getting into his model. I think it's Aidan behind all this.'

'Miranda—'

'Casey …' A sigh. 'Christa's kid's better, so she can scoot down to Marbella tomorrow morning. You're not safe out there. It feels wrong.'

'I—'

'You can ring round his Instagram followers just as well from back here.'

'Okay,' Casey muttered. 'I'll be on the first flight tomorrow.'

She couldn't settle in her hotel room, pacing to and fro. Her eyes roved over the striped wallpaper, trying to make sense of the pattern. Orange stripe, grey squiggle, yellow dash. Orange stripe, grey squiggle, yellow dash. Orange, grey, yellow, orange, grey, yellow. Then orange stripe, yellow squiggle. It drew her eye again and again. Her phone bleeped. Landon Harvey.

Just saw Jac's Insta post. I'm worried, Casey.

She remembered the Prada shorts, the Balenciaga top, and wondered if the fear was for Jackson or himself. As if he had guessed her thoughts, another message bleeped in.

This Blake guy's probably been killed, right? What if they go after Jackson next?

She rang Landon's number and he answered on the first ring.

'Aidan Gardiner's organising security for Jackson,' Casey said soothingly. 'They'll keep him safe, Landon.'

'But what if they don't? He's just a kid, Casey.'

The concern in his voice sounded genuine, and she liked him a bit better for it.

'Jackson won't stay at his own house for a bit,' she said. 'These bodyguards are professionals, I promise you.'

She waited to see if Landon would ask where his brother was staying, but he didn't. 'If anything happened to him, my parents would … Mum's having a meltdown already. She's furious with me. Furious. I should never have done it, Casey. I was an idiot. I should never … It's all my fault.'

'We'll work it out, Landon. Promise.'

She put the phone down, stared at the wall again, then got up to see if there was a join in the wallpaper.

*

Her phone buzzed again. Someone had messaged the investigations Instagram account. @georgiesnapsaway, Casey read. Otherwise known as Georgie Carlin, from the brief description in her bio. Casey had messaged her after spotting Blake Gibson in one of her photographs.

In her selfies, Georgie was round-faced and sweet-looking, although trying hard to disguise that fact with layers of make-up. She had wide blue eyes and long blonde hair graduating from dark to light. Balayage, Casey recognised, thanks to Cressida.

Blake was one of my best friends. A string of emojis. *I'm devastated. Can talk if you want.*

She had sent a mobile number along with the emojis. All Miranda's concerns resurfaced. Georgie could be anyone.

One more glance at the wallpaper and Casey had dialled the number.

Georgie sounded quiet and sad. 'We weren't close friends.' She sounded defensive. 'But we always got on really well.'

'I am very sorry for your loss,' said Casey. 'How did you know him exactly?'

'We were always at the same parties. You know what it's like out here.'

'Yes.'

'I work for an estate agent in Puerto Banus,' said Georgie. 'We sell so much to Brits that it makes sense for them to employ me. And it's great, obviously. Usually.'

'Can you tell me a bit about Blake?' asked Casey.

A bit about Blake took several minutes. Casey made sympathetic noises and copious notes. Nothing especially usable, but helpful colour.

'When did you last see him?' Casey asked when Georgie's words had run out.

'The night before he died.' She sounded surprised.

'Oh.' Casey sat up. 'I didn't realise.'

'If he's dead, that is,' Georgie added hastily. 'I mean, I hope he's not. It's so sad. But the police seem to think ...'

'Shall we call it "the night before he disappeared"?'

'Yes,' said Georgie. 'There was a whole group of us out.'

'How did he seem?'

'He was upset. That article about match fixing … We were cheering him up, having a laugh. What he did was stupid, but it was a mistake. He wasn't … a bad person.'

Georgie hadn't seen the by-line on the *Post*'s article, Casey reflected. But then, no one ever noticed the by-line.

'I'm sure he wasn't,' she said comfortingly.

'He got really drunk that night. I mean, we all did. You know how it is.'

'Oh, yes.' Casey allowed a giggle to creep into her voice, one of the girls. 'What did you get up to?'

'We started at that new bar that's just opened up near the Hermès shop. And we ended up at Neroli's, of course.'

'Of course. Who were you with?'

'The usual crowd.' Georgie sounded vague. She started listing names. Casey noted them down. One of them might remember more. 'I didn't know everyone there, though,' Georgie concluded. 'You know what it's like.'

'How did the night end?'

'Oh, it was wicked!' Georgie forgot to be sad. 'We all ended up on this really cool boat. We were *hammered*.'

'And Blake was there too?'

'No.' The bounce went out of Georgie's voice abruptly. 'He went home just before we got on the boat. It was weird. He got really arsey and took off.'

'Weird,' Casey echoed. 'And that was the last time you saw him?'

'It might be the last time anyone saw him,' Georgie said frankly.

'Whose boat was it?' asked Casey.

'Some guy we met at Neroli's.'

Casey reflected. Ross would love photographs of Blake's last night. *You're not safe out there.*

The wallpaper caught her eye again. Orange stripe, yellow squiggle.

'Where are you right now, Georgie?' Casey asked. 'Could we meet up?'

*

It was late now, the night warm and still. Along the beachfront, shop after shop sold postcards and sunhats, flip-flops and kaftans. Casey slalomed between rustling palm trees and flirting teenagers and blackboards rhapsodising about paella and tapas, panini and burgers.

She twisted away as a group of drunk Brits lurched past her, half laughing, half brawling. One of them bumped into her. *It might never happen, love. Smile, why don't you? Moody little bint.*

She had suggested the bar to Georgie, a random place pulled from Google. She was fairly sure Georgie wasn't a trap, but they would meet in a public place, under bright lights.

Georgie was already there by the time Casey arrived. Early twenties, denim cut-offs, a white top that displayed a very bronzed midriff.

'Hi.' She giggled nervously. Georgie, Casey decided, was who she said she was. A waitress appeared to take their order.

It didn't take long for Georgie to forget her nerves. Soon, she was scrolling through her photographs, talking Casey through the evening.

'There's Reese, he's hooking up with Natalie. That's her there. Don't they make the cutest couple? And that's Ezra. He was *so* drunk that night. And that's Gianna with Nova on the left, and there's—' Until Casey's head was spinning.

'Do you have any photographs of the boat?' she asked. 'The one you all ended up on?'

'My battery was flat by then,' said Georgie sadly. 'And it was so cool, too.'

'Whose boat was it?' She asked again.

But she looked blank. 'I can't remember his name. I was *wasted.*'

'Do you have a picture of the guy?'

Georgie pursed her lips. 'Like … maybe.'

She scrolled through her photographs again. It took a long time. Casey's eyes traced the pattern on the floor, painted to look like seashells.

Georgie stopped scrolling. 'It's useless, really, this one. I think that's him. But, well, look …'

It was a man's back. Casey peered closely and shuddered despite the warmth of the evening.

White-blond hair. She zoomed in until the image was meaningless pixels. That was the edge of a tattoo, just above the collar, she was sure of it. Almost sure.

'What?' Georgie's eyes were sharp. 'Do you know him?'

'No. But …'

From behind, this man had broad shoulders, wore the same trousers and T-shirt combination that all the men out here wore. The hair was longer than it had been in Regent's Park.

If it was the same person, Casey told herself. If.

Dash would raise a cynical eyebrow if she came back with this.

'Could you send me that photograph?' Casey asked casually. 'Just in case.'

'Sure.' Georgie shrugged, tapping her phone.

Casey zoomed in and out. It was impossible to tell.

'You definitely don't have any more photographs of him?'

'No.' Georgie shook her head. 'I can ask the others, but I'm the one who always takes photographs of everything on nights out. They take the piss.'

'Please ask them, all the same.'

'Okay.' Georgie bowed her head over her phone.

'What was the name of the boat?'

Another shrug. 'I didn't see, sorry.'

'Where was it moored?'

Georgie's phone was vibrating. 'No one has any photographs, I'm afraid.' She giggled and typed something else.

'Thank you for asking them.'

The phone buzzed again.

'I've got to go.' Georgie sounded coy. 'I'm meeting someone.'

'Can you remember where the boat moored, Georgie?'

But she was already jumping to her feet, excitement bubbling up.

'Rompeolas Marina, I think? Something like that?'

'And the boat itself? What was it like?'

'Big and white.' Georgie was pulling out a lipstick.

'How long was it?'

She looked blank. 'About as long as a London bus?'

'Did it have any flags on it?'

115

'Not that I can remember.' Eyeliner out.

'And there wasn't a big mast and sails?' asked Casey. 'Just an engine.'

'Yes.' Georgie was definite. 'A motor yacht.'

'Okay.' Casey tried to think what else to ask.

'The cushions on the chairs were purple,' Georgie said suddenly. 'And those things dangling over the sides of the boats, what are they called?'

'Fenders?'

'Yes, that's it. To stop you bumping into other boats. They were purple too. I remember, because they matched my dress and Nova said it made it look like I owned this whole massive boat, which was so cool.'

'Okay. Thanks, Georgie.'

'Got to run,' she said firmly. 'Bye!'

Rompeolas, Casey learned a few minutes later, was Spanish for breakwater. The marina was slightly away from the main drag of Marbella. Casey looked thoughtfully at the map.

It was probably nothing. Some guy in Marbella picking up an oven-ready party from Neroli's.

Not a trap for Blake, escaped at the last moment.

Check it out tomorrow, she told herself. In the brightness of the day.

But.

The yachts clinked in the darkness. Peering out, Casey could see how the marina had got its name. Two breakwaters stretched far out to sea like huge protective arms. A narrow gap allowed vessels to come and go. Closer to the shore, hundreds of yachts were tied up to long wooden jetties.

Casey walked slowly along the boards, staring at one yacht and then the next. *A London bus?* That was probably sixty feet long. Small by the standards of some of the Marbella yachts, but still a very expensive toy.

Big and white. It would be impossible to find.

She persevered. Green fenders, gold fenders, silver and pink.

She couldn't see any purple ones.

Even though it was very late now, there were cheerful groups on the decks of several boats, enjoying the warmth of the evening. Casey overheard English, Spanish, German, a dozen more languages she didn't recognise. The pop of a champagne cork echoed across the water. As she plodded on, people started heading for bed.

Two hours later, she had identified three boats with purple fenders. She walked between them thoughtfully.

Come back in the morning.

She texted Georgie. *Can you think of anything else about this boat? Anything at all.*

Three yachts, nothing especially distinctive about any of them. One was tied up right the way out along the breakwater, at a distance from the rest. Casey looked at it closely, with no sense of what she was searching for, then she turned and walked back towards the main harbour.

She jumped as her phone buzzed. Georgie. *I've just remembered! It had three purple stripes running around the outside!*

Thanks, Georgie! Really helpful.

It was the boat far out along the breakwater.

From one of the wooden jetties, Casey stared out at it. Its isolation was suspicious now.

Come back tomorrow, she told herself.

But it might be gone tomorrow. Might slip its moorings and disappear – to Cannes, to Capri, to anywhere.

Slowly, Casey walked out along the breakwater again. The boat lay in darkness.

Now she was next to it, craning to read its name. *High Roller.* Not helpful. Where was it registered? Barcelona. Also unhelpful. Thousands of yachts had Barcelona as their nominal base.

Casey scuffled her feet.

Go back to the hotel, she told herself. Go and find out who owns *High Roller*, safe from your laptop.

Orange stripe, yellow squiggle.

The marina was quiet, no one around.

I could hop on and have a quick look.

No. Go home. Or back to the hotel, anyway.

I have to know.

One more glance around, and she had stepped lightly aboard. *High Roller* moved gently beneath her.

Carefully, Casey made her way to the cockpit. There were no signs of a party now, everything neatly stowed away. The wood of the cockpit was beautifully polished; the words *Carpe Diem* carved elaborately above the hatch. Seize the day, a slogan for a joyous life.

Casey bit her lip in frustration. There must be a clue, a lead, anything.

She poked around, opening lockers to find coils of rope and staring crossly at the incomprehensible navigation system. Another glance back along the breakwater and then she peered into some complicated drinks cooler. Nothing there either.

Another locker, this one secured.

Sighing, exhaustion creeping over her, she leaned down to inspect yet another locker. This was where they kept the lifebelts, so they could be thrown overboard as fast as possible in a crisis. Casey pulled one out.

Carpe Diem. Black letters on orange.

She looked at it in mild surprise. This lifebelt belonged to another yacht.

She pulled out a second lifebelt. It too was emblazoned with the words *Carpe Diem*.

She stopped sharply. The motto carved about the hatch … This yacht was called *Carpe Diem*.

But someone had painted *High Roller* on the side.

Get off! a voice screamed in her head. *Get out of here at once.*

She jumped to her feet. Only a few steps and she would be clear. Off the yacht and back to being a tourist wandering under the stars.

Hurry.

She scrambled to the side, looking back along the shoreline.

A man, walking along the breakwater.

He might be a tourist, wandering under the stars.

And he might not.

Casey jumped down. Had he seen her?

She wavered. The man kept walking. There were lampposts all along the breakwater, casting pools of light across the water. Casey stood next to the yacht, still unsure.

The man was approaching the next pool of light. Still, she hesitated. The breakwater was narrow, no way past him, and they were a long way from the other boats. The man walked under the light. A gleam of white-blond hair – she turned and bolted. As soon as she spun around, she heard the man burst into a sprint. Casey fled.

The breakwater stretched out ahead of her. For another fifty yards, a rough road continued so people could bring provisions out to their boats. After that, the barrier narrowed to a row of huge boulders, the power of the sea surging against them to her left.

Where could she go? Only one way and that was out along the boulders, leaping desperately until she reached the end of the breakwater. If she got that far, she would have to swim for it.

If.

Casey reached the end of the little road and jumped down onto the first of the boulders. The water swirling against the base of the rocks was filled with shreds of seaweed like glistening black ribbons. The movement of the waves made them look alive, eels writhing.

Casey scrambled from one boulder to the next. It was impossible to see in the dark, impossible to … *Keep going.*

The boulders were bigger than she had realised. Huge stones positioned to withstand the tides. They were hard to climb but there was no other way, no time to …

A couple more jumps.

In the corner of her eye, she saw the man spring down onto the boulders. He was catching up with her.

Casey scrambled up the next rock, but this time as she jumped, her foot slid into a crevice, her ankle half twisting as she crunched down. She pulled it out, scrabbling against the rock with the panic of a wild animal.

I can't.

You must.

The waves were higher out here, the rocks slippery with spray. Every step was a danger, every leap a gamble. She was shouting as she scrambled – desperate, panicked yells. 'Help me. *Help me.*'

You have to stay alive.

Stay alive and someone might come and help. Someone. Maybe. There was no time to look back, her screams dissolving in the dark.

One slimy boulder to the next. Another leap. She was tiring now. Her foot landed on algae, skidding away beneath her. Her shout became a wail as she fell hard against the rock. First blood, the beginning of a death. A gazelle, limping behind the herd. And the predator, confident now, certain.

Stay alive.

The man was closing the gap with every stride he took, leaping easily from boulder to boulder. He was maybe fifty yards behind her now and she was screaming, filling the air with noise. Someone, maybe someone …

Casey hurled herself forward. This time she missed her footing, scraped along the rock and only just caught herself, her fingernails jamming painfully into a crevice. The waves were waiting just a few inches below her feet, sucking at the breakwater, chewing and gnawing. She dragged herself up and struggled on.

No time to think. Casey leaped for the next crag, pulled herself up, slithered down the other side. Ignoring the pain in her leg. Shutting out everything. The man was only twenty yards behind, springing from rock to rock. Any second now he would … Any second …

Why did I come this way? A pointless shriek in her head. *Further from the marina. Further from rescue. So* stupid.

The man was only a few feet away now. Another step and he lunged at her, just catching her top. Electric with fear, she yanked away, somehow pulling herself free, somehow … He grabbed at her again.

And Casey threw herself off the side of the breakwater.

16

The water was filled with a million shreds of seaweed. Casey dived down and swam through the darkness, the weed wrapping itself around her arms and face. To the surface for the briefest gasp of air and then down again, down again, lungs burning, heart pounding. The seaweed seemed alive now, clutching at her, clinging to her, dragging her down.

Up to the night air with weed stuck to her face so she couldn't see and couldn't breathe. She clawed at it. *Get away.* Dive down.

Swimming until her lungs burned. Then up again, to the terror of the air.

But this time, when she glanced back, the man had stopped his pursuit. He was watching her from one of the boulders, but making no attempt to chase her. Casey kept swimming, turning towards the other breakwater beyond the marina entrance.

When she looked for her pursuer again, she saw he was making his way back along the boulders. Must be planning to hunt her down from the yacht.

But he wasn't hurrying. He was stepping from one boulder to the next, taking his time. Casey trod water, trying to see, trying to hide.

Then she realised. Three figures had appeared at the end of the road, peering out into the darkness. The blond man shouldered past them and disappeared towards his boat.

A shout reached her.

'¿Estás bien?'

'Ya voy.'

Wearily, Casey started swimming back towards them. In the distance, she heard the roar of the yacht's motors starting up.

He was coming. She struggled through the water, the seaweed clogging her movements.

Nearly there.

Nearly.

In the distance, she could hear the yacht roaring across the marina, ignoring any speed limit.

Casey reached one of the boulders, scrambled frantically. She had to get out of the water, had to get out of his reach, had to …

There.

She clung to the rock, gasping for breath.

On the other side, the yacht prowled past. As Casey watched, its prow appeared through the narrow gap. The blond man was in the cockpit, looking towards her.

She couldn't make out any details of his face. Did he know who she was?

The boat headed out to sea. As she peered through the darkness, she saw the man onboard kick something that was lying on deck. Something big, something heavy. A splash.

The engines roared abruptly, the front end of the vessel rearing up out of the water. And then it was off, skimming away far faster than she had imagined from its placid silhouette.

A peace settled over the waves. The boat was gone.

She had survived.

Casey clung to the rock for a few moments, almost shocked by the silence. Then she shook her head. Get back to the beachfront. Back to the paella and the panini and the burgers. On the road, the three figures were still watching her, baffled. That was why he had run, she thought hazily. They had saved her life, those spectators.

She started climbing wearily along the breakwater.

That splash, though …

Casey hesitated at the eel-writhing water. Then she slipped back in, started following the line the yacht had taken.

Seaweed swirled soupily around her, a constant impediment, slowing her movements and exhausting her.

Where was it when ...

Here, maybe? Casey trod water again, trying to peer into the depths. But it was hopeless, the weed blurring the dark depths. She could sense confusion among the onlookers on the breakwater.

Get back to shore.

But there was something ...

Get back to the marina and the yachts.

There was something ...

Casey swam backwards and forwards, closer to the breakwater for a few minutes and then further out to sea.

Whatever it was, it probably sank straight to the bottom. Hire a boat tomorrow ...

But I have to know now.

To and fro she swam, rising and falling with the waves. Whatever it was must have drifted away, been caught by the falling tide. Must have ...

A couple of the onlookers were climbing out along the breakwater towards her, growing impatient.

Her leg began to ache where she had scraped it down the side of a rock. When she ran her hand along her skin, it felt rough, torn. The saltwater stung.

Right. There's nothing here. Go back to the beach.

I ...

Just then, something bumped against her leg.

Casey recoiled violently, jerking her limbs away, floating as close to the surface as possible.

What was ...

It took her a few seconds to edge her feet down again, feeling around in the dark water. But there was nothing ... Nothing ...

Maybe a little bit further on ...

Something touched her knee.

Again, the shudder of revulsion. That instinct: get away. Get away, and don't look.

But there was something floating a few feet beneath the surface. Something snagged in the mass of seaweed.

I don't want to …

I don't …

Come on.

Casey forced herself to reach towards the shape, feeling her way through the scraps of seaweed.

What was it …

There.

What?

Oh, no. Please, no.

But she knew, quite abruptly.

It was an arm, floating in the blackness. The brush of cold fingers, yielding, almost soft. Gagging, she felt along the arm to a torso, solid under the water. With a surge of strength, she yanked at the body, hauling it to the surface. It was motionless, weightless, lifeless in the water. Another tug and a face emerged from the depths. A face coated in seaweed, white and bloated. And a scalp, shaved close, so that she knew.

The scream filled her head until she couldn't stop herself. Couldn't stop the howls bursting from her mouth.

Blake.

Blake.

It was Blake.

17

The swim back to the breakwater seemed to take forever. Unable to bring herself to touch the corpse's limbs, Casey dragged Blake along by his shirt. The closer she got to the boulders, the thicker the weed became. It was an endless nightmare of waves and seaweed and death.

'Ayúdame,' Casey screamed. *'Ayúdame, por favor.'*

Until finally they realised, and at last one of the men splashed out towards her. And as he caught sight of the dark shape, his face reflected her horror.

After that, it only seemed to take a few minutes for the marina to fill with policemen. Blue lights flashing, police cars flickering along the rough road, a siren slicing through the night. Faces peered out of the yachts: sleepy, curious. The hush was spiked with questions. Casey folded herself to the ground.

Later, she found herself sitting in a police station, two Spanish policemen staring at her thoughtfully. Her phone had been destroyed by the seawater.

'I need to call a friend,' she insisted. 'I have to …'

Her schoolgirl Spanish tangled and slowed.

They let her call in the end. Miranda's voice answered, thick with sleep. 'Casey? What … What time is it?'

Miranda woke up fast.

'A lawyer is coming to stay with you,' one of the policemen said, in broken English, a few minutes later. 'We find a translator now.'

'Thank you.'

Casey sat in the small meeting room, staring at the wall, too tired to speak.

A lawyer arrived within minutes, brandishing a new phone for her and flitting between English and Spanish with ease. They were just sitting down for an interview when a senior policeman walked into the room.

'What?' whispered Casey, after a few minutes of frenzied Spanish.

The lawyer turned towards her with a friendly smile.

'They have found who owned the boat,' she said. 'They are asking if you know a man called Aidan Gardiner.'

18

'The police say this boat was registered in Aidan Gardiner's name,' said Casey's lawyer. Gabriela, that was her name. '*High Roller*, that is what those teenagers said it was called. The boys who helped you with the body, I mean.'

'We check out this Aidan Gardiner,' said the policeman. 'He is a gambler. *High Roller*.' He nodded meaningfully.

Exhaustion was overwhelming Casey. The lights were too bright, the sounds too loud. Nothing made any sense.

'When was it registered?' she asked.

The policeman hesitated. 'Just a few days ago, I think.'

'The yacht wasn't called that.' Casey felt as if she were speaking from the bottom of a well. 'That name had just been painted on its bow. Its real name was *Carpe Diem*. I saw it on the lifebelts.'

Gabriela and the policeman stared at her in polite confusion.

'You need to track down a boat called *Carpe Diem*. Find out who owns that.'

The lawyer and the policeman looked blank.

The yacht had switched off its transponder, Casey understood a bit later, and faded away into the darkness of the Mediterranean. A ghost ship, roaring over the waves.

By dawn, *High Roller* would have disappeared forever and a new, equally anodyne name would have been painted on that bow. Then the yacht could cruise unremarked into a marina anywhere in the

Mediterranean and no one would bat an eyelash. *Carpe Diem* would almost certainly be untraceable too.

'But it is this man Aidan Gardiner who owns the boat,' the policeman insisted.

'Maybe,' said Casey. 'Can you get hold of the actual registration documents? See if there is anything odd about them?'

'It will take time,' said the policeman.

'The registration will be fake,' Casey insisted. 'That boat was called *Carpe Diem*.'

'Ah.' Gabriela turned to the policeman with another burst of Spanish.

'Why dump the body in a Marbella harbour though?' the lawyer wondered aloud when she was done. 'We would never even have known it was there if he had not done that.'

'A warning,' murmured Casey. 'Or a threat.'

'Come back to the office, Casey.' Miranda was already there. Casey could hear Ross shouting in the background.

'I will if they let me leave.' Casey was still in the police station. As she looked out of a window, she saw that dawn was breaking. The police were bickering over the transformation of *Carpe Diem*.

'You're lucky those teenagers heard you screaming,' said Miranda. 'Came out to see what was happening.'

'I know.'

'Christa's on the case. It would be better if ...'

A long pause.

'You're in danger, Casey,' Miranda said quietly.

'I'll come back.' She heard her own voice roughened with exhaustion. 'I'll come back as soon as possible.'

Gabriela shifted from charming to forceful, and eventually – grudgingly – the police said Casey could fly home.

When she checked the *Post* website, Tillie and Christa had written up the news stories and the pages of analysis. Scrolling on, she found a first-person piece by herself and a mournful screed from the chief columnist about the beautiful game and money and death. There were dozens of emails from other journalists and several slightly tense missives from Jackson's PR agency.

Jackson himself had left several messages. *Jesus, Casey. Call me.*

Mum is doing her nut, from Landon.

On the flight back to London, Casey fiddled numbly with her notepad, turning it over and over in her hands.

Cui bono, she doodled. *Cui bono, cui bono, cui bono.* She stared vacantly out of the window, watching the puffs of white cloud far, far below.

And, finally, she started making notes.

As soon as she landed, she called Miranda.

'It's Aidan,' were Miranda's first words as she answered the phone.

'It's not.' The words sounded hollow.

'I've spoken to Gabriela,' said Miranda. 'Aidan Gardiner registered a yacht called *High Roller* a few weeks ago.'

'Someone who *said* that they were Aidan Gardiner,' Casey corrected her. 'The Spanish police are having the documents sent through to them ASAP. I'm absolutely sure they'll be forgeries.'

'Fine. What exactly do you think is going on, then? Start at the beginning.'

'Okay,' said Casey obediently. 'It starts with the Ascot attack when Aidan Gardiner was hunted down by a group of men including the one with white-blond hair and a tattoo of an olive tree on his back.'

'And?'

'The man with white-blond hair then killed Nick Llewellyn in Regent's Park.'

'If you say so.'

'And finally, the same man kills Blake Gibson within three days of us publishing an article about match fixing. He then hides the body on a yacht called *High Roller* and escapes into the Med when he catches me checking it out.'

'Two murders and one ambush,' said Miranda. 'What the hell is going on?'

'I don't know.'

'And why?'

'I don't know that either.'

'It's Aidan,' said Miranda again.

'It's not.'

'You'd told him that you were going to meet Nick in Regent's Park. This yacht, *High Roller*, is registered as belonging to him.' Miranda was flicking through her notes. 'It all looks fairly conclusive to me.'

'The yacht registration isn't confirmed yet.'

'The key thing is that this blond man killed Nick Llewellyn and Blake Gibson extremely competently. But Aidan Gardiner got away.' Miranda was thinking aloud. 'He was the only one to survive.'

'That's because I dragged him into a taxi on Ascot High Street and legged it with him. He wouldn't have stood much of a chance otherwise.'

'Yes, but it still doesn't make sense that Aidan – not by any stretch of the imagination a natural athlete – somehow manages to escape a highly organised and very aggressive attack. I think he set up the Ascot chase himself, for whatever reason, and then had the other two killed.'

'Why, though?'

'I don't know yet,' Miranda admitted. 'But this barman ambushed him in front of thousands of witnesses even though Ascot is entirely the wrong place for a planned assassination. If that man had actually killed Aidan, he would never have made it off the racecourse. Even the most inept police force would have grabbed him.'

'Unless he hijacked the winner of the four-fifteen.'

'Ascot,' Miranda said firmly, 'was a set-up.'

For a moment, Casey was back on the escalator. She remembered the barman's hand going to his pocket, the gleam in his hand as he sprinted down the street.

'Okay,' she admitted. 'Maybe you're right and there was something weird about the Ascot attack. But if Aidan wanted to find out who was behind the match fixing so he could kill whoever it was, he didn't have to involve me. He could have dispatched Jackson Harvey to the sting and then taken out the match fixer himself. He wouldn't even have had to send Jackson along, if you think about it. Landon could have pointed out Blake to him and it would all have been done and dusted, with no pesky newspapers anywhere to be seen.'

'But why else would someone attack Aidan in front of you?' asked Miranda.

'To get me to write about the attack? To get me to investigate match fixing because they knew it was Aidan's hobby horse? To get me to write about organised criminals attacking him?'

'It all seems …'

'I'm going to see Aidan right now.'

'Casey,' said Miranda. 'Please don't.'

'It doesn't make sense to me that it's Aidan.'

'It does. You just don't want to see the pattern.'

'Sod the bloody pattern.'

For all her assurances to Miranda, Casey shuddered as she looked up at Aidan's house.

He lived in a tall Georgian terrace on Cleaver Square, not far from the industrial unit where he worked. Outside, people were playing boules and drinking pints bought from the pretty pub on the corner of the tree-lined square. Laughter and gossip filled the summer evening.

'I like Kennington,' he had said, shrugging when she'd asked him about the industrial unit's location. 'It suits me.'

It was probably the first area he had lived in when he arrived in London, Casey guessed, in a random flatshare. And he'd shifted up the property ladder without ever considering a move elsewhere. And because his life revolved around the industrial unit there, it never occurred to him to escape to a mansion in Fleethurst.

She walked up the steps, squared her shoulders and knocked sharply. When he opened the door, Aidan was paler than he had been before, with dark shadows under his eyes.

'Come in,' he said vaguely.

Casey took a deep breath and stepped through the door. Outside, there were shouts, laughter, the clunk of boules. Inside, a dusty dimness. She hesitated.

Aidan pushed the front door closed. She thought he would lead the way further into the house, but instead he turned and leaned back against the closed door. A shiver crept up her spine. Aidan hadn't switched on the lights. The house was dark, his face in shadow. All at once, the boules and the pints were a hundred miles away. Her fingers curled into fists.

For a moment, he stared at her, his eyes sharp on her face. He opened his mouth, as if he was going to say something, then closed it again.

'Aidan?' Casey asked.

He stood there, his back against the front door.

She felt for her phone in her pocket. She could leap into the sitting room, dive for the windows. She could smash the glass, scream at the drinkers, get help. Why had she come here …

Aidan stepped towards her and Casey jumped away.

Her movement startled him to stillness. 'Are you …' He wrinkled his nose, pushing his glasses back into place, and all at once he was Aidan again, awkward, baffled. 'Are you all right? Sorry, I just didn't know where to start. Sorry, Casey.'

She let out a gasp of air, tried to turn it into a laugh. 'I'm fine, Aidan. Sorry.'

He stared at her, as if trying to make sense of her presence.

'Sorry,' Casey repeated. 'It's been a complicated few days.' She paused.

'I know.' Aidan tried to laugh too. 'It's been … weird.'

Slowly, Casey took in the house. It looked as if he were still unpacking, although he'd bought the place three years ago, according to the Land Registry. There were pictures leaning against the wall and cardboard boxes piled high in what might have been an elegant drawing room.

'Come downstairs,' said Aidan, when they had finished apologising to each other. 'The kitchen.'

'Okay.'

'The police came to see me,' Aidan told her, when they reached a glossy kitchen that looked virtually unused. 'They were asking about some boat in the Mediterranean. I told them I didn't know anything about it, but they said they might be back with more questions.'

'Get a lawyer,' Casey advised. 'As soon as possible.'

'But why?' He sounded worried.

'They think you might be involved,' she said bluntly. 'In Blake Gibson's murder.'

'What?' Aidan's jaw dropped. 'What do you mean?'

'They found out that someone registered a boat in your name in Marbella – the boat they held Blake Gibson on after he was killed.'

'But that's … that's …' Words failed him.

'Aidan, I need to understand what the hell is going on. If there's anything you're not telling me …'

'I don't know anything! I—'

'Blake Gibson was distorting your data,' said Casey. 'And you hated that.'

'Not to the point that I'd kill him … I'd never—'

'You knew I was going to meet Nick Llewellyn in Regent's Park, too. You had the opportunity to send someone after him.'

'But you didn't tell me Llewellyn's name. I'd never even heard of him before his death was in the papers.' Aidan wasn't getting angry. He seemed bewildered, like a slapped puppy. 'I thought the police said Nick Llewellyn drowned. That it was just a horrible accident.'

He came to a baffled silence, physically shrinking in on himself.

Don't assume, Casey told herself. *It could still be an act …*

'I'm only repeating their concerns, Aidan.'

'Their concerns?' Resentment was finally starting to simmer. 'Why would they—'

'We need to work out what the hell's going on,' she said.

'I know. That's why I *asked* you to check it all out.'

She stared at him. He looked wounded, confused, uncertain how to respond. She softened.

'Let's put it another way. We only got to know each other because you were chased at Ascot. One of my colleagues has suggested that it was staged to bring you to my attention. So is there any reason someone would want me to investigate you?'

'Well …' Aidan looked uncertain. 'Honestly, Casey, nothing really. I told you. What we do is grey, but it's not illegal … I've told you everything, anyway.'

Casey thought about the email to Griff. 'Maybe it just worked for them, however it played out. Either you'd tell me all about match fixing – in which case I would investigate that for them – or they wanted me to dig into your activities. The Ascot attack was made to look like organised crime, and they may have guessed that would interest me.'

'Maybe.' Aidan's forehead crinkled with worry. 'I don't really understand ...'

'Okay,' she said. 'Let's sit down and work it out.'

'But I've already told you everything I know.'

'Let's go through it again.'

They sat in the garden, next to a liquidambar tree. Aidan fiddled with a fallen leaf.

'I don't like it.' His voice was flat again. 'Any of what's happened. I never thought Blake Gibson would be killed. I just wanted the match fixing *stopped*. And as for this Nick Llewellyn ... If he was murdered ... Well, I don't like it,' he repeated.

'Neither do I.' She matched his tone.

'I didn't know either of them,' he said firmly. 'But still.'

He didn't like the arbitrariness of it all, Casey thought. Aidan was used to fitting people into neat data points. Assigning them to categories, to pigeonholes. His model sought to anticipate behaviour, not influence it. To make sense of the world, create some sort of order. And maybe she did that too, in her own way, with words not numbers. Writing people into neat profiles, five hundred words, a tidy summary with the corners tucked in.

'Is there any other group who might have set up that attack?'

Aidan turned away from the liquidambar, meeting her eyes cautiously. He wrinkled his nose again while he thought.

'All the bookmakers operate in slightly different ways,' he said eventually. 'Some of them will have their own intelligence operation – scouts up on Newmarket Heath to watch the gallops, that sort of thing. With something like Betfair, it's individuals setting the odds and gradually coming to a consensus. Some of the bookmakers will then use that information to set their own odds. Harness the wisdom of crowds. Because bookies aren't really calculating the result, they're calculating how people will bet on the result, and aiming to come out ahead.'

'But you didn't think it was one of the bookmaking operations,' she said. 'Back when we first spoke.'

'No. I just assumed it was the match fixers. But now ...'

'You're saying that one of the bookmakers might have benefited from the elimination of Blake Gibson? And that it might serve as a warning to other match fixers too?'

'I suppose so.' Aidan sounded defeated. 'It is possible.'

'I need a list,' Casey said firmly, 'of groups and individuals who might have benefited from me doing this story.'

'I'll get you one,' he promised. 'Do you want a cup of tea?'

She had never seen him drink alcohol. Not his thing. 'Sure.' She nodded.

When he returned, he was carrying a sheet of paper. 'That's a list of possibles.' He handed it over. 'But the more I think about it, the more I reckon it's the lot in Ealing.'

'Who,' Casey reached out for the piece of paper, 'are the lot in Ealing?'

Aidan was staring up at the liquidambar again.

'They do very similar stuff to us.' He spoke quietly. 'The same techniques.'

'What do you know about them?'

'They work with algorithms,' he said. 'Making a similar analysis of sports. They focus on football like us, and tennis, too. But that makes sense, really, because there's a lot of liquidity in those markets. If you're betting on – I don't know – curling, the number of people gambling is tiny, and any move you make is pretty visible.'

Aidan's mouth was tense, eyes dark with disapproval at the thought of the operation in Ealing.

'You don't like them?' Casey guessed.

'They sent someone into my organisation two years ago,' he said angrily. 'A junior guy, who'd only left Cambridge a few months before

I recruited him. He accessed quite a lot of our codes and data, and then just didn't turn up to work one day. He *stole* from us.'

'But surely there are confidentiality clauses in your employment contracts?' asked Casey. 'You must be vulnerable to corporate espionage, doing what you do? You could have sued him.'

'It would be a nightmare trying to enforce all that.'

Aidan didn't want his own operation analysed too closely by the British legal system, thought Casey. He operated in a grey area himself, and instinctively shied away from scrutiny.

'So what did you do?'

'We tightened things up. Siloed things a lot more than they used to be. It's a shame, but … We'd grown bigger than I realised. I hadn't really thought about it all before then, not properly.'

'How long have the Ealing lot been operating?'

'I'm not sure,' he said. 'They're expanding, though; they've set up a chain of betting shops and a website. It makes sense, really. We often can't place all the bets we'd like because the market can't absorb them. But I just don't want the faff of running a business like that.'

'Sure.'

'They tried to buy me out after the business with the junior guy,' he went on disapprovingly. 'They were aggressive about it. I didn't like it. They approached me again, a few days after that thing in Ascot. They're very … determined.'

Casey's attention sharpened. 'They wanted to buy you out?'

'Yes.'

'What's the name of the betting chain?'

'Oh.' Aidan looked vague. 'Tip Top. You've probably seen the shops.'

The bright purple shop in Kentish Town; the bright purple shirts in the Premier League.

'Who runs it?' she asked. 'Who's their equivalent of you?'

'Never explored it. But then, I suppose no one would know about me either, if that makes sense? I've never been interested in …' He made a vague gesture.

'I'll have a good look at the operation in Ealing,' said Casey. 'Did you ever try to speak to the guy who infiltrated your company?'

'Wasn't very effective.' Aidan fiddled with his teacup. 'I'm no good at that sort of thing. He just said that the Ealing lot had offered him a bigger salary so off he went. He's still working there, but in a fairly junior role.'

'He got played by someone in the Ealing organisation?'

'I think so.'

'Too bad for him.'

Tip Top was impenetrable.

'It's registered in Curaçao,' Hessa recited a few hours later, 'and from what I can make out, it's ultimately owned in the Caymans, where they won't be publishing beneficial ownership data for quite a while yet. And by the time they do, those assets will probably have been moved off to Samoa or Nevis or wherever.'

Curaçao and the Caymans, two dots in the Caribbean with impermeable privacy laws and tax codes generous to billionaires. International pressure was gradually extracting information about the ultimate ownership of assets, but the process was slow.

As Hessa, Miranda and Casey pondered Curaçao, the *Post* was falling quiet for the night. Casey had come over to the main office at the end of a long day in Parliament, Tillie heading off soon after she arrived. 'That way, you can use my desk, Casey!'

'Who owns the physical building that Tip Top operates out of?' she asked. 'The Ealing headquarters?'

'A company called Theia Incorporated,' said Hessa. 'Which is registered in the British Virgin Islands. And, of course, Tip Top could just be renting that anyway.'

'So Theia could have nothing to do with Tip Top at all, even if we could work out who owns Theia, which we can't.' Casey sighed, staring up at the ceiling. 'Thanks for trying, Hess.'

'They're growing fast, aren't they?' said Miranda. 'Tip Top, I mean. I read something in our business section about them opening more shops this year.'

While Hessa carried on working, Casey trawled through the other betting companies Aidan had listed. Finally, she shoved away the piece of paper in frustration.

'I don't know what I'm searching for.' She bit her thumbnail crossly. 'It's just an endless sequence of company names and random people. I think that ...'

She trailed off.

'You need to find the pattern,' said Miranda. 'If a pattern exists, that is.'

'Or maybe Hessa's right, and I just want a pattern to exist because otherwise I'm going mad? Or maybe I'm going mad looking for the pattern?'

'Perhaps. But if someone used you to track down Blake so they could kill him, you need to get to the bottom of it.'

Casey turned to her computer screen and started searching.

'What,' Hessa asked a few minutes later, 'are you doing?'

'I'm making another list,' said Casey, 'of all the stories we've ever done. And then I'm going to try and work out who might have benefited from them.'

By the time Hessa and Miranda arrived the next morning, Casey's list ran to several pages.

'The problem is,' she gestured with her pen, 'that it's all so sodding random.'

'That Libya story,' Hessa remembered, 'came from you overhearing a casual conversation in a club in Soho. The Bangladesh one came from a piece of material stitched into a jacket in a shop that our fashion editor came across randomly.'

'So you have to assume that neither story is relevant to this, although people can stage a conversation,' said Casey, 'or pin a piece of material into a jacket just before the *Post* fashion editor walks into a shop. But it's unlikely, in those cases. Same with Nick Llewellyn. I don't believe that Lucas Fairbairn let his location slip on purpose, but I suppose it is just about possible. With the rest of this list ...' She paused, staring at the notepad again. 'The problem is that tips come from all over the place.'

Tips: the seed that fell on fertile ground, sometimes.

'A story might be sparked by a paragraph in a trade paper,' Miranda nodded. 'Or one MP slagging off another to a political correspondent. Or anything, really.'

Intelligence flooding around the world, and sometimes a few drops channelled to the offices of the *Post*.

'Think of all the things we don't know,' Miranda would say wistfully. 'Just imagine the things we'll never know.'

'Take this one.' Casey pointed. 'Miles Foscliffe. He was Education Secretary back in the day, but we did an article about his wife having an affair with Foscliffe's bodyguard, which was enough to make him a laughing stock. Poor old git – he couldn't even resign to spend more time with his family without everyone getting the giggles.'

'But how did you find out about it?' Hessa nudged her.

'Someone slipped a letter into my coat pocket,' said Casey. 'While I was having lunch in the House. And any number of people linked to the story might have benefited from the consequences of that anonymous note being made public, not least the brand-new Education Secretary who replaced Foscliffe. The police bodyguard was sacked, too.'

'Unintended consequences,' said Miranda. 'Or were they? It's impossible to tell.'

'It's also assuming that someone is using me,' said Casey.

'How solipsistic.' Miranda grinned.

'Solip— what?' asked Hessa.

'Thinking that you're the centre of everything.' Miranda flicked her blonde hair. 'That you're the sun around which everything else revolves.'

'Quite.' Casey flipped a rubber band at her.

'Keep going,' Miranda told her, unexpectedly.

'Really?' asked Casey. 'I don't know …'

'There is something weird going on. Reverse-engineer every story you've ever written, and see where you end up.'

19

'Coffee?'

The business reporter looked up with suspicious eyes. 'What do you want, Casey?'

'It won't take long,' she said chirpily. 'But I wondered whether you could help me make sense of some short selling.'

James peered at her for a second, then reached out for the coffee. 'Sure. Thanks for that tip on Swann Hopkins the other week, by the way.'

'It worked well in the end, didn't it?' said Casey. 'You really got to the bottom of it all. Nice colour from the victims too.'

Mollified, James took a gulp of the coffee. It wasn't unusual for reporters to pass tips to other sections, especially if they were busy with their own patch. He had added Casey's by-line to the Swann Hopkins story, which not all the reporters would have done either.

'Which company are you interested in?'

'Could we have a shufti at Cormium?'

'The commodity traders? Or what's left of them after you left their chief executive for dead in Libya? Sure.'

Selby. That was his name.

'Yes, that's the one. Can we see who's selling them short at the moment?'

Short selling is essentially when a hedge fund bets against a company. If a share is trading at a pound and the hedge fund sells it short, that means the hedge fund might borrow, for example, a

thousand shares from a broker and sell them on for a thousand –
with the promise to return the shares to the broker at a specific date,
say, next Wednesday. If the shares behave as the hedge fund hopes, by
next Wednesday their value will have fallen ten per cent and they will
now be worth nine hundred. The hedge fund will then buy one thousand shares and return them to the broker, pocketing the hundred
pounds' difference. Short sellers win when prices drop.

As Casey watched over James's shoulder, he clicked on the Financial
Conduct Authority website.

'The FCA makes spirited attempts to monitor short selling.' James
spoke over his shoulder. 'But it's not clear how effective the regulator
can actually be at tracking it all.'

He was clicking confidently through the site. 'There you are.' He
pointed. 'Those three funds have all got short positions in Cormium
right now. They have to tell the FCA if they short more than nought
point one per cent of a company's shares. It's so they can try to
keep on top of market abuse. There are other places you can find
data too, including the historical stuff. I'll show you some of the
databases …'

James's seminar on short selling took the rest of the morning. After
thanking him profusely, Casey headed back to the investigations
room.

'Right,' she said to the room. 'Let's see.'

Slowly, she worked her way down her list.

'The problem is,' she said to Hessa and Miranda, who weren't
listening, 'that there are so many possibilities. It's not just that a hedge
fund might have shorted a company, it's that they might have bought
shares in their rival – and it will take me years to check all that.'

Miranda and Hessa's heads were still bent over their computers.

'I suppose it's about seeking out a pattern,' Casey went on. 'And
that means …' Her voice trailed away.

'What?' Miranda finally looked up.

'A hedge fund called Meldon Group,' said Casey. 'They've shorted
two companies I've written about in the past.'

'Never heard of them.' Miranda was searching for the hedge
fund's website. 'They're based just round the corner from the Bank

of England,' she read out once she had found the site. 'And they're a big fund with a major short-selling operation. So it could just be coincidence that they sold shares in the companies you wrote about.'

'Sure,' said Casey. She concentrated again, silent now, completely focused on her screen.

'Does anyone want a—' Hessa began.

'Bugger!' Casey interrupted. 'Meldon Group also sold Swann Hopkins short last month.'

Hessa sat down sharply.

'Does that mean—'

'Yes.' Casey met Miranda's eyes. 'It means that Meldon made close on ten million pounds in the twenty-four hours after James and I published that story.'

There was a short silence.

'Because you said that Swann Hopkins's new heart drug caused problems,' said Hessa, 'Swann's share price tanked.'

'It was Nash Bexley who gave you the Swann story, wasn't it?' Miranda said slowly.

'Yes,' said Casey. 'When we were at the Royal Opera House. And I let him know when it was going to run, out of courtesy.'

'Ah.'

'And,' Casey didn't want to say the words aloud, 'I talked to Nash about Nick Llewellyn when I was at the Opera House.'

'But what did Nick Llewellyn know?' asked Miranda. 'What did he know that might have got him killed?'

'I have no idea,' Casey said numbly. 'He never told me.'

'Is there any other link between Greville Polignac and those other stories?'

'Yes,' Casey said tonelessly, pointing to another name on her list. 'There's that story, there. Nash gave me that tip over lunch at 6 Arundel Street, just after I moved across to Politics.'

'Right.' Miranda came to stand beside her. 'And what other stories has Nash Bexley given you?'

'At Ascot …' Casey was fiddling with the silver necklace around her neck. 'That was when I was told about Lucas Fairbairn and Esther Amaral being in a relationship.'

20

'You?' Lucas Fairbairn stared at Casey. 'You want *my* help?'

She had waited for him on the green sweep of Highbury Fields, halfway between the Tube station and the little cottage. She pounced as he walked along a shortcut gouged out by a thousand commuters.

'Yes.' Casey tried to sound more confident than she felt. 'You know I'd only ask you if it was important, Lucas.'

Lucas Fairbairn pressed a hand to his forehead and spun away from her. 'You've got a nerve,' he said. 'You really have.'

Casey waited until he was facing her again, and then repeated the words. 'I need your help, Lucas.'

'I asked *you* for *your* help when you were about to publish,' he said. 'I begged you not to ...'

Please don't mention Esther. Please.

'It is not an aspect of my job that I enjoy—'

'You could have fooled me. Your voice ...'

'I am sorry.'

'Esther was fired from her job,' he said. 'She dedicated years of her life to her career and now it's completely trashed. Did you know that? Or do you not even glance back at the wreckage as you sprint on to the next target?'

Unintended consequences, thought Casey. Although some outcomes were more predictable than others.

'I am trying to work out why I was tipped off about you and Esther being in a relationship.' She spoke sedately, hoping to calm Lucas down. It didn't work. He raked his hands through his dark auburn hair, a flush creeping up his freckled face.

A group of children were playing rounders fifty yards away, shrieking as a small boy sprinted between the bases. It was only the presence of the children, Casey guessed, that was preventing him from losing his temper completely.

'Get away from me.' He managed to keep his voice low, spitting the words with an only just controlled venom. 'You stay the hell away from us.'

As he strode away across the neatly cut grass, Casey sat down and sighed. A breeze blew through the trees and a plane drew a long silvery scar across the sky. She lay back and closed her eyes. The grass was scratchy under her legs, the sun warm on her face.

Footsteps. Casey opened her eyes sharply as a pair of feet stopped beside her.

Lucas Fairbairn stood a few yards away, squinting his light brown eyes against the sun.

'Why?' he said. 'Why the hell do you want to know? What do you think has happened?'

Casey sat up. 'I'm not sure how to explain this.'

'Try.'

'Did you see the story I did recently about match fixing?'

'I read a bit about it,' he said warily. 'That guy in Marbella and the Fleethurst footballer.'

'The guy in Marbella was killed. I think someone wanted me to identify him so that they could get rid of him.'

'That ...' Fairbairn looked tired under the freckles. 'That doesn't really make sense.'

'I know,' Casey said earnestly. 'But there's something else.' She looked at him for a moment. 'Nick Llewellyn?' He nodded. 'I think there was something odd about his death too.'

'What are you talking about?' Fairbairn was shaking his head, ready to walk away again. 'You think the death of Nick Llewellyn is linked to match fixing? That's insane.'

'No,' said Casey. 'Yes. Maybe. Lucas, I need to make sure there isn't a pattern here. Because if there is some sort of link between my stories, I need to know. Please. Sit down for just a moment and let's talk.'

'I don't want to—'

'I went to find Nick Llewellyn at Holloway Road,' Casey said evenly, 'because you mentioned him being there.'

'What?' Fairbairn looked stunned for a second. 'But I never—'

'"That poor fucker in Holloway Road,"' Casey quoted. '"We can all end up like that poor fucker in Holloway Road." That's what you said.'

'And you *went* there? Just because of *that*?'

'And now he's dead.'

'I don't … What …' Fairbairn faltered into silence.

'Please, Lucas. I need to understand what's going on.'

Fairbairn sighed and looked across at the beautiful Georgian terraces that framed the green. Then he sat down, folding his long limbs into an awkward shape.

'All this,' he said firmly, 'is off the record.'

'Absolutely.' Her tone fervent. 'I just want to … understand.'

'Fine. A few minutes. Where do you want to begin?'

For a moment, Casey hesitated. 'I'm looking for a consequence. An outcome from your story that might appear to be completely unintended … Because it's that consequence that might be the key to the whole thing.'

'So …' Fairbairn rolled his eyes. 'Fine. Five minutes.'

'I'll have to ask some odd—'

'Fine.'

'Do you gamble?' Casey asked bluntly. 'Have you got an account with one of the gambling firms?'

'What? No.' Fairbairn was adamant. 'It's never appealed.'

'What was Esther working on? Before she was fired, that is.'

'That's … I can't talk about it,' he protested. 'Client confidentiality. She wouldn't give me any details anyway.'

'But it's exactly the sort of thing I need to understand,' said Casey. 'What if it was Esther who was the real target? You're obviously the more interesting story from a newspaper's point of view, a useful sort

145

of bait to get things on the front page. But what if she was the actual target, not just collateral damage?'

'Bait? Collateral damage? Do you *hear* yourself?'

'I need to understand, Lucas.'

'For God's sake.' Fairbairn kicked at a clump of grass. 'Fine. As it happens, Esther was working on project finance for some Spanish infrastructure company. Focusing on a bridge, if you must know. It was insanely boring. In fact, it is one of the very few things that she has found remotely amusing about the last few weeks: the fact that the Spanish bridge borefest continued absolutely unaffected by her departure. Her old firm slotted in another compliance officer to replace her, and her departure caused barely a ripple. As a matter of fact, she's now thinking about a completely different career long-term because, really, how much of your life do you want to dedicate to reviewing the collateral warranties for a bridge in Spain that you'll never even see?'

'Fine,' Casey admitted. 'Esther wasn't the target.'

'No,' Fairbairn snapped. 'She was not.'

'How do you think the source found out?'

'What do you mean?'

'Someone,' Casey explained, 'told me that you and Esther were in a relationship. How did they know?'

'Well, who told you?'

Never reveal a source.

'I can't tell you.' Casey looked at her hands. 'You know that.'

'Really?' he retorted. 'You want every jot and tittle of my life, but not even the vaguest hint about the person who sold me out?'

'I'm sorry,' said Casey. 'I just can't.'

She still wasn't sure about Nash's role in the cobweb of stories.

'Should we go to Nash Bexley?' Miranda had asked back in the office, as they all peered at the FCA website. 'Give him a good going over? I could do it for you, Casey, if you want? The pompous, manipulative creep.'

'*If* we've got it right,' Casey had said. 'Because even if we're spot-on, Nash will never just cough to this. He's a very sharp operator.

We'll need proof, real proof. Not a couple of coincidences. Plus, if we're right, this started quite a long time ago. Nash was still working at the *Post* when we did the Nick Llewellyn story. So unless he was running all this alongside his *Post* job, which I don't think is possible, it was someone else who began it all. That makes Nash a worker bee. A well-paid worker bee perhaps, but not the main target.'

'I guess you're right,' Miranda had sighed. 'But be careful, Casey.'

'If you tell me who told you,' Fairbairn was playing the persuasive MP again, 'it might give me a clue as to how they found out.'

'So you don't know?' asked Casey.

'No,' he said. 'Esther and I have spent hours thinking about it, of course. Wondering who … But we were so careful. So very careful.'

His arm round her waist, her hand on his back. Smiling at the receptionist. Grinning at each other.

The briefest of kisses.

Not quite as careful, Casey thought to herself, as all that.

'They might have put a private detective on you,' she said. 'I suppose they didn't actually have to be quite sure, either. They could just dispatch me to collect conclusive evidence.'

'How handy,' his voice dripped sarcasm, 'that you were there.'

'Okay.' Casey was fiddling with a blade of grass. 'You were a Treasury minister. What were you doing while you were working there?'

'Got your notebook ready?' he asked cynically.

'This is all off the record. The only way I will use any of this is as background, to get to the bottom of why you were targeted. That's it, I promise.'

Lucas Fairbairn exhaled loudly. The children were playing tag now, racing in and out of the trees.

'Well, it was only the usual sort of stuff,' he said. 'I wasn't exactly the Chancellor of the Exchequer. Things were assigned to me.'

'Like what?' Casey nudged him along.

'Oh, you know, decarbonisation of the economy and green finance. Spending review stuff. An analysis of the Financial Ombudsman's work. Some of it was very nearly as exciting as the mezzanine finance agreements on a Spanish bridge.'

'Was there anything that was your particular project? Something you were pushing the Treasury to look at?'

'What are you actually interested in?' he asked. 'It'll be much quicker.'

'Anything about gambling regulations?' she asked.

'Not really. That was Miles Foscliffe's focus. Until you did him over.'

'Miles Foscliffe?' Her head jerked up.

Baz's voice echoing sharply in her mind. *Fossil's never really recovered from that story you did on him ages ago … His wife, having an affair with that bodyguard …*

'How did you know about Fossil's wife anyway?'

'An anonymous letter.' Casey rubbed her face.

'So, basically, you have no idea.'

'Nope.'

'Miles Foscliffe wanted extra protections for problem gamblers,' said Fairbairn. 'One of his kids lost a fortune on those sites, and although Miles tried and tried to get him banned from them all, the kid kept managing to get back on them.'

Casey scratched at the dusty grass, avoiding his eye. 'I didn't know that.'

'No, you wouldn't.'

'What was your hobby horse, then?' she asked.

'It really wasn't very interesting.'

'Tell me.'

He shrugged. 'I thought that the government should have another look at short selling.'

Casey caught her breath.

'What?' Fairbairn's eyes were fixed on her face. 'That's it, isn't it? You think it's something to do with short sellers.'

'There is a hedge fund,' Casey spoke carefully, 'that has appeared a couple of times in our research.'

'Which hedge …' He broke off. 'You won't tell me, of course.'

'It's partly to protect you,' she protested. 'These people may be dangerous … It might be better that you don't know.'

'It's rather more helpful,' he said bitterly, 'to know your enemy. I'm not a child, Casey.' He was still studying her face. 'You don't actually know what's going on, do you? You've just got a few random names, and you've no idea who's behind it all, or if anyone even is.'

'Pretty much,' she acknowledged. 'I've got a few pieces of a jigsaw, and to be honest, I'm not even sure they all belong to the same puzzle.'

'How comforting.'

'Why were you focusing on short selling?' she asked.

'Oh, it was …' Fairbairn's gaze wandered to the past. 'Stupid, really. My father set up a company when I was a kid. It was doing well, growing fast. He floated it, and for a few years everything went brilliantly. Then one day he woke up to a research note from one of the big investment banks, warning that the company was in trouble. Then more rumours started flying around. There are supposed to be ethical walls in these big banks, but you've got one team putting out research notes while on the next floor you've got the short sellers. I mean, how can you be sure? Investors began to get worried, saying they needed their money back. I remember my father coming home, night after night, his face completely white. He said it was like fighting some faceless vampire: every time you faced down one piece of nonsense, the next one reared its head and, in the end, it becomes a self-fulfilling prophecy. My father's company collapsed. He lost everything. The whole family did, really.'

'Can't have been fun.'

'It wasn't.' He kept his face blank. 'So you see, that's why I was interested in the issue.'

'I'm sorry.'

'He was a good father,' Lucas said forcefully. 'In a lot of ways, he was wonderful. Before all that, he and my mother would dance around the kitchen together, laughing. They would dance for hours. Rock and roll.'

'I'm sure he was wonderful.'

'You think that someone tipped you off about me and Esther just to stop me clipping the wings of a few short sellers?'

'Maybe. I don't know. It's possible.'

'We were so stupid,' he said. 'I was so stupid.'

She could see his thoughts grinding down the same groove again, as they must have done a thousand times.

'Why did you do it?' she asked suddenly. 'You didn't need the money. Esther must have been earning a decent amount as a compliance officer and an MP's salary isn't small.'

'I wasn't in a relationship with her when I moved in.' He shook his head. 'I only took the room in the first place because she was a friend of a friend and I needed a place in a hurry. The friend I was living with at the time was moving abroad, and someone suggested Esther. And it's perfectly legit, renting from someone random. But then ... then I fell in love with her. It was slow at first, hard to know the exact moment that it changed. And I suppose I was ... greedy.' He stared at Casey angrily. 'That's what you're thinking, isn't it? That I was greedy.'

'I suppose. Yes, a bit.'

'Would you turn it down? I was paying Esther rent, and I wasn't going to stop doing that, because that wouldn't have been fair on her. Most people wouldn't say no to free money like that.'

'But they expect more from ...'

She thought about the boy, and the father crumbling to dust. There were always reasons, you just had to look.

'I know. I *know*.' He slammed a fist into his other hand. 'I did one stupid thing. One!'

'Why didn't you and Esther just get a place together?' she asked. 'Then you could have claimed half and that wouldn't have broken any rules.'

'It's her family,' said Fairbairn slowly. 'They're Sephardi Jews. In North London, there's a big community. They wouldn't have accepted her being in a relationship with anyone who wasn't Sephardi. When her sister married out, they cut off all communication, behaved as if she was dead. Sat shiva. It's brutal. Esther didn't want ...'

'Were her family okay about the article?'

'No,' he said. 'No, they weren't. I don't think they'll ever speak to her again.'

150

21

'Miles Foscliffe,' said Casey, 'was campaigning against online gambling. Lucas Fairbairn was on the warpath against short selling. It's a pattern of sorts. Maybe.'

'Once is a fluke,' Miranda recited, 'twice is a coincidence, three times is a two-thousand-word feature.'

'That does at least,' Casey tapped a copy of the paper, 'explain our page-three lead today.'

'Yes, silly season seems to be stretching on a bit this year.' Miranda turned a page in her notebook. 'Okay, so you have two stories where a tip to you ended up with a campaigning MP taken off at the knees.'

'It doesn't sound great when you put it like that, but yes.'

'The Fairbairn story came from Nash Bexley of Greville Polignac, and the Foscliffe one from a note left in the pocket of your coat, so we have no idea of its origins.'

'Yes. But I was having lunch in Parliament at the time, so that reduces the candidates to a few thousand.'

'Nash Bexley has a parliamentary pass, doesn't he?'

'Yes.'

'Yet another story was sparked by the attack on Aidan Gardiner at Ascot, which may or may not have been staged.' Miranda was drawing a diagram in her notebook. 'And as a result, you tracked down Blake Gibson, who was then killed. Nash Bexley is loosely connected to that story too because he had invited you to Ascot. If it was staged, they'd have to know when you'd be where.'

'And then there's Nick Llewellyn, who drowned in Regent's Park,' said Hessa. 'You think his death may be linked to a story you and Miranda did several years ago.'

'Nick's death is definitely linked to the attack on Aidan Gardiner,' Casey insisted. 'By that man with white-blond hair.'

'You think you saw a tattoo on his back,' said Miranda.

'I did.'

'We also have three companies that appear to be interlinked,' Miranda continued.

'Meldon Group is a hedge fund in the City that's made a fortune betting against companies I've written about,' said Casey. 'Tip Top started out as a betting intelligence operation in Ealing and then expanded into high-street shops and online gambling. Greville Polignac is a public affairs company in Westminster.'

'What does Meldon Group actually do?' Hessa asked. 'I know they're short sellers, but do they specialise in any area?'

'They're a quant fund,' said Casey. 'Short for quantitative. They do exactly what Aidan does with football, but instead of building an algorithm to gamble on sport, they've created algorithms for every-thing. Share prices or currency value or derivatives … anything, really. Same tools, different market.'

'So it's what Aidan does?' Hessa said.

'But to the power of a hundred. Computers think faster than humans, and they can process data from all over the world in seconds. So a quant fund feeds all that information into their algo-rithms, and buys and sells shares off the back of it. That data can come from anywhere. They might track how many cars there are in a manufacturer's parking lot because that tells you how well the cars are selling and, by extension, how the economy is doing. They track planes, too, so when Occidental Oil's corporate jet was spot-ted in Omaha airport, they guessed that Warren Buffett might be making a bid and bought shares before the price rose. God, one guy I know even had a camera trained on the MI6 building round the clock because if there was a light on in a certain room on the sixth floor late at night, it meant some drama was kicking off in the Strait of Hormuz, and the price of oil was about to spike. The art lies in processing the data, and that's what Meldon does rather well.'

'If this isn't limited to just one interest, like football,' Hessa said gingerly, 'it could be quite an operation.'

'Yes,' said Miranda. 'Makes Aidan's outfit look practically shoe-string. The other thing is that he has simply built his firm the capacity to react faster to something everyone can see. The cricketer catching an edge or the footballer breaking a leg. But these other companies may be accessing intelligence illegally – and cashing in.'

'We've got no real evidence that they've done that,' said Casey.

'We know it happens elsewhere. Private detectives discover something, pass it up the ladder, and eventually, somehow, it ends up in a newspaper.'

'Because we've got our whole schtick about protecting sources,' said Casey moodily, 'they can leak us whatever they want and know that we'll cover for them.'

'The way that Mossad keeps dumping a zillion gigabytes of banking data on the *Sunday Sentinel*,' agreed Miranda. 'Keeping their investigation team – such as it is – tied up for months on end. I suppose it also means Mossad can pull the plug on them whenever they fancy, which can't be entirely unhelpful. And the fact that they outsource all their unbelievably tedious data analysis to the *Sentinel* – of all papers – will never not be funny.'

'That sort of thing.'

'Keep going,' said Miranda. 'Kick the tyres on all the stories.'

'I think Miles Foscliffe is a dead end,' said Casey. 'We never had any idea who was behind that story.'

'Foscliffe himself may know. Or the ex-wife. Or even the ex-bodyguard.'

'How about checking in with Selina Armstrong?' suggested Hessa.

'Nick Llewellyn's ex?' asked Miranda. 'See if she knows anything more about Orbmond. Where is she at the moment?'

'Nick said she was living in Devon,' said Casey. 'Close to Sir Reginald's pile. That's how Nick ended up representing the constituency in the first place, because it's where the Armstrongs lived.'

The golden son-in-law, back then. Swept to a safe seat, the future bright.

'And Daddy bought them a house near his own,' Miranda hazarded.

'You guess right.' Hessa spun her laptop towards them. 'We've still got their address from an MPs' expenses story and she doesn't seem to have moved. It looks very nice indeed.'

Postbridge House *was* very nice indeed, Casey thought, as she peered across the fields. Queen Anne, and perfect in its simplicity. The bricks were russet and the house's cream quoins emphasised its symmetry like the seams on a well-tailored dress. In the warmth of late summer, the house seemed to glow against the English green of the rolling hills.

Casey approached the house cautiously, walking slowly up a long drive lined with beech trees. She always preferred parking nearby and walking up to a house. Even if she were kicked out, walking justified a dilatory departure. She suspected, also, that the lack of a car made her look slightly pitiful. Harmless, even.

'Have you ever had to run?' Hessa had asked.

'Once. Or twice. Yes.'

As she walked, Casey assessed the situation. The drive approached from the left, ending in a turning circle in front of the house. Beyond that, lawns rolled away, delineated by geometric box hedges.

A woman was sitting on the grass, keeping an eye on four children. Even from a distance, Casey could see it wasn't Selina. When Nick Llewellyn was smeared across the front pages, Selina had shoulder-length hair, in an expensive shade of blonde. She had a doll-delicate beauty, with cheekbones that suggested generations of impeccable breeding. Selina was the sort of woman who went from pretty to elegant over the decades, never putting on an extra ounce.

Even if Nick Llewellyn's indiscretions had broken Selina Armstrong utterly, thought Casey, she still wouldn't look like the woman sitting on the lawn. Selina would be around forty and this woman must be about the same age, maybe a few years older, but any similarities between them ended there. This woman wore baggy denim shorts

and a blue shirt – oversized, almost as if it had been bought for a man – with old pink espadrilles. Her skin was that of a smoker who enjoyed relaxing in the sun. She looked comfortable, confident, and not especially interested in the opinions of others. Her long coarse hair was a rich red-brown streaked with grey. It was tied back by an emerald green headscarf in which threads of gold and sequins glimmered. On the immaculate lawns of Postbridge House, she looked incongruous.

Beyond the woman, the children were playing a complicated game of hide and seek, ducking behind the trees that edged the garden. They ranged between five and ten years old, guessed Casey, and two of them were probably Arlo and Saskia, although she couldn't have identified them. Within hours of Nick Llewellyn's death, Sir Reginald Armstrong had sent stern lawyers' letters to every media organisation in the country reminding them of his grandchildren's right to privacy, and so there were no photographs of the Armstrong children on file.

Was this a nanny? Casey wondered. But as the woman noticed her approach, there was a cool certainty to her wave that made Casey think not.

Casey sent back an ambiguous gesture and headed straight for the house.

As she approached the turning circle, she found she could see into the drawing room. *I remember parking the car on the drive and looking at the light behind the curtains in the drawing room …*

There. Selina Armstrong was sitting at a polished mahogany desk, head bent over a letter. Casey had no difficulty identifying her now. As seen on every news bulletin, the hair was the same blonde it had been years ago, the make-up immaculate. Selina's silk shirt was the colour of a caffè latte and it was paired with an ecru linen skirt. Apart from a huge bunch of dahlias on the desk, purple and scarlet and gold, the room was decorated in creams and fawns, framing Selina perfectly.

Feeling this awful sadness descend …

As Casey made her way towards the front door, her feet crunched on the gravel. Selina looked up.

'Can I help you?' The tone wasn't helpful. Selina stood up and walked across the room, speaking through the open sash window.

'I'm a journalist,' Casey said calmly. 'And I am investigating the death of your ex-husband.'

Selina raised her head and sharply drew breath. But it took her only a second to regain her composure. 'I have absolutely no comment to make about any of that. Please leave at once.'

'I'm looking at the events surrounding the Orbmond articles. I'm trying to understand exactly what happened. I know it's—'

'I've asked you to leave.'

'I think there was more to the Orbmond story than people realised at the time. I would like to—'

'I've told you to—'

'Is everything all right, Seels?' It was the woman who had been sitting on the lawn. Casey hadn't heard her coming across the grass. The woman was tall, Casey realised, a forceful presence.

'Yes,' said Selina firmly. 'This person is just leaving.'

'I'm a journalist,' Casey introduced herself to the newcomer. 'And I am working on a story about Orbmond.'

'Orbmond?' The woman frowned. 'If Selina wants you to leave her property, you really ought to. Right now, please.'

'It's important,' said Casey. 'I believe Nick Llewellyn was murdered and I think it had something to do with the Orbmond stories.'

'What?' Selina instinctively craned around to look for the children. 'What on earth are you talking about?'

'The kids are fine, Seels,' said the tall woman. 'They're designing a treehouse.'

Selina straightened up and faced Casey. 'Please leave,' she repeated. 'Right now or I will call the police. Your coming here is harassment.'

This wasn't the first time Selina had faced down journalists, of course. Standing in her elegant drawing room, she had the angry eyes and the determined jaw of her tycoon father.

'Don't you want to know why Nick was killed?' Casey asked.

'The police will find out,' said Selina. 'It's their job. You, get out.'

The tall woman folded her arms.

'Okay, okay,' said Casey. 'I'll go.'

She turned away down the drive, leaving the Queen Anne elegance behind her. After twenty paces, she glanced back. 'Could Nick's death have had anything to do with the Tip Top betting chain?'

It was a guess, almost.

Both women stared at her, Selina's face unreadable. A small boy was walking up behind the tall woman. Maybe seven, with gold-blond ragamuffin hair and grazed knees. Bright blue eyes, watchful. Arlo.

'It was just a thought.' Casey shrugged and kept walking.

She was almost back to the road, the shadows of the beech trees lying like bars across the drive, when she heard quick footsteps behind her. It was the tall woman, tugging a bra strap back onto her shoulder.

'What exactly,' the woman's eyes were steady, 'do you know about Tip Top?'

22

'Dawn!' the tall woman bawled as she and Casey returned to the house. When a middle-aged woman holding a duster appeared, she added: 'Could you pop out to the garden and keep an eye on the kids for a few minutes, please? Me and Selina have to have a chat with …' She waved towards Casey.

Dawn nodded wordlessly and headed off to the garden.

In the drawing room, Selina was waiting, standing by the window again.

'Do sit down,' the tall woman said hospitably. 'I'm Leah Mulroney.' She gave no further details.

'I'm Casey Benedict.'

There was an exasperated gasp from Selina. 'Casey *Benedict*. You were one of the journalists on the original Orbmond story.' Her voice rose. 'It's because of you that—'

But Leah hushed her with a gesture.

'What do you want to ask about Tip Top?' she said to Casey.

'I'm investigating a series of stories that may or may not be inter-connected.' Casey avoided the question smoothly. 'And one of the things they have in common is a link to Tip Top.'

'How?' Leah cut to the chase. Her vowels were from the Thames estuary, in sharp contrast to Selina's RP. She had an unusually expressive face, her countenance flitting from suspicion to amusement to alarm almost simultaneously.

'Not long before he died, Nick told me about his gambling habit.' Casey addressed Selina. 'He told me how he'd … got things wrong.'

Selina flinched.

'Why are you looking at Tip Top now, though?' Leah was implacable. 'What have they done?'

'It may all be coincidence,' said Casey, 'but Tip Top's name keeps cropping up. I've been told that the company carried out corporate espionage against a professional gambler I know. That gambler was then attacked at Royal Ascot. While I was investigating the attack, I identified a match fixer. Finding out his identity is useful to Tip Top because his activities skew their calculations. Pursuing that led me to a hedge fund, which I believe is involved in insider trading, and a public affairs company, who've been doing some very odd things.

Selina and Leah processed her words.

'It's a bit flimsy,' Leah said crushingly. 'Isn't it?'

'Finally, Nick told me he used to bet with Tip Top.' Even to Casey, it sounded slightly lame.

'From what you told me,' Leah said to Selina, 'Nick would bet with anyone.'

Selina nodded. She had regained her equilibrium. 'Exactly. It all sounds extremely tenuous.' She spoke distinctly, addressing herself to Casey. 'And I don't see how it's relevant to me.'

'Were there any other links between Tip Top and Nick?'

'I—' Selina looked away, clearing her throat. Both Leah and Casey watched her with interest.

'Are you all right, Seels?' Leah began. 'I can—'

'I don't see why this has anything to do with me,' Selina snapped. 'Or – more importantly – my children.'

'The match fixer,' said Casey, 'is dead. The incident at Ascot was an extremely well-coordinated ambush. And, of course, Nick himself is dead.'

Dead. The word hung in the air, ugly among the creams and beiges and the brilliance of the dahlias.

'If you think there is any real risk to Selina and her children,' Leah said, 'you need to go to the police.'

'I've already spoken to them,' said Casey. 'But they agree with Selina. It's tenuous. So that's why I am here. To try and get to the bottom of it all. You don't have to talk to me, but it is the only way I am going to work out what is going on.'

Selina was shaking her head. 'You don't know—'

'I believe the same man ambushed the match fixer and attacked Nick.' Casey weighted every word. 'I believe he is truly dangerous, and I need your help.'

Leah glanced at Selina. 'Seels?'

She had one hand pressed hard against her mouth. Casey realised she was trying to stop herself from crying.

Leah realised it too and turned back towards Casey. 'You're wondering why I'm here, aren't you?' she said chattily, hauling the conversation in a different direction.

'No,' Casey insisted.

'You are.' Leah smiled and shrugged. 'You can't work out how two people like me and Seels ended up being friends.'

'How did you meet, then?'

'I had my two girls,' Leah jerked her chin towards the garden, 'with my husband. But I had a son back when I was eighteen and his father was a bit of a dickhead, to put it mildly. My boy got into gambling when he was just fourteen – about a decade ago now – and it … There's a support group for families, you see? I go along quite a lot, because it helps a bit. Not much, but a bit. And one time, I bumped into Seels. And we just hit it off over a cup of stewed PG Tips. God knows why.' A bark of laughter. 'But we did.' Over by the window, Selina was listening, still blinking away tears. 'Our kids are roughly the same age, too,' Leah went on. 'And we started spending a bit more time together and slowly we became proper mates.'

'I'm glad,' said Casey.

'And the other thing we have in common,' Leah's tone changed sharply, 'is that we want to see the fucker behind Tip Top roast in hell.'

Selina smiled at the burst of belligerence. Casey was abruptly taken back to her first glimpse of the golden couple flitting around the room at party conference. They'd had charm, Selina and Nick, indisputably.

'I lost touch with a lot of people,' Selina said quietly. 'After Nick. But Leah …'

'People,' Leah observed, 'can be fuckwits.'

Selina moved away from the window, sitting down in a pale pink armchair. She perched on the edge, ankles neatly crossed, ready to leap away at any moment.

'There's another link between Tip Top and Nick, isn't there?' Casey asked her. 'I'm absolutely sure of it. Please tell me.'

In the end, it hadn't taken long for her to guess the connection. But she needed Selina to confirm the link. The information had to come from her.

'I blocked Nick from all the gambling sites,' Selina said abruptly. 'We did it together when I first found out how badly things had … Self-exclusion, it's called. But Tip Top was a new site back then, and I suppose one of its adverts must have appeared under Nick's nose. He ended up opening an account with them.'

'Okay. Then what?'

'He managed to rack up a debt of thousands, so fast,' said Selina. 'He didn't tell me about the new losses. I know why. By then, I was so *angry*. Bit by bit, you're turned into the person you never wanted to be. This furious, nagging *bitch* …'

Selina had a silk cushion in her hands and was twisting it around and around, unconsciously.

'So he didn't tell you about the Tip Top debts?'

'He only told me afterwards,' she muttered. 'After the newspaper articles. After everything.'

'Told you what?'

'That he was being blackmailed,' said Selina flatly. 'He told me that someone had found out he owed Tip Top a fortune, and guessed he was totally screwed. And, of all things, this blackmailer just said that if he would sort out some government funding for Orbmond, the gambling debt would go away.'

Casey breathed out slowly. Selina looked down at the silk cushion as if confused to find it in her hands.

'What's Orbmond?' asked Leah.

'A large company, something to do with satellites.' Selina sounded tired.

'Nick had received a donation from Orbmond's chief executive, so lobbying for them to get a big chunk of government funding was a conflict of interest,' Casey explained quickly to Leah. 'When it came out, he lost his job.'

'She wrote the story.' Selina nodded at Casey.

'The Orbmond executives always insisted they hadn't asked Nick to lobby for the funding. But that just seemed implausible. We wrote the articles very carefully so that we didn't actually accuse Orbmond, just Nick.'

'It destroyed the company anyway,' said Selina. 'The hint of scandal was enough. The funding was pulled and they were relying on it.'

'I see.'

'How?' There was anger in Selina's eyes. 'How did you get Nick's emails?'

'I can't …' Casey looked down.

She wasn't protecting a source, this time. Printouts of the emails had come through the post in an anonymous white envelope. Casey had investigated the emails, proved that they were genuine, and run the story. She had wondered, briefly, who posted them – an enemy of Llewellyn's? An Orbmond rival? – but at the time it hadn't seemed to matter.

It hadn't until she was staring at Orbmond's name on the Meldon short-selling list, almost willing the black and white letters to disappear.

'Nick had taken a donation from Orbmond and gambled with Tip Top,' said Casey. 'That was why they targeted him. Simply because they could.'

'But why?' asked Leah.

'I believe that this hedge fund made a lot of money out of it all. They made money when the share price went up as the funding was announced, then even more when it went down.'

'And whoever put pressure on Nick knew about his outstanding account with Tip Top.' Leah worked it out. 'And that should have been confidential information. So you think it proves Tip Top and this hedge fund are working together.'

'Basically, yes. Although, of course, it doesn't prove it to the level that I can write about it. It's supposition, really.'

'So as part of their gambling business, Tip Top's also creating a nice little database of people they can pressure in different ways,' Leah pointed out. 'Useful sideline.'

'But not everyone would be able to do what Nick did,' Selina objected. 'He was unusual in being an MP.'

As Selina spoke, Casey heard Ross's voice, loud in her head. *Everyone has a front-page story in them, Case. Everyone. You just have to work out what it is and get it out of them.*

'You'd be surprised,' she said to Selina. 'Do you have any hard evidence that Nick was being blackmailed by someone linked to Tip Top?'

'No. He only told me a couple of days after you'd done your story. We were back here, trying to get away from it all. I was screaming at him, saying I had been reasonable about the betting, reasonable about how he was chipping away at the foundations of our lives bit by bit. But that I hadn't known he was a crook too … And that I couldn't … I wouldn't … And he was crying, saying he was sorry. That he had been so desperate …'

'Could he have made it up? To try and shift the blame?'

'I don't think so,' said Selina. 'It didn't make me any less angry anyway.'

'And now Nick's dead,' said Leah flatly. 'So it's not as if he can tell us anything else. Honestly, Seels. What that man did to you …'

But Selina was staring out of the window, towards the geometry of the box hedges. 'You never knew him, Leah. You never knew what he was like.'

'I've met the sort.'

Selina walked over to the window and looked out across the beautiful gardens. The sun had gone in now, the colours of the garden muting. She put out her hand, touching the glass.

'I've been thinking about him a lot since he died. Awful, isn't it? How you can only let yourself remember how much you loved someone after they're dead. You couldn't when they were still alive. When they were still … a danger. Only when they're safely dead can you love them again.'

'Seels ...'

'There were others, you know?' Selina was almost speaking to herself. 'Other men I might have married instead. Sensible types. The sort my father would have preferred for me. But Nick ... He was exciting and fun and he could make me laugh ... so much.'

'I'm sure he did.'

'I never liked gambling. Nick and I would go to the races when we were younger, but I never really saw the point. Nick ...' She was trying to explain, searching for the words. 'He was my gamble. I could have had ordinary, I could have had nice. But I thought we might be ...'

Through the window, they could hear the children shrieking with laughter. They were closer to the house now, little feet crunching on the gravelled drive.

'It was the one great gamble of my life,' said Selina. 'And it lost me nearly everything.' A small smile. 'But I'm still not sure that I regret it.'

23

Miranda pushed her chair back and kicked her legs up so they rested on her desk. She enjoyed posing like that, thought Casey, and smiled.

'Okay,' said Miranda. 'So you think you've found another connection between Meldon and Tip Top?'

'Someone from Tip Top blackmailed Nick Llewellyn,' said Casey. 'We know that now. And then Meldon used that intel to make money as Orbmond's share price went up and back down again.'

'Or someone with access to Tip Top's books anyway. And you also think that Nash Bexley passes on information to Meldon, which they again use to make a fortune from short selling.'

Casey nodded.

'And because of the ties between Nash Bexley and Meldon and Tip Top, you think that mentioning Nick Llewellyn to Bexley was enough to get Nick killed off?'

'Yes,' Casey said firmly. 'In case I got him to spill the beans about being blackmailed.'

She imagined the man with the white-blond hair tracking them both through the green of Regent's Park, pouncing the moment the opportunity arose. Had he checked first that Nick hadn't told her about Tip Top's blackmailing? Probably. And then killed him nevertheless, in the coldest blood.

'I mean ... perhaps,' said Miranda.

'I know,' said Casey, 'what you're thinking.'

'Luckily for you, you don't.'

'No!' Hessa appeared in the investigations room doorway, shouting back over her shoulder, 'I'm not bloody doing it, Ross.'

'For fuck's sake, Hessa!' the news editor bawled across the newsroom. 'I don't see what the problem is. We'd provide you with excellent lawyers.'

'No.' Hessa was stern. 'I draw the line.'

'You'd only be in for about a week. And it would only need to be a very small crime.'

'Ross, no.'

Miranda looked up, mildly interested. 'What does Ross want?'

'That murderer who's got vague royal links,' Hessa said. 'She's on remand in Bronzefield. And Ross wants me to get myself *jailed* in order to get the first interview, because it's the only way he can think of getting to her. I mean, honestly ...'

'I could do it.' The home affairs editor was wandering past. 'Maybe for GBH of – let's see – a news editor.'

'You could,' said Hessa, 'but I'm not sure you'd be sent to HMP Bronzefield with all the other ladies.'

'Ah, yes.' He shrugged. 'Probably wouldn't work so well.'

'Plus very hard to deny it was premeditated.'

'Also true. On the plus side, after five minutes of Ross in the witness box, no jury would convict.'

Ross appeared in the doorway. 'Hessa—'

Miranda stood up and closed the door in his face.

Ross hammered on the glass panel.

'How *did* Ross's sensitivity and diversity training go last week?' asked Miranda.

The entire newsdesk of the *Post* had been ordered to attend several sessions after Ross sent a particularly egregious email about a Muslim MP to the home affairs editor, who had taken enormous joy in forwarding it to HR.

'It was an *accident*,' he'd insisted to Ross later.

'We've just had a really good tip in about a bomb-maker in central Syria,' Ross had replied. 'Just outside Tiyas, lovely this time of year. I've personally booked your flight.'

'Diversity training wasn't an overwhelming success,' said Hessa. 'They brought in some external company to run the session, and five minutes in, Ross fronted up the trainer about some tweet she'd written in two thousand and fourteen and said he'd splash the paper on her company's hypocrisy if she didn't wrap up the daylong session in time for morning conference. It was all over by nine-thirty a.m.'

'The HR boss went ballistic.' Miranda was laughing. 'But Ross told him that he'd inform Mrs HR boss precisely what happened at the last Christmas party if he didn't hop it too. Mr HR boss went green and hasn't come out of his office since.'

'Ross is an utter disgrace,' said Hessa. Then, brightly, 'So, how'd it go with Selina Armstrong?'

'There's a tighter link between Tip Top and Nick Llewellyn than we realised,' Miranda began, before stopping and opening the door a crack. 'Do bugger off, Ross, you absolute goon.' She closed the door again. 'But it's all anecdotal from Selina. Nothing concrete.'

Ross disappeared back to the newsdesk. 'Probably gone to report me to some terrorism hotline,' said Hessa gloomily. 'You have to promise to get me out, okay? But that's encouraging about Tip Top, right?'

'Not so much of the apophenia,' said Casey sardonically. 'Maybe.'

'I read some more about that,' said Hessa. 'Pareidolia is the visual equivalent. Elton John in a cloud or the Virgin Mary in a cheese sandwich.'

'Fascinating. But I still can't prove any of this. Is it Adele in a hot cross bun or Piers Morgan in a cinnamon roll or is it just a slightly wonky selection of baked goods?'

'Astonishing how many of our stories fall into this particular bracket,' said Hessa.

'The three companies do appear to be interacting with each other,' said Miranda. 'Tip Top generates a list of people who might be vulnerable to blackmail and in – for example – Nick Llewellyn's case, that allowed Meldon to cash in.'

'Greville Polignac also passes information to Meldon,' said Casey.

'Okay. Although I'm not sure if we can prove it's the company doing that. Could just be Nash freelancing.'

'Maybe. Tip Top and Meldon do essentially the same thing,' said Casey. 'Apply clever algorithms to a huge amount of data. While Greville Polignac is a conduit, hoovering up intel and spraying it out again.'

'Between Tip Top, Meldon and Greville Polignac,' Hessa observed, 'they've got the worlds of politics, finance and sport all covered. That's pretty extensive.'

Miranda stood up and stretched. 'Let's go old school: motive, means and opportunity for these attacks. Means is fairly obvious in all three. What's the motive for attacking Aidan Gardiner?'

'Scaring him?' Casey suggested. 'Tip Top tried to buy him out. They might have thought that scaring the shit out of him would make him more inclined to come under the Tip Top umbrella.'

'Maybe,' said Hessa. 'Or did they just want you to write about him? *Betting boss in organised crime attack at Ascot.* It is one way of taking out one of Tip Top's main rivals.'

'Basically,' said Miranda, 'we still have no real idea about that. Right. What's the motive for killing Nick Llewellyn?'

'To stop him telling us about the Tip Top blackmail,' said Casey.

'Fine. Opportunity?'

'They could have found him by following me,' Casey admitted. 'I had also told both Aidan and Nash Bexley that I was speaking to him.'

'Nick was probably relatively easy to track down,' said Hessa. 'Especially if your tattooed friend was passing himself off as a helpful citizen caring for the homeless.'

'Fine.' Miranda nodded. 'And what's the motive for Blake Gibson's murder?'

'Once we had identified him, it made sense for Tip Top to take him out,' said Casey. 'They had the same motive as Aidan. Match fixers screw up their data.'

'I suppose so,' said Miranda. *'Pour encourager les autres.'*

'If you're a crook, you're less likely to go into match fixing,' agreed Hessa, 'if the last person was splashed all over the *Post* and then had his throat slit.'

'It's not the most appealing career path.'

'And with Blake's death,' Casey went on, 'they also appear to have set up Aidan. Two birds with one stone, I guess.'

'But we are still nowhere near working out who's behind it all.'

'We'll find a way.' Casey's voice was firm.

'How?' asked Hessa.

'Yes, Casey,' Miranda said pointedly. 'How?'

24

Casey spent several days staking out the three offices.

Greville Polignac occupied two large Georgian houses in the warren of terraces behind Millbank, three minutes south of the House of Commons. The dark brown brick was perfectly set off by white sash windows and scarlet geraniums cascading from window boxes. The railings were freshly glossed, and every few minutes the main door – black-painted and surrounded by ornate plaster mouldings – opened and another couple of besuited lobbyists trotted off towards Parliament.

When Nash emerged, surrounded by his own keen little group, Casey ducked behind a car. She had visited these offices before, to interview one of Greville Polignac's clients. That time, she had waited in the reception area, perched on one of several huge ergonomic chairs that had been upholstered in a startling shade of pink. Greville Polignac's logo flickered in turquoise neon behind the glossy white berm of the reception desk. Opposite the desk, a vast photograph of racehorses surging towards the winning post dominated the room. The whole effect was ostentatiously cool and deliberately designed, Casey guessed, to clash with the grandeur of the exterior.

In sharp contrast, the Tip Top office was on an unremarkable street close to Ealing Broadway Tube station. The dingy office block must have been infill after World War II bomb damage to a drab row of

Victorian semis. Image here was irrelevant. Customers never knew this site existed, let alone saw it. The windows were frosted so that the office turned blind eyes to the world. There was less pedestrian traffic here. Once the workers arrived, they didn't surface for the rest of the day. As Casey watched the men – they were almost all men – file away for the night, she wondered which of the hunched shapes was Aidan's turncoat.

Sighing, she hopped on the Elizabeth Line, emerging to the bustle of the City. Again, the contrast between the offices was dramatic. Only a few hundred yards from the neo-Classical glory of the Bank of England, Meldon Group operated from an ultramodern block. Behind a sheet of black glass and steel, the hedge fund looked as friendly as the north face of the Eiger. Here, work carried on until late in the evening, lights just visible behind the panels of darkened glass.

'Not much in common then,' said Miranda, when Casey reappeared in the office. 'No overarching personality between the three businesses.'

'No. Except for one thing: all three of those buildings are owned by companies linked to Theia Incorporated.'

'Does Theia own anything else?' asked Miranda. 'Any other properties in the UK?'

'Not that I can see. But you can't search that way round. You have to have the address first.'

'What does Theia mean anyway?'

'Bit obscure,' said Casey. 'It's the name of one of the Titanesses in Greek myth. It seems to refer to the brightness of the sky. Not the sun itself – that was Helios, one of Theia's sons – but the lustre of the whole sky.'

'"The brilliance in silver,"' Hessa was reading aloud from her computer screen. '"The glow in gold."'

'She's the goddess of sight, too,' said Casey. 'Someone who sees more than the rest of us do, maybe?'

'And who runs these companies – the day-to-day operations?'

'Unclear. There are no profiles anywhere, nothing like that. The websites don't give anything away, either.'

'PRs spend all their time trying to get us to write glowing articles about their own CEOs,' Hessa remarked. 'We don't really have time to think about the ones who don't want publicity. Just because we don't write about them doesn't mean they don't exist.'

'Yes,' Casey agreed. 'And some PR companies will do the exact opposite of PR. Accept a nice sum to ensure you're not in the papers, ever.'

'So you're assuming that the three CEOs all report to one person,' said Miranda. 'Whoever is behind this Theia group.'

'Yes.'

'But Theia is a BVI company? So we can't find out who is behind that.'

'Nope,' said Casey. 'But there is someone there. We have a target now, at least.'

Miranda went in first: to Greville Polignac.

'Nash Bexley's doing a talk at the University of the West of England next Tuesday,' Hessa had announced after a few minutes of research. 'A lecture on the role of public affairs in creating effective legislation, whatever that means. Kicks off at eleven a.m.'

'Perfect,' said Miranda. 'It's a good two hours from London to Bristol, so he'll be safely out of the way for the whole of Tuesday morning.'

They hadn't overlapped for long at the *Post*, Nash and Miranda, but Casey had watched the former political editor work a room. He didn't forget a face.

On Tuesday, with a polished smile, Miranda presented herself as a senior executive at an up-and-coming healthcare company based in Bracknell. The company wanted to organise a roundtable with one of the health ministers, she said. Really push the brand forward. In preparation, Casey created a website for the imaginary company, and Hessa organised some branded pens.

'I dropped in a mention of that story James is running tomorrow – Woolland Reed having major problems with their new cancer drug,' Miranda said afterwards, as she disentangled herself from the recording equipment. 'It'll be interesting to see what comes of that.'

Six hours later, the Meldon Group informed the FCA that it had taken out a small short position in Woolland Reed.

'So Greville Polignac feeds information to Meldon, not just Nash Bexley. It's a little bit more proof that these companies are interlinked,' said Casey.

'But we need rather a lot more,' Miranda said drily.

'I know.' Casey was going through the footage Miranda had filmed as she was shown around Greville Polignac. *I love your offices! We're just about to get ours redone. Can I have a quick tour?* Frame by frame, Casey assessed the layout and the decor of the conference rooms, the arrangement of the desks and the gossip by the watercooler. 'Anything that links the three offices,' she muttered to herself. 'There has to be some sort of connection.'

'When's Hessa going in?' Miranda asked.

'Tonight.'

Lammas Cleaners – perfection every day.

On a late-night visit to Ealing, Casey had noted the name on the side of a little van parked up in the Tip Top office's driveway. A quick search of Lammas Cleaners' Facebook page revealed the company had a standing need for new staff.

'Tillie?' Casey had looked up from her computer. 'Could you get yourself down to Ealing and offer up your services? Try to get in as soon as possible. Night shifts only, I'm afraid.'

'Oh, I'd love to,' she said, 'but I'm tied up literally every night this week. There are a few drinks parties Ross wants me to go to. Sorry!'

Ross, Casey knew, was enjoying the hints and clues Tillie picked up over her cocktails.

'I'll get over to Ealing,' Hessa sighed. 'Shunt across the details, Casey.'

'Easiest interview ever,' Hessa reported back a few hours later. 'She made me laugh, the woman in charge. Romanian, I think. Asked if I had any experience and then interrupted herself and said she'd stick me on hoovering, any moron could do that.'

'Lammas is a small company,' said Casey. 'With any luck, you'll be rota-ed to Tip Top fairly soon.'

It took Hessa only two nights to manoeuvre herself onto the Tip Top shift. 'The other girl was brutally hungover,' she said, laughing the next morning. 'I offered to cover her just this once.'

The laugh became a yawn.

'Thanks, Hess.' Casey grinned. 'I'll start trawling through the footage now.'

'And I'll ring Lammas,' said Hessa, 'and tell them I'm really sorry but I've been offered a better job over in Acton.'

'And then go and have a nap.'

'God, yes. Although maybe I should hang onto that job, given the amount I get paid here.'

Hessa had recently moved into a tiny studio flat, Casey knew, after scraping together the deposit.

'Are you enjoying your new place?'

'Adore it. I've finally escaped my family. Not that I don't love them, but doing my own thing is bliss.'

'Well, take the rest of the day off and enjoy that peace.'

'My name's Gemma,' the woman greeted Casey in the plush reception area. 'I work in the HR team here. And you must be – er – Cassandra?'

'Cassandra Benson, yes. Sorry I've only got copies with me.' Casey thrust a sheaf of papers at Gemma. 'I left the originals at my parents' house last weekend!'

'It's no problem.' A beaming smile from Gemma. 'We'd need to see your passport or driving licence before you start, that's all. It's just a temporary role, of course, but we have to do the checks all the same.'

Back at the *Post* offices, the head of graphics had quickly and cantankerously adapted Casey's driving licence and a random water bill. 'Just run it through the crap photocopier again before you head out? That will blur it nicely.'

'No problem.' Casey grinned at Gemma now.

'Great!' she said. 'Welcome to Meldon Group. Let's get started!'

An hour later, Casey had used every excuse she could think of to extend her exploration of the hedge fund. After the basic interview, she had expressed an interest in the conference rooms, the office kitchen, the break-out areas. As they walked past the little groups loitering around the watercoolers, she had slowed down, trying to make out every face.

Her task was made slightly easier by the fact that a large part of the Meldon Group's office space was open-plan, rows of desks striating the large room. Each workspace had a cluster of computer screens, similar to the ones in Aidan's Kennington operation. But the Meldon offices were far sleeker than the industrial unit. Here, the decor was silvered, glossy, with huge blown-up photographs providing bright splashes of colour.

'Where does that lead to?' Casey pointed to a heavy steel door.

'That's one of the secure zones,' Gemma said cheerily. 'Where they write the code for the fund. The algorithms, you know? The codes themselves are hugely valuable, so there's all sorts of security built into that area. There's a biometric finger scanner to get in and a weight sensor too, so you can't walk in and out with extra stuff, like your phone or whatever. I'm definitely not allowed in there!'

'Amazing,' Casey gushed. No one walked off with the nuclear codes here, she thought.

'The guys in that room,' Gemma said conspiratorially, 'don't look like they see sunlight all that often.'

'I'd love to see the roof terraces.' Casey smiled at Gemma, at the end of the office tour. 'I've heard they're amazing.'

Gemma, who was obviously not focused on getting back to her desk, grinned in reply.

'Sure, why not? I love the view up there anyway.'

Glass executive boxes lined the room, each with a nameplate in that special brushed aluminium. As they headed towards the lifts, Casey strolled at a deliberately leisurely pace down the row of nameplates, not especially hopeful that the tiny camera embedded in her navy-blue business suit would be able to pick up the little Helvetica names.

'Who owns the company?' she asked as the lift doors hissed closed. 'Meldon Group itself.'

'I don't actually know his name.' Gemma's brow furrowed. 'It's all very discreet.'

'They often are, hedge funds.'

The lift doors opened silently to a huge rooftop terrace. Topiaried hedges lined narrow gravel paths, and the view over the park was worth millions.

'It's beauti—' Casey was stepping forward when Gemma grabbed her arm.

A tall man with sleek grey hair was standing fifty yards away, deep in conversation on his mobile phone. He had his back to them. Before Casey could get a proper look, Gemma had pushed her back into the lift.

'That's the founder,' she stage-whispered as the elevator doors whisked closed. 'He won't want to be interrupted. Sorry!'

The lift hummed straight down to the ground floor. 'I'd better get back to my desk now,' trilled Gemma. 'Lovely to meet you, Cassandra. We'll let you know as soon as possible, okay?'

'Thank you, Gemma.'

Casey found herself back on the street. For a second, she peered back up at the sheer black glass. So close. And still so very far.

Her phone went as she was walking back towards the Bank of England and its Corinthian columns.

'Where are you?' Jackson's voice.

'City of London.'

'Nice. I'll come and join you.'

'I'm undercover, Jackson.'

'As you'll remember, I aced that too.'

'Yes, it's so helpful the way you fade right into the background.'

'I can provide a distraction. If things get really desperate, I'll even take my top off.'

'Any opportunity.'

'That members' club, up in Shoreditch. I'll meet you there in an hour.'

Casey paused in the shadow of the Bank. 'I can't, Jackson.'

'Why not? I promise I'll keep my top on. Unless you ask nicely.'

'It's … complicated.'

'It's really not, Casey.'

'I don't want to be—'

'A "WAG"?' His tone put quotation marks around the word.

'Yes. No.'

'Casey.' Exaggerated seriousness. 'It's one drink.'

She felt silly for a moment, then laughed. 'I have to get back to the office anyway.'

'Casey. Come on.'

'Speak soon, Jackson.'

25

Outside the *Post*'s offices, the road had been narrowed in a vague attempt to even up the eternal battle between motor traffic and pedestrians. On the empty swathe of brand-new pavement, the council had positioned a series of granite blocks to serve as benches. The granite was embedded with swirls of metal: not comfortable.

As Casey approached the office, a figure stood up. Tall, formidable, flowing russet hair tied back with a crimson bandana. Leah Mulroney.

'Fancy a coffee?' she asked, as if they had arranged to meet.

'That would be great.'

Casey bought two lattes and they strolled down the road towards the park. Overnight, the last of the summer had been swept away. A cold wind blew a chaos of rusty leaves ahead of them and shoppers were wrapped in hastily unearthed winter coats. Leah wore a long green coat embroidered with golden flowers, and purple fingerless knitted gloves. She took long strides, Casey hurrying to keep up. Every few seconds, Leah blew on her coffee.

'You're struggling to prove the main drive of this story, aren't you?' Leah spoke without preamble. 'Yesterday, the police told Selina they hadn't got anything new on Nick's death, for example. And I haven't seen anything in the papers about that fixer in Marbella for ages.'

'No,' said Casey. 'There's very little to go on. It is … frustrating.'

'So you need to build up the little bits of evidence, don't you? Prove it that way around instead.'

'Yes.' Casey felt tired. 'Maybe.'

'Well, I was thinking, what if you could find more people who were being blackmailed by Tip Top?'

Casey considered. 'It might be helpful. I don't know how to find them, though. I suppose the whole point about blackmail is that people desperately don't want to talk about whatever it is.'

'Right,' said Leah. 'But maybe there's a way of tracking them down all the same.'

Casey stopped walking. 'What's your idea?'

'I told you that Selina and I met at a support group. CasiNo.' Leah mocked the pronunciation. 'It's a stupid name, and I take the piss out of them quite a bit, but it did actually help us. It's for gamblers, but it's also for the people around them. Their friends, their families. When my boy ... my Owen ...'

She broke off, looking up at the rustling plane trees. Casey waited. Leah cleared her throat.

'People just say whatever they need to say at these meetings,' she went on. 'If you've lost everything, or your husband can't stop betting, or whatever it is. They're' – Leah spiked the words with a twist of a smile – 'safe spaces.'

'I can't go along to one of those,' said Casey. 'They're anonymous. They have to be, so that people can speak freely.'

'But no one would ever guess who you were. And no one would ask, either. People quite often come in and sit at the back and never say anything at all.'

'No, Leah. It's not—'

'Either way,' Leah interrupted her, 'I can go along. And I can talk about Tip Top, just casually, you know? I might drop in the idea that Owen had mentioned blackmail and that a journalist had asked me about it, and I was thinking it might be a good idea to get his story out there. People *know* me at these things. I've been going for years. They *trust* me. If someone else was being blackmailed, they might come to me. Tell me if the same thing had happened to them.'

'I don't—'

'You could keep them completely anonymous anyway. You just have to listen to what they have to say.' Leah's eyes glowed with determination. 'It would help you build up the picture. And that's what we need to do.'

'I really don't—'

'Well, I'm just telling you out of courtesy anyway.' Leah pulled her bandana off her head and shook out the mass of hair. 'I'm going to do it either way. I've got to, Casey. It's …'

'There are rules—'

'I'm not a journalist,' Leah said simply. 'They don't apply to me.'

She had finished her coffee and stood there looking down at the gritty dregs in the empty cup.

'Leah—'

'I'll start with the group in Battersea. You get a good mix of people there. From all over the place. Then, perhaps … Islington. You'd get some City types there. And Chelsea, maybe. My girls are back at school now. I need something to do when I'm not at work.'

'I don't even know what you do,' Casey said, realising.

'I'm a healthcare assistant,' said Leah. 'I help fix people. It was just a shame I could never fix my own son.'

26

'What do we know about this Theia person?' Miranda addressed the room randomly.

'He's very rich,' Hessa said simply.

'But he may not be the sort of person to show it off,' said Miranda. 'Like Aidan Gardiner, for example. If you passed Aidan in the street, you'd never guess he was worth a fortune. Even his house in Kennington … It looks like success, but not world domination.'

'But maybe this person is more focused on money than Aidan is?' Casey suggested. 'Aidan's an observer. A superpowered observer, but an observer nonetheless. I think this person is more proactive, more aggressive, enjoys the power. I think they actively like manipulating people. Find it interesting.'

'They use attack as the best form of defence too, and quite ruthlessly,' said Miranda. 'Foscliffe and Fairbairn were a threat so they were destroyed. It was clinical.'

Casey was doodling in her notepad. She had spent most of the previous night staring at the ceiling of her flat, her mind flicking through the options until it was a blur. When she finally slept, she dreamed of seaweed coating her face and woke to the sound of her own screams.

'What do they collect?' she asked abruptly.

'What do you mean?' asked Hessa.

'Almost every very rich person I've ever come across enjoys collecting things. They get started and suddenly they're obsessive. Because that's their mindset anyway – they can't do anything half-heartedly. Art, vintage cars, yachts, land, whatever. There's always something. And there'll always be someone around to enable that. Your canny art dealer, your cute estate agent. Even Aidan's started collecting footballers, if you think about it.'

'Well, what else are you going to do?' asked Hessa wistfully. 'With your billions.'

'You're talking about hobbies, basically.' Miranda rolled her eyes.

'Sort of,' said Casey. 'But on a grand scale. You don't celebrate your billions by taking up crocheting.'

'But how do we identify this obsession?' asked Hessa.

When she had arrived in the investigations room that morning, Casey had nicked Hessa's and Miranda's laptops. Now she sat them all in a row, cueing the footage from the three offices.

'Obsession,' Miranda threw a piece of Blu-Tack at Casey, 'can be surprisingly easy to spot actually, Hess.'

Casey ignored Miranda, all her attention focused on the three screens.

'There just isn't a common denominator between those offices,' Hessa sighed. 'I've watched them all several times.'

The footage spooled silently. Casey drank her coffee and then was surprised to find the mug empty.

'Antiquities,' she murmured. 'Private jets. Wine.'

'Stamps?' Hessa was laughing. 'Star Wars memorabilia? A harem?'

'I'd collect jewels,' said Miranda. 'A magpie hoard of rubies and sapphires.'

'I bet you would.'

Casey got another round of coffees and then sat down again. The cameras continued to make their jerky way around the offices. When one ran out, she started it again.

Her phone bleeped. Lucas Fairbairn, probably sitting in his Parliamentary office. *The more I think about it, the angrier I am. If there's anything I can do to track down whoever is behind all this, please let me know. L*

Casey smiled to herself and typed a reply. *Will do. And thanks.*

Back to the undercover footage. And finally she gave a sharp intake of breath. Miranda looked up.

'Photography,' Casey was saying. 'Racehorses. *There.*'

She had paused all three screens. Hessa and Miranda stood and made their way over to her.

'What am I looking at?' asked Miranda.

The screens were frozen on the Greville Polignac reception area, a conference room at Tip Top and the big open-plan office at Meldon Group.

'The photographs,' said Casey. 'On the walls.'

In Greville Polignac's reception, the racehorses were blazing towards the winning post. They were stretching for the line, torn between terror and that desperate urgency to win.

In the high-ceilinged main office of Meldon Group too, the horses were sprinting to the post, frantic to be first, because nothing else mattered. *Nothing.* They were images to inspire the Meldon worker bees, Casey thought. Competition incarnate.

'And then there are those.' Casey pointed to the Tip Top conference room. On the wall was a series of cityscapes, the views out over a jigsaw of buildings.

'That's London,' Hessa guessed, pointing at one image. 'And that looks like an American city.'

A sweep of skyscrapers, jagging into the sky.

'It's New York,' said Miranda. 'That's the Empire State building.'

'And that one?'

That photograph was the odd one out. Big ugly buildings, probably apartment blocks, a palate of beiges and greys.

'Not sure.' Miranda peered closer. 'That could be almost anywhere.'

'The picture frames are all the same,' said Casey.

'They're all aluminium,' said Hessa doubtfully. 'But that's hardly unusual.'

'It's more than that.' Casey was dialling an extension. 'Stan? Would you be a star and pop into the investigations room?'

Stan was the *Post*'s picture editor, and not known for his sensitivity. Casey suspected it had been obliterated by thousands of photographs in razor-sharp focus. A mother after a bomb blast, holding her dying child: nah, the resolution's off. A man with his leg ripped open: fine, bit overexposed though. They used to think cameras stole the soul, but maybe it was the photographs. Every snap, a chip.

Stan was shouting down his mobile as he appeared in the doorway. 'Tell Dick Pic that I need the Downing Street photographs in the next three minutes or he's fired. What?' Stan shrugged at Casey as he terminated the call with a stabbing finger. 'If you're a snapper called Richard, what the hell do you expect?'

'These photographs,' Casey gestured towards the screens, 'are they all by the same person?'

'Do you have a clearer image?' Stan would have that engraved on his tombstone, Casey thought. There was a pause as the picture editor peered closer. 'Mind you, the images from those buttonhole cameras are a lot better than they used to be, aren't they?' Another shrug. 'Yeah, I see what you mean. It could be the same photographer.'

'Can you be sure?'

'If I had the originals in front of me instead of these crappy stills.' Stan was always blunt. 'Good photographers develop an individual style. You get a sense for it. I could tell Dick Pic's stuff easily, for example. Although I'd deny calling him good, obviously.'

He paused, concentrating hard for a moment. Miranda smiled at him. 'Go on then, Stan. Impress us.'

'Right.' He grinned back suddenly. 'First thing, this isn't a professional job, so it's a bit odd these pics are being hung in offices. This is a decent amateur, but not a pro.'

'How come?'

'Well,' Stan pointed to one of the racehorses, 'whoever it was, they weren't expecting these pics to be blown up to this size. They're over-sharpened here and here.' He pointed briskly. 'Easy to do, and it looks okay on a smaller image. But at this scale, you can make out a sort of pixelating effect.'

'All right.'

'Next thing is that they've vignetted the images and overdone it a bit. Darkened round the edges and the corners, basically. Photography students do it a lot, because they think it makes things moody, arty.'

'I see,' said Miranda.

'There's also a similar composition in all of them.' Stan warmed to his theme. 'Lots of sky, the focus in this area here. But the main thing …'

He paused, enjoying his moment.

'The main thing?' Miranda gave him his dues.

'Come with me.' Stan bowled out of the investigations room.

He led them briskly to the *Post*'s production suite, complete with large, high-resolution computer screens. Within moments, he had several of the photographs up on the screens.

'What are we looking at?' Casey asked.

'Well,' Stan took on the air of a magician pulling a rabbit out of a hat, 'look here, and here, and here.' They all peered closely. There was a tiny smudge – the same small blur, almost invisible – towards the top left-hand corner of each photograph. 'He's got a bit of dust on his camera mirror,' said Stan, as if that explained everything.

'Camera mirror?'

'You open up any standard digital camera,' he expanded, 'and there'll be a mirror inside. And if you get a piece of dust on that mirror, it'll show up on all your photographs even if you're changing the lens between shots. It'll stay there until you give your camera a proper service, which lots of amateurs never do.'

'So they're all by the same photographer?'

'Yup.'

'Stan,' said Miranda, 'you're a genius.'

'I do my best.' He made no pretence at modesty. 'I do my very best for you ladies.'

As he spoke, Stan was distracted by more images flashing up on his tablet. 'Good *boy*,' he growled, waving the screen at them. 'Yet another Cabinet Minister trotting up Downing Street with a top-secret document under his arm. They really are useless.' Stan zoomed in happily on the photograph, until the pixels danced and blurred. 'Mind you, it does seem to be the only way that the government briefs us at all these days. You'd think they could leave a few documents in Houses of Parliament photocopiers, like the good old days. Bit classier, that …'

And he was gone, hurtling back towards the picture desk.

Casey dialled another number. 'Griff? Can I steal you for a couple of minutes?'

The sports correspondent slouched in a few minutes later. 'Crisp?' He proffered a bag of salt and vinegar.

'Which racecourses are those?' Casey pointed at the stills.

'That's Goodwood,' Griff said immediately. 'And that's ...' He screwed up his face. 'I'm fairly sure that's Epsom.'

Casey was already searching online. Images of Epsom racecourse taken from a dozen different angles.

'It's the same place,' Hessa confirmed. 'Look at the angle between the white rails and the stands. The rise towards the finish line there. And that row of billboards. Easy.'

'Can you recognise any of those colours?' Casey asked Griff.

The jockeys all wore silks, bright and deliberately distinctive. An emerald cross on amethyst. Chocolate and lime stripes. A Barbie-pink slash across sapphire blue. Designed to identify a horse's owner from half a mile away, through fog.

'Those colours there.' Griff clicked his fingers at the Goodwood photograph. 'That's that Middle Eastern sheikh. And the maroon and green diamonds, that's an Irish pharmaceuticals heiress.'

Casey was hunting again. 'They both had horses running at Goodwood in May and August last year,' she muttered. 'And on four different days the year before. And that's assuming the photographs were taken in the last couple of years. They might be older, of course.'

'Both of them have a lot of horses.' Griff upended the packet of crisps straight into his mouth. 'That's how I know the colours.'

Casey had pulled up the list of runners. Beside each horse's name was a brief description of its colours. Again, she peered closely at the bunch of horses sprinting for the line.

'There.' She pointed at the last. 'That photograph was taken during the three-thirty-five at the August meeting last year. That's the only race when that exact line-up of colours was racing.'

'Nice one,' said Griff.

'The other one,' Miranda observed, 'is trickier.'

'Yup.'

There were only two horses in this photograph, and barely an inch between them as they flashed towards the finishing line.

Barely an inch after a mile or more: the gap between triumph and despair.

'Can you recognise those colours?' Hessa asked Griff.

'Nope. But that's the Champion jockey riding the chestnut.'

'Okay.' Hessa was making a spreadsheet of all the days of racing at Epsom for the last five years. 'Strike those, for starters.' She marked them off.

'Why?' asked Griff.

'Weather data,' Hessa said smartly. 'Look. On those days, it was overcast in Epsom, but the sky in the photographs is a lovely clear blue.'

'Fair enough.'

'On those days,' a few more keystrokes from Hessa, 'the Champion jockey was racing at Newmarket and York, not Epsom. That leaves these race days.'

'Knock out those races.' Griff pointed.

'Why?'

'Because none of the horses in those races were wearing blinkers,' he said. 'And the bay in that photograph is.' He watched Hessa raise an eyebrow. 'The brown horse with a black mane and tail. They list the horses wearing blinkers in the racecard because the punters like to know.'

Hessa pulled a face. 'Fine. That leaves us with ... Champion jockey wearing white stars on cerulean ...'

'Cerulean.' Griff rolled the word around his mouth. 'Nice word.'

Hessa ignored him. 'That photograph was taken in June two years ago,' she concluded a minute later.

'So what does that tell us?'

'I don't know exactly.' Casey was generating a list of names. 'Except that maybe the person we're looking for had a horse in that race.'

'Or they owned a horse running that day,' said Miranda. 'You might not be messing about with a camera as your white-hot hope was actually racing.'

'True,' Casey sighed. 'Or they could just be a racing enthusiast who popped along for the day.'

'And the other thing is,' Miranda said regretfully, 'a fascination with photography doesn't really align with our analysis of this guy being a numbers obsessive.'

'You may be right.' Casey crumpled up a piece of paper. 'You may be right.'

'I'm starting to see,' Griff said, 'how your stories take so goddamn long to appear in the paper. Got to fly, ladies. My article's actually being printed tomorrow, if you can imagine that.'

'Yeah, yeah, bugger off.'

As Griff disappeared from the office, Casey's phone buzzed again. *Come to the coffee shop next to your offices? I've got someone I'd like you to meet.*

Leah, Casey thought, was a sight more efficient at investigating than anyone at the *Post*.

The woman standing next to Leah was about a foot shorter than her. 'This is Michelle,' Leah shouted over the steamy hiss of the coffee machine. 'I bumped into her at a meeting last night.'

Michelle was about five years older than Leah, Casey guessed, and lacked her innate exuberance. Michelle looked beaten down by life, with dark roots and a round, tired face. Her eyebrows had been overplucked in the nineties, and she punctuated every sentence with a laugh, even when she hadn't attempted a joke. Diffusing any tension, Casey diagnosed: half apologetic. A habit that had become a nervous tic.

'Hello,' she said. 'I'm Casey.'

'I'm Michelle. It's nice to meet you.' A jittery laugh. 'Leah said you'd like to talk to me about …'

'It would be incredibly helpful, yes. Thank you so much for coming along to meet me.'

Michelle looked at her feet and carved out circles on the coffee-stained floor. Her trainers were worn, her jeans frayed at the heel.

'I've seen Leah at these meetings before. And when I heard her talk about …' The words trailed away into an uneasy giggle.

'We don't have to rush anything,' said Casey. 'It's absolutely up to you.'

'Michelle's been coming to the meetings for a while now,' said Leah. 'It's about her son, Liam.'

Michelle glanced up, her eyes apprehensive. 'Liam's … Liam's, well …' Her eyes filled with tears.

Casey paid for the coffees and led Leah and Michelle over to a quiet corner. They sat down and Michelle mopped her eyes.

'I don't know where to start.' A querulous laugh. Michelle fiddled with a wooden stirrer and shredded her napkin.

'Liam's in jail,' Leah said bluntly.

Michelle's eyes flicked to meet Casey's in alarm. 'Leah said you wouldn't write about me personally. That you just wanted to know as much as possible about …'

'About Tip Top,' Leah clarified. 'Yeah, Casey only wants to understand what's going on, Mich.'

'You don't mind if I don't tell you my surname?' A skittish laugh. 'Well, I can tell you what it is. But you have to promise not to put it in the newspaper. Please?'

'I won't, Michelle. I won't publish anything without agreeing it all with you in advance.'

'Liam's Liam Briggs-Nelson, then. Me and Chris combined our surnames. I was Briggs, Chris is Nelson.'

'Okay.'

It took a few more minutes, peppered by Michelle's laughter, an octave higher now, but finally she started speaking.

'Gambling's been a problem since Liam was really young, you know? I blame it on the computer games. The loot boxes.' Michelle saw Casey's expression and expanded her explanation. 'In lots of the computer games the kids play these days, there are these things called loot boxes. The kids use real money to take a chance on them and see what's inside. Sometimes it's something pointless, but other times they win something that's important for the game. The prize might help them get to another level or something. I never really understood it all.'

'It's gambling for kids,' said Leah. 'Junior roulette. Baby blackjack. Getting them hooked on the dopamine hit before they've even hit puberty. Bing, bing, bing.'

'Liam used my husband's credit card.' Michelle sounded bleak. 'This was right back when he was thirteen. Suddenly there were all these payments on Chris's credit-card statement and we had no idea where they'd come from. We gave Liam such a bollocking when we worked it out, explained to him that it was real money. That spending it on these stupid games meant we couldn't do anything nice with him and his sister, or whatever. Money was always ...'

'Tight.' Leah finished her sentence. 'Same with us, don't worry.'

'We changed all our passwords, thought we'd nipped it in the bud. But it turned out ... Chris was always such a softie with Liam.'

'How old is Liam?' Casey asked.

'He's twenty-three now,' said Michelle. 'He got a good job straight out of school. Coding, that's what he's good at. I could never make sense of that, either.'

'And then what happened?'

'We only understood after ... He'd never stopped gambling. He started with football, and soon he was betting on anything. Greyhound racing, when he doesn't know the first thing about bloody dogs.'

'I'm sorry.'

'You can't *see* a gambling problem, you know? I'd probably have been able to tell if he'd been hungover to the back teeth, or shooting up, or whatever, but there was nothing to *see*.'

'I know,' said Leah. 'I know.'

'Just before the trial, he was crying down the phone to me. Said he was so ashamed and embarrassed. He'd run out of money completely towards the end, would have nothing left at all at the end of the month. He'd taken out loans, the whole bit. But even so, even when he had nothing, he'd get his monthly pay packet and find himself logging on for a quick go. And within minutes, a whole month's money would be gone, just like that. He didn't know how to tell us it had all gone to shit. I was so proud of him, you see. I'd tell all my friends, "Oh, Liam's doing so well. He's got such a good job." He thought his luck would change somehow. That he could make it all better.'

'Those sites are designed to draw you in,' said Leah. 'They're all fun cartoons and music. Chatbots that tell you jokes as if they're your mate.'

'Liam said that the sites deliberately played jolly music,' Michelle was breaking a wooden stirrer to shards, 'so that even when you were losing, it still *sounded* as if you were winning. Click, spin, click, spin, jingle, jangle, good times. He didn't even realise how much he was losing half the time.'

'They're so young,' said Leah. 'These companies design the games deliberately to draw them in.'

'Maybe.'

'And there's so much money in gambling. One website boss was paid over four hundred million pounds last year. Four hundred million!' Leah spaced out the words. 'For one year's work. I can't even—'

'So what happened next, Michelle?'

She hesitated.

'Tell her, Mich,' Leah urged. 'It'll help, I promise.'

'Liam stole.' Michelle spoke very quietly, as if she might be able to make the words disappear. 'He began to steal from his own employers. He managed to access their bank accounts and transfer a bit of money to his own. He thought he'd be able to use that to win back everything he'd lost and replace the money in the company's account. He was so ...' Michelle tipped her head back. 'He was so *naive*.'

'And he lost?'

'Of course he did. Of *course*. And then he transferred a little bit more from the company account, and then a little bit more. And suddenly he was a hundred grand down.' The impossibility of the sum reverberated in Michelle's voice and she fell into silence.

Leah broke through the hush. 'Tell her about Tip Top.'

'What?' Michelle looked vague. 'Oh, yes, Tip Top. Liam'd lost a lot of the money to Tip Top, you see? And one day, he got a phone call.'

'From whom?'

'He never even knew,' said Michelle. 'But it was someone who knew all about his losses with Tip Top, knew how much he'd lost and when. And this man said he could make them all go away.'

'It was definitely a he?'

'Yes.'

'Accent?'

'I don't know. I can ask. Next time I—'

'What did he want? This man?'

'He wanted access to what Liam was working on.'

'What was that?'

'He was working at this electronics company called SportWatcher. Not a big one, but they're very good at what they do. They develop wearable tech.' Michelle used the phrase hesitantly.

'Oh,' Casey said simply. 'Oh, I see.'

'We're always on the hunt for better data,' Aidan had explained back under the liquidambar in his back garden in Kennington. 'We need it as fast as possible and in a format that is really easy to process. Take tennis, for example. You can monitor unforced errors or double faults or whatever, and feed those into the model, but everyone else is getting that information anyway, so there's no real advantage. You have to look elsewhere, but unless you're getting that data really fast, it doesn't help you either. Because it doesn't matter if you're getting the richest data in the world if it comes with a time delay of ten seconds. Ten seconds is basically yesterday for us.'

'Right.'

'So we need to find data points that can be analysed and transmitted to us in real time.'

'I see.'

'Look …' And he had tried to sketch it out for her on a piece of paper, and the hours had flown past.

'What do you mean,' Leah took a gulp of her coffee, 'wearable tech?'

'When footballers are on the pitch nowadays,' Casey said, 'they wear trackers. You can see them sometimes, sewn into the back of their shirts. They transmit their GPS position, their heart rates, their temperature. You can see how many sprints they're making, you can tell how they're moving around the pitch. If the sensor's in their boot, you can tell how often they're kicking the ball, and how hard.'

And when a player was starting to tire, Casey thought, or when he wasn't playing to his usual standards. And that would tell you precisely how the betting market was about to shift five minutes before it did. Five minutes: a lifetime.

'Exactly.' Michelle was nodding. 'And this guy told Liam that if he built a backdoor to that data, the Tip Top debt would disappear. If Liam hacked his own company.'

'And he did it?' Casey asked. 'Liam gave them access to all the data being generated by the footballers as they were actually playing?'

'Yes.' Michelle's face sagged. 'And not just footballers either, loads of sports. The company was well protected from hackers, but Liam was actually working there. He'd helped build the wretched defences.'

'And Liam took this man's word for it? That the debt would be wiped out?'

'Yes. He can be a bit naive, like I said. And I suppose he also thought that he could shut down the backdoor if the money didn't come through after all.'

'But the Tip Top debt was wiped out?'

'Yes. Liam said he remembered accessing his account the morning after and it felt like a sort of miracle.'

'How did he end up in jail then? Did SportWatcher catch him?'

'Sort of. Even after all that, Liam still couldn't stop gambling. Not just with Tip Top, but with other betting sites too. The idiot. The stupid, stupid idiot! He kept on transferring the money, and SportWatcher caught him in the end. It was so predictable, the whole thing. They reported him to the police and he got three years. Three *years*.'

'I'm so sorry, Michelle.'

'It was his own bloody fault. But he's ruined his life now, hasn't he?'

'It's the betting companies that are to blame.' Leah's voice was quiet. 'These kids can't stop themselves.'

'What happened about the hack?' asked Casey. 'The backdoor?'

Michelle laughed drily. 'He never told SportWatcher,' she said. 'The man who called him up had said he must never breathe a word of it to anyone, ever, and Liam didn't want to get into any more trouble either. As far as I know, they still have no idea.'

27

'Okay, okay,' said Miranda. 'It's more than a coincidence.'

'But what does it actually prove?' asked Casey. 'Someone at Tip Top was blackmailing people, fine. But we're still no closer to finding out who's behind it all.'

Casey had brought Miranda and Hessa cappuccinos from the coffee shop. Leah had said goodbye with a defiant gleam in her eye, and Casey was sure she would be off patrolling another meeting that evening.

'I'll try to find out if Liam can tell me anything else about the man who called him,' Michelle had promised before she left the coffee shop. 'I'm going to visit him on Friday. You never know ...'

But all three of them knew: it was unlikely.

'We need to coax this person out of hiding.' As she spoke, Casey zoomed in and out of the stills from the Tip Top offices in Ealing. 'Trap them.'

'Difficult though, isn't it?' said Miranda. 'He seems to have quite an efficient group of heavies around him, and I'm quite keen not to attract their a— What is it?'

Casey had frozen, still staring at her laptop.

'This photograph.' Casey pointed at the screen. 'I've just realised that it was taken from the Meldon Group offices. The rooftop gardens. Not the direction I got a glimpse of – that was south towards the river – but the other way.'

Hessa leaned over her desk.

'How do you know?'

'Geolocation. Bellingcat – that team of investigative journalists – use it all the time to verify footage from places like Ukraine,' said Casey. 'I think originally investigative geolocation evolved because of a child rape case or something. Some utter scum was filmed abusing a child, and you could just make out the view from the window behind him. The idea is that you take everything you can see in that view, and cross-reference it to a map or satellite images or whatever you have available, and that way you can work out where it actually happened. And then you send the police around to the door of the child rapist. Or whoever else you might fancy sending.'

'Clever.'

'It is.'

'Doesn't it take forever though? If you're looking at some featureless streets in some random city you've never even been to?'

'It does, although if you get a posse together to trawl, it's much faster. It's a team effort essentially, almost a game. And if one of your gang knows a view anyway, you harness the local intelligence. You see here.' Casey pointed to the image on the Tip Top conference room wall, enlarging a map on another screen at the same time. 'You can see that rooftop there, and the way it correlates to that street, there. And then you can just make out a fragment of that church down there in the left corner.'

'Okay,' said Miranda. 'So whoever took that photograph has been up on Meldon's terrace.'

'Exactly.' Casey turned to the next image. 'And not many people have had access to that rooftop. So now I just need to work out where the rest of these photographs were taken.'

It took less time for her to trace the New York photograph.

'There.' Casey pointed at a map of the Plaza district of Manhattan. 'This photograph was taken from that building.'

'I'll take your word for it,' said Miranda.

The photograph was the classic Manhattan scene. The sun just breaking over the jagged skyline. Steam rising from vents. The middle of an icy winter, taxis and town cars hurrying through the dawn.

'So the first thing is working out the angle of the streets to each other, although on a grid like New York, that doesn't tell you a huge amount,' Casey said. 'But you can make out the Empire State building in the photo, and it's fairly easy to extrapolate roughly how many blocks you are from that. Then you just trawl the streets on Google Earth. You can see a cluster of American flags there and a launderette there, so pretty quickly you can tell that this photograph was taken from this building here.'

'And who owns that office?'

'Steady on.' Casey grinned. 'That office block is over forty storeys high. And it's divided into at least fourteen different workspaces.'

'Oh, excellent.'

'But you can use basic trigonometry to work out roughly how far above street level the photographer was when he or she took the picture. About the thirty-fifth floor, it turns out.'

'I always hated trigonometry. So who owns the thirty-fifth floor of that building?'

'That's where it gets annoying. It looks like it's a serviced office. Companies can hire it by the week or the month or whatever.'

'So ...'

'Fortunately for us,' said Casey, 'Bellingcat and his lot more or less invented chronolocation too.'

'Chronowhat?'

'Not just working out where a photograph was taken from, but working out when it was taken too.'

'Casey—'

'You look at the shadows in the photograph. Then you line them up with things you can identify from a satellite. So if you have two trees throwing a shadow, you measure how long the shadow is, and where it points, and from that you can work out roughly when the photograph was taken. Time of day and time of year. 'Course, you can only do it when the sun's out.'

'Of course.'

'Besides, it's especially easy with this photograph.'

'Why?'

'Manhattanhenge,' said Casey.

'Manhattanwhat? Casey, you really need to get out more. Or less. I'm honestly not sure which.'

'The Manhattan solstice,' Casey explained. 'The city of Manhattan is laid out on a grid, which is tilted slightly off the east–west axis. That means that twice a year sunrise aligns with the Manhattan grid, and another couple of times a year, sunset does too. Tourists gather to watch the sun rise, looking straight down a canyon formed by skyscrapers.'

'Stonehenge for skyscrapers.' Miranda understood.

'The sunrise alignments,' Casey read aloud from a website, 'occur on two separate dates that bracket the winter solstice – one usually around early December, with the second in mid January.'

'Fine,' said Miranda. 'So when was this taken?'

'You can see Christmas decorations, in the windows there and there, so it's probably December.'

'Could just be late taking them down. I took my Christmas decorations down on Valentine's Day this year.'

'Gave you something to do, I suppose.'

'Shut up.'

'I will soon,' said Casey. 'But look. If you go back through Google Images of that area, checking the dates that each photograph was uploaded, you can see that this block here had scaffolding up for an entire year for a major refurb, and it only disappeared in February of this year. But there's no scaffolding in the Tip Top photograph, so we have to go back beyond the date it was put up. Then that shop there stopped being a Gap and became a homeware shop in August three years ago. And that restaurant there closed down just after Christmas three years ago. I found a short article about a nest of rats being discovered under the countertops.'

'Delightful. So the photograph had to have been taken in December three years ago,' said Miranda.

'Exactly.'

'And who,' asked Miranda, 'was operating out of that office then?'

Casey rolled her eyes in frustration. 'I can't find that out online. I'll see if Matteo can work it out.'

Matteo was the *Post*'s US editor, based in New York. 'I get to deal with Ross like all the rest of you fuckers,' he would whine to the newsroom. 'Except he starts calling me at four-fucking-a.m. my time. And that man at four a.m. on a hangover is actual hell, I tell you.'

'Okay,' said Miranda. 'What about the third photograph? It's the odd one out.'

Casey turned to the ugly apartment blocks. 'I'm not sure yet,' she admitted. 'Let me have a go.'

Hours later, Casey was no further forward. She pushed her laptop aside.

'I need to think about something else.'

Miranda waved a bag of fruit pastilles in her direction. 'Right. There are three routes to this person that we know about, aren't there? Tip Top, Meldon and Greville Polignac.'

'What do you mean?'

'Well, you need to get to the person at the top. So you're going to have to find someone to take you to him. Or her. Probably undercover, but there may be another way.'

Casey considered it, head on one side. 'Yes, you're right.'

'So, which route? Can we twist Nash's arm?'

'I'm not sure we can twist it hard enough,' Casey said, a note of regret in her voice. 'We have lots of coincidences, a lot of links between Greville Polignac and – say – Meldon's short-selling habits, for example, but Nash would probably be able to wriggle off the hook.'

'And Nash,' Miranda said thoughtfully, 'knows a bit too much about how we operate. He'd spot our lack of real evidence a mile off. Do we still have nothing on the CEOs of Tip Top and Meldon?'

'There's very very little about Tip Top's CEO in the public domain,' said Casey. 'Setting up the chain of shops was smart. Aidan himself bets through Tip Top quite a lot of the time, because they offer the best odds.'

'We know that Tip Top has accessed the data of that wearable tech company and swiped Aidan's intel,' said Miranda. 'So they're ruthless crooks too.'

'Our source is the very distressed mother of someone who's currently serving a not inconsiderable period of time in jail for theft,' said Casey. 'It's anecdotal, and unreliable at that. We can't use it.'

'Anthony would *love* the idea of Liam Briggs-Nelson in the witness box,' Miranda said. Then, becoming serious, 'Liam'd be ripped to pieces.'

Anthony was the *Post*'s lawyer, who would go through every word of any investigation before it was published, occasionally ululating with horror. He divided the rest of his time precisely between Le Gavroche and the Connaught.

'And then there's Blake.' Miranda spread her arms wide, palms to the sky. 'Who is unhelpfully dead.'

'Thoughtless of him.'

Seaweed coating her face, screams echoing in the night.

'Quite,' said Miranda, after a short silence.

'I need to know more about what Meldon does,' said Casey.

'Sure,' said Miranda. 'But who the hell's going to tell you?'

28

'I can't talk about this stuff over the phone,' the Russian shouted. 'Are you crazy, Casey?'

'Okay, okay, I'll come to you.'

'Perfection,' he bellowed. 'I'm having a party tomorrow night. You can be guest of honour.'

'Or something like that. Where's the party?'

'I'll get my PA to call you, sort you a hotel room. Or stay with me, whatever.'

'The party's in London, right?' Casey said, remembering a previous misunderstanding.

'Of course not,' he yelled. 'It's at the house in Venezia, *bella*. See you tomorrow!'

'Fine.' Miranda rolled her eyes as Casey put the phone down. 'Go to Venice.'

'It doesn't have to be Sergei. I'll find someone else to talk to. Quite a few people have left Meldon over the years.'

'But you already know Sergei,' said Miranda.

'And the flights to Venice are cheapish tomorrow morning.' Hessa had been listening in.

'I imagine I'll be the only person at that party who's flown out on EasyJet.' Casey grinned.

'Probably.' Miranda smiled back. 'But there we go.'

*

Casey had met Sergei Kiselyov during a riot in Paris. Students, enraged. Neither of them was there for the protest, but the aggression of the battle pinned them into a doorway. They stood watching police and protesters surge to and fro, heads bobbing as if they were viewing an especially furious tennis match. Out of habit, Casey filed a couple of paragraphs to the foreign desk.

'They're pulling the ambulances back,' the Russian had noted after a few minutes. 'That's not good.'

'They must think someone's got a gun,' Casey observed.

Oxygen canisters can explode to cataclysmic effect. When the ambulances roll away, it is never a good sign.

Sergei had grinned at her with an odd sort of recognition.

A short while later the storm had swirled past, leaving a trail of smashed windows in its wake.

'Drink?' asked Sergei.

And so they found themselves in one of the little bars off the Place de la Bastille, drinking red wine and cackling over nothing.

'What are you doing in Paris?' he had asked in the end, because the conversation had rolled in ridiculous circles and who and where and what and when hadn't seemed especially important, for once.

'I'm a journalist,' she said. 'I came over here to interview someone.'

And he paused for just a second. 'Well, we cannot all be perfect.'

Sergei ran a hedge fund, she found out slowly, specialising in something he called 'alternative data'.

'We take information from all over the world,' he explained simply, 'and we use that information to make money.' A wolfish grin.

'How?'

'Galileo,' he said unexpectedly, 'and his telescopes and Venice.'

'What?' She was laughing.

'Galileo – he was a genius, just like me.' He grinned. 'And four hundred years ago, he discovered the moons of Jupiter, and the phases of Venus, and the stars of the Milky Way.'

'I'll take your word for it.'

'And the reason that he found all these beautiful things was because he took this brand-new invention, the telescope,' Sergei rolled the consonants around his mouth, 'and he made it even better.'

'More wine, Sergei?'

'Of course. But it was very expensive, all this research, and Galileo, he needed more money. So one day he took the senators and the traders right to the top of the campanile in the Piazza San Marco – you know it? It's the bell tower of the basilica there, the highest point in Venice.'

'I've visited Venice.'

'From the top, the traders could see right out into the Adriatic. With Signor Galileo's telescopes, they could see the merchant ships as they came over the horizon. And from the flags on the ships, they could tell where they were coming from. And from the way the ships were sitting in the water, they could tell how heavily laden they were. And after an hour or so, still using their new telescopes, they would be able to make out the names of the ships. In that way the traders would be able to work out what was about to arrive in the market. Silks and spices, brocades and peacock feathers.' Sergei rolled the words around his mouth.

'And then what did the traders do?' Casey was enjoying his esoteric ramblings.

'They would rush to the Rialto,' he said, 'knowing that a ship heavily laden with silk was about eight hours away, and that meant the price of silk was going to fall. So they would short the price of silk. It was early futures trading, essentially.'

'Bring out your ducats.'

'Exactly. With his telescope, Galileo could show the traders the future. And it is the same for us. By analysing what we know today, we can make a guess at tomorrow.'

'Galileo ended up under house arrest though.'

'Indeed. Knowledge can be dangerous.'

'So how do you harness this knowledge of yours?'

He smiled and took another gulp of wine. 'In a million different ways.'

Sitting side by side under the cafe's striped awning, they gazed at the exquisite houses on the opposite side of the road from their little crowded bar. From the first floor up, the houses had the most elegant facades, with rows of graceful shutters. With a blaze of gaudy neon at ground-floor level – from the bars and the *tabacs* – they looked like dignified courtiers wearing the bawdiest of shoes.

'And so you come to Chipotle,' Sergei was saying.

'Sorry?' Casey shook her head. 'Did I miss a step?'

'Chipotle is a very ordinary chain of restaurants mainly in Canada and the US.' Sergei was shaking his head as he poured more wine. 'In two thousand and fifteen, they had an outbreak of food poisoning – *E. coli*. Then they had Norovirus and a federal criminal investigation ... you name it. A disaster.' He waved wildly at a passing waiter. '*Encore du vin, s'il vous plaît!*'

'Not good for Chipotle.'

'Not good for Chipotle. Not good at all.'

'So you could tell that Chipotle's share price was going to fall?'

'Yes,' Sergei agreed, 'but everyone knew that already. How far were the shares going to fall? *That* was the crucial question.'

'So you sent someone to count how many people were going in and out of Chipotle?'

'In the old days, yes.' He nodded seriously. 'You'd send some underling to stand outside the Apple store and see how many of their customers came out with the new iPhone.'

'Hours of fun.'

'Exactly. But this time, Foursquare – you know the app? Lots of kids use it to check-in when they go to a shop, a park, a restaurant, what-ever – could produce that data. So long before Chipotle announced its results, Foursquare was able to say that their sales would be down thirty per cent. Because they could see from their data how many people had checked into Chipotle a year ago and how many people were checking in today. And just like that, we could work out exactly how much Chipotle's sales had gone down and how far Chipotle's shares were going to fall.'

'Clever. So you run a hedge fund?'

'I do indeed.' He grinned broadly. 'Campanile Alpha. Well, I wasn't exactly going to name it after Chipotle.'

Unlike Aidan, Casey thought, Sergei thoroughly enjoyed showing off his success. Standing outside his palazzo in the heart of Venice, she felt as if she had stepped back into the Renaissance. The house overlooked one of the wider canals, its faded pastel stucco reflected in the water. To one side, a spur of the canal led to a staircase, this house's own private exit to the waterways.

The peace of the surroundings clashed with Sergei's boundless energy. As soon as a maid had shown her into the house, he was striding across the grand hall. 'Casey,' he shouted, 'welcome to beautiful Venice!'

'Sergei, this place is incredible!'

The frescoed ceiling was thirty feet above her head and hung with an ancient Murano chandelier that dominated the room. To her left, a red marble staircase soared up to a gallery radiant with gold leaf.

'It's not bad, hey?'

'How long are you here for?'

'A few days, maybe?'

Sergei got bored easily, Casey knew, but each of his houses was comprehensively connected so that he could work as effectively in Venice as he could from Paris or New York or Sydney.

'Although I need to go back to Mayfair all the time just to keep an eye on them,' he would grumble. 'Idle buggers.'

'The struggle is real.'

'Yeah, yeah.'

Sergei was tall, with close-cropped black hair and a face made up of sharp angles. Around thirty-five, he was thin and fizzed with ideas. His very dark eyebrows turned up at the ends, giving him a quizzical look.

After the riots in Paris, they had stayed friends in a saw-this-and-thought-of-you way. When Casey was trawling LinkedIn for associates of Meldon Group, she'd felt a burst of relief when she came across his name.

'Why Venice?' she asked now.

A contented shrug. 'I like to climb the campanile with Galileo's ghost.'

'And you can't travel back to Russia, I suppose.'

For a moment, there was a deep sadness in Sergei's eyes. 'No,' he said. 'No, I cannot. What they are doing ... It is horrific.'

Sergei had an EU passport, Casey knew, courtesy of a Hungarian grandmother and a substantial investment in the Budapest property market. A golden passport, worth far more than its weight in platinum.

'I'm sorry.'

'Let's go up to the roof.' His natural bounce had returned.

The marble steps led them to a spacious terrace with glorious views over the terracotta roofs of Venice. The maid reappeared with a jug of some sort of fruit juice. 'I am reformed character,' Sergei announced. 'Until later tonight.'

'Delicious.'

'So,' he threw himself into a white linen hammock, 'what do you want to know, Casey?'

She sat down in the hammock opposite his and rocked herself to and fro.

'You started off at Meldon Group,' she began, 'and then set up on your own.'

Sergei blew out his cheeks. 'Meldon Group. Now, there's a name. Why are you looking into them?'

'Curiosity. What was it like working there?'

He grinned. 'I certainly learned a lot.'

'Tell me.'

'Casey ... You don't ask much.'

'Please, Sergei.'

He swallowed some fruit juice and grimaced. Standing up, he stepped over to a small fridge and removed a bottle of vodka. Casey shook her head when he waved it at her. He shrugged and poured himself a large measure.

'You must be careful, Casey. Meldon ... They are not good people.'

'I am being careful. I just need to understand who they are. Tell me.'

A slug of vodka. 'Where to begin? Okay, as you probably already know, Meldon's a quant fund specialising in alternative data. So that means it hoovers up datasets from everywhere and uses that information to generate alpha – that's the ability to beat the market. In hedge funds, if the market goes up five per cent, you need to be going up twenty per cent. If it falls ten per cent, you're okay if you only drop five per cent, right?'

As he spoke, he started to perk up. Sergei always enjoyed telling a story.

'Not that I ever drop five per cent,' he went on airily. 'But others …'

'Of course, Sergei.' Casey rolled her eyes at him.

'So, okay. Meldon gets its intel from all over the place. Satellites, so they can monitor activity in – say – ports, because that tells you a lot about how an economy is doing. The R number was worth a fortune during the Covid pandemic, although a lot of the quant funds did very badly at that time because it was so' – a frenetic gesture – 'not like anything that had gone before. And then there's oil.'

'What about oil?'

'The oil market tells you a lot about what the world economy is doing.' Sergei waved his glass of fruit juice wildly. 'Most of the time, the more oil the world is using, the better the economy is doing. But because most of the figures are announced by governments, that means the information is usually crap and definitely out of date.'

Casey thought of Aidan and his casual dismissal of ten-second-old football data.

'So what do you do instead?'

'Well, because the data is shit, there are specialist companies that track the oil market,' Sergei said. 'So, for example, they track heat spots all over the world. When you extract oil, you flare off the natural gas. So if rebels in Libya storm an oilfield, and the heat spot disappears, you know they've shut down production, and from that, you work out what will happen to the oil price.'

'And how do you get this data?'

'Hedge funds buy it,' he said simply. 'So if you're running a company that sells anything from shoes to bananas to sports cars, you can package up your data and sell it to a hedge fund. Because if the sales figures for Ferraris suddenly go through the roof, someone somewhere is making a lot of money.'

'And they use that to extrapolate …'

'Exactly. Nowadays, if you're smart and you've got a start-up,' said Sergei, 'you price in the value of your data from the beginning.'

And Tip Top, Casey thought, was squeezing every last drop of value out of its data.

'What's it worth?' she asked Sergei. 'All this precious data?'

'It depends,' he said, 'on how detailed it is – like the credit card info for fifty thousand people isn't that interesting, but the credit card info for five million is. And then there's how often it is published. Once every three months isn't that interesting, once an hour is. And if it correlates very closely to the value of a share price or something, then you're going to be making a lot of money. If someone offers us – say – five years of data, and by going back through it, we can see that every time their data predicts that the value of copper is going to rise, the value of copper does indeed go for the moon, then you're in business. We are definitely going to want your next five years of data.'

'So how much?'

'A few thousand dollars for some datasets,' another grin, 'and a few million for others. And then, of course, you can sell your data to ten thousand different hedge funds. Why do you think every single website you ever visit asks for permission to use your data?'

'I hadn't really thought about it like that.'

'Nope.' Sergei looked out happily over the Venetian rooftops. 'People really don't.'

A few hours later, the party was well under way. 'Carnival-themed,' Sergei's PA had informed Casey tersely, 'although obviously I've told him that the carnival isn't on for months.'

'Obviously.' Casey grinned.

The beautiful rooms were filled with swirls of feathers, spectacular hats, silk capes embroidered in scarlet and indigo and gold. The rising babble of Italian clashed with the eerie blankness of the masks. Champagne spattered the marble floor.

'I've always thought that carnival,' Sergei said, 'should be all year round.'

'How do you know all these people?'

'I meet them here and there.' He waved his hand. 'Doorways in Paris, or wherever. Come this way. It's too hot in here.'

They took the little flight of stone steps that led down to the spur of the canal. Two boats were tied up there, bobbing gently in the darkness.

'Imagine,' Casey said wistfully, 'whisking through the night to your lover.'

'The canal doesn't smell too bad at the moment either,' Sergei said unromantically. 'It was terrible a couple of days ago.'

They sat on the steps, a bottle of limoncello between them.

'What were they really like then, at Meldon?'

'Casey, I think I preferred it when you were talking about love and romance.'

'Tell me about Meldon.'

'After I left, I had a posse of men following me around for months.' Sergei poured them a glass of limoncello each.

'Private detectives?'

'Ex-spooks, I guess. Hedge funds live in fear of someone stealing their codes – signals, they call them.'

'But you hadn't taken the codes?'

'No.' Outrage crossed his face, then he relaxed back into a smile. 'But at the same time, I had come up with most of their best ones, and it wasn't like they could extract them from my brain, although I am sure they would have liked to give it a try.'

'They weren't happy when you left?'

'They hate it when anyone leaves.' Sergei's accent thickened. 'Paranoid, you know? And they made my life hell for a long time afterwards. I wouldn't mess with these people, Casey. They are not good people. Not good at all. They still … I know they are still on manoeuvres.'

'Where do they get their data from, then?'

'Meldon? Like I said, all over the place, same as us.'

'And it is all legit?'

There was a long pause. Sergei was watching the light flickering over the water. 'Some guys are just after money. Fair enough. Like me, I guess. But some want more. Some are after power. Meldon ... It wasn't just about money. There was more. They wanted to know everything.' He brightened. 'Mind you, I'm not sure British newspapers are in any position to lecture hedge funds on stealing information. And the *Post* flogs off its readers' data to anyone who asks.'

'Sergei.'

'Casey.'

'Meldon broke the rules, then?'

'I could not swear to it.'

'But they must have compliance officers, like everyone else.'

'Sure, everyone has to have their compliance guys, who are meant to take care that a fund is following all the rules and regulations and blah-dee-blah, but do they understand everything that goes on? You're kidding me.'

Because those guys, Casey thought, only got to live in a nice house somewhere off the North Circular. If they could understand an algorithm in the way Sergei could, they too would be spending a couple of days at their palazzo in Venice before skipping on to New York or Sydney or Bali.

'You collect houses, don't you? That's your thing.'

'Well, yeah.' He peered up at the stucco walls. 'They're not going anywhere. Although this one might if they don't get their shit together with that flood barrier. And they're so pretty, don't you think?'

'Do you believe that Meldon steals data?'

'In a company like that, no one knows what anyone else is working on. They ban the teams from talking to each other, even when they're outside of the office. So, yeah, they could be.'

'Who's behind Meldon?'

'I don't know,' said Sergei. 'I know the CEO and the guys who ran the day-to-day stuff, but the main brain behind it all?' A shrug. 'I've never been certain ...'

'You must have some idea.'

'Nope.' He shook his head.

'I need a name,' she insisted.

'I can try,' he said. 'But honestly, no one at Meldon knew who it was.'

'I think the person behind Meldon is dangerous.' Casey looked Sergei straight in the eye. 'I'm investigating a series of deaths connected to that hedge fund and a couple of other organisations, too. I need to know who is behind Meldon.'

Sergei stared at his glass of limoncello. 'Tell me, then,' he said. 'Tell me what I can do to help.'

And so she told him.

When she had finished, he grinned at her.

'You'll do it?'

'Yes, Casey, I'll do it.'

'Thank you, Sergei.'

He checked his mobile and stood up. 'Someone has just arrived,' he said. 'Someone who would like to talk to you.'

'I'm exhausted,' said Casey. 'I might call it a night.'

'Casey. It's a beautiful night in Venice. Live a little.'

They walked up the steps and back into the house. Inside, the volume had risen, the rooms a riot of silks and satins. Before they entered, Casey tied her mask over her face, twirling the ribbons through her fingers. It was a *volto*, the classic Venetian mask in smooth white porcelain. There was gilded filigree around the eyes and the china lips were painted gold.

She had found the mask lying on her bed earlier, blank and promising. Beside it was an exquisite crimson dress and cloak. Slipping them on, she had danced, half doll, half human, laughing expressionlessly before the mirror.

Now Sergei was leading her across to a tall figure. A man, his *volto* painted in scarlet and green. There was a tricorn on his head and a gold brocade cloak flowed from his shoulders.

'My lady.' An elaborate bow.

'Who ...' But Casey was laughing, swept away by the carnival madness.

'A dance, madam?'

She allowed herself to be led onto the dancefloor. She felt protected by the mask, smiling to herself under the porcelain.

It didn't take long to guess who this was. The man moved with an athletic confidence, a total certainty of his body's abilities. Below the mask, his skin was almost black.

She peered through the mask's eyes. 'Jackson?'

And he laughed and whirled her around the room.

'Miranda told me you were here,' he explained when at last they stopped dancing. Casey leaned against the wall, catching her breath. 'She saw that I was playing in Bologna and got in touch. It's only an hour down the road.'

'She would.' Underneath her mask, Casey's cheeks were aflame.

'I wanted to see you again anyway.' The mask lent his words a strange sincerity.

'Well, now you have.'

'Champagne? Might as well.'

Their eyes met. 'All right.'

As they made their way through the crowd, Jackson was very close to her. He put his hand on her waist and she jumped away.

'Don't be an idiot,' he murmured.

'That's your speciality, is it?'

'Casey.' He was laughing inscrutably. 'Why can't you relax? You're attracted to me.'

'You are attractive.' She shrugged. 'It doesn't mean anything.'

'And it has to mean something for you.'

'Yes. Perhaps.'

'Always on the hunt.'

'It's easier, I find.'

A man in a Plague Doctor mask prowled past, the long nose sharply outlined against the frescoes.

'If I'm with you,' Casey couldn't find the words, 'I can't be me.'

'My girl in the shadows.'

'Maybe.'

'You need someone who's happy in your shadow, then?'

'No,' she said. 'That's not it. But someone who won't try to shape me. Who won't expect dinner at seven-thirty and the laundry folded.'

'I have people for that.'

'That's not what I mean.'

'I know.' A Colombina in a half mask painted gold and silver danced past them. Jackson watched her twirl. 'Miranda said you'd lost someone.'

It was too sudden. Casey's eyes filled with tears. She spun away from him, crashing off a capering Harlequin.

'Casey.' Jackson caught up with her. 'Wait.'

The mask half blinded her. She tugged at the ribbons, but they were knotted, impossible to untie. She could feel her tears hot under the mask.

'Leave me alone, Jackson.'

'I'm sorry. I said the wrong thing.'

'I ...' She let him put his arms around her but turned her face away.

He held her steady, waiting. After a moment, she looked up. Behind the porcelain mask, his eyes were oddly compassionate. Moving without haste, he stroked a finger down the porcelain of her cheek, and then over the gold paint of her lips. His eyes on hers, he traced his finger along the edge of the mask. She felt a shock as he reached the warmth of her skin. Very slowly, he slid his hand down her throat until it was touching the top of the crimson dress, then he hooked two fingers over the neckline and pulled her closer.

'Come with me,' he whispered. 'Take off your mask and come with me.'

29

Casey stood outside the little cottage in Islington, next to a neatly pruned bay tree. She took a deep breath and pressed the doorbell firmly. Quick footsteps made their way to the front door.

Enquiring dark eyes: Esther Amaral. Casey could see Lucas Fairbairn behind her, looking nervous.

'I've had an idea,' said Casey.

'There are two ways of approaching this.' After landing at Heathrow, Casey had stopped off at Miranda's house in Queen's Park. 'One option is that we find a way to mess around with Theia's operation.'

'What do you mean?'

'We find someone to kick up a fuss about short selling or gambling websites. Probably an MP. A tethered goat, if you like. And then we wait and watch for a response. Thanks for dispatching Jackson to Venice, by the way. That was very thoughtful.'

'You're welcome.' Miranda pursed her lips. 'But I'm not sure that's a great idea. Our tethered goats seem to have a slightly unfortunate habit of ending up as mincemeat.'

'True. And we'd also have to hope that Nash Bexley comes to me with the plan for destroying the career of the tetheree rather than taking it to someone else.'

'When, for all we know, he may be spoon-feeding stories to several hacks,' said Miranda. 'That particular goat might get fed to Jessica Miller, for example.'

Jessica Miller ran the investigations team at the *Argus*. She and Miranda smiled at each other in public.

'We could find someone completely clean.'

'No one,' Miranda stood up and flicked on the kettle, 'is completely clean.'

'And if they can't take them out professionally,' Casey admitted, 'they may just take them out altogether.'

'Yeah, I'm not sure you're going to get people queueing up for that role. And I can't see how effective it would be either. I think Lucas Fairbairn could convince a fellow MP to have another go at short sellers, for example, but even if Nash then comes to you with a story about how our tame MP's having affairs with four constituents and a kunekune pig, I'm still not sure that necessarily proves our point. It's the same problem we keep having. How do we prove it's all more than coincidence?'

'Right,' said Casey. 'But the other option is a bit more complicated.'

An eye-roll. 'Of course it is. Tell me.'

'You're Casey Benedict?' Esther Amaral's eyes narrowed. 'You ... We don't have anything to say to you.'

She started to close the door.

'Lucas,' Casey called past her. 'Lucas, I've thought of a way we could get to them.'

Esther hesitated, glancing back over her shoulder.

'What is she talking about?'

Lucas froze for a second, watching Esther's face. 'I was going to tell you—'

'What, Lucas?'

'Casey's been trying—'

'You've been *talking*? To *her*?'

'You know I—'

'Even though she—'

'Esther, I know—'

'Lucas!' Esther's rage erupted. 'What the hell are you thinking? After what she did to us? This woman … She ruined our fucking lives.'

'I am sorry,' Casey muttered behind her. 'I—'

'Esther, I know how angry you are,' Lucas interrupted Casey, 'and it's completely right that you are.'

'So why did you talk to her, Lucas? Why let her—' Esther's fist thumped against the doorframe.

'Someone stitched us up, Esther.' Lucas's voice rose too.

'I'm aware of that, thank you.'

'Someone did all this to us quite deliberately, and I want to find out who it was and why the hell they did it.'

Casey couldn't see Esther's face as she looked round at Lucas, but the woman's back was tense, her hand clenched on the open front door until the knuckles turned white. For a moment, Esther didn't say anything at all.

'I am also worried that this person could be very dangerous,' Casey said quietly.

Esther turned to face Casey again.

'What?' A frustrated exhalation. 'What on earth do you mean?'

'I am investigating the activities of several organisations,' Casey tried to explain. 'I believe that Lucas's interest in short selling was enough to attract this group's attention in the first place, and that was why I was told about your relationship with him. I was given the story to wreck his career, quite deliberately.'

Esther pushed a hand through her long dark hair as she considered. 'Even if that's true, they've done their worst with us already. What could they possibly do now?'

Casey regarded her calmly. 'I think there are several deaths connected to these organisations, and those may be only the ones I know about. I think this person remains a very real threat. To you, to me, to anyone they target. We need to stop them.'

Esther tilted up her chin. 'It all sounds very far-fetched to me.'

'It is far-fetched. But that doesn't mean it isn't true.'

'Please, Esther.' Lucas took a step closer to his girlfriend. 'Let's just hear what Casey has to suggest.'

'No, I can't—'

'She thinks they killed Nick Llewellyn.'

Esther stopped. 'Nick Llewellyn? That guy who …'

'Yes,' said Lucas. 'The man we used to talk to at Holloway Road.'

'But … why? Why would they do that?'

'We don't know,' said Lucas. 'Look, it could all be bullshit. I have no idea anymore. But whatever you think of Casey, she is a good investigative journalist. And if she believes there is something bad going on, maybe we should …'

'Nick Llewellyn,' Esther said slowly, and Casey could see a sort of affection emerging. 'But he was a sweetheart. Do you remember? He would …'

Nick always had charm, Casey thought.

'Yes,' said Lucas. 'Nick wasn't a threat to anyone. You saw him.'

'And they *murdered* him?'

'That's what Casey believes.'

Esther tapped her fingers against the front door. Then she pulled it further open. 'You can come in for a minute.' Her voice was icy. 'We'll hear you out, but …'

'Thank you, Esther. Thank you very much.'

'What's your second option, then?' Miranda had asked briskly.

'Well, we know they target problem gamblers. There's Nick Llewellyn,' said Casey. 'Then there's Liam Briggs-Nelson, the guy who ended up in jail after ripping off SportWatcher, the sports data company he worked for. They both ran up huge debts with Tip Top and they were both blackmailed.'

Miranda poured boiling water into two teacups. 'So it's likely there are other Tip Top victims out there.'

'Leah Mulroney messaged me while I was out in Venice,' said Casey. 'She wants to meet up with me ASAP. Says she's found a couple more people who've been targeted by Tip Top. Bear in mind, she's only been digging for a few days.'

Miranda raised her eyebrows. 'So what are you suggesting?'

'Well, it's obvious, really. We need to find someone who can run up a big debt with Tip Top.'

*

'Me?' Esther snapped. 'You want me to start *gambling*?'

Anger was bubbling up, only just contained.

'Well, there are two things we'd need you to do, really.' Casey tried to sound nonchalant. 'I'd need you to start gambling, and I'd also need you to apply for a job.'

'Apply for a job where?'

'You were a compliance officer, weren't you?' said Casey. 'For a big pension fund.'

'Yes, but …'

'Esther's looking into other opportunities,' said Lucas. 'I told you about that, Casey. She's had enough of that sector, wants to move across to …'

'Yes, but before you do that, Esther, is there any chance you could apply for a job as a compliance officer at a hedge fund?'

Back in Venice, Sergei's guffaws had rung across the darkness of the canal. 'We're recruiting for what now?'

'Campanile is in the middle of recruiting a compliance officer,' Casey had said patiently. 'I went through all the recruitment ads after I saw that you used to work for Meldon.'

'Are we?' The corners of Sergei's mouth tugged down comically. 'I guess, maybe. I have people who take care of that side of things, Casey.'

'I know you do – but I have an idea.'

A gondola had rowed past the front of the house as she spoke, sending ripples across the canal, piercing the darkness with sparkles of light.

'You want me to recruit someone specific to fill this role?' Sergei guessed.

'Someone very specific.'

'What's their name?'

'Well, I haven't actually asked them if they'll do it yet.'

'Casey.' Sergei lit another cigarette. 'I think one day I'm going to throw you in the Grand Canal.'

'Yes, but you'll do it? Sort them getting the job?'

'Yes, Casey. All right, I'll do it.'

*

Esther shook her head. 'You want me to go and work for a hedge fund called Campanile Alpha?'

'Yes.'

'I don't think I've ever heard ...'

'They're very low-key.'

'But that's not my sector, my area's more ...'

'You'll get the job, Esther.'

'And simultaneously, you want me to start losing money on a website called Tip Top? Running up massive debts on my own credit card?'

'Yes. It would be best to start that straight away, to be honest. It'll look better if you lose the money over as long a period as possible. And at the same time, you can update your LinkedIn profile with the Campanile job.'

'I don't ... I don't understand.'

'To be honest with you, I've never worked out what a compliance officer actually does.' Miranda had plonked two cups of tea down on the kitchen table in Queen's Park.

'They're in charge of making sure that a hedge fund follows all the zillions of rules and regulations that are out there,' said Casey. 'A sort of internal police force, if you like. Because the hedge funds don't want the regulators crawling all over them routinely, but at the same time, history has shown that they can't be left to their own devices either. The compliance officers have to report any breach of the rules to the regulator.'

'And what if they don't?'

'If the hedge fund is caught out doing something naughty, it's the compliance officer's head on the block.'

'Fun. So why's it relevant to us?'

'Hedge funds like Meldon and Campanile place massive importance on security,' said Casey. 'You have to if your main asset is basically a string of symbols and figures.'

'You don't want the algorithms walking out of the building on a flash drive.'

'Nope, you really don't. So they've built secure zones inside the offices, with incredibly sophisticated defences. People have been sued for breaking contracts, and one or two of them have even ended up in jail.'

'So what's the plan—'

'The point of a compliance officer is that they need to be across everything that the organisation is doing. Audits and all that. And to do it, they must have access to everything.'

'If you say so.'

'And Campanile must be a target for Meldon,' Casey went on. 'They were furious when Sergei Kiselyov walked away. He says they still send private detectives to follow him, and that's only what he knows about.'

'I hope they didn't spot you in Venice. But that means ...'

'Exactly. What if one day, they were trawling through the lists of people who've lost thousands with Tip Top, and they came across the compliance officer for Campanile?'

'But I couldn't go into hundreds of thousands of pounds of debt on an *app.*' Esther looked at Casey angrily. 'I've just lost my job. We're okay for now, but I have to be careful.'

'I know someone who will fund it,' said Casey.

'What? Who? You're insane.'

Casey had called Aidan not long after her plane had landed. He had sounded detached. She knew, by now, that he disappeared into his own mind when he was writing long stretches of code, so she spoke quickly, concisely.

'Sure,' he'd said distantly when she stopped speaking. 'I'll put up the money. No problem.'

'Gambling someone else's money is about forty-three different types of money laundering.' Esther still sounded furious.

'I know.'

'And I'm an MP,' Lucas howled, a wary glance at the street outside. 'I can't—'

'I know. Look, I can go away and come up with another plan.'

'Won't they think it's a bit of a coincidence?' he asked. 'It being Esther who suddenly pops up on their systems. Their last target's girlfriend.'

'They might,' said Casey. 'Not least because compulsive gambling tends to affect young men more than other groups, so she doesn't particularly fit the profile. But equally, they know that Esther's had a catastrophic few months, and compulsive gambling can be triggered by trauma.'

'Yes, and we all know who we have to thank for that,' Esther said pointedly.

'It'll all depend on what this woman is like,' Miranda had said, laughing, as she looked around vaguely for some biscuits. 'Of all the bloody jobs you don't associate with impulsive, erratic behaviour, I'd put compliance officers fairly high up the list. It's quite a tricky one to pull off.'

'Sure.'

'Can't we just recruit one of the hedge funders themselves?' asked Miranda. 'One of the guys who writes the algorithms for Campanile? Get him to offer to leak the codes after a losing streak?'

'It needs to be someone in financial stress,' said Casey. 'Those guys earn literally millions and millions a year. The amount they'd have to lose to Tip Top to be under even the smallest amount of financial pressure would be eye-watering. Someone like Esther can be plausibly vulnerable.'

'Maybe.'

'And the point is that we destroyed her life. They'd never in a thousand years guess that she'd be working with us.'

'Well, she may not want to. You've never even spoken to this person, have you?'

'No.' In her mind's eye, she saw Esther powering down the Islington street, off to race around the park. She saw the decisive stride, the head held high. 'But she's tough and bright.'

'She's a compliance officer, Casey. Her whole life is spent making sure that everyone else follows the rules. She's the head girl who dobs you in for smoking behind the bike shed.'

'Yes, but she's thrown over the rules and regulations to be with Lucas. There's a rebel in there somewhere.'

'Maybe. She may be regretting that anyway.'

'And the thing is,' Casey was growing more confident, 'despite everything that's happened to her in these last few weeks, Esther's … well, she's survived.'

Esther was standing by the pretty fireplace now, fiddling with some Art Deco candlesticks. Casey perched on the edge of an olive velvet armchair.

'You don't have to do it,' she said. 'Honestly – it was just a mad idea. I'll come up with something else.'

'Like what?'

'I don't know. But there will be a way. There is always a way. Besides,' said Casey, 'I've put you through quite enough already. I am sorry, Esther. I am really sorry about everything.'

'It was your job. You did what you needed to do.'

'I know.'

'And would you do it again?' Esther arched an eyebrow.

Casey hesitated, then raised her chin. 'Yes. I'm sorry, but I would.'

Esther was still staring at the candlesticks. Casey watched her reflection in the mirror. One mistake, that was all it had taken to splinter this woman's life to shards.

'You think I should do this as a sort of atonement, don't you?' Esther caught her eye in the mirror.

'What do you mean?'

'I mean that we did something wrong, and this is a way of redeeming myself.'

'I hadn't—'

'You had.'

'I hadn't thought of it exactly like that,' Casey conceded. 'These people are killers. And they exploit others when they are at their most vulnerable.'

'That sounds oddly familiar.'

Casey met Esther's eyes in the mirror again. 'Well, perhaps that is why I am asking you. Maybe it is the chance for revenge.'

'Repentance. Penitence.' Esther murmured. 'Revenge. All the old words.'

Her fingers closed convulsively on a candlestick. Casey was watching her closely in the mirror. There was something in Esther's expression. Part sadness, part resentment.

A smack of realisation.

'You didn't know, did you?' Casey was appalled. 'You didn't know that Lucas was still claiming the cost of renting the room.'

A flinch from Lucas, a glint in Esther's eyes. For a moment, she didn't say anything, just glowered at the candlestick. Then she put it down, very carefully, and turned towards Casey.

'It hardly matters now, does it?'

Casey's mind blurred with chaotic images. A cake box, beribboned. Rainswept beeches looming as an indicator flashed. Guinea fowl and pancetta and prunes.

Esther hadn't known.

'Of course it matters,' Casey said desperately. 'I never thought … If you didn't know, if you had nothing to do with the story, you should never have been named. Your photograph should never have been used. You should—'

Esther was looking down at her as she sat in the armchair. 'It's rather too late for that, Casey.'

'But …'

'But what?'

'Your family. Your job.'

'I'm not unaware of this, Casey.'

'I could …'

'What? Undo it all? Fix everything?'

'I could correct the article, so at the very least …'

'You can't undo what you've done, Casey.' Esther refused to cry. 'That's the point.'

'But—'

'No smoke without fire, that's what they say, isn't it? This will never disappear for me. None of this will ever disappear into the past.'

'I could clarify—'

'That just makes it worse for Lucas. And it doesn't … it doesn't fix me.'

'Esther.' Lucas's voice was hoarse. 'Please let her. I hate that you—'

'You and I know the truth at least.' Esther's voice was fierce. Half rage, half love. 'That's something.'

'But it was my fault,' he said. 'All my fault. I should—'

'No, Lucas. We've discussed it.'

'I'll change the article,' said Casey. 'I have to.'

'Don't you dare.' Esther spat out the word, anger bubbling up again. 'What you've done is unfixable. Don't try to put some pathetic little sticking plaster over it.'

'I'm sorry,' said Casey. 'I should have ... I am truly sorry, Esther.'

'Your arrogance,' she said. 'Your arrogance in assuming you knew me. That you knew what was going on in my head.'

'I got it wrong. Completely wrong. And I never knew ...'

'And now you have the gall to ask me for a favour. Because it's all about helping you, isn't it? You and your precious career.'

'I shouldn't have asked you. I'll think of something else.' Casey stood up to leave.

'I should have told you before you published,' said Lucas.

'Yes,' Casey said. 'You really should have.'

'I didn't realise,' he added. 'Not until it was too late. You didn't give us much time to think.'

'When you first got in touch with us,' Esther said, 'I panicked. All I could think about was my family. What it would mean to them that Lucas and I were in a relationship. And you'd have published that anyway, right? That we were together.'

'We wouldn't have named you if—'

'My family would have known anyway. Guessed. The photographs of the house, for starters.'

'I'm sorry.'

'So, you see, you can't just come in here and blackmail me.'

'It isn't blackmail.'

'Guilt trip, then. Because I don't feel guilt, Casey. Not a scrap. But you should. You really should.'

'I am sorry.' Casey moved towards the neat front door. 'I'll go now.' She fumbled with the latch.

'Stop,' said Esther. Standing in front of the fireplace, she looked almost regal, defiance in every move.

'What?' asked Casey.

Esther stared at her, emotions flickering across her face. 'How bad are these people? Really?'

Casey shrugged. 'Bad enough that I thought it was worth coming here.'

Esther nodded. 'They fucked up my life.'

'They couldn't have done it without me.'

'Okay.' Esther fixed Casey with an angry stare. For a moment, the word made no sense to Casey.

'Okay, what?' said Casey.

'Okay,' said Esther. 'I'll do it.'

30

Esther began losing money to Tip Top within a few hours. She was decisive, thought Casey. Tough. Once she had committed to the scheme, she embraced it with energy and determination.

'Use this phone to set up a Tip Top account,' said Casey, handing her a burner, a pay-as-you-go mobile that wasn't registered to anyone's name. 'Don't use it for anything else.'

'I don't know much about online gambling.' Once she had downloaded the Tip Top app, Esther stared with bemusement at the site's flashing lights, the welcome banners. 'And you're absolutely sure this guy will cover my losses?'

Casey had rung Aidan again and put the phone on speaker.

'But this man could be absolutely anyone,' Lucas protested after Aidan had said his piece. 'Sorry, Aidan, I know you're trying to help.'

'I'll get my lawyers to set up an escrow account.' Aidan spoke casually, still sounding distracted. 'I can get all the paperwork to the *Post* in a few hours. Along with an agreement that the money will transfer to you at the end of all this. It'll be rock solid, I promise.'

'This,' Lucas tugged at his shirt sleeve, 'is going to be very hard to explain to the Standards Commissioner.'

'Why?' Esther asked, once Aidan had hung up. 'Why is this man doing this?'

'He hates match fixing,' said Casey. 'It's an obsession for him. And we also believe that he's one of the people who's been attacked by this group.'

'You *believe*?'

'I'm sure. I saw it happen.'

'How dangerous is this?' Lucas fixed Casey with a stare. 'Really?'

'I've been very careful,' Casey told him. 'And I promise I will continue to be very careful.'

'But they must know you're investigating them?'

Casey paused. 'There's nothing at all to link us at the moment. And we are going to keep it like that.'

As soon as the paperwork for the escrow account was dropped off at the *Post*, Esther went to work.

'What should I gamble on first?'

'Go for roulette, bingo, slots. The games of chance. Long-term, you're guaranteed to lose.'

'Why does anyone ...' Lucas shook his head.

'This,' said Esther, 'is when I accidentally win a million, and we're last heard of heading for Rio, Lucas.'

'Can you even play poker?' he asked. 'We've never ...'

Esther's eyes gleamed. 'A lot better than you, chum.'

'Well, that's not what we want, is it?' Equally pert back. 'You're in it to lose it.'

'My excellent poker skills,' she pouted at him, 'mean that I can lose with conviction.'

'A bit like my beloved party at this evening's vote,' Lucas sighed. He glanced at his watch. 'I have to run, darling. Got a meeting. Good luck. Or the opposite of luck, whatever that is.'

'None of it is luck,' Casey said, almost to herself. 'Only statistics that permit you the odd beat of hope. Lady Luck, in the mirror backwards.'

'What?' Esther looked round as the front door closed on Lucas. 'Okay, where do we start, Casey?'

She shook herself back to the Islington sitting room. 'You have to make sure that your gambling appears realistic. Sites use artificial intelligence to monitor customers.'

'Hmm?' Esther was concentrating on the app.

'Online poker is a massive market,' said Casey. 'But mathematicians have created programs that can win fairly systematically, and bookmakers know that if the rest of their clientele realise they're playing a machine and have no genuine chance of winning, the whole massive online poker market will dissolve overnight.'

'And what does that have to do with AI?'

'The sites use AI to monitor playing, to ensure that a rogue program doesn't creep in. They shut down bots all the time,' Casey explained.

'Not much chance of them thinking I'm artificial intelligence.'

'Exactly. Mind you, they're also supposed to use AI to identify problem gamblers and stop them betting.'

'Not doing a fantastic job on that, are they?'

'Nope,' said Casey. 'That is one very specific area where AI doesn't seem to be progressing particularly fast.'

'So that's why you want me playing.' Esther's attention was still fixed on the little screen. 'You need a real person to lose this money.'

'Exactly.'

A few days later, Esther attended an interview at Campanile Alpha's sleek headquarters in Mayfair.

'One of the Campanile HR team met me,' she explained afterwards, 'and took me straight to a suite of offices. And halfway through, this Russian guy walks into the meeting and the HR guy almost had a coronary. "Hello, Mr Kiselyov! How *are* you, Mr Kiselyov? Is there *anything* I can help you with, Mr Kiselyov?" And this guy just went, "It is such a pleasure to see you again, Esther. Campanile would be so very lucky to have you working here. Would you please send my regards to your mother?" So, yeah, I think I've got the job.'

Within days, she was installed in the Campanile offices.

'Just as I was starting to enjoy my time off, too. So now what?'

'Now, you go about your business,' said Casey. 'Head down.'

'Doing a thorough audit of Campanile's activities?'

'I don't think you need go that far. How's your Tip Top account doing?'

'I'm down thousands.' Esther sounded cheerful. 'Had a particularly bad run at roulette the other night. My credit cards are in flames.'

'And don't forget to update your online CV.'

'Oh, I won't.'

31

'You've been staring at that photograph for two hours now,' said Miranda.

'I'm aware.'

'You're being obsessive.'

'Takes one to know one.'

Casey pushed back her chair and stretched her arms.

'That photograph,' Miranda told her, 'could have been taken in any suburb anywhere in the world.'

Miranda stood up and walked over to Casey's desk to take another look over her shoulder. Casey was staring at one of the three photographs on the wall in the Ealing Broadway conference room. Several concrete-built apartment blocks squatted dismally beside a scruffy road. They were five storeys high. Unmown grass softened their bleak lines, a few trees dotted the grass.

'Literally anywhere,' Miranda repeated. 'Any temperate climate.'

'Actually not. That sort of apartment block is called a Khrushchyovka.'

'I'm sorry?'

'In Russia, in the early nineteen sixties, hundreds of thousands of people moved from the countryside to the cities,' Casey explained, 'creating a catastrophic housing shortage. To solve it, the Soviet government created prefab concrete apartment blocks that could be put up incredibly quickly. It was all done under Nikita Khrushchev, hence the name Khrushchyovka.'

'I suppose the Russian winter would focus the mind.'

'Quite. See the shape of the windows, the concrete panelling, the balconies? Some of the residents of this one have glassed in the balconies and turned them into a sort of winter garden, by the looks of things. The Khrushchyovkas were only meant to be used for twenty-five years or so. Lots of them are in a pretty dire condition now.'

'How many of them were built?'

'That's where it gets a bit complicated,' Casey admitted. 'Hundreds of thousands of these bloody things were slapped up right the way across the Soviet Union and various satellite states. There were sixty-four thousand built in Moscow alone.'

Miranda started to laugh. 'Well, that should fill your afternoon nicely.'

Casey groaned. Her phone rang. Archie. 'Casey, you couldn't watch the Home Affairs select committee hearing this afternoon, could you? We'll need seven hundred words.'

'Sure, Archie.'

Casey listened to the Home Affairs session through her headphones and made half-hearted notes as she clicked through images of Khrushchyovkas. By analysing the shape of the roofs and the distances between the apartment blocks, she had worked out what this street would look like from a satellite.

'Are you trawling through every suburb in Russia?' Miranda grinned at her.

'If only it were just Russia.' Casey pulled a face back. 'I'm looking at Lviv right now, and I've got the whole of Belarus to do next.'

'To each their own.'

Casey's phone went. 'Hello, Matteo,' she greeted the New York editor. 'All okay?'

'I've tracked down who operated out of that office, Casey.'

'Who?'

'It was a bloody nightmare trying to work it out. It's taken sodding days.'

'Who, Matteo?'

'A company called Trelawney.'

'Trelawney?'

'Leather goods, apparently,' said Matteo. 'Not for long, though. It's folded.'

'Leather goods?'

'Handbags, I guess.'

'Who ran the company?'

'An English girl called Allegra Mayhew. She's back in London now. Was only over here for a while, by the looks of things.'

The name meant nothing to Casey. Thanking Matteo, she hung up and pondered the name for a few minutes. A bit of Googling revealed some minor press attention for Trelawney and that Allegra Mayhew was now working for a PR company in London. The handbags turned out to be eye-wateringly expensive and not – to Casey's eyes – very attractive. Making a note to ask Cressida about them as soon as possible, she went back to the Khrushchyovka.

It was many, many hours later that Casey sat up sharply. 'There,' she said. 'Right bloody there.'

Miranda rubbed her eyes. It was late now. The office lights were motion-triggered, and had gradually switched off around them. Only the newsdesk was still bathed in a glow.

'Where?'

'That photograph was taken in a suburb to the south-east of Budapest.' Casey pointed to the map on her screen. 'Panelház, that's what these blocks are called in Hungary.'

'How on earth can you tell?'

'You can see a little bit of that pedestrian crossing there.' Casey gestured to a patch of white paint. 'And that road sign there. And the angle of that telephone line there.'

'Wonderful.' Miranda rolled her eyes. 'And what, exactly, does this tell you?'

Casey spun the Google image until she was looking at the building on the opposite side of the road. 'That the photograph was taken from outside that building.'

It was another anonymous block, concrete and ugly. But this building was not residential. Instead, it appeared to be an office. There was space for a few cars to park in front of it, but no nameplate visible anywhere.

'I'll ask Irina to check it out.' Casey was typing an email. Irina was the *Post*'s stringer in Budapest.

'Right.' As she pressed send, Miranda leaned forward and closed Casey's laptop so that it almost snapped shut on her fingers. 'Time to go home.'

By the time Casey arrived at the *Post* office the next morning, Irina had emailed to say she couldn't find out anything about the Budapest office block. *Do you want me to bang on the front door? It won't take me long to get over there.*

Not yet, typed Casey. *Thanks.*

Any time.

'This man is bloody invisible,' Casey grumbled when Miranda arrived.

'He's not, he just doesn't want to be seen. Subtle difference.'

'A name. I just need a *name*.'

'Why don't you cheer yourself up,' Miranda sounded as if she were offering a cross child a cookie, 'by working out when this Khrushchyovka photograph was taken?'

'You can't even use chronolocation on this photo,' Casey grumbled, 'because the sun's not out, so there aren't any shadows. It's grey, grey, grey … Anyway, it's all just an interesting academic exercise at this point, isn't it? I'm not getting anywhere at sodding all.'

'I'm sure you'll think of something,' said Miranda.

Casey huffed then concentrated again. 'It was taken some time in summer two years ago,' she said a few minutes later.

'How do you know?' asked Miranda.

'Well, there are lots of leaves on those trees, for starters,' explained Casey. 'So that knocks out about six months a year in Budapest, give or take. But really it's because of the height of the trees. Five years ago they were a lot shorter. And that one there was cut down last year …' As Casey spoke, she sat up sharply. 'Miranda, I've thought of something.'

'I thought you might.' Miranda looked smug. 'In the end.'

'This guy,' said Casey. 'Or woman, whatever. He's very rich, and we think he enjoys the finer things in life, right?'

'I suppose we can assume that.' Miranda nodded.

'So I reckon,' Casey tangled her fingers together, 'that he'll have a private jet.'

'Okay.' Miranda nodded again.

'Toby,' said Casey. 'I need Toby.'

Toby was the *Post's* star data journalist; algorithms as familiar to him as nursery rhymes. Now he slouched into the investigations room, clad in his usual slogan T-shirt and torn jeans. Pale, with his head almost completely shaved, he chewed gum relentlessly. He had helped Casey out with stories several times in the past.

'What do you need this time, Benedict?'

'It's a slightly tricky one, Tobes.'

'What I love.'

By the time she had finished explaining, Toby's smile was broad.

'Dash'll need to sign off on better computers,' he said. 'It's a huge amount of data to crunch. Can't do that sort of thing on Microsoft Excel.'

'I know,' Casey matched his smile, 'a guy.'

'What,' Miranda raised an eyebrow, 'are you two up to?'

'Well, we've tracked planes before, right?'

'Sure,' Miranda agreed. 'Follow the tail numbers.'

Occidental Oil's jet on the tarmac of Omaha: enough to make a share price leap.

The CIA, shifting suspects around the world. Dubai to Afghanistan. Thailand to Diego Garcia. And Morocco to Guantanamo – or hell, of course.

And a small plane, once, flying in and out of a tiny airport in the Sahara.

Those big bold numbers, so easy to trace.

'We've used the planes to track the flights,' said Casey. 'But what if we turn that around and use the flights to track the planes?'

Miranda tapped her desk with a pencil. 'Come again?'

'We can buy the flight data,' explained Toby. 'There are companies that have been tracking almost every single flight around the world for years now.'

'And that helps us how?'

'Once we have the data, Toby can build a system that will identify which plane flew to all these places,' said Casey, 'on these specific
dates.'

'Because you know this person was in Manhattan around December
the fifth three years ago,' Miranda worked it out. 'And they were at
Goodwood in August last year, and Epsom in June two years ago.'

'And Budapest at some point in the summer two years ago,' said
Casey. 'And I think I saw him on the roof of the Meldon offices, when
I was being shown around by Gemma from HR, which puts him in
London nice and recently. There may not have been many planes that
followed that precise trajectory.'

'Although obviously it may have gone anywhere else in the world
in the meantime,' Toby interjected.

'But when they were travelling to Manhattan, the jet could
have landed at any of the airports near New York,' said Miranda.
'Westchester or Teterboro or anywhere, really. Same goes for
Goodwood or Epsom. To get there, they might have landed at
Heathrow, Northolt, wherever.'

'Sure. Toby's algorithm will have to factor that in.'

'And they may have upgraded their private jet at any time, so now
they're using a completely different aircraft. And even if this person
happened to be in London for the races in Epsom, they could have
landed weeks earlier and then stuck around for a while after.'

'Yup.'

'And we're not even sure that the person who took the photographs is the target,' Miranda added. 'It could be someone completely
different.'

'It could be a mate,' said Casey. 'A business sidekick. A wife or
brother, maybe? But I am sure it'll be someone close to the person
we're after.'

'It's a very long shot,' said Toby. 'Definitely. But it could just work.'

Miranda grinned. 'Well, you might as well give it a go.'

Toby worked through the night and the day and the night.

Sergei, laughing, dispatched additional computers to the *Post*. 'We
buy that flight data anyway,' he said. 'I'll get it to you.'

'It's depressing, really,' Toby said, as he downloaded the data. 'Thirty years ago, newspapers had access to more information than anyone else, and the fastest reactions to it, too.'

'And now,' Casey said, 'we're not even in the top ten industries on either count.'

'Nope.'

Casey was dozing on the sofa when Toby shook her shoulder.

'I've narrowed it down to eleven planes,' he said.

'Eleven?' she asked.

'A lot of private jets yo-yo between New York and London, appaz.'

'Bugger.' She sat up.

'Can we eliminate any of those planes?'

'You can certainly have a go,' he said. 'I'll send you the list.'

'Could you print it out for me?' She was thinking slowly, just woken up. 'With the dates and destinations of all of their flights?'

'Sure.' Toby shrugged.

A few minutes later, he was back with a sheaf of paper.

'Okay.' Casey stared blankly at them.

'So what are we looking for, Ms Benedict?'

'I'm not sure yet.'

'Coffee?'

'Yes.'

By the time Toby got back to the investigations office, Casey had the pages spread out on the floor.

'Honestly,' he grumbled. 'Printing out this stuff is properly Stone Age.'

'Shh.'

She straightened up.

'I need to know more about racehorses,' she said vaguely.

'Private jets, racehorses,' said Toby. 'Someone's living their best life.'

He swigged his coffee as he watched Casey work. She studied the papers, tapped on her keyboard, studied the papers again.

'This plane.' Casey waved one of the sheets at him a few minutes later. 'It's been in Paris on the first Sunday in October for the last three years.'

'Maybe it loves Paris in the autumn.'

'Your singing is terrible, Toby.'

'I know.'

'And then it was parked up in Louisville on the first Saturday of May this year.'

'Should I have heard of Louisville?'

'The Prix de l'Arc de Triomphe is run in Paris on the first Sunday in October every year,' said Casey. 'The Kentucky Derby is run at Churchill Downs on the first Saturday of May. Louisville International airport in Kentucky is seven minutes' drive from Churchill Downs.'

'Do you just memorise this stuff?' Toby asked. 'To one day score a memorable victory at the local pub quiz?'

'That's exactly what I do, Toby, yes.'

'So that specific plane probably belongs to a racing fanatic. And because of a few photographs of horses, you think your guy is into the gee-gees?'

'Yes, but crucially that plane's also been in and out of Budapest several times.' Casey read down the list of airport call signs. 'It would tie in with having an office there. Or some specific reason to be there, at least.'

'It's a Gulfstream.' Toby pulled up an image of a sleek silver plane. 'How delightful.'

'A G600,' Casey read aloud between sips of her cooling coffee. 'Now who the hell does it belong to?'

'It belongs to yet another bloody BVI company,' Casey howled as Miranda arrived a few hours later. 'This is like wandering around in an endless fog.'

'Not helpful then?'

'It operates out of the same small office in Road Town as Theia,' said Casey grudgingly. Road Town on Tortola, the biggest of the British Virgin Islands. 'So that's something. But I need more.'

'Where is that plane right now?' asked Miranda, after she had listened to Casey's grumbles.

'Athens,' she said. 'But it's been moving around so often that even if I flew to Greece right this minute, it would probably be gone by the time I arrived.'

'Even you can't pursue a plane around Europe,' Miranda agreed. 'You need to get ahead of it.'

'How, though?'

'It's very tenuous.' Miranda was reading through Casey's notes. 'I mean, I'm all for wild goose chases, but hunting down a jet because it's been to New York and London and Kentucky feels a bit ...'

'I know.' Casey looked mournful. 'I can't ...' She snatched the notes back off Miranda. 'Toby, I've thought of something.'

An hour later, Hessa handed them each another coffee.

'Melbourne Cup day,' Casey was murmuring. 'The Dubai World Cup at the Meydan.'

Miranda looked up. 'What are you up to now?'

'I couldn't see a common denominator,' said Casey.

'But?'

'On each of these race days – whether in Melbourne or Dubai or Paris – there was a jockey wearing identical silks. White stars on bright purple. And those horses are owned by various companies, which all operate out of the same BVI address as Theia. I was actually there when one of the horses was running at Ascot. Active Risk, it was called.'

'Active risk is a hedge-fund term,' Toby explained to Miranda. 'Then there's Seeking Alpha – another hedge-fund name. That one ran in Dubai a few weeks ago.'

'White stars on purple,' said Casey. 'Bright purple. Tip Top purple.'

Miranda was grinning as she read through the list. 'When I said make it less tenuous ...'

'I know,' said Casey. 'I *know*. But it's a link, isn't it?'

Miranda rubbed her eyes. 'Okay. We have Tip Top, Meldon and Greville Polignac, which all operate out of Theia-owned offices. From the photographs on their walls, you've identified two more addresses linked to those companies, one in New York, one in Budapest. You've also identified a jet that moves between these destinations. Furthermore, this plane travels to race days where Theia-linked horses run. So we are concluding that the plane is Theia – or someone close to them – and so are the New York and Budapest offices.'

'Yes. And that's only the tip of the iceberg, I'm sure.'

'How do you mean?'

'Well, the companies we know about are absorbing the most extraordinary amount of data, some of it legitimately acquired, some of it not. The more I look at it, I think that Tip Top and Meldon are just a way of funding the overall enterprise. Between them, they're pulling in probably hundreds of millions a year, but they're only one part of the whole operation.'

'The overall enterprise is what exactly?'

'I don't know yet,' Casey admitted.

'But whoever heads up the empire is a ruthless fucker, who quite happily kills off anyone who gets in his way.'

'Yes, and that white-blond man is either the head of Theia or else acts as his assassin.'

'And they've been using you as one of their tools? Whether it's to take out MPs like Lucas Fairbairn, or to run stories that they can profit from, or to hunt down troublesome match fixers?'

Casey winced. 'Yes.'

'Just you, I wonder? Or do they have a hack in every outlet?' As Miranda was speaking, she was reading through the G600's list of journeys. 'That plane usually goes to Budapest once a month,' she said eventually. 'And it hasn't been there for over three weeks.'

'I could ...'

'You could.'

32

The temperature was hovering around zero. Casey walked down the street, noting the familiar road sign, the telephone wire, the pedestrian crossing. The road was greyly quiet, the blocks of flats looking as if they had been plonked out of identical moulds.

In other cities, some of the Khrushchyovkas had been remodelled with colourful insulation and bright new windows. But not here, not these. These blocks were joyless and crumbling.

Walking back, she peered surreptitiously at the office building again. Frosted windows glared at the Hungarian twilight.

Nothing.

In the late afternoon, she watched as the office workers left. They were mostly male, with pale faces, the odd piercing. They dressed casually in jeans, scruffy jackets, trainers. They carried battered rucksacks and stared at iPhones. There was nothing distinctive about any of them, and no way of knowing what they were doing in the unremarkable building.

The next morning, she watched them arrive. Approaching them would be unwise, she guessed, the habit of secrecy deeply ingrained. And that was even before she crashed into the language barrier. She scuffed her shoe to and fro on the pavement peevishly.

She had been in Budapest for two days now. The very day she flew to Hungary, the Gulfstream had taken off from Athens and headed north. Casey had stared at her laptop with a surge of hope before the plane veered west, landing in Reykjavík a few hours later.

Iceland? Miranda messaged.

God knows, Casey messaged back. *Although I suppose there are a lot of data centres in Iceland. Might be something to do with those.*

Why Iceland??

Those massive data centres need a huge amount of power, and they can also overheat very easily. But Iceland makes so much electricity from geothermal and hydro that it's basically free energy. And it's obviously easier to keep a centre nice and cool in a country called … Iceland. There are data centres scattered all across the far north nowadays. Finland, Sweden, Russia.

Good to know.

At lunchtime the next day, Casey wandered past the office again. One man came out, walking towards a small coffee shop. A few more emerged in ones, twos, threes.

Thin blond hair, glasses, black duffel coat, bright purple rucksack, grey trainers.

Sandy hair, torn jeans, blue anorak open over a bright purple T-shirt.

Dark hair, clipped close, black trousers with a key chain dangling, lighting a cigarette, bright purple hoodie.

Bright purple, she thought.

Bright purple.

Tip Top.

She followed a group of them to the coffee shop, not understanding the fluent Hungarian as they bought sandwiches, hot drinks, crisps. Then she sidled closer to the bright purple rucksack. She could just make out a small logo. TT, with a lightning jag.

'Tip Top.' She grinned and pointed.

The man looked blankly at her so she pointed again, grinning brightly. 'Tip Top. My boyfriend uses this site.'

His eyes cleared. 'Tip Top, *igen.*' The Hungarian accent was near impenetrable.

'Do you work for them?' Casey mimed typing. 'Near here?'

'*Igen.*' And she didn't know if he had understood a word.

The barista handed over the man's coffee and there was nothing more to say.

Casey watched as the bright purple rucksack walked off down the street, and then she sat in the little coffee shop for the rest of the lunch break, watching for the small logo, the flashes of bright purple, her fingertips tapping the table in frustration.

As she emerged from the fug of the coffee shop, Casey's phone buzzed again: Miranda.

That plane took off from Reykjavík half an hour ago. It's heading straight for Budapest.

33

Casey sat in an airport coffee shop, staring into the sky above Ferenc Liszt Airport while demolishing a wide variety of Hungarian pastries.

Eventually, she was rewarded with the sight of the G600 skimming in with an ear-splitting roar, its tail number sharp against the grey of the sky. It *had* been heading for Budapest. She let out a sigh of relief. But a moment later the plane had taxied into the distance and she couldn't think of a way of identifying its passengers as they left the airport. Dozens of expensive cars whisked in and out of Budapest's international airport every few minutes. It was impossible to guess which one held the G600 travellers.

So instead of waiting fruitlessly, she tore herself away from the airport and made her way back to the Budapest suburb.

Surveilling the anonymous office had also proved to be challenging. There was no cafe close enough to watch from. There was no bench. There wasn't even any litter. She tried dropping a tin can with a motion-activated camera in it and, within minutes, a grumbling street cleaner had swept it away.

Instead, Casey had decided to present herself as an architect writing a book on the history of the Khrushchyovka. The day before, Mrs Horváth on the third floor had been delighted by the interest shown in her flat. Through the language of hand gestures, she had told Casey to return whenever she wanted to examine any aspect of the apartment.

Now Casey tapped on the door, a box of chocolates in her hand.

She had timed her arrival carefully, calculating exactly how long it would take to drive from Ferenc Liszt to the dreary suburb. The apartment was small and it wouldn't take long for even the most ardent Khrushchyovka fan to inspect every room.

Inside, Mrs Horváth's apartment was cramped but neat. There were two poky bedrooms, with the windows at an awkward height. The kitchen and sitting room were small and shabby, softened only slightly by the dark purple and navy wall-hangings made by Mrs Horváth herself. She had also made the patchwork quilts on the beds, Casey deduced from the proud gestures. The rooms were lit by lamps fringed by orange shades. After the blandness of the street, it was cosy and bright.

Casey and Mrs Horváth smiled at each other, and Mrs Horváth began making tea.

Casey had brought a measuring tape and started noting the size of the small spaces in a notepad. Every time she heard a vehicle in the street, she edged towards the net-curtained windows.

The car she was waiting for, when it arrived, was so quiet that she almost missed it. Mrs Horváth was just handing her a cup of black tea when she heard the expensive hum.

'Köszönöm,' Casey murmured her thanks, and smilingly made her way to the balcony.

It had been boxed in, making a sort of conservatory where Mrs Horváth could sit in the sunshine, safe from the cold wind. A cat sat in a patch of sun, tabby fur glistening in the light.

'Lovely kitty.' Casey stroked the animal as she peered down at the road.

A black Maybach, incongruous against the drab surroundings, had pulled into the small carpark in front of the office block.

Casey felt that surge of joy – or was it relief?

A smart Maybach, here, just over an hour after the G600 had landed. The right plane, the right address.

Probably.

Maybe.

Hope, anyway.

Sensing her tension, the cat leaped away from her, landing on the floor with a soft thud. Moving across to the windows, Casey caught a glint of interest in Mrs Horváth's sparrow eyes and turned back to the flaking windowsills, faking fascination.

She just made out the back view of a tall man disappearing into the office's reception area. Scribbling in her notepad, she wrote down the car's number plate.

A few minutes later, she bade a grateful farewell to Mrs Horváth and her cat, and scurried down the stairs.

One quick text to a freelance photographer waiting around the corner – *He's in the building, get in place ASAP please because I am not sure how long he'll be in there. Mrs Horváth is expecting someone to come and photograph her apartment. Take flowers!* – and she was hurrying to her hire car, parked a couple of streets away.

A few minutes later, she was on Üllői út, the long avenue that led to the centre of Budapest. If her target headed straight back to the airport, there would be no chance of tracking him any further anyway. She would just have to watch crossly as the G600 cruised away from Hungary.

But if he headed into central Budapest, this was the route he would take. She pulled over and crossed her fingers.

It was almost two hours before the freelance photographer texted her. *Got him coming out to the car. He's just left. Good luck!*

As she waited hopefully for the Maybach, Casey stared at the series of photographs sent through by the freelancer.

The man was tall and broad-shouldered. Late fifties, maybe. The hair was steel grey, and there were taut lines running from the corners of his eyes to the edge of his mouth. It was a face that looked as if it were rarely softened by a smile. She couldn't make out the colour of his eyes from this photograph, but he appeared tough, ruthless, very effective. The man she had seen on the Meldon roof terrace? Maybe. Then she felt a thud of realisation.

Coral petals and lavender feathers and a rainbow whirl of ribbons.

I'd like you to meet the founder of …

A tall man pouring champagne, with laughter in his eyes.

She had *met* this man before. At Royal Ascot, all those months ago. Dropping in on Nash's lunch party, Rosamund thrilled to see him. The founder of … The name floated just out of reach.

He looked tougher here, the Ascot sleekness rubbed away.

She texted the photographer again. *Take the long route home, in case they spotted your camera.*

Sure thing.

The photographer would be fine, Casey knew. Irina had recommended him. *He spends most of his time up mountains in Chechnya,* she had messaged. *Don't worry about him.*

Casey inspected the photograph again.

Who are you? She zoomed in. *What are you? And what are you doing here?*

It was easy to spot the Maybach when it purred past. Casey joined the stream of traffic, dropping in a couple of cars behind it.

The Maybach drove smoothly to Andrássy út, a spectacular boulevard lined with neo-Renaissance mansions and very expensive shops. A few hundred yards from the statue-spiked drama of the Opera House, the Maybach turned onto a quieter street. It indicated briefly and pulled into an underground carpark that had somehow been installed under a magnificently Baroque house.

Out of the corner of her eye, Casey saw a good-looking woman with long red hair walking down the street towards the house. A man trailing behind her moved like a bodyguard. The woman waved as the car pulled in and, as the carpark's security gate rolled closed, walked up the steps to the house. Fingers tapping on the steering wheel, Casey carried on up the street and then headed back towards Andrássy út.

Pulling over, she dialled a number.

'Sergei? I need another favour.'

'Another one?' He exaggerated his outrage. 'Do you want me to write your articles for you too, Casey?'

'Not right now.'

'Well, what do you need?'

'Do you know anyone who works at Tip Top in Hungary?' she asked.

'The betting company?'

'Yes. They have an office in the outskirts of Budapest. There's a group of companies who operate out of the same place, and I need to speak to someone who works there. One of your maths superstars might know someone?'

'Hmm.' A pause. 'I don't think so.'

'What about that Hungarian grandmother? There must be someone, Sergei.'

'Casey, I—'

'I'll be very careful.'

'I'll see.' He sounded dubious. 'Maybe a friend of a friend of a friend. Maybe.'

'Thank you, Sergei.'

A few hours later, she was sitting on a bench on Gellért Hill, overlooking the lazy curves of the Danube. Beneath a cold blue sky, the city – half the sprawling hills of Buda, half the flat plains of Pest – looked ravishing. Tourists and influencers – there seemed to be dozens of them all over Budapest – teetered on the edge of the viewpoint, grinning manically at their selfie sticks. One girl wore only a tiny red playsuit in the wintry chill, smiling fixedly as her friend took a hundred identical photographs.

Casey was so distracted that she barely noticed the man walking towards her. But as he sat down next to her, she recognised him immediately.

The dark hair, clipped close, the black trousers with the key chain: she had watched this man walking into the coffee shop earlier. The bright purple hoodie had been swapped out now and he lit another cigarette as he sat down beside her.

'Antonin,' he grunted.

It's not his real name, Sergei had messaged earlier. *But he'll know what's going on.*

'Thank you for meeting me, Antonin.'

A shrug. 'It is nothing.'

A pretty bride was posing in front of the viewpoint now. She was young, maybe twenty, dressed in an explosion of lace and taffeta. Her groom stood awkwardly to one side, trying to smile as his bride pulled a dozen confident poses. The photographer snapped hectically.

'You see them everywhere.' Casey pointed. 'These happy couples.'

A nod. The bride twirled away at last, the groom following hesitantly.

'So how long have you worked at Tip Top?' Casey asked.

'I've worked in that building eighteen months. But I don't work at Tip Top. That is just one part of the organisation.'

Antonin's accent was stronger than Sergei's, and his words were slower to fit together. Not a man, she guessed, who wasted time on small talk.

'And what do you do there?'

The dark brown eyes met hers thoughtfully.

'Antonin worked in Russian intelligence for years,' Sergei had told Casey before she went to the meeting. 'I've known him for a long time. He was on the cyber side. He left because he fucked something up, but I reckon he did it on purpose to get out. The group he was working for, they're not people you choose to leave, if you see what I mean?'

'I do.'

'He's been in Budapest for a few months, but it's very difficult now for Russians in Europe, so he doesn't want any trouble.'

'Sure.'

'He'll meet you, but he says to leave your phone in your hotel. And no recordings at all. And don't fuck him around because he will know and he will walk.'

'Okay.'

'He's very good. Russian analysts are some of the best in the world. I offered him a job, several jobs, but he wanted to go to Budapest.'

*

246

Now Antonin leaned forward, blowing out a stream of cigarette smoke.

'What do you want?'

Casey held his stare.

'I want to know exactly what that organisation is up to in Hungary.'

Antonin shrugged. 'Tip Top is gambling. The rest …'

'Tip Top don't have a public presence in Hungary, from what I can make out.'

'Sure.'

'What do they do, then?'

'Why do you want to know?'

'This person.' Casey showed him a photograph of the man walking out of the anonymous office. 'I want to identify him.'

Antonin looked closely at the photograph. 'The boss.'

'What's his name?'

A long silence. 'I don't know.'

'And what is he doing here?'

'I think it is better for you not to know.'

The words weren't quite a threat. A warning, Casey thought.

'I need to find out,' she said.

Antonin lit another cigarette. 'That office, it's several organisations working together. Tip Top, it just brings in the money for everything else. It's the ATM, almost.'

'The cash point?'

'The Tip Top money means the group can concentrate on other things,' Antonin said. 'Also they take what they learn from Tip Top and use it. On everything.'

'What do you mean?'

'Betting is easy money.' Antonin knocked ash off his cigarette on the edge of the bench. 'A tax on stupid, they call it. If a betting company lets you gamble, it's because you're going to lose. They close the accounts of people who win too much.'

'What are they learning from Tip Top, then?'

Antonin examined the glowing tip of his cigarette. 'Machine learning, artificial intelligence. I don't know what you call it.'

'Can you try to explain it to me?'

'It's looking at,' a wide gesture across the river, 'everything and learning from it. It's looking at the patterns across the world and working out what they mean. In the end, it's working out what happens next.'

'How?'

'Machine learning is computers teaching themselves, perfecting the way to carry out certain tasks.' Antonin struggled to explain. 'Then you take what they've learned and put it in all sorts of situations.'

Casey tried to follow. 'I don't ...'

'We look at business, social media, anything. Build up more and more intelligence. And then you can use that however you want.'

He was simplifying things for her. Trying to explain the impossible complexity of his work.

'Can you give me an example?'

A long drag of his cigarette. 'Okay, so, take Tip Top. They gamble on soccer, right? And you have years and years of Premiership games recorded already, so you set your computers to watching all these millions of hours of football, and gradually they learn to work out who will win.'

'How?'

'It's so many things,' he said. 'The computer might analyse the body language of the players, the sound of the crowd, the speed of the sprints. Whatever. It's up to the computer to prioritise what it deems important. And from that, you set the prices for betting.'

'I see.' That, thought Casey, combined with the SportWatcher data, would make Aidan's predictions look amateurish.

'Then it's working out who to target for their adverts. Gambling addiction, it can be genetic.'

'So you look for fathers who slapped down their paycheck on a throw of the dice?'

'It can be done.'

'What does the group do more broadly?'

'Anything. Everything. Developing systems that read the price of every product in every online supermarket anywhere in the world, and updates in real time as prices change. Others that analyse every company report published anywhere in the world, because when you pull it all together, you can know more about the economy than anyone else. Although companies, they know we do that now, so they leave certain words out of their annual reports. Words like "challenging". He grinned suddenly. 'Or "difficult". Tesla once put a section of their report in a Jpeg, and the computers missed it because they were only scanning text. Not next time, though.'

'And then you build trading models that operate off that information,' said Casey, 'and all the other data streams, and pull in hundreds of millions.'

'Exactly.'

'They'll know more than anyone else in the world.' Casey was speaking to herself. 'They'll know where problems are brewing, where economies are struggling, where politicians are vulnerable. They'll know everything.'

'Eventually, yes. Don't forget, there are only – what? – eight billion people in the world. He's starting to get a pretty good knowledge of who they all are, what they have and what they want. Or what they think they want. Or what he wants them to want.'

'And what will he do with that information?'

'Make a fortune, I guess.'

It was Aidan's model, Casey understood, but exponentially so.

'He's breaking the law though,' she said. 'He's taking major risks. And surely he already has all the money anyone would ever need. So why's he doing it?'

'Curiosity?' Antonin blew out a cloud of smoke.

Power, Casey thought. Because if knowledge is power, this man is on the verge of predicting the future. Of taking advantage of events that haven't even happened yet.

'He could do anything,' she said. 'He's obsessive.'

A shrug. 'Who knows? No one in Hungary is going to stop him. He wouldn't be operating in Budapest if they disapproved.'

Hungary, with its ancient ties that pulled both east and west.

They sat in silence, contemplating the city. Casey's thoughts were racing. She was about to speak again when she was startled by a Russian swearword. Antonin was shuddering. Before Casey had even turned her head, he was on his feet.

'Shit!' he said. 'Shit, we need to go.'

34

Antonin was looking towards the entrance to the hermit's cave, which burrowed into the hillside a few hundred yards away. Casey followed his glance.

A jolt of recognition.

It was the same woman she had seen before, tall and beautiful with long red hair flowing down her back. Twenty-five-ish, Casey guessed. She had been waving at the Maybach as it turned into the underground carpark. She wore a long white coat with an expensive hint of fur at the neck. There was a camera around her neck. A Nikon, Casey thought. Extremely good, and not cheap either.

'Who is she?' Casey asked Antonin.

'I don't know. But she almost always travels with this guy, wherever he goes. A girlfriend, I suppose. A wife, maybe.'

'We should go, Antonin. Thank you—'

But he had already gone, hurrying away across the wooded park. With her hand to her face, as if she were rubbing her eyes, Casey glanced back towards the woman and gasped as she found the camera lens pointed straight at her.

Urgent thoughts flashed through her mind.

Don't be photographed.

Don't be caught.

Get away.

Catching her breath, Casey turned away from the hermit's cave and walked north.

Who is she? What is she doing?

Casey's stride lengthened instinctively, speeding up. The urge to run was spilling through her limbs.

No.

You have to look casual.

You have to look casual, and hurry.

You have to hurry and hurry and hurry.

The contradictions flurried around her head. And there was another thought too, overwhelming everything else.

Make sure she doesn't follow Antonin.

Fighting the impulse to sprint, Casey sauntered along the path. There was a small market here, selling a tourist-trap chaos of post-cards and Matryoshka dolls and baseball caps. *Baseball caps.* Casey made for the colourful stalls.

The woman was fifty yards away from her now, and Casey sensed she was hesitating: to follow Antonin or hunt down Casey?

Casey slowed even more and the decision was made. Antonin, moving at speed, must already have disappeared among the greenery of Gellért Hill. Casey caught a movement in her peripheral vision: the woman was following her.

The little market was crowded, too small to vanish in, tourists moving slowly between the bright awnings of the stalls. Casey edged through the press of bodies, grabbing a baseball cap here, a scarf there, keep the change, bright smile. *Köszönöm.*

Hurry.

A windchime, mirrored, dangled from the next stand. Casey peered into it for a second. Behind her, the woman was making her way through the crowds. There was a gleam in her eyes, obsessive, manic. Clutching that camera, with a speck of grit deep in its heart. Casey had the odd feeling that this woman knew her from some-where, would hunt her forever.

Don't be ridiculous.

Casey scurried down the nearest path, scruffy trees on either side, glimpses of the river below. Yanking off labels, she pulled the baseball cap over her face, wrapped the scarf almost to her nose.

The woman must be calling in reinforcements, unknown faces, the enemy multiplying like bacteria.

Don't be photographed.

Head down.

Hurry.

Maybe if she could make it to the broad embankment, the river flowing quietly beside her, she could lose herself in the buzz of the city. Casey dodged around a patch of scree and allowed herself to run, sprinting down the stony track. But the speed only fuelled her panic, her sense of isolation. There was nothing but unfamiliar paths, the echo of footsteps, an icy wind tearing at her throat.

Run.

Slowly, relentlessly, the path was curling to the left, leading her back towards the hermit's cave. Casey felt disorientated, unnerved, lost in a nightmare of endless paths and unseen pursuers.

Where am I? Where should I go? And who – who – is the enemy?

The narrow paths twisted and turned, offering enchanting views of the city one second, a thicket of wintry trees the next. Just as Casey needed to run and run, leaving all this behind, she was inexorably drawn back to where she had started.

She had to find crowds, a swarm of people, but this park was empty; she was alone and a thousand miles from home. She abandoned the path and plunged sharply down the hill, her feet slipping away beneath her. Ducking past scrubby trees, twigs whipping her face, an ankle jarring, tree roots like traps. *Too fast, too fast, don't fall.* Until there, at last, was the embankment, traffic purring, everyday normal. Casey turned left, scurrying north up the river. Any minute now, she would be safe, a tourist again, looking out over the swirls of the Danube and wondering about a coffee. Any minute. Any minute. Hurry.

A swirl of white and a dash of red in the corner of her eye.

Her, again, finding her way easily down the paths.

And Casey had been spotted, a target, panicking.

Who is she? My phone, useless back in the hotel room ... No camera ...

Casey bolted, giving up any attempt at pretence. Fear was suffocating, a hand tight across her mouth. She slipped and the road slapped up at her. For a second, she skidded across the cold tarmac, skin ripping, hands torn, and then she was scrabbling to her feet, dashing along the riverside again.

I've got to know who she is. Who they are.

Her thoughts were the ricochet of a pinball.

Escape was impossible, there was nowhere ...

Who is she?

That camera. That Nikon.

The racehorses and the skyscrapers of New York. The roofs of London and the dismal grey of the Budapest suburb. What did they mean?

Faster and faster, Casey sprinted over the cobbles, trying to crush down the panic.

Was this what it was like for her targets? An unknown enemy circling closer and closer? Fighting to escape when a glance was enough?

Ahead, she saw a van pull up. A man glancing down the embankment in her direction. Was he ...

Find another way. Where then? Where?

She thought she could hear the tap of heels not far behind her, inexorable, unrelenting. She imagined the swirl of white, the flash of red.

A Medusa who freezes her victims to pixels, trapped in the light forever.

Delirious.

A sign – Buda Castle – pointing to the right. She sprinted up the hill as fast as she could.

And behind her, the van began to move again.

35

The gardens in front of Buda Castle were packed with tourists. The castle itself – once a palace of the Hungarian kings – gleamed above them in Baroque splendour. Casey sprinted into the gardens and jerked to a halt.

Crowds here, at least. Where to go, where to hide? The museum? A warren of art and beauty. But there were guards and barriers, and she didn't know the way through.

She stepped forward, trying to think. She needed a photograph of the redheaded woman, but there was no way of snapping her without a camera. Hunter and prey, all at once.

That driver would abandon the van and hurry here. Others would be on their way. Casey stared around frantically. She had only seconds.

To her left, yet another bride was posing, towering over her new husband in her six-inch heels. To Casey's right, an influencer was posing with a bunch of pink roses. As a friend snapped pictures obediently, the influencer threw them in the air. The ground was already scattered with petals. Beyond the roses, a tourist waited patiently for a clear shot of the castle.

Cameras.

In seconds the redhead would appear.

Casey turned to the influencer, praying that she spoke English.

'Oh my *gahd*,' Casey squealed loudly. 'Have you heard that Angelica Deneuve is in Budapest?'

The influencer stared at her blankly.

'I just ran into her! She's coming this way for a photoshoot in front of the castle! She's just signed up for the next Tom Cruise film, you know? And everyone's saying she'll get an Oscar for her work on *First Frost*.'

Tourists all around were listening now, edging closer.

'She's coming right now,' said Casey. 'Incredible red hair and wearing the most amazing white coat and black boots.'

She moved on, murmuring as she edged through the crowds, leaving the tourists craning their necks.

Have you heard? Angelica Deneuve is doing a photoshoot here ...

Just the most stunning red hair ... Yes, my absolute favourite actress.

She's got such a sensational look ... Opposite Brad Pitt, right?

It took only seconds, the buzz spreading from influencer to tourist to bride to museum staff. When the redhead turned onto the promenade, a wall of cameras was waiting. Casey saw the strange eyes widen, the hesitation in the stride, and grasped the few seconds of confusion. She raced away behind the cameras, running down the hill towards the river. But as Casey hurried towards the bridge over the broad River Danube, she glanced back. The woman was staring after her.

36

'So now we have photographs.' Miranda touched one of the print-outs. 'But still no names.'

'We're getting closer,' said Casey. 'I know it. And I met that man at Ascot, so he's got to be connected to the Greville Polignac lot somehow.'

She kept staring at the photograph. There was something about the woman's face that she recognised.

Something.

Casey had left Budapest as soon as possible, waiting only for the pink roses to appear on Instagram. She didn't have to wait long. Within a few hours, delightful photographs of pink petals flying through the air in front of Buda Castle's columned glory had been splashed all over social media. They were #hungarianheaven and #rosesinBuda and #baroquenhearts.

Smiling to herself, Casey had contacted the influencer through the investigations team's Instagram account – now changed to @iheart-worldadventures – and asked if she was available for a coffee. *I'd love to talk with you about a really exciting collab with one of my clients. Could be great for you both!*

In a chic little cafe just off Váci Utca, it took precisely three minutes to get the influencer to scroll back through her photographs to the shots of the fictitious Angelica Deneuve. The influencer cheerfully forwarded the lot to Casey.

Although it turned out the influencer's rates were higher than Casey's client could manage, they parted on excellent terms. When Casey left, the influencer was photographing the cafe's macaroons and asking how the manager felt about swapping lunch for exposure.

Casey zoomed in and out of the photograph until finally she exclaimed: 'I know where I've seen her! She was at Ascot too. I saw her talking to Nash. Just in the distance, but …'

Miranda glanced at the photograph again.

'She's very pretty.'

'Rosamund didn't like it, I remember.'

She lined the photographs up side by side. The man coming out of the Budapest office and the redhead at Buda Castle.

'Bloody hell.' Casey pushed the images away sharply. 'I need names.'

'How many thousands has Esther lost now?' Miranda changed the subject.

'Many.' Casey grinned. 'Many, many thousands. Also, I had another thought.'

'What,' Miranda looked resigned, 'was it?'

Casey had the printouts of the G600's flight path spread out in front of her again.

'There.' She pointed. 'In the summer, that Gulfstream spends a lot of time flying in and out of Ibiza, so I reckon this guy's got a house on the island. Look. A long weekend here, a week there.'

Miranda studied the printout. 'Makes sense, I guess. Do you want to go out there and wave his photograph around? Someone always knows.'

'It's not quite the right season for Ibiza,' said Casey. 'The pattern switches to Geneva airport in winter, so I guess he's got a chalet somewhere near there too.'

'I have got to get into crime one day. I could do with a scattering of luxurious houses around the globe.'

'You do have a highly transferable skillset.' Casey nodded. 'It is an option.'

'Tracking him in Switzerland's trickier though,' said Miranda. 'There are a lot of ski resorts around Geneva. He could be anywhere.'

'I'll take your word for it.'

Miranda had grown up with ponies and sailing and at least one skiing holiday a year, of course.

Casey had only been skiing once, helping her pursue a Bulgarian gun runner around Zermatt.

'I can't ski,' she had said before they flew out.

'You can spend the first day with a ski instructor,' Miranda had said airily. 'After that, gravity can be your guide.'

'Thank you so much, Miranda.'

'I'm just not sure how you'd narrow it down to the right resort.' Miranda was peering at the G600 printout.

'Not sure *yet*.'

'Who was this woman?' Miranda fixed Casey with a stare. 'And why was she photographing you and Antonin? How did she know to do that?'

'I don't know.' Casey's enthusiasm was starting to seep away. 'It's a problem.'

'Is your Budapest contact okay?'

'Yes, so that's something.'

Sergei had heard from Antonin. No, he wasn't worried. Yes, he'd probably get out of Budapest for a bit.

'I feel awful,' Casey had said.

'I told him we'd always have a job for him,' Sergei said. 'Don't worry, Casey. Antonin is a big boy. And he's dealt with worse than this, I promise you. Don't use your phone to contact anyone sensitive, by the way.'

'I swap burners all the time.'

'And wipe all your social media.'

'I never had any in the first place.'

'And be careful, Casey. Be very careful indeed.'

'Was she tracking Antonin and me or did she just get lucky?' Casey wondered now. 'Did she recognise me from Ascot? Are they watching me?'

'We have no idea how much they know,' said Miranda. 'Which makes it all very dangerous.'

'I don't like it.'

'Me neither,' said Miranda. 'I don't like it at all.'

Later, Casey made phone calls. Leah had found two more people who might want to talk about their experiences with Tip Top. Aidan had identified three more footballers whose playing patterns suddenly defied logical explanation.

'Someone's taken Blake's place already,' he grumbled. 'It's endless.'

Selina was: 'Fine, thank you, Casey. No, I haven't had any more thoughts about Nick, I'm afraid. No, put that *down*, Arlo.'

Jackson asked her to meet him at Mimi's that night.

Busy. Sorry. She was reading back through her notes as she texted.

Casey, come on.

Allegra Mayhew, she read in her notes. Trelawney.

Catch up soon, Jackson. Bye.

Jackson was typing something else, but Casey was already halfway across the newsroom.

'Trelawney?' Cressida raised an eyebrow when Casey arrived at her desk. 'I just about remember them.'

'Do you know this Allegra Mayhew?'

'Vaguely,' said Cressida. 'She works in PR now.'

'Did she set up Trelawney on her own?' asked Casey.

'I can't remember. Is anyone else mentioned in cuts?'

'Not that I can see, but I went through the accounts and some BVI company put a decent chunk of cash into the company.'

'And then lost it when they folded,' said Cressida thoughtfully.

'Did Allegra Mayhew come from that sort of money?' asked Casey. 'The sort of family that wouldn't mind blowing a few hundred thousand on a non-starter?'

Cressida pursed her lips. 'Wouldn't have thought so. Allegra works pretty hard nowadays. And her boss is meant to be an absolute dick. Not the sort of person you'd work for if money didn't matter.'

'Like Ross.'

'That's not a salary.' Cressida applied more Russian Red lipstick. 'That's danger money.'

'Do you know Allegra well enough to ask where the money came from for Trelawney?'

Cressida pulled a face. 'She might think it was a bit odd. Happy to give it a go, though. Let me get back to you.'

'Sure.'

Casey headed to her desk. After a couple of fruitless hours probing Trelawney's finances, she yawned and rubbed her eyes. Time to go home, she told herself. Time for bed. And that was when her burner buzzed.

37

'Meet me in half an hour?'

'On my way.'

Even before Sergei's warning, Casey had set up an entirely separate phone for Esther. For face-to-face meetings, she had adopted an old-fashioned tactic, writing down a list of locations scattered between Mayfair and the little Islington house for every day of the next month.

'If we meet on the first of the month, we meet at the Nereids in the British Museum,' Esther had read out. 'On the second, we meet by the Eros statue at Piccadilly Circus.'

'And if it takes more than a month, I'll post you a new list.'

'Post?'

'Have you ever heard of a postbox being hacked? Quite.'

Today's meeting point was a specific bench in Barnard Park, a largish patch of grass just to the east of King's Cross. After following an elaborate route to the park, Casey waited in the gathering dusk as commuters hurried past. Esther arrived in running shoes and Sweaty Betty leggings, bouncing from one foot to the other.

'I thought it was the easiest way to throw people off.' She grinned. 'You can jog down alleys, and that means no one can follow you in a car. And I'm fast.' Esther was enjoying her own strength. 'It would be very bad luck if they sent someone who was able to keep up with me.'

'You're wasted on compliance, Esther.'

'Oh, I know.'

'Just don't get mugged. What's up?'

'Someone called the batphone.'

'Who?'

'I don't know.' Esther's bounce faded. 'I'm sorry, Casey. I was at my desk at Campanile and I just panicked. After all our practice …'

'Don't worry. It's tricky all this, especially the first time.'

'I'm so annoyed with myself.' Esther grimaced. 'I just said, "Sorry, I'm at work at the moment and it's a terrible line. Can you call me later?"'

'Which is perfect,' Casey said soothingly. 'And they will call back, Esther. They've taken the bait, which is just what we wanted. What sort of voice was it?'

'Just ordinary. I don't … A normal man's voice.'

Normal to Esther was North London middle-class, thought Casey. Not a regional accent, then. No foreign intonations.

'Maybe leave the burner at home from now on,' said Casey. 'Then you know you'll be able to speak when they call. I always feel self-conscious anyway, on those calls. You don't need your new Campanile buddies listening in either.'

'You know how it …'

'You can do all the practice calls in the world,' Casey smiled at her, 'but when it's real …'

'Won't they think it's weird that I have two phones?'

'If you were a real problem gambler,' Casey explained, 'you might well be hiding a phone from Lucas, have various secret email accounts and so on.'

'I suppose.' She sounded deflated.

'You don't have to do this, Esther, if you're finding it all too stressful. You can just forward the calls on to me, and I'll deal with everything.'

'You can't take over yet. If they are going to ask me to do something to Campanile, you won't know enough about how the company operates. And all the compliance stuff – you don't know any of that either.'

'I can learn. And I am sure Sergei would let me look around Campanile.'

'No.' Esther was decisive. 'I'll do the first call and see what they want. You can always take over later.'

'Okay. And don't forget to record the call.'

'I won't. I want to get these buggers.'

'Go home now, then,' said Casey. 'Wait for the next call.'

38

Even though she knew Esther had left the burner at home, Casey spent the next day staring at her mobile.

She jumped when a message came through. Jackson. *Mimi's was awesome. You should have come.*

Don't you ever work? she messaged back. *I mean, play football.*

Yeah, yeah. I might go again tonight. Come? Landon says hi and better luck getting me killed next time.

Casey didn't answer, just sat fiddling with her silver necklace. Eventually, she made her way to Cressida's desk. It was Fashion Week and barely any of the team were in. Popping into the office between shows, Cressida wore Isabel Marant and a harassed expression.

'Where do I casually run into Allegra Mayhew, Cressida?'

'You don't.' Cressida glanced at her watch. 'She'll be flat out like the rest of us this week.'

'Tonight.' Casey was unabashed. 'Where will she be?'

There was a stack of invitations on Cressida's desk. Making an outraged noise, she grabbed them while simultaneously clicking on her calendar.

'It's the Solenne party tonight and Allegra's company does the PR for it. So that's where she'll be.'

'Great,' said Casey. 'Can I nick your invite?'

'No chance. It's non-transferable and the Solenne party is … *it.*'

'Cressida, there will be loads of parties tonight and there's no way you can get round them all. Please?'

'I'd give it to you.' Cressida looked at her watch again. 'But the Solenne security team makes the secret service look like sloppy amateurs. You'd never get in, and even if you did, you'd be booted straight out again. Plus Allegra won't have time to sit and natter tonight. She'll be handling all the celebs.'

A thought floated into Casey's mind.

'Okay, no worries.'

Cressida eyed her suspiciously. 'What, exactly, are you planning?'

'Nothing.' Casey grinned. 'I'll see you later.'

'It's interesting.' Casey grinned at Cressida in a mirror a few hours later. 'Allegra really does seem to have all the time in the world to chat to me.'

'You,' said Cressida, indistinctly because she was applying lipstick, 'are a ratbag.'

'True.' Casey stroked on another layer of mascara and then reached for one of the Solenne-branded hand towels. 'So very true.'

'I knew you'd want to see me again,' Jackson had laughed down the phone when Casey called him. 'Knew it.'

'It's work,' she said.

'Any excuse.'

'Okay, it's fun too.'

'Exactly.'

'But only fun. And you have to keep your top on.'

'Casey. Fine.'

She had explained what she needed from him and then sat waiting. She could imagine the phone call. Jackson's PR team, in that dismissive tone. *Jackson, yeah? He's around, might want to pop by.* And Allegra's team, simply delighted to help.

As they arrived, Jackson posed in front of the banner with the Solenne branding over and over again, so that no one could miss it. The snappers loved it. *Over here, Jackson. Big smile, yeah?*

Casey loitered to one side of the frenzy, well out of the way of the photographers. She identified Allegra easily from a snap she'd found on her agency's website. Allegra looked delighted by the coup.

It was so easy to drift into conversation with her.

'*Love* your handbag.'

'Oh, thank you so much. I designed it myself actually.'

'No way! That's amazing.'

Casey let the conversation drift in circles, because Allegra would want to keep Jackson's maybe-girlfriend or PA or whoever she was entertained while the cameras flashed, and soon the PR was telling Casey all about her previous short-lived venture.

'It didn't work out in the end, which was a shame. But we had a lot of fun.'

'Did you run it by yourself?' Casey asked idly, eyes on Jackson.

'Oh, no, with an old friend of mine. We did it together.'

'Who was she?' And she kept her eyes vague as Allegra hesitated. Hesitated and then thought, what did it matter? Hesitated, and remembered she wanted this conversation to go on for as long as possible.

'A friend of mine called Rosamund,' said Allegra. 'Rosamund Bexley.'

And the shock ran all the way down Casey's spine.

39

Thirty-six hours later, Casey was waiting obediently in the chill of Speakers' Corner. The traffic throbbed around Marble Arch.

7.30 a.m., the message had read late last night and Esther was always punctual.

Casey called Miranda while she waited.

'Do we really have to do this thing with Esther now?' Miranda was saying. 'If we already know roughly who's behind Theia.'

'But we *don't* know who is behind it.'

'We have Rosamund Bexley in New York three years ago. She's either Theia or she's very close to them.'

'The handbag company had been wound down by then, but it still held the lease on that building. Someone else could just have been subletting the space.'

'It's not going to be a coincidence though, is it? We've got enough clues now. This thing with Esther, I don't—'

'It wasn't Rosamund who took those photographs,' Casey said stubbornly. 'It's that redhead, and we still have no idea who she is.'

'Have you worked out who Rosamund's parents are? If she has any siblings?'

'No,' said Casey. 'If it's Rosamund's father who heads Theia, I can't find anything about him anywhere. I don't even know what his name is.'

'The marriage certificate should have her maiden name,' said Miranda. 'And what about her birth certificate?'

'I know,' said Casey impatiently. 'But they didn't get married in this country, and I can't find a birth certificate either. I don't think she was born here. I haven't been able to work out where …'

'Archie must know where Nash got married. Nash was his bloody boss then.'

'I asked. He doesn't. He remembers that they went off somewhere abroad but no idea where. He said Rosamund's father was obsessed with privacy so the wedding was tiny.'

Casey had felt a pang when she heard that. Hyacinths twisting towards a slanting winter light. Love, and the wedding he wanted.

'It won't be impossible to track him down,' said Miranda.

'But who's going to tell us? We certainly won't get it out of Nash or Rosamund. It might be hard, Miranda. Impossible, even.'

Miranda sighed. 'What did Archie know about the father, then?'

Archie had chewed a biro as he thought back. 'I never met her father,' he said slowly. 'Nash was in awe of him. Wary, too. Rosamund was the same, now I think about it.'

'What was his name?'

Archie sucked on his lower lip, tapping the biro on his desk. He shook his head.

'But Nash was nervous of him?'

'Nash'd sort of try and laugh about the old man when he and Rosamund were summoned for a weekend or whatever. But you could tell that they were dancing to his tune.'

'And then Nash went to work for him?'

'Well, he went to work for Greville Polignac. I didn't know there was a link between Greville Polignac and Rosamund's family until now.'

'Can you remember anything else about her family, Archie? It's important.'

'I'm trying, Casey. But it was a long time ago.'

'Anything at all.'

Archie stared at his biro. 'He was obsequious – Nash. He was the son-in-law, marrying into a very rich family, and he knew his place. Sycophantic, I suppose. He rang me up once after he'd left here, actually. When you and Miranda were doing one of your big investigations. Said I had to get Dash to pull it, because it involved a client of his and you'd got the wrong end of the stick. Of course, I told him I couldn't. And he would have known I couldn't, so I don't know why he even asked.'

'That's odd,' said Casey. 'Which story?'

Archie muttered in frustration. 'I can't remember.'

'Do you have any way of looking it up?'

'Can't think how.'

'Please try.'

'I will. Nash really pushed me, too. He sounded ...' Archie paused. 'He sounded scared.'

As she told Miranda about her conversation with Archie, Casey caught sight of Esther cycling towards her. She said goodbye to Miranda and watched Esther cycle straight past her, heading for a wooded patch of Hyde Park. Casey followed.

'Here.' Esther handed her a flash drive. 'I recorded the whole call.'

Even after the cycle ride, she was paler than usual, and there was a slight tremor in her hand as she handed over the small device.

'What did they say?'

Esther was trying to smile. 'It went just as you hoped. They want a load of the signals Campanile has developed. They had it all worked out. How I would get into the secure zone. How I can copy the algorithms. How I could get the information out of the Campanile building.'

'Esther ...' Casey breathed out, feeling a glow of success. 'Well done. And thank you. Thank you very much.'

'The man who called me ... I was scared of him.' Esther was frank. 'Even though I know ...' She gestured widely. 'I know that I'm not in debt to Tip Top. I know I'm not deceiving Lucas. I know that, but ...'

'But this man threatened you?'

'Yes.' Esther nodded. 'He was so sure that I was going to do what he asked. That I was desperate enough to do anything. That he could command me. I can't imagine ... I cannot imagine what it would be like to be under that man's control.'

'You're not,' said Casey firmly. 'And this finally proves that Tip Top is blackmailing people. It's brilliant, Esther. Really brilliant. When does he want you to do all this?'

'He wants it fast. Wants me to have everything by this evening.'

Not letting people stop and think. Not letting them come up with an escape plan.

'Would you be able to access Campanile's secure zones that fast?'

'If I had to. Yes, probably.'

'And you know what to do now?' asked Casey. 'Like we discussed?'

'Yes.' Esther looked resigned. 'Although I still think it's mad.'

'It is mad.' Casey allowed herself a smile. 'But it might just work.'

The vast airport terminal echoed around Casey, the polished white floor stretching away towards the gates. Tourists milled about, business travellers cutting a fast path through the throng.

The First Class lounge was quiet, though, plush with silver and grey chairs. The sofas were piled high with lavender cushions. Discovering that she was hungry, Casey made free with the buffet.

'Does it have to be the First Class lounge?' Dash had grumbled.

'Yes. We need space and quiet.'

After demolishing the buffet, Casey moved across to one of the neat little pods that had been designed for urgent – they were always urgent – meetings. Then she sat down and waited.

Half an hour later, Esther joined her, flushed and nervous. She wore a scarlet business suit, bright among the silver and lavender.

'I did it,' she said. 'I turned on my phone the moment I got off the Tube.'

'Great. I don't know if they are actually tracking that phone, but if they are, then you're doing exactly what you said you would.'

Leaving the Campanile offices, Esther had hopped on the Piccadilly line straight down to Heathrow's Terminal 5.

'Right.' Casey met her eyes. 'Are you ready?'

A firm nod.

Esther got the burner phone out of her handbag and dialled a number. As she waited for it to be answered, she breathed in and out very fast. By the time a male voice answered abruptly, Esther was almost hyperventilating, sounding convincingly panicky.

'They caught me!' she shrieked. 'They caught me and I had to run … I have to get out of London or they'll … I'm going right now. No, I'm not telling you where I'm going … I'm scared, I'm so scared! They told me Sergei Kiselyov has links to the Russian mafia … That he would … No, I won't. I won't!'

Casey could just make out the voice at the other end of the call, catch the odd word. The man sounded brusque, increasingly angry.

'Fuck you,' Esther spat. 'I'm getting out of the UK right now. I know what happens to people when they steal these codes … Prison or worse. And after all the stuff with Lucas and the press … I can't … I *can't*. I'm going to Geneva.'

An eruption from the other end of the line.

'I don't care what you think.' Esther's voice grew spiteful. 'I know a guy who works in a hedge fund out there … He'll want these signals … He's got money. And I'll get away from all this … I've had enough. I can't do it again. The last few months …'

Anger at the other end of the call. A vivid, molten fury.

'Well, you can't stop me, you blackmailing bastard. I'm already at the airport. I'm gone, as far as you're concerned.'

Esther ended the call with a jab of her finger and breathed out slowly.

'Well done,' said Casey.

'I'm fairly sure,' Esther said calmly, 'that there will be someone waiting for me in Geneva.'

40

People were smiling, 'Welcome Home' banners flapping. Couples were kissing and crying with joy. The chauffeurs, smart in their uniforms, held up iPads, the names in large font. *M. Landolt. Mme. Hill.* Taxi drivers – prosaic in old jeans – held up scrawled pieces of paper. *M. Clarvis. Julian Meier.*

Just a few steps to the end of the barrier. Casey hesitated.

They would be … They must be …

I hope they … Please let them …

I wish I could go home.

She walked slowly down the line of people, to where signs pointed to trains, carparks, taxi rank.

A deep breath and she stepped out into the crowd.

It only took seconds. She felt a jab against her back, a whisper in her ear. Although she had expected it, the gleam of white-blond hair in the corner of her eye made her shudder.

'Walk towards that door on your left. Walk slowly and smile all the way.'

So she did.

'The waiting will be boring,' Casey had warned Esther.

'Seriously, Casey? After all this, I can cope with a few hours of boredom.'

While they spoke, Casey was wriggling into the scarlet suit in an airport bathroom in Geneva's arrival zone. It was beautifully cut, the pencil skirt ending precisely on the knee. The shoes were black patent leather.

'You wanted the most distinctive thing in my wardrobe.' Esther shrugged. 'I never get around to wearing it normally, but …'

'It's perfect.'

'I don't wear that much make-up.' Esther peered at herself in the mirror. 'Do I?'

'Noooo.' And for a second they could have been any two women giggling in the restroom mirror.

'But your hair looks great,' said Esther. 'I love it like that.'

Casey had already been back to the salon to undo the Marbella bleaching. Her hair was dark brown now, blow-dried to the same smooth gloss as Esther's, a thick fringe hiding half of her face.

'You like it because it's exactly the same as yours. Now find somewhere to sit for at least six hours, okay? A quiet corner, just the other side of passport control. Head down, completely invisible. Miranda will meet up with you ASAP.'

Esther wore beige chinos, a grey sweater. Her hair was twisted up with a purple plastic clip.

'Casey, I don't … Okay.'

'Buy a few novels.'

She was just about to leave the bathroom when Esther put a hand on her arm. 'What if they—'

The sentence hung in the air, and all the nightmarish possibilities flashed through Casey's mind.

'They won't,' she said lightly. 'I'll be fine.'

'They might. And your colleagues – they might not be able to track where you're taken.'

'It'll be fine, Esther.'

'Promise me that if they … Tell them who you are. Tell them you're a journalist. Don't …'

'I will,' said Casey, and she almost believed it.

The man had a hand on her arm now. He marched her across the concourse, to where a line of cars stood queueing to pick up passengers. All around them, people were heaving piles of luggage and awkwardly shaped skis. Casey carried only a handbag, black and shiny.

As they waited, sideways glances confirmed it. This was the barman from Ascot. The killer in Regent's Park. The hunter on a breakwater in Marbella. He exuded an overwhelming sense of physical power, but he was not the boss. His aide-de-camp, who sorted problems before they appeared, she guessed. Tough. Ruthless. Murderous.

I need you to take me to the boss.

Would this man recognise her? At Ascot, he had been focused on Aidan. In Regent's Park, on Nick. In Spain, she'd been an intruder, indistinct in the darkness. The thick make-up, the dyed hair. Would it be enough?

She spotted another black Maybach inching forward in the traffic, identical to the car in Budapest. The windows of this one were blacked out too. She could just make out a chauffeur sitting in the front, face impassive.

The car stopped beside them.

'Get in.'

For a second, Casey breathed in the chilly mountain air, with its undertones of petrol. Around her, people were laughing and chatting. Two worlds, overlaid.

Then she leaned forward and climbed into the depths of the Maybach.

41

The doors locked with a soft clunk as the car moved away. The chauffeur was sealed off by a wall of smoked glass.

Close to, the blond man didn't look like a thug. He was younger than she'd thought, in his late twenties, perhaps, though he addressed the chauffeur with an air of calm confidence. In a town car where she would expect to see someone dressed in a business suit and a neat tie, he wore ski clothes, colourful and warm.

'Let me go,' said Casey.

'I'm afraid I can't, Esther,' he said, quite politely. 'Not for a while, anyway.'

'People know where I am.'

'Do they?'

'You have to let me go.'

'I'm going to need that flash drive first, Esther.'

'You can't have it. And why should I—'

The man sighed and stared out of the window. They were heading into the middle of the city, Casey saw, and it was snowing hard already. Winter had swept across Europe early this year and, all around Geneva, the mountains were white. The city itself purred on, designed for snow.

'Where are you taking me?'

From Casey's research, Meldon Group didn't appear to have an office in Geneva. There was an outpost in Zurich, the other Swiss city that revolved around the financial industry, but nothing in Geneva. She hoped, desperately, that she wouldn't be taken to another anonymous office block, another dead end. The G600 was parked up in Geneva's airport. Surely they would …

'I need that flash drive, Esther.'

'I don't have it.'

His head came around sharply.

'That would be very unfortunate.'

A shrug, sarcasm. 'I'm sorry about that. I didn't expect to be met at the airport.'

He turned back to the window. He was convinced she had the flash drive, she thought, and his calmness sent a tremor through her. This man was absolutely confident that he would get what he wanted.

Now the Maybach was slowing as it edged through the narrow streets of central Geneva. Soon they were beside the river that wound its way through the town. In the distance she caught a glimpse of Lake Geneva, slate grey under the louring clouds. The wind was catching the landmark fountain as it blasted water almost five hundred feet in the air. The jet arced across the lake, whipping to and fro as if it were alive.

The car drew to a halt next to the grey concrete of the Mandarin Oriental hotel.

'Esther?'

He waited until she met his eyes.

'What?'

'We are going to go into this hotel now, but you are not to cause any drama, do you understand? I don't want to hurt you, but you have created many' – a pause – 'inconveniences today.'

'I'm so sorry.'

'You are going to give me the flash drive,' he said calmly, 'because you have very few other options. Your reputation in London is already destroyed. Your family has rejected you. You have lost thousands and thousands of pounds gambling on stupid games. You have stolen from Sergei Kiselyov, and when he catches up with you, he will have you put in jail. If all this becomes known, your boyfriend will have to abandon you in order to have any hope of rescuing his political career.'

Casey stared straight ahead. The desperation Esther would feel, the terrible loneliness, flooded over her.

'I won't give it to you.' Stubborn.

'You don't need me as an enemy, Esther.' The words were almost gentle.

'I don't care anymore. What else can you do to me?'

He pulled out his phone. 'It might help if you looked at this, maybe.'

He hit a button and a suburban street flashed up. Someone was pointing a camera at a house. The footage looked live: a delivery van pulling over, a gardener pruning a hedge. North London, Casey guessed. Golders Green. It must be the Amaral family home, and she let Esther's despair snake through her heart.

'No,' she muttered. 'No, please.'

'You understand now,' he murmured, 'why it is so important that you are quiet as we walk through the hotel? That you smile and laugh, as if you are on the most delightful holiday?'

'Yes.' A whisper. 'Yes, I understand.'

'Good. Now follow me.'

The lobby of the Mandarin Oriental was all grey marble and black ironwork screens that gave the impression of privacy between different areas of the large space.

The man walked confidently across the marble to a bank of lifts, pulling a keycard from a pocket. Casey followed him, her smile broad, her footsteps hesitant.

As the lift doors closed, the man hit the highest button. The penthouse? But as the lift doors opened onto a rooftop, she understood. A silver helicopter waited on a big bright H, the rotors already spinning. The pilot glanced at them briefly as they approached and then turned back to the flight controls.

'Come,' the man said, and again she followed wordlessly.

Up on the roof, the wind was icy. Dressed only in the brave red suit, Casey's breath was whipped away. She found herself shivering within seconds.

The blond man climbed into the helicopter and strapped himself in. He looked around at Casey, and casually pulled the phone from his pocket.

'Hurry up, Esther. Hurry up or—'

Awkward in the pencil skirt, Casey pulled herself into the helicopter.

'Buckle up.'

The helicopter took off with a roar. The quarter-moon of Lake Geneva tilted away to the left as the helicopter accelerated: they were flying east.

As they juddered along, Casey was almost distracted by the beauty of the Alps unfolding beneath them. Covered in snow, the mountains jagged up towards the helicopter, white peaks and jumbled falls of rock. The clouds had lifted, the blue of the sky breaking through.

'What's your name?' she shouted over the thud of the helicopter.

'Leon,' he shouted back, and it might be a lie.

He was wearing a headset to communicate with the pilot. This was a large helicopter, two rows of three seats facing each other in the cabin, with the pilot screened off in the cockpit ahead. Casey sat in the seat furthest to the left, facing forward. Leon also faced forward, a single empty seat between them. They probably used this helicopter for heli-skiing, Casey guessed, flying high for the virgin powder.

'Give me your handbag,' he yelled.

Casey hesitated. She didn't want to hand it over—

His aggression shocked her, even though she half expected it. In the split-second that she hesitated, he had ripped the handbag from her hands. The civility tore like tissue paper.

'Stop that—'

He was already yanking open the bag, crouching over it, an animal feeding.

But there was nothing in the handbag to satisfy him. Make-up and a wallet holding only cash. The mobile was a cheap pay-as-you-go and the set of keys might have opened any door. She had left her own passport with Esther, sloughing off anything that might identify her.

Leon searched systematically through the handbag's pockets and came up with nothing. He looked up at her, his eyes narrowed. The menace was a sudden forcefield, a physical threat. Casey began to shake again.

'Where is your passport?'

'I dropped it,' she forced defiance into her expression, 'as you shoved me across the airport concourse. Someone will find it and Swiss efficiency will be set in motion. They'll be able to work out where you kidnapped me. There'll be CCTV.'

He raised his eyebrows but moved on relentlessly.

'Where is the flash drive, Esther?'

'I told you, I don't have it.'

'And I told you, that is very unfortunate.'

'Where are we going? Where are you taking me?'

'What have you done with the flash drive?'

'I'm not telling you.'

The response was immediate. Reaching past her, Leon pressed a button beside the helicopter door. It jerked open fast, the icy wind rushing in.

'Stop it,' Casey shouted. 'What are you doing—'

The blast of air swallowed any thoughts, a roar of sound and fear. There was nothing beside her, nothing to grab onto. Nothing but empty air, down and down to the snow-covered mountains. The void yawned, gravity clutching at her until she felt she was falling already. The headwinds screamed viciously cold, stripping away the last warmth from her bones.

'Stop it,' she yelled. 'Close the door.'

Her harness felt insignificant, useless. It was a few nylon straps, nothing. She yanked at it, pulling the straps as tight as possible, turning to Leon.

'I don't have the flash drive, I swear. It's not here, it's not—'

Ignoring her, he leaned forward calmly and lobbed the handbag through the open door. The freezing headwinds ripped it away instantly. Casey caught only the briefest glimpse of it tumbling towards the sharp crags of the mountains.

There were no houses here, she noticed hazily. No roads picking their way cautiously through the Alpine ridges. No one would ever find the pathetic scraps of that handbag. No one would ever notice …

'Tell me,' Leon bawled, his face a mask of rage. 'Tell me where you left the flash drive.'

The ice was biting through her pathetic red suit, tearing into her core.

'I can't.'

'You must.'

'I won't.'

'Fine.'

He spoke a few words to the pilot – in a language she didn't recognise – and the helicopter pitched hard to the left. Casey screamed, the wind ripping the sound from her mouth.

When she opened her eyes, the aircraft was tilting sharply. Below her, there was nothing for hundreds of feet, all her weight thrown onto the narrow nylon straps. She dangled over the void, her hair whipping around her face. Something small fell out of the helicopter and disappeared into the emptiness. One of her shoes was ripped away, sucked into the blur. Casey screamed and screamed.

Leon was above her, his face twisted into a mask of rage.

'Tell me where it is, Esther.'

'I can't.'

'You will.'

He was reaching down towards her, his hands tearing at the harness.

In her mind's eye, Casey saw the harness open. Saw that split-second as she began to fall, almost slowly at first. Impossible to reach, impossible to save. That moment when flying turns to falling, a body tumbling through the air, cartwheeling wildly, faster and faster.

She tried to fight him off. But it was impossible. He was far stronger, far more powerful. His hands were on the clasp, and she was scrabbling desperately, hopelessly. He would kill her. Watch impassively as she plunged out of the helicopter, her whole being a scream. And then the helicopter would level out, quite indifferently, fly on mechanically, and no one would ever find her, no one would ever know …

Leon's hands were on the safety button. She tore at his fingers, ripped at his face.

Tell him who you are.

Tell him.

Tell him.

No.

The harness jolted open, and Casey slipped forward, too terrified to make a sound now, grasping frantically at the arm straps, her whole body hanging out of the helicopter, her legs kicking wildly in the thin air.

Any second, she would lose her grip, those few millimetres opening up into forever. Here and not here, torn away and lost. That gap between life and death, almost nothing.

Casey wrapped herself around the shoulder straps, clinging on with every ounce of strength.

'Please—' A lost battle.

'Tell me where it is.'

His grip was relentless. He would pick her off, twist her from the harness, as if she was a shred of rubbish, a minor inconvenience.

Tell him.

Tell him.

No.

'I posted it to myself,' she screamed.

The hands paused. 'Where?'

'To a hotel in Geneva. It'll be there tomorrow.'

His face was inches from hers, his eyes boring into her.

'Tomorrow?'

'Yes. I didn't want to travel with it. I put it in the post in central London. You can have it as soon as it arrives.'

'Which hotel?'

'The Coralex. It's a small one in the centre.'

He stared down at her and then spoke a few words into his headset. The helicopter jerked upright and Casey fell back into her seat, unable to breathe, unable to think, clutching at the harness, ramming it together. The red suit had torn. She was shaking with cold and fear.

The door slid closed. Leon was staring out of his window, eyes on a distant peak.

Casey gripped her seat, and jammed her fingers under a handle, and the helicopter flew on disinterestedly.

She should have felt a moment of relief as they landed beside a sprawling chalet. She had done it. She had tracked him to his house.

In the distance, she could make out the Matterhorn, a broken incisor gnawing at the sky. And the sun was setting to the west, so she would know this place again. Know roughly where it was in relation to the famous Swiss mountain. She would come back here and find someone who knew his name, at last. Her cover just had to survive a few hours.

She was too tired for euphoria, too scared of what Leon might do. Too ...

Then she saw him. Standing on a terrace, looking out over the helipad.

The steely grey hair, the taut mouth, that sense of contained power. Even from a distance, he was formidable.

Him.

'Who is that?' She pointed up to the terrace.

There was no reply. The helicopter rotor slowed to a grumble.

Casey kicked off her remaining shoe. Trying not to wince, she jumped down into the snow and made her way to the entrance of the chalet.

A man was walking down the wide pine staircase. Casey stared up at him, eyes furious.

'Miss Amaral, how kind of you to ...' He stopped sharply. 'You're not Esther Amaral,' he said slowly. 'You're that journalist. You're Casey Benedict.'

42

Run. The word exploded in her head.

But there was no way of escaping this house in the snow, barefoot and miles from anywhere. It would be hopeless to try. Deadly.

Beside her, Leon's head had jerked round. 'She must be Amaral,' he said. 'We tracked her all the way from the office in Mayfair. Dark hair, red suit. They sent me photographs.'

But there was an edge of uncertainty in his voice, and somewhere a tremor of dread.

'I don't care what you think. She's not Amaral.'

There was no eruption, no blaze of violence. The older man's expression was unreadable as he reached the bottom of the stairs. Close to, his face was craggy and tanned, deep grooves around his eyes. His mouth turned down towards a tense jaw. The steel-grey hair swept straight back above strong eyebrows. He was tall, dominating the space, and his voice was a rumble. When he paused at the bottom of the stairs, his stillness was that of a hunter watching his prey drift closer.

'Are you carrying any of your recording devices, Miss Benedict?' he asked. 'Any of your clever little cameras?'

'I had a tracker,' she said coolly. 'But your sidekick here – Leon, I believe he said his name was – lobbed it out of the helicopter.'

'Leon. So … impulsive. After your efforts in Marbella, I'd hoped for better.'

'She told me the package was being delivered to the Coralex in Geneva tomorrow,' Leon replied, on the defensive. 'We can get it there.'

'I'm not sure,' the man said, 'that we should entirely depend on Miss Benedict's word in these matters.'

The anger was dissipating slightly now, the fury tamped down.

'You're Rosamund Bexley's father.' Casey risked fuelling it again. 'We met at Royal Ascot and you gave me that story about Lucas Fairbairn. Nash mumbled your name as he introduced me, which I thought was a mistake at the time.'

'I was interested,' he said, 'to meet you. Curious, one might say.'

'Why?'

'And now you know where I live.' He ignored her question. 'I presume you have my photograph, too?'

She nodded defiantly.

'You really are very determined, aren't you, Miss Benedict? I suppose you know my name?' He was watching her face closely, must have detected a tell-tale flicker. 'Ah, I see that you still don't know that.'

'I'll find out. We've got you now. We have photographs, we have locations. Even if it's something as simple as Jackson Harvey slapping your photograph on Instagram and asking his millions of followers if they can name you for fifty thousand pounds, I will find you.'

'I could ...' Leon began, his meaning clear.

'No.' The man's voice was sharp. 'If you've managed to throw her tracking device out as you were flying over the mountains, they'll know the exact direction the helicopter was travelling when it fell. Pointing like a bloody arrow straight towards this house, you fucking idiot.'

The swearword was a split in the rock, a glimpse of the lava boiling below. Leon ducked his head.

'I'm sorry—'

'But just to avoid you messing around on Instagram or anything else that comes into your strange little mind, Miss Benedict, I might as well tell you,' he went on. 'My name is Pascoe Knox.'

Pascoe Knox. She burned through a million headlines – and came up with nothing.

'I—'

'But you will never write a story about me, Casey. I promise you that much. You will never publish a single word about me.'

He turned and walked away.

After Knox had disappeared, Leon led her to a small bedroom at the back of the house. He pulled her along, just roughly enough to make it clear: cross me again, and I will hurt you. I will hurt you badly.

The door slammed behind him. She heard a lock turn, a bolt drawn across. No escape that way.

The small room offered no solutions. There was a single bed, made up with clean sheets and a bright red blanket. Navy blue curtains, a tiny en suite bathroom. Staff quarters, at a guess.

A set of French windows led out to a little balcony. Casey pushed them open and let the Alpine air cool her fears. The mountains rose up sharply behind the house, she realised, the rear walls of the chalet just a few yards from a rocky cliff. Too far to jump, she calculated. The neighbouring balcony was out of reach too.

She looked up the cliff. At the top of the rocks, a fringe of pine trees peeked over the edge. It felt claustrophobic, oppressive.

The minutes ticked past slowly. Casey sat on the bed for a while and then stepped out to the balcony again, ignoring the rocks looming above. A movement to the right of the house caught her eye. A ski lift, a private one, serving this house only. Steel benches, each able to take two people, were clipped to a long cable that circulated continuously. At the bottom and top of the lift, huge wheels would be turning the cable.

This lift ran close to the chalet before rising up behind the house. Pylons spiked among the trees, a row of steel footsteps disappearing towards the horizon. The chair lift was running smoothly, silently, but she couldn't see anyone riding it. They must have already disappeared up the mountain.

A few minutes later, the lift stopped equally silently, the chairs bouncing at the sudden halt. Simple engineering, highly effective.

A sharp knock at the door.

*

It was a different man who opened the door for Casey. Tall, dark hair, a subservient manner. He checked her over thoroughly before marching her up a flight of stairs.

'There are no cameras on her,' he told Knox as he pushed Casey into a white armchair. 'No recording devices at all.'

'Thank you.'

The man bowed and moved away.

The surge of temper appeared to have dissipated for now. Knox was seated at a long oak table, which had been carved from one massive piece of wood, unevenly beautiful. He typed on a silver laptop, ignoring Casey. She took the opportunity to stare around the room.

It was an extraordinary space. The central part of the chalet was three storeys high, the two wings slightly lower. The top floor of the middle section was one huge drawing room, rising up to soaring beams. The front of the building was a wall of glass giving panoramic views south across the valley. Huge cream sofas were set around a blazing woodfire at the centre of the room, a stainless-steel chimney whisking away the smoke. Beyond the glass wall, a wide veranda wrapped around the exterior.

The space was so large that Casey didn't notice the redheaded woman at first. She was sitting on a sofa, looking out over the panorama, wrapped in a fur blanket.

'Viva.' Knox nodded, noticing the direction of Casey's glance. 'Casey.'

'Hello.' Viva gave her a childlike smile.

The woman seemed distracted, as if half listening out for someone else. A silver chess set sat beside her and she was fiddling with two of the pieces. There was something in her movements that again made Casey think of obsession, compulsion, uncontrollable urges. She wondered again about the relationship between Knox and the redhead.

On the wall to the left was a series of black-and-white photographs. Racehorses galloping through frosty mornings, being unsaddled in clouds of steam, that almost unnoticeable mark in the top left-hand corner of each.

'Did you take those?' Casey pointed. 'They're great.'

Viva's face lit up. 'Yes,' she said. 'We often go and watch the horses exercise. I love it. Magical animals.'

'Viva was just heading downstairs.' Knox shut the laptop.

'Was I?' Viva smiled charmingly. 'All right.'

She stood up, letting the blanket fall back to the sofa. 'Goodbye, Casey. It was lovely to meet you.'

Knox stood up. The earlier tension was gone from his eyes, Casey noted. He had had time to recalibrate. He waited until Viva had disappeared then walked across to where Casey sat. For a minute, he stared down at her, eyes narrowed. Then he sat down in a large armchair, stretching out his legs.

'So,' he said, 'what exactly are you going to accuse me of, Miss Benedict?'

'Greville Polignac, Tip Top and Meldon Group.'

'Those are some of my operations, yes.'

'You've been using data from those companies for insider trading,' she said bluntly. 'Each of these outposts gathers intelligence and then passes it to the next organisation so that it can be fully and illegally utilised. For example, information sourced from politicians by Greville Polignac is passed to Meldon Group, which can then exploit that knowledge.'

Knox regarded her thoughtfully. 'I'm not sure you can prove all that, Casey.'

'Several people have been blackmailed,' she said. 'After they ran up debts with Tip Top, they were forced to steal information for you, which was then used by Meldon to make a fortune.'

'Again, I am not sure you'd be able to substantiate that.'

'We have recordings of one of your employees threatening Esther Amaral.'

'Really? Which one?'

'And then of course Leon just tried to kill me,' said Casey. 'In your helicopter.'

'Are you sure?' Knox asked politely. 'Were there any witnesses?'

'When I return to the UK, I'll send you a proper right-to-reply letter, so that you can respond to all these allegations. We were struggling with your identity, but now we know it.'

'How very fortunate.'

'Leon killed Nick Llewellyn.' Casey dropped the pretence of civility. 'He also killed Blake Gibson. Operating under your orders.'

'Why on earth would I order their deaths?'

The question was archly posed, but Casey answered it seriously. 'You thought that Nick Llewellyn would tell me about being blackmailed by Tip Top. And Blake Gibson's murder was a warning to other match fixers. Mess with us and you're dead. The other reason you had Gibson killed was because you can't bear someone interfering with your data. You're like Aidan Gardiner on that particular point, although Aidan just took his concerns to CleanBet rather than – well, you know – slitting the match fixer's throat and dumping him in the Med.'

'Again,' Pascoe Knox shrugged, 'I don't believe your lawyers will let you publish that article.'

His calmness was making her uneasy.

'We've got plenty to publish,' she said firmly. 'And more evidence will emerge once we start the ball rolling. It always does.'

Knox leaned his head back against the armchair. It was a gesture of relaxation, not tiredness.

'I'm certainly interested in the transfer of information,' he said. 'The movement of intelligence – the way those tiny pulses of light fly around the world faster than we can think. It's more powerful than anything humanity has ever even been able to imagine before.'

His eyes gleamed.

'That's all fascinating,' said Casey. 'Now—'

'But there's no particular secret in that,' Knox went on. 'Meldon Group, for example, buys data from all over the world. Then we analyse it, combine it with other datasets, extrapolate a bit further. Meldon alone is pushing right against the edge of all that can be known.'

'How illuminating. And if you'd like to sit down for a proper interview, we'd be happy to write up your thoughts further.'

'But you can gather this information everywhere.'

'I know all about your operation in Budapest, too,' said Casey. 'Your research into artificial intelligence. I know what you're doing.'

'We get information from satellite companies, from opinion polls, from Facebook.' Knox spoke as if she hadn't. 'From health companies, from fitness trackers, from insurers. All quite legal. Mostly.'

'Yes, we know—'

'I find it utterly fascinating,' said Knox. 'If the price of sugar is going up in Eldoret and the price of maize is falling in Juba, what does that mean? If some agritech company makes a breakthrough on genetically modified rice, who will that ultimately benefit? If a super-tanker is heading for Latakia but suddenly changes direction, does it have anything to do with a terrorist attack on the Ceyhan pipeline? A million data points a second, analysed by the best computers in existence. Because it's all consequence, not coincidence.'

Despite herself, Casey was listening. 'If you tug on this thread, what happens to the tapestry over there?' she said. 'Patterns in everything, everywhere. The butterfly effect, mapped out weeks in advance.'

'Exactly.' There was an odd moment of understanding between them. 'We have the capacity to know. So why not?'

Theia, she thought. The brightness in the sky. All-seeing, all-powerful. Lethal, really.

'It drives you mad, doesn't it?' she said. 'The idea that there isn't a pattern to everything.'

'Not mad,' he replied. 'Not quite. But none of it is random; people just need to believe that it is. They don't like to realise that the only reason they're fighting a war is because the price of wheat rose above these predesignated parameters and that was because the rainfall in Sulaymaniyah dropped below eighty millimetres last March. But, actually, that is precisely why they're getting stuck into their little freedom fight this particular morning. And because they've picked up their antique Kalashnikovs, the effect on the oil price will be ...'

He waved carelessly.

'I suppose you've factored climate change into all this.'

'Oh, yes.' He grinned. 'Absolutely.'

'I'm delighted someone will profit.'

'None of it is random,' Knox said again. 'If you track arms sales and ration-pack distribution and tank movements and refugee migrations, you can predict exactly where young Igor is going to have his leg taken off by a landmine. Underpaid, illiterate Igor has to believe it's random, brutal fate. But it's not. It never was.'

'It's certainly intriguing, but unfortunately it's also substantially illegal. So ...'

'As I said, we get our information from product reviews or web scrapers or—'

'You get it from everywhere,' she said. 'I understand.'

'But,' the voice grew even smoother, 'we get some of our most valuable intelligence from newspapers.'

Casey's head jerked up. 'What did you say?' she asked.

'Only that we get information from newspapers.'

'If you mean that your bots mash up newspaper articles in some groundbreaking way,' Casey tried to ignore the alarm ringing in the back of her mind, 'I think you'll find—'

'That's not what I mean. Of course, it's a free-for-all *after* the articles have been published.'

'What do you mean,' asked Casey, '*after* they're published?'

'Intelligence devalues the moment it's published, doesn't it? Even you know that, Casey. It's why you're so desperate to be first. It's information *before* publication that gives one the edge.'

'Which newspapers?' she asked. The alarm bells were screaming now, inexorable. 'Which newspapers are you ...'

He smiled at her. 'More specifically, I mean the *Post*.'

'How?' she asked. 'How the hell do you get information from the *Post* before it's even published?'

'To be absolutely precise, Casey, it comes from you.'

43

Afterwards, she found it hard to piece together the conversation, time fraying at the edges. The wind was blowing against the wall of glass, the blast too loud in her ears. It was the dragon roar of the races swallowing her up all over again.

'What do you mean?' she managed. 'What do you mean, it comes from me?'

Knox stood and picked up the slender silver laptop.

'Even though newspapers are pretty slow at delivering actual news these days,' he tapped on the keyboard, 'they still have their uses. As a microphone, rather than a serious investigative operation.'

'I don't—'

Knox angled the laptop towards her. He was clicking on a file marked *Casey Benedict*.

'And obviously, you've been very helpful to us all along.'

Photographs popped up on the screen.

Casey at Ascot, in the oyster silk dress: smiling up at Knox as he told her about Lucas Fairbairn.

Casey at the Royal Opera House, a glass of champagne in one hand: Knox whispering in her ear.

At 6 Arundel Street, smiling over the table at Nash Bexley.

'What are these—' Ice was edging its way up her spine, her hands beginning to shake.

Another click. Emails between her and Nash.

Great work on Fairbairn, Casey! The git had it coming. Catch up soon.

Thank you for your help, Nash.

Another click.

Hi Nash – that Swann Hopkins story's going up online this afternoon, just FYI. It'll be in the paper tomorrow morning. Best, C.

Ordinary emails, sent without thought. The tone friendly, familiar. Winding their way back through months – years, even.

And they looked …

'But I didn't …' Casey said slowly. 'I didn't …'

'Oh, this is my favourite bit.'

Footage, slightly wobbly. A buttonhole camera, Casey diagnosed, filming at Royal Ascot. Casey and Nash, standing at the bottom of the escalator, chatting.

Aidan Gardiner appeared, a blur making for the escalator.

Rosamund's most particular, Casey could remember Nash's words that day. *You head up, I'll follow.*

At a gesture from Nash, Casey was following Aidan. The camera tracked her following him up the escalator, caught her engaging him in conversation.

'But,' said Casey. 'But …'

'Oh, and that's just the start of it.'

'I don't see—' she started.

'Because one day,' Knox tapped the computer again, 'we realised that – very handily – newspapers put together a whole list of stories for tomorrow's papers.'

The newslist, the newslist, always the newslist …

'So what—'

'Take these images, for example.' Another click.

It was a photograph of a computer screen, showing a list of articles, with the names of journalists tacked on the end.

Wednesday 15th
At least 67 people have died after a plane crashed in … [Henry]
Antibiotic resistance breakthrough as … [Heather]
Gradibus CEO to resign after … [James]

EXCLUSIVE: The Post *reveals that Treasury minister Lucas Fairbairn … [Casey/Miranda/Tillie]*

These were Ross's newslists. Casey recognised the font and the layout – and the relentlessness.

All the reporters could access the newslist from their terminals – so that they knew who was doing what and when, and ensured that the news editors weren't pitched the same story repeatedly. There were newslists for News, for Business, for Sport.

'How did you get those photographs?' Her voice was hollow.

'They were sent to me by an unregistered phone,' Knox said lightly. 'But the location data will show the photographs were sent from inside the *Post*. And when you see those images alongside your emails, it's all very clear.' Now Knox was clicking through more emails between Nash and Casey. The tone was chatty, gossipy, fatal.

'You can guess how valuable an information stream from the *Post* might be to, say, Meldon Group,' said Knox. 'Knowing exactly when *Post* stories would be published, and what they would say.'

'You stitched me up. You're making it look as if …'

'Mmm,' Knox murmured. 'But it rather takes one to know one, doesn't it?'

'So that's your plan?' Casey tried to sound defiant. 'If I publish this article, you'll make it look as if I was working for you?'

'You *were* working for me.'

'A useful idiot.' The bitterness rose in her throat.

'It's touching, really,' said Knox. 'Doing it for the glory, not for the fortune. You spend your whole life gouging out information for the greater good – well, I think you enjoy the chase, too, if you're honest – but you never stopped to realise that the information was worth millions. Or if you did, you never thought to monetise it.'

But someone had. Someone at the *Post* had known. Photographed their computer monitor and pressed send.

'I'd deny it all,' Casey said. 'Admit I got played.'

'But it's not just you, is it? Your editor won't be delighted when it's revealed that the *Post* has been involved in market manipulation for months. Could it even survive that?'

Knox stood up. The sun was breaking through the clouds, shafts of light turning the mountainside to a patchwork of blues and silvers.

'You can carry on fighting your unwinnable fights if you want.' He looked out over the peaks. 'But not against me, Casey Benedict. You publish one word and I will take you down. I will destroy you forever.'

44

Knox walked over to the expanse of glass. The sun was edging towards the horizon.

Casey sat as if turned to stone. She found that she was shaking, her whole body trembling. Nausea washed over her and she pushed her fist hard against her mouth.

Knox was watching a skier on the other side of the valley, she realised. Off-piste, carving down the side of the mountain, joy in every movement.

Casey cleared her throat.

'It's not just about the money, is it?' She forced her voice not to shake. 'You must have billions. You hardly need more.'

He didn't respond, stayed looking out over the mountains.

'Your systems must almost be able to predict the future by now,' she said. 'And who gets to use that information? The Russians? The Chinese?'

He turned around and moved towards the woodfire. There was a glimmer of a smile in his eyes.

'Very good, Miss Benedict.'

'Russia, I'd guess.'

'I'm hardly going to tell you.'

She thought of his computers, absorbing intelligence from all over the world. Everything from the price of eggs in Montevideo to the cost of petrol in Benin City. From the number of containers loaded onto a ship in Yantai to the number of cars driving over the George

Washington Bridge. And spinning it into gold. Because when the next big war was fought, it would be over this. Intelligence, knowledge, power. And Knox would be king.

'I won't give you all my secrets, Casey,' he continued. 'Not even if you can't do a thing with them.'

'Why me?' Casey's throat felt dry. She wanted to stand up, but she wasn't sure her legs would hold her. 'Or do you just target journalists randomly? Enjoy that sense of control.'

He contemplated her.

'What did you think of Viva?'

The change of subject wrongfooted Casey. 'She seemed … fine.'

'She's my daughter.'

'Your *daughter*?' Casey's eyes flickered. 'I didn't realise …'

'She and Rosamund have different mothers. Rosamund doesn't approve, of course. Never did. I married her mother young. Too young. But Viva's mother …'

'I see.'

She remembered Rosamund's face when she had spotted Nash talking to Viva at Ascot. Not jealousy over Nash, then. Jealousy over a father, twisting towards the light.

'We had two sons and a daughter,' said Knox. 'They took their mother's surname.'

'Viva and … ?'

'Leon is my younger son.'

Casey's mind swirled. 'He …'

'Viva had a breakdown a few years ago. She's never really recovered. She has good days and bad days. Complicated grief, they call it.'

'Oh.' She couldn't think of anything else to say.

'Today isn't a good day,' he said. 'She's been a bit … upset today.'

'I'm sorry about that.'

'Not quite there, is she?' A mask of sarcasm. 'A bit damaged, wouldn't you say?'

'She did seem a bit confused. Maybe.'

'Viva travels everywhere with me nowadays. She has to, really. She'll never live an independent life again. That day in Budapest, when she saw you. It was unusual for her to be out on her own. She's … broken.'

The van, Casey thought. It had been coming to Viva's assistance, not hunting Casey down.

'I'm sorry—'

'My daughter,' he said, and for a moment, agony glinted. 'My precious, wonderful daughter. She was studying photography at university, you know? Before all this. Loved it, lit up like a firework when she talked about her course. She was this glorious, beautiful girl, who bounded into every room as if it were a new adventure. And now I can't let her out of my sight.'

'I really am sorry. But I don't see why—'

'You walk away when stories are finished, don't you, Casey?' It wasn't a question. 'You file your article, maybe the odd follow-up or two, and that's it. Then you're on to the next thing, the next furore.'

'No.' The word was out of her mouth before she could stop it.

Knox was throwing another log on the fire, watching the sparks spiral up the chimney before sitting down again. In the calm, she could sense the storm coming.

'You might revel in the glory for a bit, gloat over the headlines. Rip open a magnum of champagne or two. But that's that,' he said. 'You throw a grenade into someone's life, and you never even think about the consequences. You don't think about the hush after the explosion. The seconds before people start to scream.'

Collateral damage? Do you hear yourself?

'I do,' she managed. 'You don't know …'

'Bullshit,' he snapped. 'You just destroy life after life. I've followed your work for years now. Careers destroyed. Families torn apart. Lives ruined.'

Nick Llewellyn, bright blue eyes peering from a sleeping bag.
Esther Amaral, humiliated, wrongly, her own family casting her out.
Miles Foscliffe, clinging onto the wreckage of his dignity.
Oliver Selby and a shallow grave in Libya.

'I don't … I don't mean to.'

'You don't even stick around to bear witness to what you've done. It's just a few more drops of ink. Black ink on your heart.'

'Look what Leon has done,' snapped Casey. 'He's a killer, a murderer.'

'Leon sorts things out.' Knox shrugged. 'In his own way.'

Interpreting his father's fury, Casey guessed. Turbulent priests, put to the sword.

This bloody match fixer in Marbella. Wiped out.

We need to shut down Nick Llewellyn. Drowned.

Lacking Pascoe Knox's sophistication, but she couldn't deny the efficiency.

'But Leon enjoys killing people. He's a madman.'

'Leon,' Knox shrugged again, 'has his own demons. Grief affects people in different ways, after all.'

'Tip Top causes plenty of grief,' Casey spat. 'Careers destroyed. Families torn apart. Lives ruined. Sounds familiar, does it not? At least I'm trying to ...'

'What?' He laughed at her anger. 'Reveal the truth? Fight for justice? At least I know what I am, Casey. Spare me the sanctimony.'

'So what's your point?' She glowered at him. 'Yes, what I do has consequences. Holding people to account is necessary.'

The words tripped off her tongue, too familiar.

'It's journalism as bloodsport,' said Knox. 'Demolition as entertainment. Every one of your stories causes pain and misery for dozens of people, and you don't even bother to learn their names.'

'Like Viva's, I suppose?'

'Yes.' His jaw clenched. 'Like Viva's. Like Leon's.'

Casey looked at him again. The shape of the head, the angle of the cheekbones. A memory echoed. Who did he remind her of ...

Abruptly she was on that path again, following the footsteps across the Sahara. A huge blue sky, the red of the rocks, a fizzling blackness of flies.

Blood smearing, a metallic glint in the air.

And a child. A *child.*

And a shallow grave, left far behind.

'I know who you are,' she said at last.

For a second, the pain in his eyes was unbearable. A father, in despair. She could almost see flashes of his memories. That first smile. Crawling, so proud. Those first staggering steps. Every day, every milestone. A baby, a boy, a man.

There's nothing random about any of us, she thought. We are the consequence of a million tiny actions. And one day, any day …

'I know who you are,' she said again.

'My son.' It was a hiss. 'My eldest son. You left him out there to die.'

'Not on purpose.'

Nothing random.

'My son. My *boy* …'

'I couldn't …'

'To get a story.' His eyes blazed. 'A fucking story.'

'He murdered a child.'

'That's what you claimed, at least,' he said, 'in your wretched newspaper. For all I know, you set him up.'

'I saw it,' Casey said. 'I watched it. And just watching it was the worst thing I ever did.'

'So you say.'

'It's the truth. You know what he did.'

'The truth?' he sneered. 'What do you know about the truth? Viva went out there to search for him. To the Sahara. *Christ*. So dangerous, but she had to *know*. Nothing to find, of course. Never even got to say goodbye. But that's why I keep her so close. In case she disappears off to … God knows where.'

'I couldn't have guessed …'

'Yes, you could. At the very least, you could have given a thought to the fact that someone would miss him, that so many lives would be ruined.'

'You don't know that I didn't.'

'You cared, did you?' There was contempt in his voice. 'Sure you did.'

His eyes bored into her until Casey looked away. The logs in the fire crackled loudly, the only sound in the room. Slowly, Knox's fury drained away, leaving only the dregs of sadness.

'Leon has that tattoo of an olive tree,' Casey said slowly. 'On his back. Oliver … Olive … In memoriam?'

'I thought …' Knox studied the floor in silence, then shook his head, clearing it. 'For a while, I thought I had lost Leon too. He disappeared a few weeks after we lost Oliver. Even with all my resources, I couldn't find him. He was gone. For a long time, I thought I had lost both my boys. Both my sons. But one day, like a miracle, Leon came back. The Prodigal Son, walking through the front door so casually. I still don't know where he went for all those months. Some slum, some squalid nowhere. But he was back, and that was all that mattered. Then slowly, I realised that he had changed. I think he will always be different now. He adored Oliver. Idolised him. His big brother. His North Star.'

Oliver had dreamed of death, thought Casey. And Leon had followed so very closely in his big brother's footsteps.

'So you let Leon emulate his older brother?' she said. 'Murder whoever he wants?'

Knox ignored her. He stood up, threw another chunk of wood on the fire.

'And what happened after that?' Casey made the words crisp. 'You decided to set me up?'

Knox calmed slightly. Considered. 'Not exactly. At first, I wanted to understand you. To make sense of what had happened. I wanted to know how your mind worked, I suppose.'

'And you found out?'

'I think so,' he said. 'And I liked the idea of using you, of course.'

'You didn't anticipate me coming out here.'

'No.' He smiled. 'But it's another piece of intelligence. Another data point. You've surprised me on several occasions. Finding the fictitious *High Roller* – not that Leon covered himself in glory there. Tracking down Nick Llewellyn. How did you know to do that, by the way? I couldn't work it out.'

She stared at him, refusing to give away a word. 'And what will I do next?'

He looked straight at her, any civility draining away.

'You'll do as I say,' he said simply. 'You'll do exactly what I want. And it will break you into a thousand pieces.'

45

It was Prime Minister's Questions and the Commons was in full flow. MPs bayed at each other: pantomime villains and slapstick laughter and he's-behind-you gags. From the press gallery, Casey could see Lucas, far back on the green benches, occasionally getting to his feet as the script required.

The journalists stared down from the gallery. Thumbs up, thumbs down, another reputation thrown to the lions.

Casey flipped through her emails again.

Aidan: *Any news?*

Esther Amaral: *I need to get back to England. The coast is clear, right?*

Sergei Kiselyov: *Casey? I'm a compliance officer down and a little worried. Call me.*

Jackson: *Mimi's?*

Casey shut her emails, the flood of exhaustion washing over her. She felt like a spider trapped in a bath, trying to climb shiny white walls again and again. Until boiling water was almost a relief.

PMQs was drawing to an end now. Casey joined the chaos of journalists scrambling back to their offices.

Her phone rang silently. Leah Mulroney's number. She ignored it.

He's wrong, she thought. I won't break. He's wrong, he's wrong, he's wrong.

Right.

*

After being dismissed by Knox, she had spent a sleepless night in the chalet. By morning, she had sunk into depression.

In a strange parody of an expensive holiday, a maid brought her breakfast and a neatly ironed stack of clothes, along with a new pair of shoes. Casey had changed, defeated.

You'll do as I say.

And it will break you into a thousand pieces.

She had watched from the balcony as Knox and a couple of men disappeared up the mountain on the ski lift. They reappeared a few hours later, schussing down the snowfields back to the chalet. She wondered, vaguely, how long they would keep her there. If she didn't appear at the Coralex within a few hours, Miranda would start to panic.

The same thought must have occurred to Knox – or been delegated, at least – because an hour after he had finished skiing, Leon appeared at her door.

'Come.'

As they made their way down through the house, Casey heard the roar of the helicopter starting up. Viva and Knox were already on board, Viva smiling sleepily, the Nikon in her lap.

'Get in.'

Casey hesitated, sharp memories of that icy vortex of terror jagging up.

Leon pushed her hard in the back. They wouldn't do anything in front of Viva, surely? She didn't know, but there was no alternative anyway.

The flight was calm. She could sense Knox's eyes on her as they flew over the mountains. Ignoring him, Casey watched Viva instead. She was talking desultorily with Leon. Occasionally, there was a gleam of laughter, a flash of understanding in her eyes. But the thoughts were too disjointed, too fragmented. Viva would start a sentence and drift off. Occasionally, she took a photograph out of the helicopter window, handling the camera with a confident muscle memory. But then she would stare blankly at the results, fiddling aimlessly with the settings.

There was a fierce protectiveness in Knox's eyes as he looked at his daughter. Casey found herself wondering about Rosamund.

Rosamund, when this daughter – the other daughter – was kept so close, so beloved.

Because it was this son who was entrusted with tasks and forgiven his errors. It was this daughter who went everywhere with Knox. Her pictures, blown up and adored. Even to the New York office, which had been Trelawney's once. Snapping from the window, mine.

A *kintsugi* sort of love. Broken, and treasured, and fixed with gold.

This daughter was *loved*.

This daughter.

The helicopter started to descend over Geneva.

They dropped Casey at Departures, the Maybach disappearing towards the ultra-private end of the airport where the G600 would be gleaming on the runway. She called Miranda, hearing the relief in her voice. Waited at a coffee bar in the airport, and when Miranda appeared at a run, told her everything as fast as possible, the words spilling out, a sort of confession.

You were working for me.

Useful idiot.

Miranda had listened, a wince in her eyes.

'The photographs he showed you ...'

'They make it look as if I'm one of their team,' Casey said flatly. 'Right in the middle of it all. There may be more that I didn't see. I'd be destroyed, Miranda. And the *Post* would be a joke.'

'We'll find a way.'

'He's been doing it for so long. I don't know when it started. I hadn't been able to make sense of that Ascot attack, not really. Was it to track down some match fixers? To scare Aidan into selling to Theia? It was both of those things, but mostly it was to film *me*, their trained monkey, leaping to their bidding. I reread Nash's email inviting me to Ascot. *There's someone I particularly want you to meet. He's very much an expert on gambling* ... and of course he'll still have that email. For all I know, Knox was *watching* as I chased Aidan across the Royal Enclosure. I think he found it funny, in some revolting way. Part of the day's entertainment. A power play.'

Miranda didn't interrupt the stream of words, just listened.

'It was all a game for him. Tying me in knots.'

'He's fixated on his son's death,' said Miranda. 'Just like his daughter. Only it shows up differently in the father.'

'He's obsessed with the idea that I didn't care Oliver Selby was killed. That I never thought about him, just went on to the next thing.'

'Well, did you?'

'I didn't hold a requiem mass, no. But I didn't want him to die.'

'Knox is obsessive, Casey. He's mourning his son. Don't let him—'

'But how can I escape him? He has all these companies playing off each other. Nash at Greville Polignac. Tip Top. Meldon Group. Oliver was probably involved too, when he was alive.'

Oliver Selby, chief executive of Cormium, with access to that flood of information about commodities all over the world.

'Casey ...'

'Knox enjoys manipulating people,' said Casey. 'It's all planned in advance. All of it. I looked back at that Orbmond deal, the story that took out Nick Llewellyn originally. Knox made money as the share price went up, and again as it fell. But on top of that, losing the government funding sunk Orbmond. They were a specialist satellite company that carried out incredibly sophisticated monitoring of everything from how many cars there were parked outside a supermarket in Tucson to how many lights are on overnight at Chinese factories. And when Orbmond went down, most of its IP and satellites were bought out by a company linked to Theia. His reach is endless, Miranda. Endless.'

'Intended consequences.'

'Exactly. He probably learns from each of these experiments, treating us all like lab rats. Apply pressure *here*, see what happens *there*. And then feeds it all into his computers.'

'Why use Nick Llewellyn then? For Orbmond?'

'Probably just because they could.' Casey rubbed her eyes. 'Because he had taken a donation from Orbmond and was on Tip Top's list. But we'll never really know. It could have been anything, from whatever

Nick was up to as an MP, to Sir Reginald Armstrong being an old mate who got fed up with his wayward son-in-law and wanted Selina out of the marriage.'

'Tricky.' Miranda took a sip of coffee.

'And now Knox wants to dictate what I write,' said Casey wildly. 'He can control me completely. I'll have to leave the *Post*. I'll have to …'

'We'll think of something.'

'No,' said Casey. 'We won't.'

'Casey …'

'He played me right from the start.' The anger had gone out of her voice; her head drooped.

'Everyone Knox targets ends up having their reputation destroyed.'

'I know. Let's go home.'

After landing, Casey had made her way back to the flat in Tufnell Park, hearing the silence crack as she unlocked the door. As soon as she was inside, the silence formed again, an emptiness she could almost touch. Every time she moved, it broke and reformed. The squeak of a door, the roar of a kettle, the tap of a pencil. And then a spiral back to stillness. Again and again, until she felt as if she would never escape.

She put on music, but the silence was still solid at the edges. Swelling like mushrooms in the gap between two songs, the lull between two notes.

The ghosts rose again, clustering around her bed as she tried to sleep. So many of them, forgotten and locked away. Now they returned, hollow-eyed, resentful, relentless.

Endless ripples of sadness. Parents, their memories ripped away. Children and their shipwrecked lives.

Your son's a creep.

Your mother's a slag.

Small Arlo Llewellyn, with his grazed knees and his watchful blue eyes. His father ruined, his mother humiliated. A whole childhood drowning, sobs into a pillow. Unfixable, those years. Irreplaceable.

A glimmer of silver.

I didn't mean it.

A glint of red.

Yes, you did.

And those eyes, flecked with grey and green, blue and gold. Fixed and staring at nothing.

Not my fault, she said to the walls.

Not my fault, she told the rooftops.

Your fault.

Your fault.

Your fault.

I know.

She walked back to the *Post*'s scruffy office after PMQs. Leah Mulroney was calling her again.

One day soon, that phone would ring and it would be Leon, or Nash, or one of Knox's other lackeys, telling her what to write.

Casey sat down at her desk. *Leah Mulroney*, her phone shouted again.

Leah would not give up, Casey thought. She was probably standing outside the *Post* offices even now, ignoring that uncomfortable bench.

It had been two days since Casey had flown back from Switzerland. Two days since she'd climbed on the plane in Geneva and watched the mountains tilt away. She'd gone back to work because there was nowhere else to go.

She looked at her phone's display again. Another missed call. It wasn't fair to ignore Leah. It wasn't …

The little office was empty just then. Archie was interviewing a Cabinet Minister. Baz had headed to a select committee hearing. The sketchwriter was following a shadow education minister round a children's centre in Sowerby Bridge: 'If you're allowed anywhere near kids, that is? And it's not pronounced like that either, you plonker.'

And Casey had tried to smile and tried to laugh and tried to disappear.

She clicked on the newslist, to see what she was expected to write up.

Thrilling.

Someone at the *Post*, she thought. Someone at the *Post* is selling information to Pascoe Knox.

Who, though?

Even the thought was disturbing. Flogging off the paper's life-blood to the highest bidder. Ensnaring the newspaper in a scandal that might be unsurvivable. Because even a mole hunt could tear it apart.

Neither she nor Miranda had mentioned the leak since the flight back from Geneva, treading warily around the unexploded bomb.

'We need to work out who it is,' Miranda had said, as they waited for the plane to take off.

Casey had stared out of the cabin window, names floating up, her mind shying away.

'I don't know. I don't even want to think about it. You, Miranda? Of course not. Ross? He can't bear the *Post* being scooped on a down-page four story, let alone allowing someone to trawl his newslist.'

'Sure. How about Dash?'

'Impossible.'

'Who's a possible then? Hessa? Tillie?'

'It could be anyone with access to those lists, Miranda. And that's everyone. Baz the Whitehall editor? He showed me the Tip Top website on his computer, and I know he spends a lot of time gambling. Could he have got in too deep and someone rung him up with a clever way out? Maybe. Or Hessa? She's paid peanuts but managed to move into a new place a few weeks ago. Then there's Archie. He and Nash worked together for years when Archie was Nash's deputy, and Nash pushed for Archie to get the pol ed job when he left. So they're old pals and who knows? Or there's the home affairs editor. He's pissed off with everything, all the time. He might finally have had enough and be busy featherbedding his departure. I hate ... I hate even the idea of it.'

'It does feel disloyal,' Miranda admitted, 'even to consider names. If they ever found out …'

'It's what Knox wants. He wants us to tear ourselves apart over this. He'd find that entertaining, too.'

'If you knew the timestamp the newslist had been sent through to Knox, we could pull the reporters' security-pass data and see who was where when,' said Miranda thoughtfully. 'Or we could identify who had logged on to the newslists at that specific time.'

'Yes,' said Casey. 'But I didn't see enough for that.'

'We need to work it out.' Miranda had closed her eyes for the short flight back to London. 'We have to.'

Now Casey sat in the Westminster office, colleagues' names whirling through her head.

Betrayal.

It was unbearable.

Leah Mulroney rang again.

Casey watched her phone screen until the number rang out. Then she dragged herself to her feet, closing the door on any curious ears that might be on the alert in the corridor. Ten seconds later, Leah rang again, and this time Casey answered it.

'Casey!' Leah's voice reverberated down the line. 'I've been trying you for bloody days. What's going on? Where have you got to with this sodding story?'

'I …' At once, Casey wished she hadn't answered. 'I haven't got any further on it, Leah. I'm sorry. And I don't think I am going to be able to get any further either.'

I'm sorry.

I'm sorry I'm sorry I'm sorry.

'But …' Leah paused only for a second. 'You have to, Casey. We need to show the world what Tip Top has been up to. Don't be so bloody defeatist.'

'It's complicated. But the thing is that I can't *prove* any of these things. And I've got things wrong too, me personally, while investigating this story. I just … I can't see a way of getting it published.'

'I don't understand.'

'Tip Top's only a part of what this man's doing, Leah. There are several companies, all working together, all manipulating data. Tip Top funds everything else.'

Leah digested this. 'Has to be worth taking out Tip Top though, doesn't it? Follow the money – that's what you lot say, isn't it? And if Tip Top's only a small part of it, just think what's going on with everything else. You have to stop them, Casey.'

'This guy's worth billions, Leah. He'll fight every single word we publish, and I can't prove it's not a series of coincidences.'

'But you know it isn't. You know the truth, Casey.'

'The truth isn't enough, Leah.'

'But you *have* to publish it,' she insisted. 'Look at what these people have done to Selina's life. To Nick's. To Owen's ...' Her voice softened, uncharacteristically.

'I can't, Leah. You don't understand and I can't explain. But I've screwed things up. I'm not going to be able to do the story.'

'Casey ...'

'I am sorry, Leah. I am truly, truly sorry.'

'Tonight.' Leah's voice sharpened again. 'Come to the meeting tonight. I'll send you the details. There's a bloke I want you to meet. Come for the last few minutes and I'll introduce you.'

'I can't, Leah. I'm not allowed.'

'If you're not writing about any of it, then you're not acting as a bloody journalist either,' Leah insisted. 'So you might as well come along.'

'I mustn't, Leah.'

'You *owe* me.'

'Leah—'

'Casey ...' There was the briefest catch in her voice. 'Come tonight. Just once. Please.'

'I—'

'What harm can it do now?'

'All right,' Casey found herself saying, although she couldn't understand why. 'Just this once. For a few minutes.'

Just off a busy street in Hammersmith, it must have been an old cinema. Or maybe a disused bingo hall. One little duck and Valentine's

Day, Dirty Gertie and legs eleven. Half laughter, half luck, and better than sticking it all on red, maybe.

Maybe.

She stared up at the ugly building and the gilded gargoyles glared down. Thumbs up, thumbs down. Do come in, madam.

'The meeting will run from seven to eight,' Leah had said. Now there was less than ten minutes left, and Casey had kept her promise, but only just.

Inside, the decor was utilitarian. A whiff of bleach, worn lino on the floor, the lighting bleak and shadowless.

There was a scribbled sheet of paper tacked to a set of double doors.

CasiNo, 7–8 p.m.

The double doors hissed as she pushed them open. It felt as if everyone in the room turned towards her. Casey muttered something and sank into the nearest chair.

They had been laid out in a rough circle, with twenty people – maybe twenty-five – scattered among them. A man who had been standing when Casey walked in looked towards a woman. Her chair had been placed slightly apart. She must be leading the meeting.

'Well,' he murmured, 'I think I've said everything I need to say.'

'Sorry,' Casey whispered. 'Sorry.'

'Don't worry,' a woman sitting a couple of seats away whispered back. 'People come and go the whole time.'

'Thank you.'

'Does anyone else have anything to say before the end of the session?' The group leader glanced around hopefully.

'I do.' A woman got to her feet in one smooth movement. She wore a long coat of brightly printed scarlet silk. Mauve boots. A mass of red-brown hair held back by diamante clips. Leah, clear-eyed and fearless.

She stood for a moment, in perfect silence, the shabby room her stage. And then she started to speak.

'He stole from me.' Leah raised her chin, unashamed. 'Owen, my beautiful son, he was a thief.'

There were nods, glimmers of recognition, all around the room.

'I would open my handbag after he had gone out,' Leah's voice rang out clearly, 'and the cash would have disappeared from my wallet. Not a huge amount. Twenty quid. Thirty, maybe. A pathetic amount, really. But still. I started hiding my cash, or only getting out exactly what I needed. Then he went for my cards, so I hid those too. I tried to pretend that everything was normal. I would smile at him, say, "Tell us about your day, Owen." One day, his sister – she's nine now – came to me crying because her room was a mess and she couldn't find her birthday money anywhere. He'd turned her bedroom upside down. Gone through her sock drawer, her doll's house, the toy box. You don't realise what you're looking at. You think teenagers – nights out – the odd drink – it'll be all right, it'll be fine. It wasn't until I was looking at this pretty little room, all pink, fairy lights tacked over the bed, that I realised … I realised that our family was being ripped apart.'

Leah paused and fixed her gaze on the ceiling. An electric bulb hung bare.

'I confronted Owen about it, and he told me everything. Well, almost everything. I was relieved that it was gambling. Just gambling. We could fix gambling, right? Not like it was drugs or something. I feel so stupid about that now.'

The woman next to Casey was shaking her head. She had her hands clasped in her lap, knuckles white, fingers red.

'We fought about it. He was clever, Owen. Too clever. But gambling took all his energy, all his … intelligence. He left school, got a job. And the gambling just got worse.'

Leah ran her hands down over the brightly coloured silk, until they were folded neatly over her stomach.

'I remember when he was eight, long before the girls were born. We went to the west coast of Wales. Just the two of us, such a magical place. But I didn't know how strong the tides were. We were down on the beach one morning. Early, no one else about. Such a beautiful morning, all blue sky and sparkles. Owen, of course, rushed straight into the sea. But there was a riptide and it caught him. He was battling but I didn't even realise. I was grinning at him from the shore, think-ing I had an eye on him, drawing shapes on the sand, picking up bits of driftwood. And suddenly I realised that he was drowning. I got to him somehow. But I couldn't … I didn't know … I didn't know about rips. We clung to each other, and I fought and fought. But he was only little … My boy. My beautiful boy. He was crying, and screaming, and saying, "I'm sorry, Mummy. I'm sorry." And it just went on and on, until everything was salt and exhaustion and clinging on to Owen, thinking: This is the end. This is how I die. And then all at once we were out of the rip, and I was dragging us both out of the sea. And he was still saying, "I'm sorry, I'm sorry," so I knew he was alive. And all I could think was that I'd rather drown with you, my boy. I'd rather drown than be left on the beach alone.'

There was the briefest glitter in Leah's eyes. For a second, she pressed her lips together, then she continued.

'But with gambling, I couldn't pull him out. I couldn't break the rip. It pulled him further and further, no matter how hard I clung on. And one day …' Leah looked down at her hands. 'There's a little park at the end of the road. Just a few bushes, a few trees, nothing much. One morning, my neighbour knocked at my door, and said, "You have to come. You have to come now … It's Owen." *It's Owen.* I hear those words again and again. *It's Owen.* I ran down the road. Ran as fast as I could. And there was my boy, my beautiful boy … Hanging from the tree, like a piece of meat in the butcher's. His legs, just dangling …'

The woman next to Casey was biting at her knuckles now. Gnawing at them, an animal in a trap. Hurting herself, deliberately.

'That's what happens.' Leah's eyes met Casey's firmly. 'Families left on the beach, alone. You have to do whatever it takes to stop this.'

The meeting broke up not long after that. Against one wall, there was a trestle table with biscuits – digestives and custard creams on a thick white plate – and jugs of lemon squash.

Casey stayed in her seat, thinking.

It didn't take long for Leah to head her way. She was towing a man behind her as if she were a dog heading for a park.

'This,' Leah indicated over her shoulder at the man, 'is Jeff.'

'Hello,' said Casey.

'There's a burger bar just round the corner,' said Leah briskly. 'Why don't we all head there and we can have a proper chat?'

They sat in a row at the counter in the burger bar, surrounded by mirrors and bright rows of lightbulbs and perky neon slogans. Jeff was looking thoughtfully at his brioche bun and strawberry surprise milkshake. He hadn't resisted Leah's manoeuvrings, but he didn't seem exactly enthused.

Jeff was about fifty, tall – even taller than Leah – and thickset. He looked as if he had played a lot of rugby in the past and had his nose smashed in several times. His hair was receding, and his face – rounded over the cheekbones, with a prominent brow – had a shine to it, as if it had been carefully polished. He wore a brown leather jacket and the sort of jeans that would have sent Cressida screaming out of the door.

'Jeff,' Leah began, 'went bankrupt two years ago.'

Jeff's head jerked. Casey was getting used to Leah's approach now. Ripping off the bandage with the very first sentence. The worst, out there from the start.

'Casey's brother is a gambling addict,' Leah went on cheerily. 'She knows all about what you've been through.'

That was a lie. There was no hint of addiction anywhere in the family. Not that Casey would know; anything can look perfect from a distance. Peering through the windows, you can't make out spite.

'Did your brother bet with Tip Top too?' Jeff's voice was quieter than Casey had expected, softer.

She hesitated, not sure of Leah's story.

'Yeah, he did,' Leah said rapidly. 'Bastards.'

'And you're a journalist?'

'Yes,' said Casey, before Leah could jump in. 'And this is all off the record, Jeff. And, honestly, please only talk about what you're comfortable with.'

Leah glowered at her over the Cajun fries.

'I'd be fired if they knew,' he said simply. 'They'd fire me at once. And I'd deserve it.'

'Start at the beginning,' Leah ordered. 'Tell her where you work.'

'I work at the Bank of England ...' Jeff let the words trail away. 'In the City. You promise you won't name me, will you? You promise?'

He was pleading. There was a vulnerability in his eyes that belied the broad shoulders, the broken nose.

'Take me through it,' said Casey. 'Just explain the whole thing bit by bit.'

Jeff fiddled with his burger bun, picking off sesame seeds. 'I'm not an economist or anything like that,' he said. 'I just work on the fibre optics side at the Bank. Any big building in the City needs blokes like me, keeping all the technical stuff running. We're the IT guys, basically.'

Leah nodded at Casey. *Hear him out.*

'But then I got into gambling,' he said. 'Well, you'll know all about that, with your brother. And Leah's ...'

'And you lost a lot of money?'

He nodded, defeated. 'I'd messed about with gambling for years, and then everything went wrong at the same time. My wife left me and took the kids. There wasn't much left after the divorce, so I was renting this crappy room in a crappy flat. And it was just a way of not thinking about any of it. It was all my fault, of course, but other blokes drink, right? So I figured at least I wasn't waking up with a hangover.'

'Sure.'

'The gambling companies would take me to football matches. The races. Fun days out, making a big fuss of me. It was the only bit of fun left in my life, really.'

'If it's worth them taking you to the races,' said Leah, 'or their special box at the footie, you have to wonder how much these companies are making out of you.'

Casey thought of lunch at Ascot, the box at Covent Garden, the sense of alchemy as the notes spun to gold. 'Yes,' she said. 'I know.'

'I lost track of how much I was losing,' Jeff said bleakly. 'It wasn't just Tip Top, you see? It was lots of different companies, lots of different credit cards. I was betting on anything from eSports – that's video games, basically – to virtual horse racing. Virtual horse racing. What

314

even is that? I feel … stupid. You *know* you're going to lose overall. But I was in the worst trouble with Tip Top, definitely.'

'Any reason why?'

'Oh, they were just clever about things. They'd give you bonuses at random times, while you were playing. Free bets, that sort of thing. It's almost like they knew when you were gearing yourself up to log off and would sling you something to keep you hooked.'

'They probably did know you were about to log off,' Leah said darkly.

'Yeah, maybe. Their big thing was scorecast bets. You know the sort of thing – twenty to one that Fleethurst Wanderers win three–one at the weekend, with Jackson Harvey scoring the first goal. And it sounds good, doesn't it? Because we know Fleethurst are on a roll at the moment, and Harvey's been knocking it out of the park recently, so a big score and Harvey getting the first sounds plausible.'

'But?'

'Well, the reality is that it's fifteen to one that Fleethurst wins at exactly three goals to one, and five to one that it's Harvey who scores the first goal. And if you understand statistics, you know that as soon as you start combining probabilities of multiple events, the odds lengthen very quickly. So they can offer twenty to one, knowing the chance of exactly that combo happening are actually way out past fifty to one.'

'I see. So what happened to you?'

'Well, it was the same as with Leah's boy,' said Jeff, and there was a gleam in Leah's eyes, just for a second. 'Things were getting worse and worse, until it was all I thought about from the moment I woke up to the last thing at night. I wasn't sleeping much by then, anyway. I was getting so many letters about my credit cards. I couldn't open them, couldn't face it. Loads of calls – horrible ones – from debt collectors. I was panicking, and that made me gamble even more, because I thought, "I just need a few wins, and then I'll be back on top. I just need …" But of course … Then one day, I got a call. This man said, "I can make your Tip Top debts go away." And I'd have done anything by then … Anything.'

'What did he want in return?'

'Well, that was the thing, you see. It was so easy. All he wanted was a fibre-optic cable.'

She could feel Leah's eyes on her: expectant, hopeful.

'Tell me,' Casey said to Jeff.

'The Bank of England holds press conferences, right? Your news-paper always sends someone, for example. And the Governor talks about interest rates and the economic outlook and inflation.'

'Sure.'

'And then there's a video feed that anyone can watch. You'll see bits of it on the news.'

'Okay.'

'But this guy wanted me to install an audio feed.'

'Oh,' said Casey simply. 'I see.'

Hedge-fund managers think in terms of milliseconds: a thou-sandth of a second. An extraordinary amount of invisible effort goes into shaving milliseconds off data transfer, because it can be worth billions. Hedge funds set up whole new offices to ensure they are the closest to a stock exchange. One group ran a cable straight through an entire mountain range to save a few milliseconds between Chicago and New York. The cost? $300 million. Made back within months.

She remembered Meldon's Eiger-like glass facade, just a few streets from the neo-Classical columns of the Bank of England.

'Do you get it now, Casey?' Leah's voice broke into her thoughts. 'Do you see what they're up to?'

'How much faster would that audio feed be?' Casey asked Jeff. 'For the press-conference information?'

'Five seconds, maybe?'

Five seconds. Five thousand milliseconds. A lifetime to a hedge fund like Meldon.

'And you did it?' Casey asked.

'I did.' Jeff was shamefaced. He tore a chunk off the sesame bun.

'And the Tip Top debt disappeared?'

'Yes. The day after I'd installed the cable, I logged in and my account had been credited with everything I'd lost. I could withdraw it, just like that. I couldn't believe it.'

'Must have been quite a moment.'

'It was. But then ... I still ended up going bankrupt, didn't I? Stupid idiot that I am. I'd run up debts everywhere else too. The amount that I owed Tip Top was big, but it was only a part ...' He took a long swig of strawberry surprise. 'My wife went tonto when I told her I wouldn't be able to pay her maintenance. I haven't seen my kids since ... And I don't know when ... If ...'

He scrubbed the back of his hands over his eyes.

'Do they still have access to the cable?' Casey asked.

'As far as I know.' Jeff was tearing up his napkin. 'I don't work in that section anymore. The Bank moved me, after the bankruptcy. They were good, though. Kept me on in a different section when they could have sacked me.' He looked shamefaced at the thought. 'I've never heard from that man again.'

'Wouldn't someone at the Bank of England notice an extra cable running from the press-conference room?'

'They hadn't noticed for the several months that I was there.' He shrugged. 'The Governor of the Bank of England is hardly going to be grubbing around on the floor figuring out which cable leads where, is he?'

'So it's still ...'

'Yeah. Yeah, I think that it probably is.'

'Marvellous.' Miranda tipped back her chair. 'So now if you run the story, your reputation will be destroyed, and if you don't, you're covering up major market manipulation. Excellent work, Casey.' Miranda examined her Perle Burgundy nails. 'Outstanding.'

'It was an accident,' said Casey. 'I felt like I'd let Leah down, and that if I just popped along to this meeting for a few minutes ...'

'So now we know that Pascoe Knox is illicitly accessing information from the Bank of England, the *Post* and that sports company Liam Briggs-Nelson used to work for.' Miranda ticked off the list on her purple nails. 'What's it called again?'

'SportWatcher,' said Casey miserably. 'And it's anyone's guess who else.'

'And at any moment, they may start ordering you to write whatever they want.'

'Yes.'

A long sigh. 'Are we any closer to working out who is actually leaking the newslists to Knox from here?'

'No. I don't like thinking about it.'

'Neither do I,' said Miranda. 'But we need to know.'

She stood up and looked out over the newsroom. It was late in the evening, only a few reporters left at their desks.

'I need to resign,' said Casey.

'No.' Automatic.

'We can't just give up either.'

'No,' Miranda agreed. 'We can't, thanks to you.'

Casey sat up sharply. 'I know,' she said. 'I know what we can do.'

'What?'

'It'll be ... tricky.'

'Colour me shocked.'

46

She was relieved to see him in the end. The helicopter landed in front of the chalet, the blades swirling the snow into a blizzard. They shoved him out, pushing him so hard that he fell to his knees, crashing down in the dirty snow. He scrabbled to his feet, pathetic in the gloom, dwarfed by the gleaming helicopter.

'They might just kill him, you know?' Miranda had said.

That split-second when flying turns to falling.

Casey had met Miranda's eyes squarely. 'They might.'

And Miranda had paused, in the quiet of the office, and then dropped her eyes. 'Okay.'

The helicopter had soared in over the mountain range. A gleam of silver, at first, high in the darkening blue of the sky. Then the roar grew, the echo juddering off the rockface.

It was only when they dragged him from the helicopter that she knew for sure: he had survived this far.

'What if he's not there at the other end?' Miranda had asked. 'What if Hessa watches them all take off from Geneva but he isn't there when they land?'

'Then we start looking for him.'

'Casey—'

'The helicopter will fly in a straight line.'

'You haven't told him, have you? You haven't told him what they did to you on the flight from Geneva.'

'And are you going to tell him?'

A pause. 'No. No, I'm not.'

As they yanked him away from the helipad, he fell heavily to the ground again. *Fight back*, they had told him. *You have to struggle. You have to resist.*

And he did, desperately. Smart shoes slipping on the path, a frantic scramble that he was never going to win. His limbs lashed out, awkward, unpractised. *Not me. Not this.*

Until Leon turned casually with a punch that Casey almost felt. A crunch to the jaw, knees crumpling. And now he was down in the cold, shocked and stunned.

Because this is real.

And this is rage.

And this is unforgiven.

They dragged him to his feet again. The resistance was pitiful now. An arm, trying to shove Leon, that was swatted away. Fingers clawing, a playground effort. His feet slid along the path in defeat.

They dragged him all the way to the chalet and the door opened and swallowed him up.

The camera caught it all.

'That's Nash Bexley,' Casey told the camera. 'That's Nash Bexley being taken into the house of Pascoe Knox.'

It had taken a week to set it all up.

'If Nash Bexley recognises any of the names of the people who approach him,' said Miranda, 'we're screwed before we even get started.'

'Nash will only know about the political stuff, I hope. Just the intel that goes through Greville Polignac. Knox must keep the companies siloed. It would be too risky otherwise.'

'Let's hope so.'

They had gone to SportWatcher first, the tech company that employed Liam Briggs-Nelson before he was jailed for three years.

Griff Aitken knew the chief executive of SportWatcher, it turned out.

'Harvey Powell?' The football writer had looked up from his screen. 'Yeah, I can put you in touch, no probs. Why?'

And as he listened, a broad smile spread over Griff's face.

'Liam Briggs-Nelson did what?' The shock on Harvey Powell's face was slow to subside. He sat behind his expensive desk, shaken out of his prosperous complacency.

'We're absolutely not saying that we have any proof that Liam Briggs-Nelson built the backdoor to the tracker data,' said Miranda smoothly. 'Just that we've been told he may be aware of its existence.'

'Liam Briggs-Nelson – currently a resident of HMP Standford Hill – is aware that someone hacked our sensors?' Harvey Powell dropped his head into his hands. 'The sensors worn by dozens of Premiership footballers every bloody Saturday. Christ, it's a data-security nightmare. I need to report it. I need to …'

'It's up to you whether you tell anyone,' said Casey. 'Ideally, you'll take your time thinking about what to do next. Maybe a couple of days, for example.'

'And during that time, you want me to bump into some lobbyist guy at a drinks thing in a restaurant next door to Parliament?' Powell sounded bewildered. 'And get him chatting? I don't understand …'

'It might seem slightly eccentric,' Miranda agreed. 'But I promise it will all make sense in the end.'

Griff wasn't trying especially hard to hide his grin. 'You just have to trust them, mate,' he said to Powell.

'It all sounds insane.'

'It means you can close the backdoor without any … wider ramifications,' said Casey.

The shock was easing now. There's the drop, and there's the safety net. It was an easy choice, usually.

'If I could get my hands on Liam Briggs-sodding-Nelson,' Powell was starting to grumble. 'I'd—'

'If you report Liam to the police over this,' Miranda pointed out, 'you'll have to reveal that SportWatcher has been responsible for one of the most serious data leaks in sporting history.'

'Still—'

'At the end of the day, the focus of this story,' Miranda's voice was silken, 'can either be on the criminality of the people exploiting the data from several different companies, or it can concentrate on SportWatcher and its disastrous data leak. It's completely up to you. We will be publishing an article on this subject either way.'

'And Liam's serving three years already,' said Casey. 'And there's no proof whatsoever that he did anything, just that we understand he is aware there might be a breach.'

Harvey Powell gave a long sigh. 'The little git had it coming.'

Then it was time for the next phase.

'Selina says she'll do it.' Casey could almost hear Leah's grin down the phone. 'She'll come up from Devon tonight and take him to her posh tennis club tomorrow morning. The Hurlingham, I think she said?'

'Brilliant.'

Casey called her later. 'Thank you, Selina.'

'I'm only doing it for Nick. And Arlo and Saskia, of course. What's this man's name, again? The chap I'm taking to the Hurlingham?'

Casey imagined Selina in Postbridge House's elegant drawing room. Gazing out over the topiaried hedges, ankles neatly crossed.

'He's called Jeff Billingham. He works at the Bank of England and he's another problem gambler.'

'Fine.'

The next morning Casey waited, staring fixedly at her phone. When Selina Armstrong's number flashed up, she pounced.

'I had to kit him out completely before we went in,' were her first words. 'His tennis shoes looked as if they'd hiked across the Gobi Desert, for heaven's sake.'

'Thank you, Selina. I really appreciate it. How did—'

'He's awfully shy too. And I dread to think what his tennis would have been like. But luckily, he didn't have to play. Just sit and drink coffee.'

'And it went well?'

'Casey, it went perfectly! I pop into the club whenever I'm in London, and Nash Bexley's there practically every morning. This time I just flagged him down and said he must meet Jeff.'

Casey could imagine it.

Nash! Haven't seen you in aaages. How are you? Have you met Jeff? He works at the Bank of England, and he's been telling me some fascinating *stories.*

Nash, pausing politely.

'And then this Nash Bexley person told me all about this new tennis racquet,' Jeff said happily, afterwards. 'Gave me his business card as he left, and everything.'

'Perfect, Jeff. Brilliant. Email him straight away.'

After that, Miranda rang Greville Polignac, passing herself off as Aidan Gardiner's terrifying PA.

'But I don't have a PA,' Aidan had said worriedly. Casey had gone over to the Kennington industrial unit to explain the plan, walking past the rows of computer monitors.

'I know that.' She swiped an ancient Jammie Dodger. 'But they won't.'

'Mr Gardiner has a window at eleven a.m. today.' Miranda's tones were clipped. 'He would be grateful for some advice on digital services taxation policy and Nash Bexley has been specifically recommended.'

'Won't they want to know what I do?' Aidan asked Casey. 'Who I am?'

'That's the miracle of having yourself as a PA. People assume that if someone's got people making calls for them, they're worth a few moments on the phone. To be honest, we use it to get tables at restaurants too.'

Nash rang Aidan's mobile promptly at 11 a.m.

'You just have to keep him on the line,' Casey urged. 'That's all. Put him on hold for ten minutes if you want.'

'But I still don't understand why,' Aidan protested.

'Because I reckon you're one of the sources of information they use.'

'What?' He looked flabbergasted. 'How?'

'Tip Top are almost certainly tracking all your bets,' said Casey. 'That way they get most of your intelligence for the relatively small amount it costs to lay off the bets. With every bet you place, you're telegraphing your company's assessment of a match.'

'You … What?'

'You told me that several of the exchanges would rather not take your business, right? Because you win too much, and that harms the odds for other punters.'

'Ye-es.'

'And you also told me that you bet through Tip Top quite a lot because they offer the best odds.'

'I suppose so.'

'Well, if you think about it, they've probably worked out which are your company's accounts but decided to let you carry on betting. That way they can figure out exactly what you're up to and piggyback your algorithm. You think Ravenna's going to win. You think Tshakhuma's got it in the bag, and so on. Then they lay off your bets. Easy.'

Aidan worked it out. 'Bastards.'

'So just keep Nash talking on the phone this morning.'

'But why?'

'You'll see.'

Then it was time for the last jigsaw piece. The next morning, Miranda and Casey waited in Dash's office, around the corner from the main newsroom. Dash was sitting at his desk, his mouth a thin line.

A few minutes after nine, they heard Ross's voice. 'Morning, Tillie. Dash wanted to see you. Pop to his office now?'

Tillie was at Dash's door in seconds, a flurry of glossy hair and big brown eyes. 'Dash, what can I do—'

The words ebbed away as she saw Casey and Miranda sitting on the old sofa. She whipped around to see Ross closing the door.

'Tillie.' Miranda's voice was ice-cold. 'Tillie, what have you done?'

47

For a moment, Casey thought that Tillie might actually make a run for it. She stood in front of Dash's desk, legs shaking, eyes beginning to glisten.

Casey stared at Tillie as if she was seeing her for the first time. The watch on her wrist: that was a Rolex. The diamond studs in her ears: those were chunky and real. The Loewe shoes, the Bottega Veneta handbag: Tillie had hardly been hiding it.

Tillie's eyes flitted around the room and met hers. Casey forced herself to look implacable. She watched the thoughts skim across Tillie's face. Thoughts that Casey had watched a hundred people try to hide. Deny it? But what do they know? *How* do they know?

Casey carried on staring, and Tillie's face crumpled.

'Tell us.' Ross spoke through his teeth. 'Tell us everything you know. Right now.'

'I—' Tillie's eyes flickered round the room, seeking out an escape.

'You've been photographing the *Post*'s newslist,' said Dash. 'And sending it to Nash Bexley.'

'I wasn't—'

'You've been working under Nash Bexley's orders for months.'

'I didn't—'

'We know you did.'

'I didn't … mean to.'

'The thing is,' no one could be more sarcastic than Ross, 'that's just not possible, Tillie.'

'How did it begin?' Miranda asked. 'Tell us the truth, Tillie, or ...'

'I don't know whether—'

'Tell us.' Dash's voice whipped through the air. 'Tell us right now, Tillie, or I will call the *Post*'s lawyers and the police right this minute.'

'It wasn't criminal ...' Tillie stopped. She wasn't sure, Casey saw. She didn't know.

'It's breach of confidence,' said Ross. 'So that gets you fired, for starters. But more importantly, it's stealing the *Post*'s intellectual property. That's theft, Tillie, and it very definitely is criminal.'

Still she tried. 'I'm going to talk to my lawyers. You have no right—'

'If you don't want to be sacked on the spot,' said Dash, 'you'll tell us everything you know right this minute.'

A flicker of hope in Tillie's eyes. Behind her, Ross rolled his eyes.

'How did it start?' Casey asked. 'Come on. We know most of what you've done already, but this is getting dangerous. What exactly is going on?'

Tillie turned to Casey again. 'Why should I trust you?'

The words stung. Casey shot her a level stare. 'Who else can you trust?'

Tillie fiddled with the Rolex and then realised what she was doing. She looked up at Casey, almost embarrassed.

'Come on. We don't have much time, Tillie.'

'You forget that I've heard you use these lines before.' Tillie tossed her head, but there was something uncertain about the gesture.

Casey met her eyes steadily. 'We can start to fix this right now.'

'I don't think I ...'

'How did it begin?' She said again.

'I don't know! It just ...' The burst of words was followed by a silence. Slowly Tillie began to disentangle her thoughts. Her shoulders slumped. 'I bumped into Nash at a party at my aunt's house.' She hesitated. Casey waited. Tillie filled the silence. 'We got talking. He was saying how grand the house was, and how it must be fun coming from a family like that. Teasing me.'

326

'And?'

'My mother's one of two sisters.' Tillie shrugged. 'They're very close, always have been. But my aunt married someone who happened to be incredibly rich, and my mother … not so much.'

It had been a very comfortable upbringing, all the same. Tillie had gone to expensive schools and never worried about the bills. But there was bitterness in her voice. She had grown up within touching distance, but not quite *there* – in her mind, anyway.

'You told Nash all that?'

'I'd had a few drinks,' Tillie ran a hand through the expensive highlights, 'and I was fed up.'

'And what did he say?'

'Nothing then.'

'But later?'

'We had lunch. He said he was always on the hunt for political intelligence. Advice, that's what he called it. And that they'd pay. And things sort of went from there.'

'I'll say they did,' said Ross.

'When did you start sending him our newslists?' Dash asked.

Tillie bridled. 'I never wanted to do that.'

'But you did,' said Ross. 'So when did you fucking start?'

'I don't know.' Tillie was fidgeting with the Rolex again. 'A few weeks ago, maybe. I never meant …'

'Give me the phone you used.'

Tillie was reaching for the burner mobile by the time she realised it was unwise. Ross grabbed it, scrolling back through her messages.

'Fucking months ago,' he spat, and Tillie winced.

'You can't prove I sent them all,' she said with a sudden surge of spirit. 'It's just one burner phone sending photographs to another. Anyone could have sent them. Ross's fingerprints are all over it now.'

'Trust me,' Ross said. 'I'd find a way to prove it.'

Tillie wilted.

'What else?' Miranda asked.

Tillie had to turn towards her to answer, the jabs coming from every angle. 'Nothing much.'

'What, Tillie?'

'Well, we'd chat every so often. If I heard something interesting, I'd …'

'Let Bexley know?' Ross sneered.

'Nash was giving Casey stories all the time,' Tillie cried out. 'She was doing exactly what he wanted, too. They'd go out to lunch, have a gossip. How is it so different?'

'It just is,' said Miranda, and Casey hid a wince.

'How did you guess?' Tillie asked her. 'That I was … talking to Nash.'

'It was small things. Interest in various stories was fair enough. But you were just a bit *too* interested. I'd seen you chatting to Nash all the way back at Royal Ascot, although I didn't think anything of that at the time. Then Rosamund Bexley mentioned that she'd asked you to the opera because you were such fun, and it made me think.'

'I was in bloody Scarborough that night.' Tillie pouted, still bitter.

'Why did you do it?' Casey asked wearily. 'Money?'

'It's expensive living in London.' It was a whine. 'We work like dogs at this place – weekends, evenings, whatever – and we're paid bloody peanuts.'

'You could always have taken the public affairs shilling,' said Dash quite mildly.

'You were part of our team, Tillie,' Casey said. 'We trusted you. You and Hessa work so well together. You could have had a brilliant future, you could have …'

And she saw the flash in Tillie's eyes: I could have been *you*. And I am not sure I wanted that.

'You've blown it, Tillie.' Miranda made a dismissive gesture. 'You've fucked it all up.'

'I'm afraid you have,' said Dash. 'I'm sorry, but it's over.'

At first, it seemed as if Tillie would shout back, but quite abruptly, she crumpled. 'I'm sorry. I'm so sorry. I never meant to …'

Her head was bowed. She was tugging at the watch as if she wanted to drag it off. It looked like a shackle now.

'What do you mean?' Casey asked. 'You never meant to?'

'I thought … I don't know …' Tillie rubbed her eyes. 'You and Miranda, you trade information all the time, don't you? I've heard you on the phone, talking to sources. And, at first, that's what it was like with Nash. I'd mention something to him, and he'd give me a story in return. And you were *pleased* with the stories. Ross said they were great. I was happy. Everyone was happy. But then ...'

'What?' asked Ross, growing impatient.

'Then it spiralled. Nash was so nice to start off with, but then he was ... less nice. And I didn't know how to explain it to any of you. I wanted to stop. I was desperate to stop ... But it was too late. I didn't know what to do. So I just kept going, and that kept Nash happy and it kept you happy.'

'So you thought you'd photograph our newslist and send it off?' Ross asked. 'One thing just led to another, was that it?'

Tillie winced. 'I was stupid, okay?'

'You think?'

'I'm so sorry, Ross. When it first started, I really thought you'd be pleased with me.'

Thank you for your help, Nash. Casey's own emails echoed through her mind.

Casey and Miranda's eyes met. 'Nash,' Casey said quietly, 'can be very charming.'

'Exactly, Casey. You know what he's like. Please ...'

'Tillie's taken money off Knox, though,' said Miranda. 'It's well past the point of a bit of gossip, Casey.'

'Yes, but Nash probably made those transfers precisely in order to tie her in. Once so much as a penny had been paid into her account, she was compromised. It was cheap at the price.'

'She should have come to us. Those newslists—'

'Sure,' said Casey. 'I know. But it's not all Tillie's fault. She's been working here for about ten minutes. We should have kept a closer eye on her. We should have ...' She stopped talking.

'Tillie ought to have—'

'Miranda,' Casey cut her off. 'It's what they *do*. Without you realising, without you knowing, they make you complicit.'

Miranda was silenced.

'So what do you want from me?' Tillie asked, tears in her eyes. 'What do you all want?'

48

Nash Bexley ran when Casey ambushed him halfway between the Tube and Greville Polignac. The soles of his hand-made shoes clattered in the quiet of the Westminster street.

Nash, she thought, with a degree of sour pleasure, was panicking.

In her trainers, it was easy to catch up. He flinched as she sprinted up behind him.

'Casey, what are you …'

'Didn't expect to see me, did you?' she said icily.

'I … I …'

'I know. And the thing is, Nash, it's so much worse than you realise.'

The day before, the *Post* newslist had been sent to Nash as normal. It was dispatched from Tillie's burner phone, at the time she always sent it.

'You stay in that office,' Ross snarled at her, pocketing her phones and stripping out the room's computer access. 'If you try to leave, Janice will call me at once. Dash may be in a forgiving mood, but I'm certainly not.'

Janice was the editor's PA, seated just along from Dash's office.

'You can't imprison me!' Tillie's outrage came roaring back.

'I can't,' Ross agreed amiably. 'But the police certainly fucking can, so I'd settle for me, if I were you.'

With a toss of her head, Tillie sat down in one of the uncomfortable office chairs.

It didn't take long for Casey and Miranda to create a newslist to send to Nash.

'We'll lift most of the stories from the actual newslist,' said Miranda. 'And then add a few more, mainly from the business section's list.'

So they had invented a merger here, a criminal investigation there, the suggestion of a major oil leak somewhere else. James from the business desk had come up with an investigation into a leading supermarket chain finding broken glass in their frozen chickens. 'Let's say eight deaths linked,' he said cheerfully. 'And question marks over their ready meals too.'

Shortly after, they watched Meldon Group declare its short selling. A massive short position in the supermarket chain. A separate fortune staked on an energy company's share price collapsing within hours.

In the early evening, Hessa had gone to pick up Tillie from the little office. She looked mutinous.

'This is ridiculous.'

'It's worth a try, though.' Hessa shrugged. 'And right now, if I were you, I'd do absolutely anything they asked.'

They had made their way to the pub just around the corner from Greville Polignac. It was a typical Westminster place, all polished wood and dark corners. By the time Hessa and Tillie bowled in at 7.30, it was packed with special advisers and journalists.

Making her way to the bar just as one of the Greville Polignac PAs was getting a round in, Tillie burst into tears. Snotty tears, smearing mascara across her face.

I thought he loved me. I thought he …

'Come on,' Hessa said briskly. 'Cheer up. Let's go and sit over there.'

But Tillie insisted on reeling around the bar. Boring people with her story, but pretty enough to be listened to. By the end of the evening, everyone in the pub knew: Nash Bexley had been having an affair, and now the girl was pregnant.

Until finally Hessa had dragged her into a taxi. 'Come on, babe. Time to get you home.'

And as the taxi pulled away, Tillie sat up straight with a jerk. 'Urgh, I can't believe anyone believed that. Nash and me … Really?'

'Well, he is so *very* charming.' Ross levels of sarcasm.

'Hessa! Yuk!' Tillie sobered. 'Will you tell them? Will you tell them I tried my best?'

Hessa looked straight at her. 'I'll tell them, Tillie. You've been an utter idiot, but I will tell them.'

'How?' Nash was struggling to catch his breath. 'What are you doing here, Casey? What have you done, you—'

He looked up and down the Westminster street, flinching as a taxi drove past.

'The organisation you work for has been stealing data from a range of companies,' Casey said calmly. 'And you've been complicit in that.'

'I haven't—' The denial was automatic, stalling halfway through.

'It doesn't matter anymore, Nash. Because in the last few minutes, several of those streams of information have been cut off.'

'What—'

'Why don't you read through your own emails?' Casey glanced up and down the street. 'And not just the ones from me, this time.'

'I *had* to hand over your emails, Casey …' He broke off. 'What do you mean, my emails? Emails from whom?'

'Jeff Billingham at the Bank of England,' she said. 'Harvey Powell at SportWatcher, too. And your work mobile called Aidan Gardiner for twenty-seven minutes yesterday morning.'

'I don't understand.'

Nash was scrolling through his emails now, his fingers clumsy, scared. Casey didn't have to see the emails. She had dictated them.

Thanks for letting me know, mate. Will be in touch about our plans for SportWatcher when you've got things sorted out.
HP

A pleasure, Harvey. Speak soon.
Nash

'But,' he looked up at Casey, 'we only had a chat about Arsenal. I told him Greville Polignac had a box, and I'd check out some dates for him to join us.'

'Sure, Nash.'

He continued scrolling. A day later, another email.

Nash –
Helpful to chat this morning. Really useful to know.
Look forward to working with you in the future.
Yours,
Aidan Gardiner

'But ...' Nash shook his head, uncomprehending.

Dear Nash,
Thank you for your advice. Eye-opening. I'd better get that sorted ASAP.
Best,
Jeff Billingham
Bank of England

'I don't ... That man was only asking me for advice about what tennis racquet he should be using.' It was almost a whimper. 'Why have you done this?'

'Pascoe Knox's organisation has been exploiting illicit information streams from all over the world,' said Casey, 'and from a variety of institutions and companies. Jeff Billingham works at the Bank of England and was responsible for Meldon Group receiving market-sensitive information about interest rates a few seconds before everyone else. Harvey Powell's company SportWatcher was hacked and Tip Top used their data about footballers to inform the odds they offer.'

'But I didn't know about that,' Nash whimpered. 'SportWatcher, the Bank of England, whatever else ... I didn't know. And how does this Aidan Gardiner fit in?'

'I believe Tip Top's been piggybacking off Aidan's statistical modelling.'

'Can you prove that?'

'No,' said Casey. 'But it doesn't matter. What matters is that this morning, the information streams from the Bank of England and SportWatcher were switched off within seconds of each other and Gardiner closed his accounts. Plus the newslists Tillie sent to you last night were total garbage. How long do you think it's going to take Knox to track down these emails and decide you've gone rogue? And what will he do then?'

Panic in Nash's eyes. 'He'll think that I'm trying to take over his—'

'I know he will. Because it's what he'd do himself.'

Nash turned back to the emails.

'Aidan sent that message just a few minutes after you called for a long conversation yesterday morning.' Casey heard the spite in her own voice. 'Greville Polignac will have a record of the timing of that call. And you had a breakfast meeting scheduled with Gardiner this morning, didn't you? At the exact moment that all the information streams were pulled. How do you think all that's going to look, Nash?'

'They'll know you're stitching me up,' he said desperately. 'I'll tell them.'

'And you're completely sure they'll believe you?' she asked. 'That's quite a gamble. I'm not sure Tip Top would give you the best odds either.'

'But I never ...'

'Sure.' Casey shrugged. 'But as I've personally discovered in the last few days, it's incredibly hard to prove you didn't know something when all the evidence suggests that you did.'

'You bitch!'

'And then there's your affair with Tillie Carlisle.'

'My ... what?'

'She was in the Ring of Bells last night, telling anyone who would listen all about it. Saying that's why she passed you all the newslists in the first place.'

'I never ...'

'How long will that intel take to reach Pascoe Knox and Rosamund?' Casey looked ostentatiously at her watch. 'They're so good at gathering information, aren't they? Definitely by now, I would have thought.

Knox isn't the sort of person to be thrilled by someone cheating on his daughter while scheming to make his own fortune.'

'What do you want?' A hiss. 'I know you'll want something, Casey. Get it over with.'

'I've got a meeting room booked at a hotel just down the road. I'll explain there.'

49

Now Casey looked down at the sprawling chalet. Nash had disappeared into the darkness and the sun had set. Night was gathering fast. They had been lucky to be able to film him being dragged into the house.

'Right.' She turned to Richard. The photographer had ill-advisedly admitted to being a competent skier. 'Send that footage to both me and Miranda straight away, and then you head back to the resort.'

Richard was shaking his head.

'We should call the police,' he said. 'That man really belted him and God knows what they're doing to him right now. We have to call the police, Casey.'

'Nash made me promise. He made me swear I wouldn't call the police.'

'But he didn't know.' The photographer was obstinate. 'He didn't know how aggressive they would be. How they would ...'

'Nash knows precisely what these people have been up to, for years. He was aware that this was never going to be a friendly chat.'

She had wondered, as soon as Nash suggested it, whether this was an attempt to atone. A punishment he thought he could bear. Because Nash knew the rules.

'I'll be your source,' he had said to Casey as they sat in the meeting room. 'But you never use my name. Not ever. You blur any footage of me. I'm a source, and you protect me. Rosamund, too.'

'It'll be much more dangerous for you if we don't get the police involved in Switzerland,' said Casey. 'I haven't got a clue how we'll get you out of that chalet.'

'You'll find a way,' he said. 'But no police, Casey, you have to promise me. This way it will look as if you and I were working together all along. It undermines everything Pascoe's got. I'll tell you everything I know. Everything.'

'I'll think about it.'

Later, she told Dash and Ross about Nash's request.

'He's not the ultimate target,' said Dash. 'I suppose we could ...'

'It's the only way he'll help us. He says that otherwise he might as well let us write whatever we can now.'

'He's a weasel,' said Ross.

'Fine,' Dash decided. 'Get him on tape telling us every single thing he knows before he goes back to the Greville Polignac offices. But we won't name him in our articles.'

'Unless they kill him,' Ross said, as the two executives walked back towards the newsdesk. 'Then all bets are off.'

'They won't.' Dash sounded uneasy. 'They won't.'

Now Casey met the photographer's eyes. 'I promised Nash,' she repeated. 'I have to go now.'

Richard shrugged. 'Seems mad to me.'

The chalet was quiet, the peace of the mountains at odds with the violence of the scene they'd just witnessed. Set below the crags of the mountain ridge, the chalet had a Hansel and Gretel charm. Although it was still early in the winter, a thick blanket of snow lay on its sloping roofs. Icicles formed a row of fangs. Behind the house, the ground rose up sharply and all around ghostly pines loomed in the dusk.

A ski guide from the resort next door had explained the set-up to Casey over an idle beer the day before. A private ski run coiled its way down through the trees above the house, he said, and the chair lift rose up away from it. When the chalet's residents wanted to ski, the chair lift was switched on, sweeping the guests a mile or so up the mountain until they could join one of the furthest runs of a distant resort. At the end of the day, they could take the private ski run back to the house.

'They use a helicopter to ski a lot too, I think,' the guide added. 'They get dropped off at the top of the best powder in the morning. You see the helicopter often during the season, but sometimes the weather is not right for it, so they have the lift too.'

'I've seen,' Casey said darkly, 'the helicopter.'

'There is a service road to get supplies in and out,' the guide went on. 'But that goes the other way, away from this resort.'

She could just make out the road from the snowy ridge, winding away to the left of the house. From where she stood, the closest resort was behind her. In order to get to the chalet, she would have to ski down a long slope. It would not be possible to return to the resort without a long, dark walk up the mountain.

Now Casey checked that she had received the footage.

'Got it,' she said to the photographer.

'Good luck.' Richard was still unconvinced. With half a wave, he slid away silently towards the resort's ski slopes.

Casey stared down the mountain. On skis, it would take only a few minutes to make her way to the chalet.

The watershed, she thought: the ridgeline that ran between mountain peaks. A snowflake fluttering an extra inch was the difference between it ending *here* or ending *there*.

A different life, a hairbreadth away. Random, probably.

One way led to safety, and peace. The other …

Onwards.

She pushed herself forward, sliding silently over the snow.

I don't want to …

I must.

A few hundred yards from the house, Casey slid to a halt. It was dark now, the lights of the chalet gleaming on the snow. The main drawing room was lit up. Its panoramic views would have faded as night drew in, the focus shifting from outside to within. Now the central room was stage-bright, a group of men sitting around a blazing fire. There was

Pascoe Knox, standing, staring out into the darkness. There was Leon, pacing to and fro, his white-blond hair gleaming. But no Nash.

In the shadow of one of the pine trees, Casey unclicked her skis and pulled a pair of walking boots out of her rucksack. She was wearing a thick, navy blue ski jacket and warm black ski trousers.

Casey stared at the house once more, and a shiver that was half cold, half fear, snaked its way down her spine.

Call the police. Stop all this. Stop it all at once.

I told Nash I wouldn't.

But.

The wind was picking up now, whining quietly in the forest. Snowflakes drifted, ethereal and insubstantial until they bulked against the solidity of the trees.

I wish I were …

Not home.

I wish I were with you.

Casey stared down at the chalet again. The minutes were chipping the night away.

Come on.

One step. Another step. Another. And she was walking towards the chalet, the safety of the shadows behind her.

Her footsteps were muffled by snow, the darkness swallowing her clumsiness. She was leaving footprints behind, a stumbling track in the whiteness, but there was no other way.

The drifts were suddenly deeper. A lurch and she was floundering to her waist, the snow softly ensnaring her. This was a forest of traps and menace, the cold already nipping at her fingers, biting at her feet.

Come on.

Avoiding the rectangles of light on the snow, she edged her way round to the back of the house. Here, it was set almost into the cliff, only a narrow chasm between the walls of the chalet and the sharp rise of the rockface. Above the chalet, the mountainside was patchworked with berms and netting designed to block avalanches if the snow started rippling and moving; without that protection, it would form into an irresistible force, roaring down, bulldozing everything in its way.

Casey reached the rocks and looked up at the back of the chalet. The house had been designed with all the focus on the front. The grand rooms overlooked a panorama of the Alps. These rooms at the back, facing north, were smaller, functional, their view just a few feet to the rocks. These were the staff bedrooms. The kitchens. The gym, maybe, where blaring music videos harnessed all attention.

Please. Please let him be there.

Casey scrambled up the rocks towards the fringe of pine trees. It was hard climbing in ski clothes, her heavy boots slipping on ice.

But there he was: Nash, tense-faced at the window of the little bedroom.

She waved and his expression lit up.

Beside one of the scrubby pine trees, Casey sat down on a rock. She pulled open her rucksack and drew out a rope ladder. She tied one end to the pine tree, then gestured to Nash. He opened the French windows and stepped out onto the snowy balcony.

'Hello,' she whispered.

'Thank God you're here.'

She threw the end of the rope ladder across to the balcony. It missed, snicking against the side of the chalet and unravelling into the narrow gap. They both froze, the movement seeming huge, catastrophic. For a moment, the ladder swung to and fro, dislodging a flurry of snow. Then the night slipped slowly back into silence.

Swearing under her breath, Casey rolled the ladder back up. Nash was leaning against the balcony rail, arms outstretched. Again, Casey threw the end of the ladder. This time, he caught it, just, the ladder looping across the gap.

'Find something to tie it to,' Casey whispered and he nodded, disappearing back into the bedroom.

When he returned, she untied her end of the ladder and watched as the loops fell away into space.

She could see Nash was nervous as he climbed onto the rope ladder. It looked frail, jerking as he shifted his weight. But then he was finding the rungs with his feet, moving with alacrity.

Casey hurried too, picking her way down through the rocks.

Their reunion was odd. Half-delighted but the memory of his betrayal still hovering at Casey's shoulder.

'Let's go,' she muttered. 'Miranda's waiting out along the road. About a mile away.'

'Yes.'

They edged away, creeping until they were outside the glow of the house, away from its jewel-box gleam.

'This way,' murmured Casey.

In order to reach the road, they had to traverse the front of the house. For a second, Casey paused, looking up at the group of men in the drawing room.

'What are they doing?' she asked Nash. 'Do you know?'

'They're definitely rattled,' he said. 'They were working out what to do next. There's some story they want you to write, tie you in tighter.'

'Did you hear anything specific?'

'My mind was rather on other things, Casey.'

'Did they mention anyone in particular?'

From here, she could make out shapes gathered around the fire. The heads were close together. Plotting, she thought. Their body language wasn't defeated or panicky.

'I don't know what they're doing, Casey—' Nash was impatient, keen to escape the lights of the chalet.

'What do you think they'll do next?'

'I don't know.' He sounded fretful. 'Can we go?'

Casey watched Pascoe Knox stand up and stretch, then wander towards the window. He had a tumbler in his hand, looked quite relaxed in his wilderness fortress.

'They'll let things settle down,' Nash said. 'They still think it's going to be okay.'

'We've got the footage of Leon beating you up now. They don't know about that.'

But she still didn't feel certain. She watched Knox turn away, say something that made the others laugh.

'Come on, Casey. Let's get out of here.'

But still she hesitated.

'What was the article going to be about? The one they want me to write.'

'Casey …' Nash was growing impatient. 'They were talking about some guy called Sergei Kiselyov, maybe? I have no idea who he is. It doesn't matter anyway. Let's go.'

Casey's heart sank.

'What?' she asked urgently. 'What did they want me to write about Sergei?'

'I don't know! Something to do with Russians, but I wasn't really listening. I had other things on my mind, quite frankly. Come on.'

'Is Sergei in danger?'

'No. Yes. Probably. Sorry about that.'

Casey pulled back. 'Head down that road.' She pointed. 'Miranda will be waiting. It's not far; it won't take you long.'

'Alone?' He was aghast. 'What are you going to do? Casey …'

'I don't know yet.'

'You can't—'

'I have to, Nash.'

She watched him hurry away down the road. The moon was bright now, giving the snow an unearthly glow.

Nash would be fine, she told herself. It wouldn't take him long to reach Miranda and safety. It was an easy jog down a gritted road. She suspected Miranda would be furious with her for turning back, though.

Turning back.

Looking up, Casey could see that several of the group were sitting at the long oak table now. Knox was showing them something on a laptop.

She had to find a way up to the balcony, but the front of the chalet was impregnable. A solid oak door. Walls, sheer and slippery with ice. Pick the lock? And walk straight into Knox's mob. No. She glanced at the looming pine trees. Close, but not close enough. Back up Nash's rope ladder? But that would only take her as far as the small bedroom, and she would be trapped again with the bright red blankets and the navy blue curtains.

Unless the ladder passed an unguarded window?

Casey edged round the right wing of the house. The ski lift stood close to the chalet there. In the moonlight, it resembled a strange steel sculpture, a frozen metal river twisting down through the pine forest.

She crept along the back of the house and peered up the rope ladder. It dangled uselessly, close to only one window and that was barred. Casey spun away, frustrated, heading back to the front and almost colliding with the ski lift.

The ski lift.

Steadying herself, she looked up at the steel machine.

Maybe.

Madness.

But.

The lift's technology was simple. A green button to start, a red one to stop. From its base, it rose up sharply, just skimming the roofline before it glided over the fringe of pines behind the house.

She hadn't heard it start before, she told herself, when she was sitting in a bedroom right there. No one would hear it now.

When she pressed the green button, the silence seemed to tear itself apart. The motor clattered loudly as it began hauling around the heavy chairs. Cables squeaked and clanked. Casey ducked away from the roar.

But no one appeared, hurrying to check, and as the sounds of the lift settled into the night, she allowed herself to breathe.

Follow Nash to safety instead. Leave all this behind.

She allowed herself to think about it, and then shut the idea away.

No.

The ski-lift benches were about fifty feet apart, purring down the mountain towards her before being spun round on the cable and sent back up. After one jerked past, Casey stepped forward. The next appeared, tapping her neatly behind the knees, so that she sat down sharply. The seat rose from the ground, heading for the fringe of pines. The roof of the chalet appeared fast to her left, a smooth expanse of untouched snow. It was close, she told herself. Easy. Ignore the drop to the cold, frozen ground. Ignore the thought that no one knows where you are. Ignore everything and jump.

The chair lift was moving faster than she had realised, the gap closing in seconds. No time to think, no time to stop.

She jumped.

50

She landed with a thump. Below her, a slab of snow fell away, whispering as it slid down the chalet roof and breaking up as it disappeared over the edge. She was sliding with it and there was nothing to hold on to, nothing to …

Casey dug her fingers into the roof, scrabbled with her feet, and somehow slowed her desperate skid. The slab of snow stopped moving. Silence settled again. The lift purred past.

Casey lay in the snow and looked up at the sky. The stars glimmered coldly.

Time to move.

But if I move, the world may start slipping again. Sliding and panicking and plummeting over the edge.

Come on.

She scrambled up the roof. The design of the chalet meant that the incline was fairly shallow. She had landed on the roof of a side wing, so she climbed to the peak and slid down towards the next section.

Just as she had hoped, the wide verandah of the huge drawing room almost reached the neighbouring roof here.

It wasn't hard to creep across and drop down over the railings.

There.

The glass wall left her almost nowhere to hide. She flattened herself against one of the huge steels holding up the roof, and hoped that no one wandered over to admire this view.

It was easy to make out Knox's voice. She pressed record on her phone.

Budapest have tracked to …
They've pulled the feed from the Bank …
Gardiner's shut down his accounts …
SportWatcher. Unbelievable …

They talked about other companies too, links that her team at the *Post* hadn't come close to guessing. And Russian names. Proof. *Proof.* A surge of excitement, something close to joy. *Proof.* Casey stood in the cold of the balcony, making notes. Weeks of tension evaporating, as she typed and recorded, and almost forgot where she was.

A flurry of footsteps. A sharp interruption. The burble died away. Leon's voice, loud in the silence.

'Bexley's gone. Fucking Bexley's managed to escape.'

A babble, people leaping to their feet.

Knox's voice sharp, angry. 'How? For fuck's sake, Leon. How?'

It would take them seconds to work it out. Seconds to find the rope ladder. Seconds to see the ski lift turning. She spun round.

It was a bigger gap than she'd realised, from the verandah back to the roof. She was too hurried for quiet, too desperate for caution. She scrambled up onto the roof, icicles splintering away beneath her.

A searing panic. Someone would grab her legs, drag her back. She was being too loud, too clumsy, and now there were voices, shouting.

'There's someone on the roof.'

'Jesus fucking Christ!'

And Knox's voice, clipped with rage. 'Get her. Get her right now.'

Shapes appeared on the balcony. A man leaped up to the roof behind her. Casey scrabbled.

She had reached the ridge and there was only one way to escape now. Chair lifts purred past, the benches a few seconds apart. Frantically, she tried to assess their speed. A man was clambering along the roof behind her, the snow breaking up and hissing away beneath him. If she miscalculated the gap between the steel benches, she would plunge off the edge of the roof, all the way down to the frozen ground, legs snapped, bones shattered.

A bench rose past the roofline, heading up the mountainside. The next one must be a couple of seconds behind? Nothing else for it.

Casey started down the roof. It was slide-slippery, the snow slithering away in a small avalanche. She couldn't stop now, she was moving too fast. One foot skidded. Her balance gone, the edge of the roof coming up, can't stop, where is the lift, where?

It appeared, rising smoothly, obliviously. She leaped wildly and just managed to connect with the cold, smooth metal, clutching the armrest, her feet scrambling frantically for a hold, somewhere, anywhere.

The lift purred on, and she was aware of emptiness beneath her. Of the roofs disappearing to her left, the pine trees tipping dizzyingly. There were shouts from the rooftop.

'She's on the fucking lift. Stop it. Stop her.'

And then there was nothing beneath her but a thick blanket of white, as her arms began to ache.

51

The moon lit up the mountain range. The chair lift purred on, and every yard further from the house was crucial. At first, Casey tried to scramble up into the seat, but it was futile, the bulky ski jacket making movement too difficult. So she clung on, glancing back to see the lights of the chalet disappearing.

The ground seemed impossibly far away, a blur of moonlit white.

How long would it take someone to sprint round to the chair-lift mechanism? A minute, maybe?

Could they put it into reverse? Haul her back down the mountain?

Some vague memory told her it might be possible to reverse a ski lift. Hazy recall of footage of a malfunction, the lift stuck on reverse, slinging tourists out at speed. Ross had loved it, of course.

So it was possible to reverse them. And there was no way she would reach the top of the lift before they stopped it. She couldn't hold on that far anyway. Her arms were shaking already, her shoulder muscles burning.

The chair lift rattled past a pylon and the jerk made her hands slip slightly. She clutched harder, desperately.

She would have to jump. But where? Not close to one of the pylons, where the lift might be fifty feet off the ground. She twisted her head around to look forward, and gasped.

A chasm was opening up ahead of her. She was already too high, too late to let go. The ground split in half, a ravine slicing down the mountainside. There was no snow, it was too steep. Just a jumble of dark rocks, a hundred feet down, two hundred, maybe.

Not here, she screamed in her head. *Don't stop the lift here. I'll never be able to hold on. I can't …*

I'll fall.

I'll die.

The chair lift continued smoothly over the crevasse, the mechanics purring quietly.

Casey's arms shook. If it stopped now … If it stopped …

Ahead of her, the ground was rising up sharply. At the top, the chair lift just grazed the edge of the ravine before skimming on to the next pylon.

If she could hold on until there …

If the lift kept going just a little bit further.

Please, it was a prayer. *Please.*

Fifty yards to the lip of the ravine.

Forty.

Thirty. There was sheer cliff below her now. If she fell, she would hit the edge and bounce off, cartwheeling into the abyss.

Twenty.

Ten. So near. So nearly there.

She almost couldn't believe it when she reached the edge of the crevasse. Almost held on that split-second too long, so that the chair lift whisked her up towards the next pylon.

Let go.

Let go now.

She plunged awkwardly into the snow, arms stiff with cold and exhaustion. The drift was thick, which saved her. Powdery and icy, filling her eyes and mouth.

Alive. Still. Just.

For a moment, she lay there, unable to move. The chairs were flitting by over her head, steel bees in a line.

Delirious.

She could just lie here. Lie here and let the cold drift over her. Lie here and wait for the morning to splinter this terrible night.

Above her, the lift came to a jerking halt. Casey raised her head. The long line of benches was jouncing in the darkness, their forward momentum sharply interrupted.

Someone had reached the lift mechanism. Someone had hit the big red button.

The benches dangled in the air, slowly stilling. There was a pause of maybe a few seconds and then they jolted backwards. Slowly at first, then faster. If she hadn't jumped down, they would be sweeping her back into the mouth of the dragon.

Casey scrambled to her feet. How long would it take them to realise she had jumped? That all the seats were empty. How long?

She sensed someone else making the same calculation back down at the chalet. The same rushed arithmetic. When could they be sure? When could they reverse the lift mechanism and come after her?

She looked around the mountainside. She couldn't carry on up the line of the lift. She would be too obvious to anyone who followed her up. But to her right, somewhere over the ridge, lay the ski resort.

The skiers would be back there by now, enjoying a hot chocolate, a *vin chaud*, a warm bath. Warmth, not a luxury up here. But they sent out snowploughs at night. From the resort, she had watched them chugging off up the pistes, headlights lonely in the dark, sent out to smooth the snow for the expensive days of fun.

A snowplough: a rescue, maybe.

For a second, she thought longingly of the skis she had left behind, and the swooping speed they represented. But she had left them too close to the chalet. Someone would have found them by now.

No. She would have to go forward. Find her way up through the forest and across to the ski runs. And she had no idea how far it was. No idea how to …

There was no other choice.

She fought her way upright in the powdery snow and turned towards the hillside. The wind whistled through the trees and snowflakes drifted, trying to find a place to rest. Already, her hands and feet were aching in the cold, the blood slowly diverting to her core, to the organs that had to be kept going no matter what.

Behind her, the chair lift screeched. She whipped around. It had stopped again, the long row of seats jolting in the night.

They hung there for a moment, silent in the darkness.

And then they started forward again.

52

Casey floundered in a drift and came to a halt. The snow here was thick, blotting out fallen logs, holes, summer streams. Hollows opened up like traps as she stumbled along, the filigree of snow disintegrating beneath her feet.

Keep going.

In the clearings, she felt painfully visible, a struggling outline in a sweep of white. In the woods, the moonlight threw shadows from the trees, knife scars of darkness that confused the eyes.

The cold was clawing through her jacket. She had been outside for a long time.

They must be in the chair lift by now. Maybe they would run it slowly, staring at the ground for signs of an awkward leap, pathetic footprints limping away. Maybe she had a bit of time …

She scrambled up a sharp slope. At the top, the wind had blown the snow to a bald dusting. She would barely leave any footprints here and managed to run, the heavy boots slapping against the ground. When she reached the snow, she chose a new angle. Anything to throw them off. Anything to …

She slipped on a patch of ice and slammed to the ground, yelping as her hip cracked against a spur of stone.

Her phone rang, the sound incongruous in the shadows of the night. Miranda. 'Where the hell are you, Casey?'

'I had to run.' Not enough air here for her to speak freely. 'I'm climbing towards the resort.'

'You're what?' Despair in Miranda's voice. 'Casey—'

'I'll be fine. Fine. Have you got Nash?'

'Yes. Yes, he made it to the car. But Casey, what have you done?'

'I have to go, Miranda.'

She shoved the phone back in her pocket. The mountain was quiet, vast. She was abruptly aware of her own insignificance. She was a dot of nothing on the mountain's flank, the merest flicker in a million years of snow and ice. Above her, the dome of stars stared down, coldly indifferent.

Keep going.

She struggled on. Just ahead, the ground fell away sharply. It must be a watercourse, frozen in the winter.

Was this the right way?

She felt disorientated.

They tell you to follow rivers to escape the wilderness. Because for millennia, people have gathered beside water, and that's where you'll find houses and life. But twentieth-century man colonised the high mountains with bright flags and neat netting, smoothed snow and a misplaced appearance of safety. So climbing towards the pistes might be the best direction for her tonight. Might be.

A split-second decision: head for the pistes.

She scrambled along the contour lines.

The cold was vicious now, every breath choking her lungs. Her feet were numb, her movements clumsy. Another fallen tree and she stumbled over it, landing hard in the snow. This time she was slower to her feet. She was shivering, the deadly thoughts starting to creep over her. *Curl up. Huddle down. Survive.*

A trap, she told herself. If you do that, you'll die. Because even if they don't find you, the cold will curl down and drift you away. Into an icy seduction, the Snow Queen's curse. A quiet death. Gentle, maybe.

I can't go on.

You must.

She rang Miranda. 'Call the resort ... Tell them, please ... if there is a snowplough ... on one of the far runs ... ask them to wait? Please.'

Her words were breaking up now, the thoughts a fading transmission.

'Casey?' Miranda's voice was sharp. 'You don't sound … Keep going, all right? Keep running.'

'I will. Will.'

She pushed the phone into her pocket and dragged herself onwards. A bleary idea: *They might be tracking my phone.* Carefully, she placed it in the hollow of a tree. Its light glowed, then faded. She nodded firmly, thoughts blurring.

Up another rise, stumbling through a hollow.

A sound behind her; she spun around.

She couldn't see them. Not yet. She sensed more than she saw.

A flicker of light among the trees. Torches, moving rapidly. Men, two or maybe more, hustling through the woods behind her. Not exhausted, like her. Not slowing and struggling.

She was outnumbered. Outmatched.

Still a few hundred yards ahead of them, though. They hadn't crossed the ravine yet. It wouldn't take them long, but …

She ran.

The branches of the pine trees were lower here. Black and bristly, a layer of snow slipping off as she passed.

Maybe the fallen snow would cover her tracks … Maybe.

The footsteps sounded closer already. There were no shouts. No energy wasted on pointless noise. She imagined their eyes gleaming as they picked up her blundering prints.

A broken branch caught her face, tearing at her cheek, just missing her eye. The pain ripped through her. She put her glove to her face and held it up with blood on it, a red gleam on black. A sob escaped her.

It was hopeless. She could never survive.

Come on.

They must have found her tracks in the ravine. She could hear them crashing through the trees behind her, moving so much faster. The flickers of light were becoming a gleam, a torchlight finger reaching through the trees. At any second, she would be trapped in that beam.

And she had nothing.

Maybe a tree branch, swung madly, going down fighting.

Pathetic.

She felt a sudden, blistering rage that it should come to this. That these men would be able to take their vicious revenge.

That they would kill, again.

And she had nothing except for unwritten words.

The woods opened up abruptly into a snowfield, an expanse of white glittering in the moonlight.

She staggered across it, feeling visible, vulnerable. She imagined she was leaving fairy-tale drops of blood, rubies on ivory. They would see them. Know that she was weakened. Redouble their efforts.

Beneath her stumbling feet, the top layer of snow slid away, the movement almost imperceptible at first.

Casey froze instantly. Avalanches, always a danger in the mountains. A small slip gathering power and strength, down and down, until the whole mountainside was a shifting chaos of ice.

Close to the resort, they set off explosives to shift the snow when the tourists were safely tucked up in bed. Before it became lethal, a blind, all-consuming fury. Eleven minutes, they said. Eleven minutes to dig someone out, or you're looking for a corpse.

To Casey's left, the ground rose steeply. Just walking across the snowfield might be enough to trigger another slide.

If she took another step, she might be swept away in a tsunami of ice and snow.

If she took another step …

Come on.

Now, she was halfway across.

Three-quarters.

Almost there.

Almost in the black safety of the trees …

And finally she was among the dark pines, the slipping snow behind her.

The slipping snow.

She glanced up the hill.

She heard them gloating as they came through the woods. 'I saw her just before she reached the trees. We'll get her …'

'Fucking bitch.'

Still, she hesitated.

It might kill them.

They will kill me.

As soon as they reached the other side of the snowfield, they would spot her footprints turning sharply up the hill. Scrambling up through the snow, lungs burning in the thin air, every stride an agony.

They would follow those footsteps, and they were so close now. So close.

Below her, the men reached the snowfield.

They didn't notice that the snow had slipped away to the right of her footprints. It was only the top layer that had crumbled, after all, merely revealing another smooth layer of white beneath. In the night, they couldn't tell, weren't looking. They stepped out into the clearing.

From above, she could make out their backpacks. Ahead of them, the snow was lit up by head torches strapped to their helmets. Father and son, well prepared for this hunt through the backwoods.

'She'll never make it.' Knox's voice, sounding satisfied.

'No fucking way.' Leon's.

That surge of rage again.

They were halfway across the clearing, blind to anything but her footprints.

High above them, Casey started silently across the snowfield, kicking as she went. Small clumps broke away and started skittering down the surface.

She shoved hard and a whole sheet of snow started moving. It was very steep here, the snow just balanced on the rocks. Teetering. Almost …

A large chunk broke away. Slow at first, then suddenly faster. All at once, it was as if the whole mountain was moving, tonnes of snow cascading down the slope.

Casey's foothold slid away. She threw herself to one side, grabbed at a rock and clung on because her life depended on it.

For a second, she caught a glimpse of the two men staring up at the storm of snow, at the white wave of death. It bore down on them, alive, murderous, the Snow Queen rising.

It roared down the mountain and crashed over their heads.

53

They were wearing avalanche airbags. She had guessed they would be.

She had hoped that their rucksacks contained the safety devices. Or at least she had crushed the hope that they didn't.

The airbags erupted as the torrent of snow approached, triggered to cushion the men from the rage of the mountain.

She watched as they were swept away, toys tumbling in the explosion of snow. Even from here, the power of the mountain shook her. A rumbling, tearing roar, an unstoppable flood of ice and snow and stones. They were there and then they were gone, slapped away into the wilderness.

As it reached the trees, the avalanche began to slow. The slope was shallower here, the tree trunks absorbing some of the wild kinetic energy.

From the top of the clearing, she couldn't see them. Couldn't see ...

You have to help them.

But I'm ...

You must.

She scrabbled down the hill, keeping well away from the clearing. The snow looked innocent now, as if the surge of destruction was quite unimaginable. But she knew.

She fought her way through the powdery silence. They must be here. Somewhere nearby. She imagined being trapped by the weight of the snow, face down, drowning in ice. You might have a small air pocket, just enough to breathe for a few minutes. But with arms gripped by the snow, there would be no way of clearing a breathing space. The snow would refreeze, solid, immovable. The oxygen would run out, and you would die just inches from the clean Alpine air. Entombed in a coffin of ice.

They had to be somewhere …

Eleven minutes, they said. Eleven minutes.

So she dug, and fought, and shouted.

And finally she saw them.

They had both been hurled to the side of the fall, the airbags keeping them clear, just. Leon had slammed into a tree. His eyes were closed, blood trickling down his face. As she stepped towards him, she saw that he was gaining consciousness, eyelids flickering. Not dead, at least. But he wouldn't be chasing anyone for a bit, either.

Knox's leg was broken. It lay at an impossible angle to his torso. He was awake, though. She could make out small movements, hear a groan of agony. As she edged closer, his head whipped round, his eyes blazing with rage and pain.

Casey approached him cautiously. 'I'll go and get help,' she promised.

He glared up at her, his blistering anger almost tangible. Having to ask for help, unbearable. She watched him reach through the pain for the words.

'You *bitch*.'

She turned away from him. 'I'll get them to come as quickly as possible. I have to go.'

'To write your fucking story.'

She hesitated, looked back. 'Yes,' she said simply. 'Yes, I will write my story.'

He refused to accept defeat, even now. 'You killed my son.' The words sounded like a curse. 'You left him to die.'

'I didn't,' she said, and for once she knew it was true. 'He chose to be there. He chose to be there, and there was nothing I could do to save him.'

'You were just a witness,' he sneered.

'Yes, that's all I ever was.' A groan from Leon. 'I'll go and get help.'

Knox was going into shock, she could tell, his pupils dilating. She had to hurry. Had to push away the thought that she could wait just a few more minutes. Wait and watch the light fade from his eyes. He looked up at her as if he read her thoughts.

'Are you going to watch us die too? It is what you do, after all.'

'It's not what I do.'

He couldn't bring himself to ask her for help even now. Would rather die on the cold mountainside, watching his son grow still beside him. She had to hurry. There wasn't much time. She thought of her phone, nestled in a hollow half a mile back. Wondered if Knox or Leon had one on them. They must do. But she couldn't risk approaching either of them.

'Why?' Casey asked. 'Why did you do it? You have billions. You could have just … enjoyed life.'

He shifted in the snow until he could look straight up at her.

'We're the same,' he said, grimacing. 'You could just enjoy life, too … But I had to *know*. You had to know.'

'And the consequences …'

'Yes.'

Casey looked up at one of the huge pine trees. 'You spent all that time thinking about what I do,' she said. 'But did you never wonder why your son ended up out in the Sahara?'

His eyes darkened – the anger, the pain, almost beyond endurance. For a moment, she felt something close to pity, and almost wished she could take the words back.

'Of course,' he said. 'Of course I do.'

He shifted in the snow. Tiring now, the adrenalin wearing off. Casey stood up.

'I'll hurry,' she promised him. 'I won't be long.'

She raced through the woods. It wouldn't be far. It couldn't be. Miranda would have called the resort, would have used all her charm to bring out the searchers. Casey clambered up another rise and suddenly she could see a light far ahead. It was moving. Hurrying. Bright headlights, trundling down the mountainside. It must be one of the snowploughs, churning noisily through the night.

And she ran towards it. Ran towards the light.

ACKNOWLEDGEMENTS

Once again, this book feels like *quite* the team effort …

Particular thanks go to …

Laura Millar, for being my Ascot guru, and correcting my various errors in print and in life. Cressida and Danny, for giving quite possibly the best parties in the world, while also attempting to explain quantitative hedge funds. Heroic efforts all around. Becky and Ed Knox, for letting me steal your surname, and then being zen when I told you what the character would be getting up to. Jo Katz, for explaining algorithms and having very strong views on what suits Nick Llewellyn would wear. Charlie Llewellyn, for letting me steal your surname too, although I quickly realised that was a strategic error. SO many Ls. Suzy Bennett, for brilliant advice on cameras and tiny flaws. Angelika and Robert Winnett, for knowing all about Budapest. Collette Lyons and Paul Vlitos, for cheerleading practically every single day. Wendy Noble, for explaining what compliance officers do, and not wincing too hard when I explained what I wanted them to do instead. Rory and Tess Hardick, for just about everything.

Tons and tons of love to Flic Fitzgerald, Jessica Sheehan, Alex Marrache, Adam and Laura Smith-Roberts, Nish and James Goodhand, Alex and Bertie Readhead, Rachel and Bertie Vanns, Sarah Mahmud, Jasmine Miller, Alice Ross, Catriona Ward, Cressy and James McCarthy, Justine Moxham, Toby Darbyshire, Miriam Kelly and Claire Newell. Huge, huge thank yous to Andrew Gordon at David Higham Associates, Alison Hennessey and the whole team at Bloomsbury Raven. So much love to Granny and Pompom and, most especially, all the love in the world to my gorgeous Jonny, my fabulous Izzie and my darling little Jago.

A NOTE ON THE AUTHOR

HOLLY WATT is an award-winning investigative journalist who worked at the *Sunday Times*, the *Daily Telegraph* and the *Guardian*. Her first novel, *To The Lions*, won the CWA Ian Fleming Steel Dagger, and was followed in the Casey Benedict series by *The Dead Line*, which has been longlisted for the 2021 CWA Steel Dagger, and then *The Hunt and the Kill*. *The End of the Game* is her fourth novel.

@holly_watt

A NOTE ON THE TYPE

The text of this book is set in Minion, a digital typeface designed by Robert Slimbach in 1990 for Adobe Systems. The name comes from the traditional naming system for type sizes, in which minion is between nonpareil and brevier. It is inspired by late Renaissance-era type.